DEVIL GLASS

C. Robert Cales

AmErica House
Baltimore

First printing

ISBN: 1-59286-202-0
PUBLISHED BY AMERICA HOUSE BOOK PUBLISHERS
www.publishamerica.com
Baltimore

Printed in the United States of America

For Mary Elizabeth Cales
Forever best friend and soul mate
ILY 12/0

PREFACE

The sentinel stood atop the bluff watching the dark clouds gathering on the early morning horizon. He was a great warrior among the Warrior Clan, those sworn with the blood oath to stand at the doorway and fight with their last breath to protect the other clans from the death bringers. Behind him, sleeping around their fire pit were the others, each a fierce warrior, each seasoned and some scarred by many great clashes at the Seeing Stone.

He looked down at the other clans in the encampment at the base of the hill with its huge fire and constant activity. He was a warrior who understood weapons and how to kill with them. The others below in the encampment were different. Some had skills that were a great mystery to him, some spoke in strange tongues that he failed to understand; yet they were all connected by the shared dreams that brought them to this place.

The most skilled of the Stone Clan used their talents to shape stones into tools while others hammered with the tools, chipping away at the black slate cliff as their fuzzy bluish reflections danced on the face of the Seeing Stone. Others of the clan used baskets to haul away the chips of black slate that accumulated below the huge crystal.

The Wood Clan maintained the great fire around which the exhausted ones slept. They foraged for dried wood and used stone tools crafted by the Stone Clan to cut green trees. The old ones of the clan with their mysterious skills used stone tools, shells and chips of the black rock to cut away the bark and carve the green logs into totems. Some of the massive totems were erected around the camp honoring the gods who spoke to them from the dream world. Other totems bearing the warnings were fashioned with great care, ends shaped into mysterious joints to be linked together, forming a framework to encase the Seeing Stone.

He looked back at the others. They knew only of their dreams and were oblivious to the approaching storm. They usually awoke when rested and used their skill with weapons to provide meat for all the clans. This morning they would be roused from their slumber to satisfy their blood oath. Soon he would walk among them, jabbing each one in the ribs with the blunt end of his spear. When the rude awakening came they would each know fire would soon rip through the sky and open the doorway. As he walked back toward the others he wondered which of the Warrior Clan would not live to see the bright sunlight and clear blue sky again. He jabbed the first warrior in the ribs as he thought of the others of his clan that had been lost to the death bringers from beyond.

The warrior sat up with a start and immediately looked up at the sky as thunder rumbled in the distance. He threw off the blanket of skins, jumped to his feet and started gathering his weapons as others were being aroused. Soon they were all awake, gathering their best weapons and provoking themselves and others into raging fury with chants and war cries. One of the warriors poured water from a skin pouch into a stone bowl of dusty plant pigment as the others surrounded him, pummeling themselves with clenched fists amid howls and screams for the blood of the death bringers. They each stepped forward, dipped their fingers into the color and painted their faces with personal war masks as another warrior mixed water with a bowl of hallucinogenic plant dust. Each warrior drank from the dark potion before sliding down the grassy embankment toward the Seeing Stone, weapons in hand.

The other clans cowered in fear at the far side of the encampment as the Warrior Clan gathered in front of the Seeing Stone, weapons poised to strike and screaming for the bloody confrontation to begin. They all inched forward with spears ready as a bolt of lightning dropped from the churning black clouds in the distance. Red crisscrossing lines spread across the face of the huge crystal, darkened for a moment, then faded away as thunder rolled across the sky.

Rain started to fall as a crackling bolt of lightning struck a nearby tree and the air exploded with thunder. The network of red lines again spread across the face of the crystal. The lines grew darker and expanded until the entire surface of the Seeing Stone was black tinged with red. As the warriors screamed their war chant and readied themselves the color started to break apart like dark sand blown by the wind until an alien landscape came into view.

In front of the ring of howling warriors on the other side of the open doorway was a dune of coarse white bone fragments. Beyond the dune in the distance were jagged mountain peaks rising into a crimson sky.

The warriors crowded forward as the first of the winged death bringers dropped out of the sky and landed on the dune. The creature moved across the dune toward the doorway between the worlds, reaching out with its raised talons and baring its deadly carnivorous teeth. It focused its yellow cat like eyes on the ring of warriors as more of the winged carnivores dropped out of the sky and onto the dune.

That stormy morning the Warrior Clan again reaffirmed their unyielding devotion to the Blood Oath amid war cries and alien snarls. The vicious clash exploded in the doorway with spears jabbing into alien bodies and talons slicing through human flesh. The deadly struggle lasted through the early morning. When it ended one of the Warrior Clan was gone.

The other clans went back to their work in stunned silence as the warriors returned to their camp to nurse their injuries and await the next confrontation.

*Man evolved, as did his fears and
After ten thousand years he no
longer recognized the warning.*

CHAPTER ONE

Joyce Robbins relaxed on the redwood deck as she watched the colors of the summer sunset spread across the rippling lake. This was her quiet place where she could get away from the troubles of the outside world, a place where she could be alone with her thoughts. She listened to the seagulls crying overhead and wondered how they ended up in Ohio. Probably blown off course by a storm, she thought as she picked up the newspaper and turned to the business section.

The publication was a sure disappointment for anyone looking for serious news. The articles were usually poorly written reiterations of stories appearing the day before in high circulation papers like *USA Today* and the editorial section was a joke. Sometimes she wondered why she didn't subscribe to a real newspaper, but the answer was simple. As bad as it was she could still keep track of all her investments and stay current with Calvin and Hobbs, Haggar the Horrible and Garfield, which was all she wanted. It was really all she wanted out of any paper, but patronizing this one was her way of supporting the neighborhood kids that delivered it.

She had a definite soft spot when it came to kids. She never wanted any of her own, but when they came to the door peddling their candy bars or magazines or Christmas cookies for whatever organization, she was an easy touch. They were always so cute and professional, but it was the newspaper kids, a brother and sister team that really got to her.

The first time she saw them standing at her front door holding hands she melted. She always guessed her attraction to them had as much to do with the loneliness of her own childhood as anything else. She always wanted a brother or sister. Her parents tried to give her a sibling, but after three miscarriages things seemed doubtful. When she was seven, fate, with the help of a drunk driver, ended her chances forever.

She finished with the business section and folded the paper to the comics.

Many of the cartoon strips were so lame that reading them made her feel guilty, like she was wasting her time but her favorites were different. They never failed to give her a little lift and sometimes she came away with a refreshing new reflection on life. Calvin and Hobbs kept her in touch with her inner child and made sure she didn't take life too seriously, Haggar the Horrible was always there to remind her that plans rarely worked exactly the way they were envisioned and Garfield was so much like her own cat it was hilarious.

She wondered where her own cat was as she folded the paper and laid it on the table. "Sam," she called as she stood up and walked to the railing. She spotted the Lynx Point Siamese in the tall grass near a tree just beyond the deck. He was nearly motionless as he watched an unsuspecting robin searching for food near the lake. She could see the tension in the cat's haunches as it prepared for the attack.

"Samurai!" she yelled as she clapped her hands. "Leave that bird alone."

The startled robin flew off without suspecting its close call with death as the cat turned its attention to Joyce.

She could almost see a disgusted look on the cat's face.

"You know I don't allow you to kill birds," she scolded. "Are you hungry?" she asked.

The cat turned away from the memory of the kill that had slipped away and jumped up on the deck. He rubbed up against her leg as if asking for forgiveness.

Joyce opened the sliding glass door and walked into the condo with the cat running ahead. The inside of her place was a beautiful contrast of different times and places, blended together with elegant class. Large potted plants and smaller hanging baskets of foliage covered the expanse of the glass door. Several pieces of antique rattan furniture were placed across the room from a state of the art entertainment center. A five foot wooden Indian stood next to an eighteenth century roll top desk with brass trimmings, and held down one corner of a Persian rug from the same era.

Joyce pushed the power button on the receiver as she walked passed, filling the room with vintage Beatle music, compliments of a local FM station. She sang along with "Sergeant Pepper's Lonely Hearts Club Band" as she moved into the kitchen with the cat running ahead and looking back at her every few steps. He ran to his dish when she took the bag of cat food from the cupboard.

As she filled his bowl it hit her that the two great definers of time were music and politics. They segregated time into separate elements and tended to keep people in their own age groups. It was why she had nothing in common with Steve except sex, thank God. He didn't know any of the Beatles' songs, and the few things he knew or thought he knew about Vietnam came from movies. Vietnam was a subject burned into her heart by personal experience, she thought.

She set the cat's bowl of food on the floor and wondered if she acted as young as Steve did when she was twenty-five. Of course she did. A few painful memories from her college years trickled through the portals of her mind before she slammed the door on them.

The twenty some years between her and Steve kept them from enjoying the same music and sharing similar political views, but sex was a different story. God, he could be ready in an instant and stay that way for hours, she thought as she smiled to herself. Sex with him was great, but that's all there was to their relationship except for their friendship, of course. She knew he wanted more, but it just wasn't going to happen, it couldn't happen. There was no more to give. She was certain that he'd eventually meet someone his own age, someone who'd give him the emotional depth he needed and deserved. They would always be friends but there would come a time when their sexual liaisons would be nothing more than a pleasant memory.

She walked over to the entertainment center and opened one of the bottom doors where she kept her compact disc collection. The FM station played good music but after awhile she needed to hear something a little different. She scanned through most of the titles before going back to "Hotel California" by The Eagles. After fighting with the box for a moment she slipped the silver disc into the player and pushed the play button. A few seconds later the first cut from the album started coming through the speakers, taking her back to Cincinnati in the Summer of 1978.

The Eagles had played in Riverfront Stadium that August. That was back when sharing pot with your friends was like breaking bread with your family and crack was something you found in your basement wall. She turned the music up a little and walked into her bedroom.

Tomorrow was going to be a busy day, she thought, as she got undressed. She hoped the part time teaching position was going to be more fun than work. The opportunity to give college students a chance to learn the truth about the American Indians fascinated her.

The money wasn't great, but it didn't really matter. The experience would be its own reward, besides she had all the money she needed. Her stock investments and salary from the museum kept her more than comfortable and the revenue from the other condos she owned in the complex gave her plenty of money for special things like vacations or the Little League teams she sponsored at the Children's Home or help for needy families at Christmas time.

She walked into the bathroom, started the shower and looked at herself in the full-length mirror, wondering if she could still pass for thirty. Tomorrow would be the true test. Being around a campus full of young college girls was probably going to be a sobering experience. She laughed at the thought as she picked up a brush and started working it through her long dark red hair. No gray yet and no obvious wrinkles. She put the brush down and took a step back as she turned for a good look in the mirror. She supposed she didn't look too bad for her age. Her breasts and butt were still firm, her long legs hadn't lost their shape and she had good muscle tone, thanks to the Soloflex.

She adjusted the water temperature, stepped into the shower and wondered if Steve would remember to pick up a bottle of wine on the way over. Sometimes he was forgetful, but she supposed there was good reason. Whenever he came to see her his mind was preoccupied with sex, and that was just fine with her. After all, it was exactly what she wanted.

During the day downtown Lima was bustling with activity. Cars and busses filled the streets with noise and the sidewalks were jammed with pedestrians moving between a variety of stores. After business hours the same area became deserted except for an occasional tavern patron or a lawyer working late. After dark traffic picked up again as a different type of commerce started taking place. The police did their best to control the prostitutes and drug dealers, but they were still there, along with their customers. There were others who didn't deal in contraband or flesh, but relished the night as their season just the same.

Dark clouds drifted across the face of the moon as a black Cadillac rolled to a stop in front of Cook Tower. Martin Aster sat in the back of the car wearing a white Panama hat. He lit a Havana cigar, lowered the power window and tossed out the smoldering match. The driver watched him in the rear view mirror and waited for orders. Finally Martin reached across the seat and tapped the driver on the shoulder.

The driver opened an attaché case on the seat next to him, took out a fat envelope and handed it across the seat.

"Give me a couple minutes, then follow me up. Wait outside the door and be ready for trouble. If he has the goods on Grady I'm going to suggest he leave town for a while. You can deal with him if he refuses."

The driver nodded.

Martin got out of the car and closed the door as he slipped the envelope into his jacket pocket, next to a small gun. He was a short, stocky man with a prominent nose and bushy mustache. He straightened his tie as he stepped forward and pushed open the glass doors.

The inside of the building was dimly lit with only small lights above the elevator and stairway doors. He moved quickly to the elevator and pushed the up button, wondering about the money he was certain his business partner had stolen. Stealing he could understand, but killing the fucking golden goose made no sense. Grady had it made. He was making a great deal of money for his part in the operation, but it was apparently not enough. And the worst part was the bastard thought he could get away with it by juggling the books. A third grader could have done a better job of covering his tracks. What the fuck ever happened to honor amongst thieves, he wondered.

A small bell sounded as the elevator doors opened. He stepped in, pushed the button for the tenth floor and watched absently as the doors closed. He felt the car move and wondered if Grady had any idea a private detective had followed him. A cornered rat was nothing to fool with. It was best to kill them before they realized there was nowhere to go.

The bell sounded again as the elevator stopped and the doors slid open. Aster stepped out of the car and walked to the only office on the floor with light showing at the bottom of the door. The brass plate on the door identified the office of Ron Pitney, private investigator. Martin took a deep drag off the cigar, and then knocked.

"Who's there?" a deep voice asked.

"Martin Aster," he replied.

He heard a chair scoot on the floor and footsteps, then the sound of a deadbolt being pulled back.

Ron Pitney opened the door. He was a tall, heavily built man with closely cropped hair. "I expected you half an hour ago. You're lucky I didn't leave," he said as Martin walked into the office. Pitney closed the door behind him, drove the deadbolt home and went back to his desk as Martin took the chair reserved for clients.

"Do you have any information for me?"

"I do, providing you have money for me."

Martin took the envelope out of his pocket and slid it across the desk to

Pitney.

He opened the envelope and did a quick count of the money before putting it in his center desk drawer. He pulled a file folder out of another drawer and laid it in front of him on the desk.

"You're about to get more than you paid for," he said as he opened the folder. "But I wouldn't charge you extra for what I got for free." He leaned back in his chair and put his hands behind his head. "I followed Grady to Atlantic City where he stayed at the Boardwalk Hilton."

"Cut to the fuckin' chase. Did he steal my goddamn money?"

Pitney leaned forward and slapped his hands down on the desk.

"Yeah, I'll cut to the chase. I don't know whether this poor bastard stole your money or not. What I do know is that he paid a casino owner named Jimmy Swicks sixty thousand dollars, lost another five thousand, and spent a bundle of money on the woman he took with him."

Martin slumped back in his chair. Pitney's report had just sealed Grady's fate. He could feel the rage building inside of him. Cheating was a way of life, but you didn't cheat a partner that had treated you as good as family. If the stupid fucker had come to him about the gambling losses, if he would have asked for the money there would have been no problem, but now there was going to be hell to pay.

Martin sat up in the chair and looked Pitney straight in the eyes.

"You said you had more on this scumbag?"

Pitney fought to hold back a smile as he opened the folder, took out a picture and slid it across the desk.

"This is the woman he was with."

Martin picked up the picture and looked at it wearily, then snapped his attention back to Pitney. "What kind of bullshit you trying to pull here? Where did you get this fucking picture?" he yelled.

"Same place I got this one," Pitney said as he slid another picture across the desk. This one showed Grady holding hands with the woman.

Martin crumpled the picture and threw it at Pitney. "He was with my wife?" he screamed as he jumped to his feet.

"Yeah," Pitney said with a snicker, "looks that way."

Martin's face contorted in anger.

"Don't push me or I'll have your fucking legs broken."

The half smile disappeared from Pitney's face as he raised his hands chest high in a defensive gesture. "Okay, Martin, I'm sorry. I was being a little insensitive."

"I want you out of town for awhile. Take a vacation. I'll even throw in a bonus to help pay for it."

"Martin, are you fucking nuts? I've got a business to run," he said as he lowered his hands.

"I'll buy your business. You can go to the Caribbean and be a beach bum."

"Fuck you, Martin. You can't buy me," Pitney said as he got to his feet. "Our transaction is completed. Get the fuck out of my office," he said as he moved around the desk and quickly walked to the door. "You get the hell out of here and don't come back," he said as he unlocked the door.

Ralph Mason pushed the heavy plate glass doors open and walked out into the dark parking lot at the back of the museum. He was a thin scarecrow of a man with gray hair and a day worth of matching stubble on his face. The loose fitting security uniform flapped in the breeze as he looked up at the black clouds. He took a pack of Camels out of his shirt pocket and shook out one of the smokes, put it between his lips and snapped back the cover on the Zippo. The silver finish had worn off the corners of the lighter and the Marine insignia was barely visible, but the flame stood against the wind, honoring all advertised claims.

He snapped the lighter closed and wondered how soon the storm was going to hit. He didn't mind a nice summer rain, but God he hated electrical storms, especially when he was working the graveyard shift. The dancing shadows cast by the lightning were just a little too much like the dreams that had plagued him off and on for the last year. The dreams were like hallucinations from the darkest corners of his mind.

He wanted to talk with other Marines who had volunteered for the drug experiment. He wanted to find out if any of them ever suffered from bizarre dreams, but after thirty years he was lucky to remember their first names. Besides there was the document he signed identifying the program as classified and swearing him to secrecy. He was never to discuss the experiment with anyone, including any of the other volunteers, not that it meant anything to him now.

He took a deep drag off his cigarette and glanced at his watch. The worst part about the dreams was that they had left him with very little resistance to getting spooked, and that was a bad condition to be in when you had to walk through a dark museum to do part of your job. A good flashlight might keep you from breaking a kneecap on a display case, but it sure as hell didn't do much for the nerves, especially if your imagination had been tainted by nightmares. There were always shadows and dark corners just beyond the light that might conceal unspeakable things. It was real spooky to feel your imagination starting to run away with itself and knowing you couldn't stop it. Sometimes the only help was to throw back a shot of Jack Daniels.

He took the last drag off the Camel and tossed the butt into the bushes as he walked back toward the building. After another quick look up at the churning clouds he went back into the museum and locked the doors. The vestibule beyond the doors was empty except for a single glass display case, which separated the security alcove from the rest of the small lobby. A wide stairway across from the alcove descended into the lower level where many of the more elaborate Indian artifact displays were kept.

Ralph glanced down into the darkness of the stairway as he walked past and fought to think of anything except what might be lurking down there. The rational part of his mind knew there was nothing but display cases filled with relics hundreds or maybe thousands of years old, but a rational mind was useless when it came to stopping the heebie jeebies.

He stopped at the desk, picked up his cup and walked back to the coffee maker. A flash of lightning from somewhere in the distance came through the window as he poured the steaming brew. He counted to himself as he waited for the clap of thunder. When it finally came he knew the storm front was still about five miles away.

He went back to the desk and sat down with his coffee as he thought about the trip he had to make through the dark museum every hour and the location of the five time clock keys. As far as he was concerned it was nothing but a bunch of bullshit Rudy dreamed up to insure everybody was making their rounds. There was little doubt in his mind that the insurance company required around the clock security, but the time clock was just plain stupid. Sure, the timed recording made by the keys proved you were at the key location at a particular time, but so what. It was just another rule Rudy pulled out of his ass to show everybody he was the boss.

He glanced at his watch and knew he couldn't put the trip off any longer. He already had a letter in his file for late time clock punches and he wasn't going to give Rudy any more ammunition. It was already pretty clear he was looking for a reason to fire him. He supposed it was all because of a few careless remarks he made about Rudy's weight and how the Marines might go about getting it off. He never was very good at keeping his mouth shut, he thought as he took the time clock and flashlight out of the bottom desk drawer.

God he hated the midnight shift, he thought as he stood up and slipped the time clock strap over his shoulder. The worst part was that staying up all night and sleeping during the day seemed to make the nightmares come more frequently and that was the last thing he needed. A couple shots of whiskey before bed helped for a while, but when the dreams came back they were more vivid and more intense than ever. That was when he first realized he wasn't dreaming of the flying monkeys of Oz. Flying monkeys were just a little weird. The creatures flying around in his nightmares were horrid things and with each dream they got a little closer.

His hand trembled slightly as he reached for his lunch bucket. No sense in facing the gauntlet alone, he thought as he lifted the lid and pulled out a pint bottle of Jack Daniels. He removed the bottle cap, spiked his coffee and took a little swig before returning the whiskey to his lunch bucket. He took a drink of his coffee for good measure before walking out of the security station for his appointed rounds.

He turned on his flashlight and started down the steps as a loud clap of thunder shook the museum.

Samuel Prince sat at the kitchen table and folded the morning paper to the sports section. He was a small man with a dark, weathered complexion and white hair. His bushy white mustache gave him an Albert Einstein look that was enough to make some strangers do a double take.

He studied the baseball scores and wondered if this was going to be the year for the Reds. They always seemed to start off strong and then fall into the same old rut toward the end of the season. He was sure they had the talent to take the pennant on a regular basis if they could only keep players off the injured list.

He turned the paper to the business section and started studying the mutual funds, wondering why he kept putting off retirement. The work was no longer as challenging as it had once been. At one time his agenda at the museum was so full it was staggering, but now, after ten years, all the bones and artifacts were identified and the displays were completed. With the real work done the job was reduced to little more than public relations and an occasional speaking engagement.

Money certainly wasn't a problem. After twenty-five or thirty years some of his stock holdings had turned into serious investments, and Martha's royalty checks were swelling the savings account beyond her wildest dream. There was no question about their financial condition, but for some reason he couldn't bring himself to pull the plug.

Martha tied the belt around her robe as she shuffled into the kitchen. She was a thin, almost frail looking woman with short brown hair streaked with gray. "Morning," she said through a yawn as she walked up behind Samuel and put her hands on his shoulders.

"Good morning," he said as he stroked her hand. "I didn't expect to see you up before I left for work. What time did you get to bed?"

"About two thirty," she said as she kissed him on the cheek. "I hope I didn't keep you awake."

"You didn't. I must have drifted right off. I don't remember hearing the typewriter. Did you finish the article?"

"Not quite," she said as she walked to the cupboard and took a mug off the shelf. "I hope Jason doesn't call me today, but he probably will." She filled the mug with coffee, went to the table and sat across from Samuel. "He thinks hounding me until a piece is done is being a good editor."

Samuel chuckled.

"Isn't it part of his job to make sure you meet your deadline?"

"Maybe, but his zeal is maddening. He has a lot to learn when it comes to dealing with people."

Samuel smiled as he folded the paper and laid it on the table. "Maybe you're just tired of the tension associated with these deadlines. You could write another novel. I'm sure you've got some unused plots in your head."

"The deadlines are still there, it's just that they're your own instead of a magazine editor's. Sometimes I think it's time to put away the typewriter and try retirement for a while."

Samuel nodded.

"I was thinking about retirement when I was reading the paper. I know the time's right, but for some reason I just can't talk myself into actually doing it."

Martha blew steam off the top of her coffee and took a sip before setting the mug down.

"I believe there's two things that keep you working. First, you think you're still a young man. For thirty-eight years I've watched you work. If you weren't opening a tomb somewhere you were digging up bones and piecing them together. When we left Egypt and came here you stayed busy with the Indian displays, but now that things have slowed down at the museum you don't know what to do with yourself. You think you still have all that youthful energy, but you don't. Your body needs to slow down, but your mind still thinks you're thirty five, so you put off the inevitable."

Samuel finished the last of his coffee as he got up from the table. "You make it sound like I'm ready for the glue factory," he said as he put the mug in the sink and filled it with water.

"Don't be silly. We've both got a lot of good years left. We shouldn't spend them working if we don't have to."

He went back to the table and took his jacket off the back of the chair. "What was the other thing?" he asked as he picked up his pipe and dropped it into the pocket of his jacket.

Martha stood up, straightened his tie and kissed him on the lips. "You think Joyce is a little girl who needs protected from the big bad wolf. If you weren't in her way you'd probably find out she's one hell of a lot tougher than you think she is. I'm sure she can handle Rudy without your help."

Samuel smiled and kissed her back. "You really think so?"

"Of course I do. She's a redhead. There's a lot of fire behind those green eyes."

Samuel looked at his watch. "I better hit the road. You want to meet me somewhere for lunch?"

"Maybe. Call me," she said and kissed him. "I love you."

Samuel hugged her.

"I love you, too, sweetheart. Finish the article," he said as he started toward the garage.

"I will," she said and patted him on the ass as he walked by.

Steve Patterson turned the lawnmower over, looked at the bent blade shaft and wondered how he was going to fix the damn thing without Rudy finding out about it. He stood up, pulled an orange shop rag out of the back pocket of his jeans and wiped off his hands. He had the muscular build of a young athlete, with curly blond hair and a dark tan. After returning the rag to his pocket he turned the mower back upright, set the idle and pulled the starter cord. The machine shook violently for a few seconds before it died in a puff of blue smoke. Steve shook his head as he sat down on the bench. "Luther," he called. "You better come over here for a minute."

Luther came around the corner of the tool shed carrying a leaf rake and chewing on the end of a smoldering cigar. He was a tall, heavily built black man with thinning gray hair. He walked over to the bench and sat down next to Steve. "It don't sound good when it runs, do it?"

Steve looked at Luther and laughed. "Man, you really fucked it up good.

What the hell did you hit?"

"I guess I hit the top of the wall when I was cuttin' close," Luther said as he pointed out toward the street where a stone retaining wall held back the terraced lawn. "Rudy's gonna have my ass," he said apprehensively as he shook his head.

"Don't lose any sleep over that fat asshole," Steve said. "We'll take care of this somehow, but you've got to start using the trimmer when you're up next to the wall like that."

"I was just hurryin'," he whispered as he leaned forward and rested his arms on his knees.

Steve heard a familiar rumble and looked out toward the street as a red Porsche turned into the drive. He lost sight of it for a second as it passed between the retaining walls. Joyce waved as she went past and turned into her parking place.

"That be one fast lookin' car," Luther said as he waved back.

Steve wanted to blurt out that the car was faster than it looked. He wanted to tell Luther how he put the car through it's paces one night, and how many times he had left Joyce's apartment with fingernail marks in his back, but he didn't. No sense in screwing up a good thing, and he knew that was exactly what would happen if anyone at the museum found out about their late night liaisons.

"Yeah, it sure is," he said as he got up. "I'll go talk to her. Maybe she knows somebody who can get us a new motor cheap."

Joyce was climbing out of the Porsche when Steve walked up to the edge of the blacktop and rested his hand on the top of the door. He felt the stirring of sexual tension as he watched the slit in her red skirt expose most of her thigh. The sight of her long legs always had an arousing affect on him, regardless of the state of his libido.

"Hi," he said as she closed the car door. "You look nice. New outfit?"

"Yes," she said as she straightened her skirt. "I start my teaching career today. I thought I should try to make a good first impression."

"You'd make a good impression in worn jeans and a T-shirt."

"I'd make a good impression on you dressed like that, but you've had your hands on the merchandise," she said with a sensuous smile. "Stop by tonight about seven if you're not busy. I'll throw a couple steaks on the grill."

"If I'm busy I'll change my plans," he said as she turned away. Her beauty always left him aroused, but this time he felt almost weak as he watched her body move. He caught himself thinking that making love to her just wasn't enough. He wanted her heart, too. It was a thought for which he quickly chastised himself. He ran into the stone wall that guarded her emotions once, and that was enough for him. He'd spare himself that pain by keeping their relationship where it belonged.

Joyce opened one of the heavy glass doors and walked through the rear entrance into the museum. She glanced at her watch as she stopped at the security station. "Morning, Ralph."

"Morning, Joyce," Ralph responded as he looked up from the magazine spread open on the top of the desk.

"I need a quick cup of coffee. Got any made?"

"I always have fresh coffee. It's the only thing that keeps me going on this damn graveyard shift," he said as he pushed himself back away from the desk.

Joyce walked around the end of the glass display case and sat in the chair at the end of the desk. "You heard anything on the radio this morning about what's happening on High Street by Cook Tower? The police had it blocked off when I went past."

"Sure did," he said as he raised himself out of the chair. "I guess some private detective jumped out of his tenth story office window. They found him this morning splattered all over the street."

"God, can you imagine?"

"No, I can't. It probably wasn't very pretty," he said as he took a couple disposable cups out of the package in the desk drawer.

Joyce noticed how loose Ralph's uniform was fitting as he walked over to the coffee maker and wondered if he was losing weight. She was sure he didn't eat right, what man living by himself did. Rotating shifts every month probably didn't help his diet either.

Ralph came back to the desk with two steaming cups of coffee. He set one in front of Joyce as he returned to his chair.

Joyce blew across the coffee before taking a sip. "Hot," she said as she put it down and looked at Ralph. The puffy bags under his eyes made it look like he could barely hold them open.

"You feeling okay, Ralph?" she asked.

Ralph shrugged his shoulders. "Probably as good as I can expect to feel working this damn shift. Why?"

"You look so tired. Are you eating right?"

Ralph gave her a halfhearted smile. "I don't eat or sleep very well when

I'm on midnights. It's like everything in me is twisted or something. I drink coffee to stay awake, and then when I go home I can't get to sleep. When I do sleep it's usually no more than a couple hours at a time. Those damn nightmares I've been having seem to get worse when I sleep during the day."

"Would you talk to a friend of mine who's a psychiatrist if I made you an appointment?" Joyce asked.

Ralph shook his head. "I've never trusted shrinks, besides everything will get better in a couple weeks when I get off this shift," he said and took a drink of coffee.

"But that's only a temporary fix. You'll be back on midnights in two months. What do you do then?"

"I'll let my buddy Jack Daniels keep me from going crazy, just like I do now."

"I wish there was another answer for you. I don't think Rudy would need much of an excuse to put you out on the street."

"Yeah, I know, but I don't worry much about it. The dreams are a lot worse than anything that shithead could do to me, so I'll continue doing what I have to do to deal with them."

"I wish I could help you," she said.

Ralph offered a tired smile.

"I know you do. Just remember to stop by and have coffee with me in the mornings. Seeing your pretty face makes things a little better."

Joyce was surprised to feel herself blush.

"Well Ralph, I've got to get moving," she said as she stood up. "I have to be on campus in an hour and I have to see Sam before I leave." She picked up her coffee and walked around the end of the display case. "Wish me luck for my first day teaching."

"You've got it, honey. See you in the morning."

"Okay," she said as she walked across the lobby. She stopped at the top of the steps and looked back at Ralph. "The offer stands about getting you an appointment with my friend. Just let me know when you're ready."

"Okay," Ralph said as he watched her disappear down the stairwell.

The central chamber of the lower level was lit by four rows of fluorescent lights recessed in the ceiling. Two rows of large glass display cases exhibiting skeletal artifacts occupied the center of the room. Along the walls between colorful oil paintings of Indian life were smaller cases filled with stone weapons and tools. A magnificent hand painted mural of Indians hunting Buffalo from horseback spread across the far wall opposite the stairway. A door stood ajar just below one of the mortally wounded beasts.

Joyce touched some of the cases as she walked by and wondered how much time she and Sam had spent setting up the displays. Sometimes she missed the hard work and long hours of those days. She hoped teaching would bring back some of the high energy that faded from her life as demands of the museum tapered off.

She smelled cherry blend tobacco from Sam's pipe as she walked into the office. There were two desks on opposite sides of another door leading out into the lab, one cluttered with mail, the other neat and orderly. Joyce set the coffee on her desk next to the phone as she walked through the open door.

Beyond the office was a large well-lit lab with several granite lab stations, each equipped with a sink, a rack containing a variety of archaeological tools and a lighted magnifying glass mounted on the table. Samuel was at the far end of the lab trying to open the double doors leading outside.

Joyce noticed a beat up cardboard box filled with bones sitting at the end of one of the lab stations and walked over to investigate.

"Morning, Sam," Joyce said as she rummaged through the box. "Having trouble with the doors again?"

"I don't know what's wrong with the damn things," he said in a frustrated tone as he turned away from the doors and started across the lab toward Joyce.

"So don't mess with them. Give Steve a call," she said with a laugh. It was a total mystery to her how he could become so exasperated with a set of doors when he once spent several months finding a way into an Egyptian tomb.

Samuel stopped abruptly and looked Joyce over. "My, you do clean up rather well."

She stepped away from the table and turned for him. "Do you think I'll be a hit with the student body?"

"Especially with the guys," Samuel said with a chuckle. "Don't be too hard on them the first day, they probably won't hear a word you say."

Joyce laughed as she turned back toward the table. "Where did the bones come from?" she asked.

"The Sheriff stopped by Friday night after you left. They found them at the stone quarry on Sand Ridge Road and he decided this was the place to bring them. He wanted to know whether to start a formal investigation or not. I told him we'd do some testing and determine the age."

Joyce picked up the skull and rolled it over in her hands like a ball. "The skull doesn't have the physical characteristics that I'd expect to find with an Indian relic."

"Let's start off with carbon dating," he said as he walked up next to her and leaned against the table. "Take a bone chip from the lower jaw. After you get that in the mail to Columbus you can do a complete inventory of the skeleton. I want to make sure we're dealing with one set of bones before we get too far along. When everything's finished you can write a report for the Sheriff."

"Did you see Ralph this morning?" she asked as she laid the skull back in the box.

"I spoke to him when I came in, but I didn't stop to talk. Why?" he asked as he took his pipe and tobacco pouch out of his jacket pocket.

"I think he looks bad," she said as she watched Samuel fill his pipe.

"The midnight shift doesn't agree with Ralph. He falls into a rut that he can't get out of until he gets back on days." He lit his lighter and sucked the flame down into the tobacco, sending a plume of cherry blend smoke drifting toward the ceiling. "He drinks too much coffee at night, then can't sleep when he goes home. A few days of that routine runs him down, mentally and physically. And then there's those nightmares he's been having for the last year or so. They always seem to be worse when he's working midnights," he said as they walked back toward the office.

"I feel bad for him. I wish there was something I could do."

"I know. He needs help, but he's stubborn and won't accept it when it's offered. There's not a whole lot we can do for him if he's not willing," Samuel said as they walked into the office.

Joyce went to her desk and picked up her coffee. "I can't imagine having those kind of issues and not wanting help," she said as she sat on the edge of the desk."

"Ralph is a different person. I suppose the best we can do for him is just be there if he ever wants to talk." Samuel relit his pipe and glanced at his watch. "You don't have a lot of time, you better get moving. I don't think you want to be late for your first class."

"Believe it or not, I've got a few butterflies." She finished the coffee, crumpled the cup and threw it into the trash. "I hope I don't get stage fright."

Samuel laughed. "You'll do just fine," he said as he walked over and kissed her on the forehead. "A kiss for good luck."

"Thanks, Sam. I'll probably need it."

Ralph shifted uneasily in the desk chair and wondered where Bill was. It wasn't like him to be late for shift change, especially when he worked days. Nobody was late when they worked days. The chances of Rudy finding out were just too great, and that was one sure way of putting him in a foul mood. When Rudy was on the warpath it was bad for everybody, but it was pure misery for the guard on duty. Sam looked out for Joyce and didn't put up with Rudy's shit, Steve and Luther could hide, but the guard was stuck in the security station.

Ralph glanced at his watch, then got up and walked to the window. He didn't want Bill to spend the day as Rudy's whipping boy, and he didn't want to see Rudy before he left. If Rudy got too close to him all the breath mints in the world couldn't hide the fact that he'd been drinking. He started to turn away from the window when he caught a glimpse of Bill's old Ford coming up the drive.

He hurried back to the desk and grabbed his lunch bucket as he headed toward the door. It was going to be a narrow escape, no sense in waiting at the desk and taking the chance of running into Rudy at the last minute. He pushed open the door and walked out into the parking lot just as Bill was getting out of his car.

Bill was a short, stocky man with a protruding belly. He started apologizing as soon as he saw Ralph standing in the middle of the parking lot. "God, Ralph, I'm really sorry about being late, but I wasn't sure I was going to make it," he said as he rubbed his stomach. "I was up all night with my gut. Must have been something I ate. I still feel like shit. Nothing seems to help."

Ralph shook his head sympathetically. "I hope you get to feeling better. A case of indigestion isn't much fun," he said as he started walking toward his car. "I've got to go, I'm on my last leg. There's a fresh pot of coffee, but you probably ought to stay away from it. You don't need any more acid in your stomach. See you in the morning."

"Okay, Ralph, take it easy."

Bill walked the rest of the way across the parking lot to the building and opened the door when he heard a car coming up the drive. He hurried inside, hoping it wasn't Rudy. He didn't need him on his case about being late, especially this morning.

He hurried back to the security station and grabbed a cup out of the drawer. Coffee was the last thing he wanted, but a half full cup would make it look like he had been there for a while. When he got to the coffee maker he reached for the spigot and realized his left arm was aching like a bad tooth. He wondered if he had done something to it during the night.

Rudy was coming through the doors just as Bill got back to the display case with his coffee. He was a mountain of corpulent flesh hidden beneath a well-tailored gray pin stripe suit. The bottom of his gold wire rimmed glasses pressed against his rotund cheeks.

Rudy walked up to the display case and looked at Bill as he took off his glasses. "Were you late this morning?" he asked as he took a handkerchief out of his pocket.

"No...I don't think so," he said as he raised the cup to his lips. He tried to hold his hand steady, but a slight tremble was obvious.

Rudy opened the handkerchief and cleaned his glasses slowly. When he put them back on he stared at Bill for a moment. "Well, I think you were," he said as he refolded the handkerchief and returned it to his pocket. "I think you know you were late and I think you're trying to lie your way out of it."

"That's not true," Bill objected as he set the cup on top of the display case.

"Bullshit, Rodgers! I'm docking you an hour."

"You...you can't do that! If I was late it was only a few minutes."

"I can do any damn thing I want," Rudy said as he poked a finger at Bill. "And if you don't like it, you know where the door is. Guards are a dime a dozen, and losing you wouldn't mean shit to me. You better be on time from now on. This isn't the goddamn welfare department," he yelled as he turned and walked away.

Bill left the partial cup of coffee sitting on the display case and went back to the desk. He pulled the chair out and slammed it against the wall. In his book Rudy VanBurg was the biggest cocksucker in the world. Just once he'd like to meet up with him in a dark alley. Maybe he'd like sucking on the end of a two by four.

He plopped down in the chair and put a hand on his stomach, which had just taken a turn for the worse. He opened the desk drawer and took out a bottle of Tums. God he wished he could hit the lottery. His first stop after leaving the bank would be Rudy's office. He'd knock those wire-rimmed glasses right off his smug fucking face. He popped three Tums into his mouth and threw the bottle on the desk while he thought of how he'd enjoy using a ball bat on Rudy VanBurg's fat face.

Joyce downshifted the Porsche as she took the new section of Campus drive that curved back into the woods. The beauty of the small campus was something that always surprised people from other communities, especially those familiar with Lima's reputation as a hard town. Aesthetically pleasing buildings set in the midst of a forest of towering pines just didn't seem to mix with a history spotted by violent episodes with the likes of the Dillinger gang.

Sunlight filtered down through the trees as she drove passed a stone monument identifying the site of a Miami burial ground. She wondered how many of the students in her class would know about the rich Indian heritage of the area. She was certain most of the class would be comprised of engineering students wanting to pick up a few easy hours during the summer. Indian Culture probably sounded a little less boring than Ethics or Introduction to Poetry. She doubted anybody signed up for the class because of a burning desire to learn more about Native Americans. She hoped the teaching experience left her with the desire to return in the fall when the class would be available to more students.

She wondered if the campus was going to look as deserted as it did when she had her interview. She hoped not. Without students a college campus was just another collection of empty buildings. They were the lifeblood of the academic community.

She came out of the woods into bright sunlight, stopping the Porsche at a traffic sign near the facility parking lot. Ahead was Galvin Hall and the open expanse of the lawn stretching to the other buildings. A surprising number of students were sitting with books open or milling about. Four young men were engaging themselves in some type of game played with a Frisbee, while another group seemed to be playing tag football.

A flood of memories of another campus suddenly surprised her; memories she thought had been locked safely away in a special corner of her mind.

She had just turned eighteen when she met Randy outside the bookstore at the University of Kentucky on a sunny day in September. Joyce noticed him as she left the bookstore, loaded down with a pile of books and supplies. He was tall, maybe six feet with an athletic body and long sandy blonde hair down to his shoulders. He was engaged in what seemed to be a serious conversation with an Oriental student with long black hair tied back in a ponytail. As she watched him a wave of emotion sent her heart spiraling upward as if on golden wings.

She turned and sauntered in his direction, hoping for eye contact and a chance to flash a smile. She was a little too close when he ended his conversation and turned in her direction without looking.

The ensuing collision was more than she could have hoped for. Books, pencils, and paper went in all directions as Joyce landed on her bottom in the middle of the busy sidewalk.

"Oh shit!" he cried out as he bent down. "Oh God, are you hurt?" he asked as he reached out to her.

"Just my pride," she said with a smile as she took his hand.

"God, I am so sorry," he said as he pulled her to her feet.

The Oriental friend that had been talking to him was busy gathering the scattered books and supplies.

"I'm Randy Lippencott," he said as he bent down and picked up a nearby textbook. "I'm really sorry. Are you sure you're not hurt?"

Joyce laughed as she brushed off the back of her jeans. "A bruise, maybe. No permanent damage. Joyce Robbins," she said with a shake of his hand. "Nice to meet you."

The friend walked up next to them holding her books and supplies that had been scattered in the collision.

"This is my friend and roommate Kim Lee," Randy said as he took half the books from him. "Kim, this is Joyce Robbins."

"It's very nice to meet you," Kim said with a smile.

"And you also," Joyce said, returning the smile.

"I think we have a moral obligation to buy Joyce lunch," Kim said.

"No, you guys. Really, you don't owe me anything."

"Yes we do. Do you like chili?" Randy asked.

"Yes, I love it," she replied.

"Well, we happen to know a place that makes the best chili in the world."

A quick toot from a car horn severed her from her memories.

She pulled the Porsche past the stop sign and turned into the section reserved for faculty cars, still reeling from the unexpected flood of memories.

She had insolated herself from the pain of the memories for years, keeping them locked away and refusing to let them out. Now they were struggling to break free and demanding to be examined. She pulled into a parking place, shut off the engine and sat behind the wheel with her eyes closed, wondering if the pain was really still there after all these years. After all, the Vietnam War was dated material. It was a subject of which most students on campus only had dim, shadowy knowledge.

Cautiously, she let her mind drift back to that day in September when she met Randy and Kim.

Joyce sat at the table watching Randy as he finished the last of his second bowl of chili. His deep blue eyes seemed to hold some magical attraction for her own. He dropped the spoon into the empty bowl and set it inside the other bowls on the corner of the table.

"That's great stuff," he said as he wiped a napkin across his mouth. "Kim had never tasted chili until I brought him here. Now he's their second best customer."

"It was a definite change from the traditional Chinese food I was raised on," Kim said as he picked up his beer.

"Joyce, what did you think of it?" Randy asked as their eyes embraced.

"It was good," she said absently as she held his gaze with her own. "A bit overrated, but good just the same," she said with a laugh. "I don't know how you managed it, but you have chili in your right eyebrow."

Randy grabbed the napkin and wiped it across his eyebrows.

"He lives like a slob at home, too," Kim said and laughed.

"Oh, like you've got a lot of room to talk," Randy said as he presented his eyebrow for inspection.

"That's got it. You guys live together?"

"Yeah, we've got an apartment about a mile from campus," Randy said, then frowned. "What did you mean when you said the chili was overrated?"

"It was good, but you said it was the best in the world. It just so happens mine is better."

Randy and Kim looked at each other and laughed.

"Wait a minute, you two. You can't laugh at my chili without trying it."

"She's right, you know," Kim whispered.

"Okay," Randy said. "You name the time. We've got the kitchen."

"God, at the rate I'm going it'll take me six months to save enough money to buy the ingredients."

Randy opened his notebook, took out a piece of paper and tore it in half. He wrote on one of the pieces and slid both across the table to Joyce.

"That's our address and phone number. Don't lose it. Put your grocery list on the other piece of paper and Kim and I'll go to the store."

"You're kidding, right?"

"He's serious," Kim said. "We've got plenty of money. We don't expect you to buy anything. Just cook up a batch and let us try it."

"Okay," she said as she pulled a pencil out of her purse.

Joyce jumped as a tap on her car window jolted her back from the memories that seemed like yesterday. A man dressed in a campus security uniform was

28

standing next to her window. She turned the ignition key to the accessory position and lowered the window.

"Didn't mean to scare you, miss."

"My mind was a thousand miles away," she said with a smile. "Do you want to see my parking permit?" she asked as she reached into her purse.

The patrolman shook his head.

"I'm sorry," he said. "I thought you were a student."

She handed him the permit, closed the window and climbed out of the sports car.

"I really don't want to put it on my bumper."

"I can't blame you for that," the man said with a smile. "This is a beautiful car. It's a 911 turbo, isn't it?" he asked as he handed the permit back to her.

"Yes, it is," she replied.

"I thought so. Just lay the permit on your dash when you're in the parking lot."

"Thanks," she said as the officer walked back to his scooter.

She tossed the permit onto the dash, closed the door and locked it with the remote as she walked away.

She moved along the cobblestone path leading to Galvin Hall and wondered if the patrolman had really mistaken her for a student. There was always the possibility he just wanted to get a closer look at the Porsche, or maybe a closer look at her. Men were funny about cars and women. They liked to look, but didn't always want anyone to know. She guessed it had something to do with some unwritten code of masculine pride.

When she got to the building she opened one of the plate glass doors and stepped into the pleasantly cool interior. Several students were sitting in the lobby with open books while others seemed to be waiting for someone. A muscular, slightly graying man wearing a Michigan State T-shirt and jeans was standing at the bulletin board reading the class schedule.

"Good morning," she said as she walked up next to the man.

He turned her way and smiled. "Good morning, yourself. Need to look at the schedule?"

"Not if you'll tell me what room my nine o'clock Indian culture class is in."

"Let's see," the man said as he ran his finger down the list of classes. "Ah, here it is. Indian Culture, room three-fifty-four, with J. Robbins," he said as he looked back at Joyce. "Must be someone new, I don't recognize the name."

"I'm Joyce Robbins," she said with a smile and offered her hand. "This will be my first quarter in the teaching profession."

"Jerry Lansford," he said as he shook her hand. "I teach chemistry and physics to the Engineering students. I'm going up to my office, I'll show you the way."

"Alright," she said as they walked away from the bulletin board and started down the hall.

"So, this is a first for you."

"Yes. I'm really not sure of what to expect."

"You're new to the students. They'll be trying to find out how well you know the material." He stopped in front of the elevator and pushed the up button. "If you come across to them as not being sure of yourself they won't take the class seriously. On the other hand, if you look sharp, they'll work hard for their grade."

A small bell sounded just before the elevator doors slid back. Jerry watched the way Joyce's body moved as she stepped into the elevator, and in that instant he knew he wanted her. The game was on, but now was not the time for bold moves. He had at least thirteen weeks to build a relationship. Only fools rushed in, and he was no fool when it came to women. He stepped in behind Joyce, pushed the button for the third floor and watched the doors close.

"You don't strike me as a person who's right out of college with an education degree," Jerry said.

"Oh, education isn't my real job. I'm a graduate archaeologist. I guess the American Indian has become my specialty. I've worked at the Allen County Museum for about twelve years."

"Are you married?" he asked.

"No. I think you'd have to list me as a confirmed single woman. I've never met anyone I wanted to spend the rest of my life with." It was a good answer to Jerry's subtle question, but it wasn't entirely true. Her heart had belonged to a man once.

"That's nothing to be ashamed of. In retrospect, after two failed marriages, I should have had an attitude like yours," Jerry said as the elevator came to a stop. The doors opened onto the third floor where a small group of students waited. They stepped out into the hall as the others piled in.

"Your classroom is down at the end of the hall on the left."

"Thanks, Jerry," she said with a smile. "I appreciate you helping the new kid on the block."

Jerry returned her smile.

"No problem," he said and watched her turn and walk away. "How about lunch one of these days?"

Joyce stopped and turned around.

"That sounds like a good idea. It'll give me a chance to ask you about the Michigan State T-shirt you're wearing."

Jerry looked down at the shirt and shook his head. "That's a long story," he said with a sheepish grin.

"I bet it is," she said with a laugh.

Jerry watched her walk away and thought it amazing that a woman so attractive could have remained single for so many years. He wondered if she had left a trail of broken hearts. He supposed there had to be a few. He vowed to himself not to join them, but the resolve of that promise already felt vulnerable. He watched her for a moment longer before turning toward his office.

Joyce walked into the small auditorium, turned on the lights and stepped up on the platform at the front of the room. She set her textbook and purse on the desk as she looked out over the empty seats and felt her pulse quicken. Having a case of stage fright would be a bad way to start out, she thought as she stepped off the platform and took one of the seats in the first row. She took a couple deep breaths and tried to relax as she gazed toward the front of the room where she'd be working in a few minutes. She glanced up at the clock just as two girls loaded down with books walked into the room. They both greeted her as they took nearby seats in the front row and started talking about their schedules.

As she watched several guys meander through the door she overheard the girls speculating about the sex of J. Robbins and realized they thought she was another student. The guys glanced at her on their way to the back of the room. Another group of guys and two girls came through the doorway just as the clock marked the hour.

Most everyone was chatting with their neighbor when one of the guys at the back of the room asked in a loud voice if anyone knew who J. Robbins was. Another of the guys responded that it was probably some old geezer with white hair and laughed loudly.

She knew that was her cue.

"Hello," she said as she stood up and faced the class. "Sorry to disappoint you, but I'm Joyce Robbins."

All the guys howled with laughter and chided the one who had made the old geezer remark.

"I'll be your instructor this quarter for Indian Culture," she said as she stepped up on the platform. "Why don't we begin by getting everyone up here in the first few rows so I don't have to shout."

Joyce was amused to see the guys in the back of the room grab their books haphazardly and race for the best empty seats. The girls, also amused, took a little more time, while speculating on the things that could make the guys move that fast.

"That's much better," she said as she held up the textbook. "I hope everyone has managed to obtain a copy of this. If not, there's still an ample supply in the bookstore." She set the book back on the desk. "I'm not wild about grading tests, so don't expect many from me. There will be a midterm and a final, which will make up half of your final grade. The other half will be from two term papers, the first of which will be due two weeks from this Friday. I won't put limits on the size, but please remember each paper is twenty-five percent of your grade. If you'll open your books to the beginning of chapter six I'll give you the assignment for tomorrow and toss out a few hints about what I'd like to see in your first term paper."

She was surprised at how easily she was falling into her teaching job. The butterflies were gone, replaced by the sudden realization that she had total command of the subject matter, a command that would enable her to shape the minds of the students in front of her. It struck her that she was engaging an awesome responsibility and wondered if such sobering thoughts had ever occurred to her own teachers. She cleared her throat when she was satisfied that everyone had located the chapter.

"I want you to read this chapter for tomorrow. Much of it refers to the general area in which we live," she said as she sauntered toward the window. "Not many people are really aware of the rich Indian heritage of this area." She gazed out the window at the tops of the towering pines swaying in the wind. "I was never particularly aware of it until I started working for the museum," she said as she turned back toward the class. "The thing that makes northwestern Ohio archaeologically interesting is the fact that several Indian nations claimed it as their own. The ensuing conflicts were fairly bloody. That's the reason you can go into almost any unworked field, turn over a few shovels of dirt and find arrow heads."

She walked back to the desk and picked up the textbook. "I hate to say it, but this isn't the only history book to be tainted by Hollywood's image of the American Indian. The American southwest was not the only place historically significant to the Indians, yet this book only contains a few chapters devoted to aboriginal life east of the Mississippi."

She walked back to the board and picked up a piece of chalk. "To the archaeologist, Ohio is very fertile for new discoveries," she said as she sketched a map of the state. "Especially the western portion, between Lake Erie and the foot hills to the south." She tossed the chalk back into the trough and dusted off her hands as she walked back to the desk. "The Delaware Indians named this vast marsh land Quilna, which loosely translated, means black foot. Many Delaware, Shawnee, and Wyandotte died trying to control the area. It was sacred ground and nobody really knows why."

For twenty minutes Joyce continued to pace back and forth between the desk and the window while she reviewed some of her most important field discoveries since coming to Lima. When she finished a girl in the second row raised her hand.

"Yes," Joyce responded.

"Do you think it would be possible to visit the museum as part of the class?"

"I think that would be a great idea," she said. "We might have to do it on a Saturday, though. I don't think we could squeeze a tour into an hour and make it meaningful."

Joyce glanced at her watch.

"That's about all I have to say for today. Tomorrow we'll use the whole hour," she said with a smile. "Come prepared to discuss the chapter and start researching your term papers." She watched the students closing their books and wondered if they all had picked up on the idea of researching a term paper about their own backyard. A trip to the museum would probably help reinforce the subtle suggestions.

She picked up her things and shut off the lights as she followed the last student out of the room. The class had gone well, leaving her secure in the feeling that she would enjoy the experience. It was a nice break from her normal daily routine.

Samuel lifted the skull out of the box carefully and rolled it over in his hands as he did a superficial surface examination. Once he was satisfied there were no marks indicating trauma, he set the skull at the end of the table and picked up a set of calipers.

He had handled enough skulls during his professional lifetime to know these bones were several hundred years old, but that was just another opinion without supporting data. He opened the calipers and slipped them over the skull, wondering if the circumstances of a two-hundred-year-old death really mattered to anyone except an historian. It would be easy to simply inform the Sheriff's office that the bones were relics, and be done with it. It would be damn easy, but sometimes the exercise was more important than the facts it provided to the researcher. He read the calipers and wrote the dimension in a spiral notebook. He was about to take a reading on the other axis of the skull when the door leading into the office opened with a slight creak.

Samuel looked back toward the office and saw Steve opening the door.

"Sounds like your hinges need oiling," he said as he stepped through the doorway.

"Yeah, they do. I wonder if I could get the maintenance man to take care of it?" he prodded. "I could use some of his magic on the double doors while he's at it."

"Are those damn things sticking again? I think I could make a career out of keeping them working."

Steve followed Samuel to the other end of the lab and watched as he tried the doors a couple times before they finally opened.

Samuel looked back at Steve with a helpless expression. "It seems like they get a little tighter every time they get used."

Steve just stood there with his hands on his hips and nodded his head. "These doors are a pain in my ass," he grumbled as he pulled a heavy screwdriver out of his tool belt. "Pull them closed as hard as you can," he said as he bent down and put the shaft of the tool between the closing doors. They came together against the screwdriver with a bone jarring crash. Steve pushed the doors back open, stood up and started tightening the hinge plate screws. When he was finished he opened and closed them a couple times without any difficulty.

"That should take care of them for awhile. Now about my problem," he said as he put the screwdriver back in the tool pouch. "You have any idea how I can get my hands on an engine for the Snapper mower without putting a requisition through for Rudy to sign?"

"I don't know, give me some time to think about it," he said as they walked back to the table. "Why do you need a new motor?" he asked as he picked up his pipe and pouch of tobacco.

"Luther was using the Snapper too close to the retaining wall and hit the blade. The shaft is bent so bad I can't keep it running. I told him I'd fix it without Rudy finding out, but I'm going to have to replace the motor."

"I thought he had one of those weed trimmers for getting up close to the wall," Samuel said as he started filling his pipe.

"He said he was in a hurry. He deserves to have his ass chewed, but if Rudy finds out..."

Samuel packed the tobacco down in the bowl of the pipe, thoughtfully. "Let me make some phone calls. Maybe I can help you out somehow," he said as he took a lighter out of his pocket and lit the tobacco. "Maybe somebody owes me a favor," he said as they walked toward the office.

Steve followed him and sat down at Joyce's desk just as Luther came into the office from the outer door.

"Well, speak of the devil," Steve said.

Samuel turned in his chair and looked back at Luther. "Well good morning, Luther. I understand you had a little problem with the lawnmower."

"Sam, I think Bill's sick. He be white as a ghost an' breathin' real funny. Better come..."

Samuel was out of his chair and moving toward the door before Luther had finished. "Steve, call 911," he yelled as he and Luther hurried out of the office.

Steve grabbed Joyce's phone and made the emergency call.

When Samuel and Luther got to the security station Bill was slumped over in the chair with his head against the wall. "Bill, can you hear me?" Samuel asked as he pulled him up in the chair.

Bill nodded his head slowly. His face had a gray pallor with beads of sweat standing out across his forehead.

"Are you having chest pain?"

Bill nodded his head again. "Can't breathe," he whispered.

"Luther, help me get him out of the chair and onto the floor."

Luther grabbed Bill under the armpits and lifted him out of the chair as Samuel took his legs. They carried him out of the alcove and laid him on the floor. Samuel knelt down next to him and opened his collar.

"Bill, the rescue squad is on the way," he said as he took off his jacket. He rolled it up and put it under Bill's head. "Try to relax," he said as he felt for a pulse in his neck.

"You be okay, Bill," Luther said as he knelt down next to him and took his hand. "We gonna take care of you."

"The rescue squad will be here in two minutes," Steve yelled as he ran up the last few steps.

Samuel looked up at him and nodded his head. "You better go get Rudy."

CHAPTER TWO

Ralph was never certain exactly when the recurring nightmares started but he remembered having them for more than a year. They were always more frequent when he worked the graveyard shift and with each recurrence became more vivid and disturbing. The thing that faded from Ralph's memory was that the nightmares were preceded by years of less traumatic dreams, which began the day he started working at the museum.

The dreams, as well as the later nightmares, always started in the same location and under the same circumstances, alone in the museum with a summer thunderstorm approaching. The depths of the subterranean level seemed the ideal place to await the end of the storm. It was there in the basement that he always found a mysterious opening leading out onto a dune of white sand below a crimson sky, a sky in which birds soared in the distance. In the beginning it seemed to be a pleasant location where he could wait for the storm to pass.

As the years progressed there were subtle changes in the illusory mental image. The storm grew more violent as it moved closer, the white sand became more coarse and crunched beneath his steps, jagged mountain peaks appeared in the distance reaching up into the crimson sky and the birds came closer, circling overhead like buzzards.

The changes that transformed the dream into a nightmare were more bizarre and centered around the birds circling above the dune. As they descended toward him, coming closer with each subsequent dream, he saw that they were much larger birds than he thought. The dream mutated into a nightmare when they came even closer, looking like the flying monkeys of OZ. He awoke to his own screams of terror when they finally came close enough to see that they weren't flying monkeys at all.

Ralph's eyes were nearly useless as the rapid flashes of lightning transformed the darkness of the room into a disjointed, strobe like vision. His breathing quickened as he inched forward, trying to locate some familiar point of reference while he fought to drive back the panic that was closing in on his mind. From somewhere in the room he could hear a flapping sound, like the slow beating of heavy wings. The sound gripped his heart in terror and sent an icy chill running up through his spine. Stiffened by fear, he moved clumsily, knocking over furniture as he tried to distance himself from the noise. As he made his way around a corner he saw a strange light spilling out into the darkness from an opening. He ran toward the light with all his strength, and as he did a low, guttural growl found his ears from somewhere behind him. He was filled with blinding fear as he ran out through the opening and across a dune of course white sand that crunched beneath his weight. He slowed, gasping for air as he looked up at jagged mountain peaks rising into a crimson sky. He had been here before. The winged creatures circling above him in the air were terrifyingly familiar as their descending flight brought them closer. The horrid beasts started dropping onto the dune around him and closing in with their cat like eyes tracking every move he made. They snarled, exposing rows of deadly shark like teeth as they approached with sinewy arms outstretched and curved talons raised. He screamed as the first one lunged...

Ralph awoke to his own screams as he sat up in bed with the sheets clinging to his damp, quivering body. Tears ran down his face as the sound of a lawnmower somewhere in the distance reminded him it had only been a nightmare. His hand trembled as he grabbed the bottle on the night stand and swung his legs over the side of the bed. Hastily, he unscrewed the cap and raised the bottle to his lips with his hand shaking so badly that some of the whiskey missed his mouth and ran down the side of his face. The familiar taste calmed his nerves as it began purging the memories of the horrific dream from his shattered mind.

After a moment he pushed himself off the side of the bed and walked toward the bathroom on shaky legs, praying once more for an end to his personal horror. Sometimes he wished he had the guts to put an end to his own life. Death couldn't be any worse than living with the torment of the nightmare.

He gripped the edge of the bathroom sink to steady himself and looked into the mirror. It was a couple seconds before he recognized the tortured face staring back at him. He struggled for a moment to hold back the tears before he began to sob.

Martin Aster walked into the dimly lit tavern and waited for his eyes to adjust before walking over to the bar. He rested his foot on the brass rail as he removed his Panama hat and set it in front of him on the bar.

The bartender pulled a couple beer mugs out of soapy water, dipped them in rinse water and set them in the drying rack.

"Afternoon," he said as he turned toward the bar drying his hands. "What can I get you?" he asked as he draped the towel over his shoulder.

"A double shot of rye whiskey, straight up and a coke with no ice," he said as he climbed up on the barstool.

The bartender nodded as he turned around and took a bottle off the shelf.

Martin used the mirror to look over the other patrons in the bar and wondered which one was his man. Contractors were generally a rough bunch and were easy to pick out of a crowd, but this whole bar was filled with tough looking characters. These were the kind of people who would do anything for a buck without asking questions, not that there should be any. Pumping down a pond and building an oversized swimming pool wasn't unusual. Extravagant maybe, but that was something to be expected of wealthy people.

Wealthy was such an elegant term, he thought. Rich seemed more fitting. After all he wasn't born with a goddamn silver spoon in his mouth, he was a diamond smuggler. It was hard work, something wealthy people knew very little about.

"Want to run a tab?" the bartender asked as he set the drinks in front of Martin.

Martin shook his head as he reached into his pocket, pulled out a money clip and peeled off a fifty. "You know George Miller?" he asked as he laid the bill on the bar.

"Yeah, he's back there in the corner," he said as he picked up the fifty.

"I want to buy George a drink. Give him whatever he wants and the change is yours."

The bartender looked at the fifty, then looked back at Martin. "Mister, that's one hell of a tip. The next round is on me," he said as he opened the cash register, paid for the drinks and stuffed some bills into his pocket. He scooped ice into a glass, set it on the bar and reached for the bottle of Dewars. "Who do I say it's from?" he asked as he poured a healthy double.

"Martin Aster," he said and downed the double shot. He wondered what would possess a man to involve himself with his business partner's wife. It

38

had to take nerves of steel, especially when he was looting the bank account at the same time. He had to hand it to Grady; he was a gutsy son of a bitch. Martin supposed he was the one who taught him just about everything, including how to stay cool. He never dreamed it would be turned against him. The betrayal hurt. His death was going to be an exercise in pain and suffering.

Martin watched in the mirror as the bartender walked back to a table in the corner. He set the drink down in front of the man, said something and gestured toward the bar. The man nodded his head and said something to the bartender before he walked away. A moment later he was back behind the bar.

"George wants to buy you a drink and said for you to join him."

"Okay. Give me another double," he said as he picked up his hat and slid off the barstool. He waited for his drink, and then walked back to the table.

George gestured toward the chair across the table from him.

He was a tall, rugged looking man with closely cropped hair and an unshaven face.

"Have a seat, Martin Aster, and tell me why you'd buy a complete stranger a drink."

Martin pulled out his chair and sat down as he put his hat and drinks on the table. "You have a construction business, and I have a construction job and lots of money. Some friends made the recommendation that I contact you."

George took a drink of scotch and returned the glass to the table. "Who are the friends?" he asked.

Martin shrugged his shoulders. "Some people don't like to be identified and I respect their wishes. They said you were a very good man who could be trusted in certain confidential matters."

"What kind of work are we talking about?"

"I'm going to construct a swimming pool where I currently have a pond. You would be responsible for draining the pond, doing the required digging for the project, and building the concrete forms. Another contractor will be responsible for pouring the cement. I'm willing to pay you one hundred thousand dollars plus costs for your part of the project."

George looked at Martin cautiously as he took another drink of the scotch. "One hundred thousand sounds real interesting, but I've got a business partner I have to discuss this with."

Martin threw back his double shot of whiskey and set the empty glass on the table. "By all means. It's very important for business partners to keep information flowing freely between them," he said as he pulled the money clip out of his pocket. He peeled off a one hundred dollar bill and slid it across the table. "That's for your time," he said as he took a business card out of his pocket and laid it on top of the bill. "Let me know tomorrow. There's another five hundred in it for you if I like your answer." He downed the rest of his coke and wiped his lips with a napkin. "Don't say anything about this to anyone," he said and smiled. "It's going to be a surprise for my wife."

Ralph turned off the oven and carried the steaming TV dinner to the table. He set the dinner on the table and tossed the potholders aside as he pulled out his chair and sat down. He had no appetite, but knew he had to put some nourishment into his body, not that the TV dinner contained much. He wasn't even sure the dinner had cooked long enough. It was hard to get excited about food with the visions from the nightmare so fresh in his mind. The dream had repeated so many times that the memory of it was nearly as vivid as the dream itself. The memories of those horrible carnivorous jaws were getting so entrenched in his mind that it was sometimes difficult to tell if he was in the nightmare or simply remembering it. The line between real and imagined seemed to be eroding.

He lifted the foil off the top of the aluminum tray and crumpled it in his hand as he peered down at the chicken and mashed potato dinner. Although small, the chicken leg and thigh were probably edible, but the mashed potatoes looked more like a cow chip gone white with age, and the cherry cobbler reminded him of a fresh road kill.

He picked up his fork and stirred the potatoes absently. He wondered if the other Marines from the experiment were plagued by the same nightmare, or if everyone had their own private hell. Nobody ever came right out and told him the drugs were designed to affect dreams, but he wasn't stupid. Other than the general questions about possible physical discomfort and the ability to fall asleep, dreams were the only thing they asked about during the review sessions. He asked a lot of questions of his own, but received very few answers. He always pressed the doctors for information on the purpose of the experiment, but never got anywhere. They simple ignored his queries and went on asking about his dreams.

He tried to push the whole thing out of his mind as he put his fork down and picked up the chicken leg. It didn't take a genius to know he needed something in his stomach besides Jack Daniels. His body couldn't run on booze for very long, especially if he was going to hold onto his sanity. He forced himself to take a bite of the chicken, and as he did his mind conjured up the image of one of the nightmarish creatures tearing meat from his own body. He fought the urge to throw the dinner in the trash as he choked down both pieces of chicken. He was pondering the nutritional benefits of eating the mashed potatoes when the phone rang.

He pushed himself away from the table and made it to the phone on the fourth ring. "Hello," he said.

"Ralph, this is Rudy VanBurg. Bill Rogers was taken to the hospital with a heart attack this morning. The work schedule is going to have to be adjusted accordingly."

"Bill had a heart attack?" Ralph said, still surprised to be hearing Rudy's voice.

"Damn it, that's what I just said," VanBurg responded sharply. "Lewis came in at ten o'clock and is working until ten tonight. You'll be on twelve hours, beginning at ten tonight, until Taylor gets back from vacation."

"That's another three weeks! I'm already working seven days to cover his vacancy. I..I can't do that, Rudy. I have to get off the midnight shift. Let me switch with Lewis. I'll come in right now."

"Not a chance, Mason. I've got you scheduled for ten. You be here."

The conversation ended abruptly with a click from the other end of the line.

For a moment Ralph stared at the phone, as if trying to put some meaning to a mysterious call. He finally hung up and went back to the table. He put his head in his hands and prayed for Bill. He prayed, but deep inside he felt cheated. Did God make some kind of mistake? It wasn't Bill who asked for an end to his torment. He was ready to die if that's what it took to get away from the nightmares for good. He pushed the glass of whiskey and TV dinner out of the way and laid his head down on his folded arms. He began to cry, and continued to do so until his exhaustion forced him into a restless sleep.

Ned Warner stepped through the doorway of the busy Mexican restaurant and started scanning the crowd for George Miller. He was a small, wiry looking man in worn jeans with his graying hair pulled back into a short ponytail. After a couple seconds he spotted George standing next to a corner table, waving his arm. Ned waived back and started across the crowded dining room. He finally made his way to the table after dodging several scurrying waitresses and hustling busboys.

"Busy place today," he said as he pulled out a chair and sat down. "It'll take me forever to get a drink ordered."

"No it won't," George said. "I've got a beer on ice for you." He waived at the waitress and pointed to Ned as he held up his own drink that was nearly gone.

"So what's up?" Ned asked. "Your message sounded urgent."

George stirred the ice in his glass as he considered how to begin. He knew how paranoid Ned could be at times. The last thing he wanted was to make him nervous before he had a chance to sell him on the merits of the lucrative deal.

"I have a job lined up for us. I think we can pick up some serious money, but the guy needs an answer right away."

"What are you calling serious money?" Ned asked.

"One hundred thousand dollars."

Ned glanced around, as if to make sure nobody was listening, then leaned forward.

"One hundred thousand?" he whispered. "That's a lot of money. What kind of expenditures come out of it?"

"It's cost plus one hundred grand, and I get the feeling it's going to be a cash deal. The guy gave me a hundred bucks for a few minutes of my time."

Ned leaned back in his chair as the waitress walked up to the table. She laid a napkin in front of Ned, set a mug of beer on top of it and exchanged glasses with George.

"Can I get you guys anything else?" she asked.

"We're okay for now, darlin'," George answered as he handed her a ten. "Keep it," he said.

"Thanks," she said and turned away.

Ned watched her ass as she walked back toward the bar. "Now that's a work of art," he said as he picked up his beer. He took a long drink before putting the mug back on the napkin. "What kind of project is it?"

"The guy wants to turn a pond into a swimming pool. All we have to do is pump down the pond and build the frame for the concrete work."

"What about the concrete?" Ned asked.

"We won't have to mess with it," George replied as he stirred his drink. "He has another contractor that will be pouring it."

"That's unusual. How did you find out about the job?" Ned asked.

George raised his glass to his lips and took a drink. He didn't want to answer Ned's question. He couldn't think fast enough to come up with a believable lie, and the truth stood a good chance of throwing a monkey wrench into the works. He set the glass on the table and cleared his throat.

"He found me at Walt's Tavern and made the offer."

Ned looked at George cautiously. "You mean he just came to you out of the blue? How the fuck did he know who we were?" Ned asked, clearly agitated.

"He said a friend sent him."

"Who?" Ned demanded.

"He wouldn't say, but I..."

"George, are you fucking nuts? This guy has Navy investigator written all over him. Just one serial number somewhere on that equipment that we might have missed and we'd be up the fucking river."

Ned started to push his chair away from the table.

"Sit still and lower your voice," George demanded. "I had the guy checked out." It wasn't exactly the truth, but George had to say something to save the deal.

Ned relaxed a little and took a drink from his beer. "Why didn't you say so?" he asked.

"I tried, but you were busy trying to get everyone's attention."

"Sorry," Ned said with a sheepish grin. "What did you find out?"

"The guy's name is Martin Aster. He's been around town for a long time, he's worth one hell of a lot of money, and nobody seems to know or isn't willing to say what it is he does." The truth was he found Martin's name in an old county directory and decided that meant he had been in the area for a while. It was a gamble, but he felt he was a good judge of character. Martin was no more a Navy investigator than Ned was.

"Well," Ned said as he raised his mug, "here's to fast cars, fast women, and big money."

George raised his glass and clinked it against the mug. "A few more jobs like this one and we can ditch the equipment and buy a legitimate business."

"Yeah," Ned said and laughed. "A bar with a bordello upstairs."

George laughed, took a drink and hoped he was right about Martin Aster.

Joyce finished watering the last of her plants and walked over to the sliding glass door where the cat waited patiently. The cat looked up at her and cried softly as she reached for the door handle. "You go out, but leave the birds alone or I'll wring your neck."

The cat rubbed against her leg as if to assure her that birds were the farthest thing from his mind.

She slid the door open a little and watched as the big tom slipped through the opening and onto the deck where he found his favorite sunny spot. As she closed the door she looked out at the rippling lake and thought about her morning on campus. A lot of things surprised her, but nothing as much as the memories of college that suddenly broke free of their shackles and leaped into her conscious mind.

It was as if she found herself in the path of a crushing tidal wave with nowhere to run. She felt helpless to do anything but brace for the heartache. The pain was only a shadow of what it had once been. Instead of feeling the bitter agony of a love lost forever she felt sadness for what might have been.

She turned away from the door, walked over to her stereo and started looking through the CD collection. After reviewing the titles she decided on some older music by Pink Floyd. She slipped the silver disc into the player, pushed the play button and stretched out on the Persian rug in front of the entertainment center. She closed her eyes and a moment later the condo was filled with an unmistakable blend of sounds unique to only one band.

She was glad Steve was coming over, she needed him sexually, but there was something else. She needed company, needed interaction to occupy her mind. Dwelling on the past made no sense, yet she kept finding herself lost in thought as she remembered her friends and the life they had together.

She wondered if she had made a mistake by blocking the memories all these years. Time had eased the pain, but now it seemed as though she was left with a vortex of swirling emotions that threatened to draw her deeper into a mood that wasn't easily defined. She found herself wishing she could sit down and talk with Kim. He always had answers to questions that others never thought about asking. Answers that always seemed to shed just the right amount of light on a confusing world.

Joyce relaxed her body and let the abstract music flow through her mind like a cool summer breeze as her thoughts drifted slowly toward the past where happiness and sorrow seemed to lock together in a hopeless paradox. Her memories of the day she agreed to move in with Randy and Kim spilled over some barrier and filled her mind.

She had cut class and had been wandering aimlessly on the campus for about an hour when she found Kim reading his calculus book as he sat in the grass with his back against a tree.

"Hi," she said as she sat down in the grass next to Kim. "Have you seen

Randy?"

Kim looked up and flashed a bright smile as he closed the book and set it aside. "I talked to him a couple hours ago," he said and glanced at his watch. "I'm supposed to meet him here in a few minutes. We've got some things to talk about over lunch. You can join us if you want."

Joyce shook her head. "I'm not really hungry," she said as she looked away.

"Why aren't you in class?" Kim asked.

"I don't know," she said in a half whisper. "Sometimes it seems so pointless."

"It sounds like you and I need to talk. You want to get a cup of coffee or something?"

"I think I'd rather stay out here with nature, unless you're tired of sitting on the ground."

"I'm fine," Kim said as he pulled his legs up and crossed them in front of him, "but I'm a little concerned about you. What's going on up here?" he asked as he tapped a finger to her forehead.

"My request for increased access to my trust fund was turned down," she said as she watched a couple push their bicycles along the sidewalk. "I'm going to have to cut hours and get a job or drop out of school for awhile and it really upsets me." She wiped away a tear before it could betray her inner frustration. "It's just not fair," she said and looked over at Kim. "My dad wouldn't have wanted it this way," she said as a tear ran down her cheek, unnoticed.

Kim took her hand and held it in his for a moment. "You need to explore all your options. I don't really think those two choices you just mentioned are going to help. In both cases you're caving in to the problem instead of fighting."

"I have explored my options," she demanded. "I can borrow against the trust fund, but the payments would be so high that I wouldn't be gaining anything, and I can't get a student loan because of the money that's in the trust. It's just a vicious circle."

"Maybe you haven't identified the real problem yet."

"The problem is I don't have enough money to stay in school."

"Wipe the slate clean for a moment, and start out with your available money before anything gets paid. Do you have enough money for your tuition and books?"

"Yes, but..."

Kim held up his hand in a silencing gesture. "You're looking through the wrong end of the telescope," he said. "You've got the money for school, it's the money for food and housing that's the problem."

"That's about the dumbest thing I've ever heard you say," she snapped.

"Randy and I have been watching you struggle financially, and we think we've come up with a solution."

Joyce gave Kim a halfhearted smile. "I'm sorry I snapped at you. I know you're just trying to help," she said with a sigh. "What kind of idea did you guys dream up?"

"What you need is a place to stay that doesn't cost you anything. So, since we have an extra bedroom, Randy and I decided you should move in with us. We'll give you the extra bedroom and buy all the groceries if you'll cook occasionally and take care of the laundry, and stuff like that. It would really be a good deal for all of us. Randy and I don't do a very good job of taking care of the domestic chores."

"Did you guys really agree to this?" she asked.

"Yes, of course."

"Swear to God?"

"Swear to God," Kim answered. "We want you to move in with us. How about it?"

"It certainly would solve my problems, but I think it's something the three of us should discuss together."

"Great," Kim said as he got to his feet. Here comes Randy now, we can do it over lunch."

"Kim, I can't afford lunch."

"Don't be silly," Kim said as he took Joyce's hand and pulled her to her feet. "We're buying lunch. Think of it as a business meeting."

"Hi, guys," Randy said as he walked up next to Kim. "What's going on?"

"I was just discussing our extra bedroom with Joyce. She's going to have lunch with us so we can talk it over as a group."

"I love group discussions," Randy said as he took Joyce's hand. "Let's have it over pizza."

"Sounds like a winning equation to me," Kim said.

Randy jerked Joyce's hand. "Pizza okay with you?" he asked.

"Yeah, I guess so." she responded.

"Hey, lighten up. Everything's going to be fine."

"I'm okay," she said. "I just don't like sponging off of you guys."

Randy pulled her over and put his arm around her shoulder. "You're not sponging now, and you won't be if you move in with us," he said as he put his other arm around Kim's shoulder. "A couple months of picking up after this slob and you'll be thinking you got the short end of the stick."

Joyce smiled as she put her arm around Kim's shoulder and completed the circle. She kissed both of them on the cheek. "It can only work if you guys let me carry my end of the load." She said and hugged them both. "Let's go, I'm suddenly starving."

A few minutes later they walked into the Pizza Hut on the far side of campus. A waitress took them to a table in the glassed atrium overlooking the river and handed each of them a menu.

"Can I bring you something to drink?" she asked.

"How about a pitcher of Michelob," Randy replied.

"Okay. I'll be right back with that and take your orders if you're ready."

After the waitress walked away Joyce cleared her throat.

"I need to ask you guys something," she said as she looked out the window and watched a group of ducks swimming upstream. "And if you're not honest with me I'll never forgive either of you."

"Okay," Randy said. "What's on your mind?"

"I've smoked pot with you guys," she said as she continued to watch the ducks. "You always seem to have some around and you always seem to have all the money you need. Are you guys selling drugs?" she asked and looked at Randy.

"No," Randy said with a laugh. "The life style of a drug dealer never appealed to me very much."

"That is the absolute truth," Kim said. "And it's important to me that you are very clear about something. Marijuana is in a class all by itself. Just because we smoke it doesn't mean we have the propensity to use other drugs. For us pot is communion between our minds and nature. It puts us in touch with our spirit. I don't want you to ever make the mistake of getting involved with any other drugs because it's just not the same."

"That makes me feel a lot better. I don't think I could have moved in with you if you were dealing drugs."

"Does that mean you've made up your mind?" Kim asked.

"Yeah, I have, and that means you guys are going to learn how to pick up your dirty clothes and put them in the basket, or you'll be going naked."

They were all laughing when the waitress set the pitcher and mugs on the table.

"Ready to order?" she asked.

"I'm sorry," Randy said. "We've been talking and haven't even opened our menus. Can we have five minutes?"

"Sure," she said. "I'll be back in a few minutes."

"We'll be ready, we promise."

"Okay," she said as she walked away.

Joyce opened her menu while Randy started pouring the beer. "So how do you guys make your money?" she asked from behind the list of sandwiches and pizzas. When she didn't get an answer she looked over the top of the menu. "Are you guys ignoring me already?"

Randy laughed and looked at Kim.

"Do you trust me?" Kim asked.

"Yes, of course," she replied.

"We can't tell you right now, but we will," he said and chuckled. "But I promise you we don't deal drugs or do contract murders."

The sound of the doorbell snapped Joyce out of her memories and back to the condo where Pink Floyd continued to play. She got up off the floor and combed her fingers through her hair as she walked toward the door.

The memories of her friends had left her feeling slightly disoriented. She knew Steve was at the door, but she wanted to open it and find Kim standing there. She knew she was going to make love to Steve, but her heart wanted it to be Randy, and that brought home the sudden realization that she had to get a grip on her runaway emotions.

She opened the door and found Steve standing there with a magnum of wine in one hand and a handful of roses in the other.

"Hi," he said as he handed her the flowers. "Something seemed to be on your mind after you came back from school. I thought these might help."

"That was really sweet of you," she said as she put her arms around his neck and kissed him. "They're very pretty," she said as she closed the door. "Put the wine in the refrigerator while I get these in some water." She smelled the roses as she walked into the kitchen and wondered if a little romance could bring her emotions back into focus. Feeling Steve's body against hers was definitely putting things back into prospective. A small smile crossed her lips. Maybe twelve hours of nonstop passion would do the trick.

CHAPTER THREE

The old brick English Tudor sat off the highway in the middle of five acres of gently rolling lawn. A high stone wall ran around the perimeter of the estate and stopped at each side of the wide blacktop driveway. Heavy iron gates closed the gap in the wall and added the finishing touches that gave the mansion a fortified appearance. Filling one corner of the stone enclosure was what remained of a large pond.

George Miller stood beside the pump and waited for it to lose suction as he watched a big bass flopping around in the mud in a slowly disintegrating fight for life. He remembered reading an article in a sporting magazine that described fish as biological machines that continued to live and grow until eaten by larger fish, or dying of unnatural causes. If that was true, the bass was probably a hundred or so. He didn't care for the part he was playing in its demise, but knew if he wasn't pumping down the pond someone else would be. People with money generally got what they wanted, and Martin Aster was no exception.

George pulled a new foil pouch of chewing tobacco out of his back pocket and started opening it as he wondered about Martin Aster. He wasn't the typical wealthy businessman. There was something about him that made George just a little nervous. He wasn't the type of person George cared to turn his back on for very long.

He took a stringy clump of the sticky tobacco out of the pouch and shoved it into his mouth and worked it into a ball between his teeth and cheek. He looked up at the buzzards circling overhead. Maybe nature had its own way of dealing with the travesty that was taking place. The fish would die, but the birds would eat well.

Ned walked up next to George and took a pack of Camels out of his shirt pocket and shook out one of the smokes. "If you didn't mind getting a little muddy we could have one hell of a fish fry," he said as he put the cigarette between his lips.

George looked at Ned and spit brown juice on the ground next to the pump. "I know they're only fish, but I'm not real proud of what's going on here."

Ned took a Zippo out of his pants pocket and snapped back the cover. "You're right, George, they're only fish. It's not exactly murder," he said as he lit the Camel.

"How much do you suppose it would have cost Aster to relocate them to the river?" George asked.

Ned shrugged his shoulders as he slipped the lighter back into his pocket. "He probably thinks they're only fish, too. I'm not going to hang a lot of blame on the guy, especially when he's paying us one hundred grand for a couple weeks work."

"Maybe we should have a big fish fry," George said as he shut off the pump. "Why don't you get the guys to go out and pick up the biggest ones? I'll go buy a grill and some charcoal."

"Sounds good," Ned said. "Pick up a case of beer, too. We'll do it up right."

Sandy Castleman studied the line of stakes waiting to be driven deeper into the ground as he pulled the red bandanna out of the back pocket of his threadbare jeans and mopped the sweat from his face. There was nothing like a rough summer job to straighten out a rotten attitude. The school counselor's words still rang in his ears. He hated to admit he was wrong, especially when someone else was right. Working outside during the summer for big bucks sounded good, but it didn't take long to get tired of the heat and the bugs. Not long at all.

He used his fingers to comb his long blonde hair back behind his ears, then folded the bandanna lengthwise and tied it around his head. There wasn't anything he could do about the sun and the mosquitoes, but keeping the hair and sweat out of his face was bound to help.

He picked up the sledgehammer and walked over to the first stake and planted his feet. Bulging muscles in his arms and shoulders strained against the worn fabric of a faded Ohio State T-shirt as he raised the hammer and swung it in a high arc. The tool hit the mark with a solid thud and drove the length of wood into the hard clay. He quickly stepped to the next stake and repeated the action. The hammer missed the target at the third stake and threw him off balance. The second stroke of the hammer hit with authority.

After driving fifteen more stakes, he threw the hammer aside and looked at his red hands. The calluses he had earned by weight lifting did little to protect his hands from the wooden hammer handle.

A tall man wearing a green work shirt with the sleeves cut out walked up behind Sandy and put a hand on his shoulder.

"Morning, Sandy. Hands sore?" he asked.

"Hi, Jim," Sandy said as he turned around. "I don't suppose you know some magic potion I could put on them?"

Jim shook his head. "Gloves help a little, but not much. You just have to get used to it."

"Jim, when I go back to school in the fall I'm going to study my ass off. This shit is for the birds."

Jim nodded in agreement as he reached into his shirt pocket and pulled out a thin joint.

"Want to burn one?" he asked.

"Yeah, I..I guess so," he said as he looked around nervously.

Jim took a bic lighter out of his pants pocket as he put the small cigarette between his lips.

"This is some really fine Jamaican I picked up in Florida. Two or three hits is all you want," he said as he lit the joint. He sucked the smoke in deeply and passed it to Sandy.

Sandy took a hit off the tiny rocket, sucked in a little air behind it as he passed it back to Jim. "Goddamn that tastes good," he said as he exhaled the smoke slowly. "You got any extra you want to sell?"

Jim shook his head as he hit the joint. "I only brought back an ounce. It was pretty fucking expensive," he said as he passed it back to Sandy.

Sandy hit the doobie hard just before he saw Ned walking toward them. "Shit, there's Ned!" he said and handed the burning hemp back to Jim. He took a couple quick steps and was on the other side of a pine tree when Ned walked up next to Jim.

"What the hell's wrong with him?" Ned asked.

Jim shrugged his shoulders and passed the joint to him.

"Hey, Sandy," Ned called, then hit the weed. "Come over here, we need to talk."

Sandy came walking back slowly, trying his best not to look guilty.

"What the hell is this?" he asked as he held the reefer up in front of him.

"I don't know," Sandy responded nervously.

"It's Jamaican, you nitwit!" Ned said and took another hit before passing it back to Jim.

Jim watched Sandy's mouth fall open and started laughing so hard he thought he was going to piss his pants. He regained his composure after a moment and handed what was left of the joint to Sandy.

"Finish it," he said.

Sandy complied before dropping the tiny ember.

"Well," Ned said and chuckled. "I hope you two have a good buzz, because I've got a real shitty job for you."

"Aw, shit," Jim groaned. "I thought we could kick back and have an easy afternoon. We've been working our asses off."

Ned shook his head. "I didn't say it was going to be hard, I said it was going to be shitty," he said and laughed.

"Okay, what is it?" Jim demanded.

"George is out picking up a case of beer, a bag of charcoal, and a grill right now. He'll be back in time to cook up lunch," he said as he looked out across the muddy remains of the pond.

Jim and Sandy both glanced at the mud hole and looked at each other.

"You don't really want us to go out there," Sandy cried as he looked at Ned.

Ned smiled and nodded his head.

"It probably won't be as bad as you think. We should have plenty if each of you brings back three of those big bass. See you guys in about half an hour," he said with a laugh as he walked away.

"Ah shit, Jim, I can't go out there," Sandy whined.

Jim laughed. "It won't be that bad, just take off your shoes and roll up your pants. When we get back we'll hose off our hands and feet," he said as he started untying his shoes.

Sandy stared in disbelief.

"You mean we really have to do this?"

"Sure do," he said as he pulled off one of his work boots.

"Aw shit!" he said as he started untying one of his shoes.

A few minutes later they were both standing barefooted at the edge of the mud. Jim's pants were rolled up above his knees, but Sandy's would only go as far as mid calf.

"Well kid, come on," Jim said as he stepped out into the mud. "Shit!" he screamed, then laughed, and then howled. "It's cold and gooey," he yelled back to Sandy.

Sandy grimaced as he took his first step, and then screamed out as the mud oozed up between his toes. He forced himself to pretend he was walking around in pudding.

Jim was ahead moving in ankle deep goo as he closed in on a big fish that looked like it was ready to give up its fight for life. When he got there he reached down for the bass. His touch brought it fighting back, but Jim held on tight.

"I got one," he screamed as he held it up like a trophy and started walking back toward solid ground.

Sandy was finally getting used to walking around in his pudding when he saw something flopping around out near the middle. He didn't really want to go after it, but knew he had to. Besides, going that far might count for two fish, so he trudged forward. He could feel the mud getting deeper as he moved along slowly, and wondered if there were any deep bogs waiting for him. He could handle going in up to his knees, but getting his pecker in the slime was simply not acceptable. A couple minutes later he was standing in a foot of mud looking at a monster of a catfish. After some careful maneuvering he finally got his hands around the fish without getting stabbed with its spiny fins. "Yahoo!" he yelled as he held it up.

Twenty minutes later Jim was hosing himself off and telling Sandy that two fish didn't count as three fish, no matter how far he went to get one of them. After a few minutes of fruitless arguing Sandy started off around the perimeter of the mud hole, hoping to find a nice sized fish near the edge.

On the other side of the pond he spotted a large turtle sitting on what looked to be one end of a massive log buried in the mud. The shelled creature seemed to be sunning itself, totally oblivious to the destruction of the small body of water. Sandy took two steps out into the mud before the turtle raised its head and peered at him. Another step and it slid off into the mud, leaving a trail of light pink and gray on the log.

Sandy studied the patch of color as he worked his way around the end of the deadfall and wondered if it came from the animal's belly.

He found the turtle on the other side of the log, failing in its attempt to make a hasty retreat in the thick muck. As he closed in on his prey it stopped and turned to face him. The aggressive move surprised Sandy and brought a quick halt to his pursuit. The turtle snapped its jaws and made a deliberate move toward him.

The sudden realization that he was about to do battle with a twenty-pound snapper sent him reeling backwards. He screamed out as the back of his knees hit the log and buckled. He tried to maintain his balance, but he was too far-gone and did a slow motion backward roll over the log and landed on his back in the slime.

"Goddamnit!" he screamed and slapped his hand down angrily. He started getting to his feet slowly as he watched for any sign that the snapper was still coming. He stood up and looked over the top of the log. The turtle was nowhere in sight, but the patch of color on the log had changed into a number of wide slashes of pink and gray where he had rolled across it.

Amazed, he stepped forward and wiped his hand across the surface of the log. The silt wiped away easily, revealing unusual color. The mud covering him from head to toe suddenly seemed unimportant as he reached into the pocket of his jeans and pulled out a small knife. He unfolded the blade and pressed the point against the log and discovered it was too hard to penetrate. Deciding the knife was useless, he returned it to his pocket and went back to wiping away the grime. After cleaning farther down on the side of the log he discovered an area that seemed to show a design in the pink and gray surface. He cleaned more of the area and found that the design was part of larger markings. After clearing the mud from around the markings he bent down for a closer look. He became so engrossed in the log that he never noticed Jim coming around the edge of the pond toward him.

Jim walked up behind Sandy and watched him for a moment.

"We've got..."

Sandy screamed and whirled around. "Goddamnit Jim, you scared the shit out of me!" he cried, clutching his chest.

"We've got enough fish," he said laughing. "Man, you are a fucking mess. You been wrestling in the mud or what?" he asked.

"There's a face in that log!" Sandy blurted out as he came sloshing through the mud.

Jim shook his head as he watched Sandy step out of the muck. "You must be stoned."

"I'm telling you there's a face carved into that log!" he insisted as he pointed to the deadfall. "Walk out there and see for yourself."

"Are you crazy? I just got cleaned up. I'm not walking back out into that mud. Come on, I'll hose you off. Ned's cooking lunch and the beer's on ice."

"There is a face," he demanded as they walked back toward the other side of the pond. "The log isn't wood either, its rock."

"Yeah, and the moon is made of blue cheese, too," Jim said and laughed.

Ruth Aster gently combed her fingers through Grady's thick red hair as she watched him cat nap next to her in the bed. He was a different man when it came to making love. A little too predictable maybe, but the brutally aggressive nature he always displayed in business dealings was replaced by a tenderness, which was alien to most men. There were other qualities that she found attractive, like his well-tailored wardrobe, and his smooth, faultless intellect, but it was his tenderness and skill in bed that made her love for him complete.

She listened to the rhythm of his shallow breathing and wondered how much longer she would have to maintain her act as Martin Aster's loving wife and companion. She remembered how incensed she became the first time Grady mentioned his plan to her. She didn't understand how he could consider putting their relationship on hold and introduce her to his business partner, especially when the sole intent of the introduction was to promote romance. She was angry and hurt until he told her how much money she would have coming as his widow. It was like a little detour to the bank, he said. The money sounded big, and still did, but two years was a long time. She was tired of the double life she bought into and was ready to become Martin Aster's sole heir.

She felt Grady stir and watched his face, waiting for his eyes to open. When they did she put her leg across his waist and rolled over on top of him.

"Want to go again?" she asked as she kissed him.

He pulled his arm out from under the sheets and glanced at the Rolex on his wrist before putting his hands on her waist.

"I'm afraid it's almost time for you to leave," he said as he slid his hands up to her breasts. "We don't need to get careless this late in the game."

She closed her eyes and moaned softly as his long fingers skillfully caressed her flesh. "I'm tired of this game," she whispered. "When's it going to end?"

"Soon," he said as he raised his head and stroked her hard nipples with his tongue. "I'm sending something home with you tonight that will start the final countdown."

"What?" she asked as she pulled back away from his mouth.

"It's a clear, tasteless liquid. Just put it in his whiskey bottle and the deed will be done."

"I want to see it," she demanded.

Grady reached over and opened the drawer on the nightstand and pulled out a glass test tube with a stopper in the end. He held it up in front of Ruth and shook it gently. "You have to be extremely careful with this shit. There's no antidote, so make sure you wash your hands afterwards."

"Is it fast?" she asked, with a slight smile.

"Actually, it's quite slow, but it's almost impossible for this type of poison to show up during an autopsy. The doctor has to run a very specific test to find it."

"So he's not going to fall dead at my feet?"

"No," he said as he put the test tube back on the table. "He'll begin to show some very mild symptoms after about eight hours, but it will take him three to four weeks to succumb."

"What are the symptoms?" she asked.

"Dark circles under his eyes. You'll know he's ingested the poison when he gets up in the morning and looks like he's been up all night."

Ruth's smile broke into a heartless grin as she began to laugh softly.

"A funny thought?" Grady asked.

Ruth bent forward and cupped Grady's face in her hands and kissed him on the lips.

"Just an amusing thought. Martin says he's building the pool especially for me. I'll be skinny dipping in that pool, but not with him."

"Poor old Martin," Grady said sympathetically. "We should plan a farewell party for him before he leaves."

"Yeah," Ruth said cheerfully. "I like that idea. We could roast a pig and have people over. The pool might even be done in time."

"God, it would be a tragedy if he went swimming and drowned in that pool," Grady said with a serious tone.

"Why would that be a tragedy?" Ruth asked with a puzzled look on her face.

"Because I paid a lot of money for that poison."

They both howled with laughter, certain that their future wealth was only a few weeks away.

George Miller stood at the edge of the pond near the deadfall and motioned for Ned to back the tractor closer to the mud. When he saw the tires begin to sink in the soft ground he clasped his hands together. "That's it," he yelled. The tractor rocked on the heavy suspension as Ned hit the brakes.

"Pull it ahead a foot or so and you should have firm ground under the legs when you set 'em down."

Ned moved the tractor ahead and set the brake.

George walked to the front of the backhoe and rested his foot on the tire. "You think you're going to be able to get it out of there without a major operation?" he asked.

Ned shrugged his shoulders as he took a new pack of cigarettes out of his shirt pocket. "I don't know," he said as he zipped off the top of the cellophane wrapper and threw it on the ground. "It all depends on how much is there and how good of a bite I can get on it."

George spit a stream of brownish juice on the ground and wiped his lips with the back of his hand. "The damn thing's got to come out," he said as he rolled the chew over in his mouth. "One way or the other."

Ned shook a cigarette out of his pack of Camels and put it between his lips. "I really don't want to send Jim and Sandy back into that mud, but it could come to that. They might have to dig around it so I can use a chain," he said as he struck a wooden match and lit the smoke.

"See what kind of magic you can work with your backhoe. I don't want to have to listen to those two bitching about going back into that slime."

"I'll see what I can do," he said as he reached down and released the seat lock and pivoted around toward the control levers at the back of the tractor. After adjusting the seat he pulled back on one of the levers and started lowering the hydraulic legs toward the ground. He watched the movement of the heavy support beams and wondered how long the same job would have taken before the invention of hydraulics. A couple of men would have gone into the mud back then without the first complaint. Big difference between then and now, he thought and chuckled to himself. It was a shame the log wasn't another couple feet away and out of the reach of the backhoe. Watching Jim and Sandy wading back into the mud would be priceless.

The tractor lurched to one side and then leveled out as the support legs lifted the back tires into the air. Ned glanced down at the pads and made sure they were sitting on firm ground before turning his attention to the cluster of levers in front of him. He worked the controls with smooth, skillful movements that brought the steel appendage at the back of the tractor to life.

Sandy crouched down with his back against a tree and watched Ned reach out with the backhoe. He knew he was supposed to be helping Jim drive stakes, but his fascination with the log was overpowering. It didn't make any difference to him what Jim and Ned said or how much they laughed, he knew what he saw, and it didn't have anything to do with the pot he smoked. He might have had a problem with motivation in college, but that sure as hell didn't mean he was stupid. He was smart enough to know what petrified wood looked like and he was certain that's what Ned was about to pull out of the mud: a petrified log with carvings. Jim would probably shit his pants if

Ned hauled up a totem pole. Oh yeah, he who laughs last laughs best, Jimmy boy.

Sandy stood up when he saw the backhoe lurch under the load of the prize. Black smoke belched from the roaring exhaust as Ned pushed the hydraulic system toward its limit. He watched closely, waiting for movement, and finally it came. Only a little at first, then the log started raising up out of its muddy grave, bringing an amazing amount of earth with it. Sandy came to the sudden startled realization that there was much more coming out of the mud than he had expected. His discovery was only one side of something huge. What he thought was the end of the log protruding through the mud now looked to be the corner of some yet indiscernible structure. An appendage jutting out at a right angle from the new side of the thing suddenly revealed itself as the backhoe pulled more of the object from the muck. Sandy started walking toward the backhoe when he saw the movement begin to slow and finally stop while the engine exhaust continued to roar and discharge thick black smoke.

The engine slowed as Ned backed off the controls and let the structure slip back into the mud a little without losing the load completely. He saw Sandy walking toward him and motioned for him to hurry.

Sandy trotted over to the backhoe.

"I don't know what the fuck I've got hold of here, but I can't get it out like this. Run up and get the big chain out of the truck."

Sandy turned and started running around the pond toward the truck with his heart already pounding in his ears from excitement. He knew he was going to have to go out into the mud and hook up the chain, but that was no big deal. As he ran he reviewed in his mind what he had seen coming out of the mud, but nothing seemed to make sense. He had no idea what the object was. The only thing he was sure of was that they were pulling some kind of an artifact out of the mud. There would be pictures, articles, and probably some kind of finder's reward. They'd know he was somebody and not just some hick fresh off the farm.

He ran to the truck and jumped into the back without breaking stride. When he grabbed the chain it dawned on him that he wouldn't be able to run with the weight. He dropped the chain, jumped down and ran around to the cab. The keys were dangling from the ignition.

Ned held a steady hand on the hydraulic controls as he shook a cigarette out of the pack and watched Sandy get into the truck. He just didn't understand the kid. Working simply wasn't his thing. He wasn't exactly lazy, but he certainly wasn't overflowing with energy either. Left to his own devices he'd string a job out until the cows came home. The last thing he expected to see was Sandy running flat out to get something done.

He lit the cigarette and watched as Sandy chew up sod with all four wheels when he pulled away in the truck. He wondered why he was in such a hurry to go back into the slime. As he watched the truck get closer it hit him that Sandy thought the thing coming out of the mud was something special. He looked out at the load on the end of the backhoe and tried to imagine what Sandy was thinking. His eyes searched for the carvings he talked about all through lunch, but saw nothing. He saw nothing, but as Sandy pulled up in the truck he felt a tinge of excitement.

Sandy got out and jumped into the back of the truck.

"Hey, Sandy," Ned yelled over the noise of the exhaust. "What do you think I've got here?"

Sandy threw the chain down to the ground and shook his head as he leaned against the back of the truck cab. "Don't know," he said, still trying to catch his breath. "Whatever it is, don't forget who found it." He rested for a second before jumping down out of the truck. "How do you want to do this?" he asked as he grabbed the chain.

George tried to concentrate on the blue prints he had spread across the hood of his car, but the action unfolding on the other side of the pond was too much for him. He picked up the prints, rolled them up and threw them in on the car seat.

During lunch he listened to Sandy's story about the deadfall, but dismissed it as nonsense. Now, after watching Ned's first attempt at pulling the thing out of the mud he wasn't so sure. He pulled the pouch of chewing tobacco out of his back pocket and leaned against the car as he watched Sandy wade out into the muck with a chain over one shoulder. It was obvious that he really believed they were about to drag something significant out of the mud.

George stuffed a wad of the sticky tobacco into his cheek and wondered how he was going to keep a lid on things if Sandy was right. The last thing he wanted was a lot of publicity about the construction site. He was sure Ned would be totally unnerved by a bunch of strangers poking around, trying to uncover other buried treasures. He didn't think Martin would be too happy about it either. He watched Ned and Sandy for a few more minutes, and then walked over to the edge of the pond where Jim was driving a line of stakes.

Jim held the sledgehammer by the head and tapped the mushroomed end of the stake until the point had disappeared into the ground. "Looks like they're gettin' ready to pull more than a log out of the ground over there," he said as he stepped back away from the stake. He raised the hammer and brought it down with a powerful swing that drove the wooden spike into the hard clay.

"I think you and I should walk over there and get a closer look at that thing," George said and spit tobacco juice.

"What do you think it is?" Jim asked as he pulled a bandanna out of his back pocket and mopped the sweat from his forehead.

"I don't know, Jim. But if it's something more than an old piece of tree...if it's something special like Sandy thinks, I want to keep it quiet for awhile."

"Shit, George, all you have to do is tell me to shut my trap and I'll be quiet, but you've got a problem with the kid. He's pretty wound up about that thing."

"We'll walk over and take a look. If it ends up being some kind of artifact we have to make sure he understands he has to keep quiet about it for a while. This is the only contract we have right now. If the job gets shut down because somebody wants to find out what else is buried in the mud you'll be back in the ranks of the unemployed." It wasn't exactly the truth, but it was a good story.

When they got to the other side of the pond Ned was dragging a massive slime covered rectangular structure out of the mud.

Sandy ran up and started wiping mud away from one area of the form as Ned continued to drag it back away from the huge mud pit.

"Look, Jim!" he cried out as he pointed at the thing. "Look at the face!"

Jim's mouth dropped open as he looked at the area where Sandy had cleared away some of the mud, exposing what appeared to be a carved face. "Aw shit, George, that sure as hell looks like a face!"

Ned stopped the tractor, jumped down and ran back to where the others stood. He was dumbfounded as he looked down at what appeared to be an enormous log of petrified wood streaked with pink and gray. He could see features under the slime where large sections of mud had fallen away.

Sandy bent down and took his time clearing all the mud away from one of the carvings. He stood up and cocked his head to the side as he looked at the features. The artwork seemed primitive, but there was no mistaking the horrified expression on the face. He looked at George, then Jim and finally Ned and saw the same stunned look as they stared at the face.

"I think this thing was supposed to stay in the ground," Ned whispered.

"Okay," George said as he stepped back. "Come away from that thing. I want to talk to everybody."

The four of them gathered next to a tree a few feet away.

"I want everybody to listen to me very closely, especially you, Sandy. I recognize that we've stumbled upon what is probably a significant artifact, but everybody has to keep quiet about it for a while. If anybody outside of our group finds out about this the place is going to be crawling with people, and that will shut the job down. If that happens you guys are going to be in line at the unemployment office, because we don't have any other contracts right now."

"But I found this thing!" Sandy demanded. "I want the credit."

George turned his head and spit a stream of brown tobacco juice. "Sandy, I understand what you're saying, and I'm sure you'll get the credit you deserve. Nobody's trying to take that away from you. We just can't let anybody find out where the damn thing came from, that's all."

"Okay," Sandy agreed. "I'll keep quiet about it for awhile, but I want you to let me take the rest of the day to clean it up and find out what it looks like."

"I don't have a problem with that. Actually I think we'll all knock off for the day and help you."

They all walked back over to the artifact and gathered around it like doctors preparing to examine a patient.

"I think we need a water hose and some brushes," Ned said.

Jim pulled the bandanna out of his back pocket and bent down. "Some of this stuff might wipe away if we get it before it dries," he said as he ran the cloth along the inside edge of one of the long logs, revealing the colorful petrified wood beneath the mud. "See what I mean."

"Ned, you think you can get the thing leaned up against this tree so we don't have to work bent over?" George asked. "We can't have anybody out tomorrow with a bad back."

"Piece of cake," Ned responded as he turned and walked back toward the tractor.

A quiet smile spread across Martin Aster's lips as he stood in his study at the bay window and surveyed the array of construction equipment grouped together near the edge of the dead pond. The heavy machinery was ruining the well-manicured lawn, but it was a small price to pay for the sweet revenge that would come with the stately pool.

He unwrapped the Havana cigar and dropped the cellophane in an ashtray on his desk as he thought about the score he had to settle with the man he had treated like a son. The stolen money, by itself, wasn't the issue. He could have confronted Grady and set things straight if it was only a matter of some missing cash reserves, but it was more than that. Even a lustful fling with Ruth could have been worked out, but there was only one response to the kind of treachery he had displayed. Grady's betrayal hurt, and his corruption of Ruth was unforgivable.

Martin smelled the rich tobacco of the cigar as he ran it under his nose and wondered how long Grady had planned the plundering of his smuggling operation. It most certainly wasn't something he had put together in a week or two. There was no doubt that the scheme was the product of a creative genius. On that point he had to respect Grady. He learned the lessons so well that he nearly outsmarted the teacher. In the end, his undoing was his own carelessness and not a flawed project.

He moistened both ends of the cigar with his mouth as he took a gun shaped lighter off the desk and thought about Ruth and her involvement in Grady's plan. Getting to her had to have been the first item on his agenda. It suddenly occurred to him that it was possible, and even likely that the plot was in place when Grady introduced him to Ruth. On the heels of that thought came another, more sobering one. His own death was probably the ultimate finale. The thought of Ruth and Grady living on his wealth after murdering him turned his blood cold and put his revenge in a new perspective.

The elaborate plan to collect a pound of flesh from his partner for the betrayal was something that he had refined with a definite enthusiastic zeal. Now the enthusiasm was decaying into a dull pain that ripped at his heart.

He never truly loved a woman until Grady introduced him to Ruth, and then it came like a blinding bolt of lightning. He fell in love with the way her long coal black hair accented her olive complexion and dark brown eyes. He fell in love with her long, shapely legs, slim waist, and full breasts, but most of all it was her warmth and affection. It brought the kind of contentment that a sheik's treasure couldn't buy.

He pulled the trigger on the lighter and rolled the tip of the cigar in the flame as he forced himself to put the harsh realities of Ruth's treachery in perspective. Denying his love for her was difficult, but living with her, all the while knowing of her betrayal, was impossible.

Martin put the cigar to his lips and puffed on it until the tip turned into a tiny inferno. He threw the lighter back on the desk as he thought of the emotional tightrope he had to walk until the time was right. Outwardly he had to remain a loving husband to Ruth and loyal business partner to Grady.

Inwardly he had to allow the seething rage to build until it was on the brink of an explosive eruption.

Treachery or not, he loved Ruth, and because of that love she would die easily with a lethal dose of heroin. The circumstances of Grady's death would be much different. Before he drew his last breath he would know pain and suffering, and in the end he would beg for a quick death.

He sucked the cigar smoke deep into his lungs and savored the taste before blowing a whitish plume toward the ceiling. It warmed his heart to think of the panic that would fill Grady's eyes as the concrete slowly flowed in around him, choking off his breath.

Joyce pulled the photo album out of the bottom of the trunk and inspected the aging yellow masking tape that had kept it sealed for so many years. The last time she closed the cover on the photographs she thought she would never be able to look at them again. Now, nearly thirty years later, she was ready to face the reflections of friendship and love that was shattered in Vietnam.

She carried the album into the living room, set it on the coffee table and went to the kitchen for a pair of scissors. On the way back she turned on the stereo, did a quick review of her discs and picked out a collection of late sixties music that seemed to match the occasion. She went back to the couch and put the album on her lap as Three Dog Night started playing JOY TO THE WORLD.

As she picked up the scissors and started to cut away the tape she wondered how the pictures were going to affect her. The flood of memories at school left her stunned. She knew looking at the old photographs might be worse. Unlike memories, the passage of time had no impact on photographs. They were like tiny windows that always remained open onto the past. A part of her wanted to run back to the bedroom and return the album to the trunk, but there was a stronger urge to peer through those tiny windows and deal with whatever emotions were conjured up.

She finished severing the remaining tape, put the scissors on the table and opened the cover slowly. The opening page was a collage of pictures from her first day on campus during registration for the fall quarter. She laughed when she saw the long hair and clothes, coming to the surprised realization that she had totally forgotten what the late sixties really looked like. The pictures reminded her of the birth of a counterculture that lashed out against Nixon and the war in Vietnam and made "drugs, sex, and rock 'n roll" their cry for freedom.

As she slowly turned the pages she discovered subtle images of a world in change, a world where social standards set by previous generations were thrown asunder and the political establishment provoked emotional condemnation.

While Procol Harum started playing A WHITER SHADE OF PALE, she turned another page and found a snapshot of the three of them sitting together on the porch swing. They had their arms around each other's shoulders and were grinning like Cheshire cats. The photograph brought on a sudden rush of emotions and the sting of building tears. The tears that welled up in her eyes and threatened to spill down her cheeks were a mixture of shear joy for finding the picture and latent sorrow for what was lost forever. The ensuing flood of memories carried her back to the day she moved in with Randy and Kim.

Joyce ran ahead and opened the door as Randy and Kim struggled up the front steps with the cumbersome footlocker.

"Is there anything else in the truck?" she asked as they eased their load through the door.

"No," Randy groaned. "This is the last thing."

"Set it down for a minute," Kim said. "I need to rest before we start up the steps."

"Yeah, me too," Randy said as he put his end down. "I had no idea a footlocker full of clothes would be this heavy."

"Sorry," Joyce said apologetically. "I threw a couple books in on top of the clothes. I didn't think about the weight."

Randy shook his head. "A couple books didn't increase the weight that much. The footlocker is just heavy, that's all."

"I don't know," Kim said as he rested his foot on top of the trunk. "I think Joyce has a tendency to minimize things." He looked over at Joyce and smiled. "How many books did you put in there?" he asked.

"I don't know," she replied with a sheepish grin. "I didn't count them."

"Joyce, you put all your books in there, didn't you?" Kim insisted.

"Yeah, I guess I did," she said with a triumphant smile. "Want me to take them out?"

"Not now," Randy said as he grabbed the handle on his end. "I'd rather make one trip up the steps and be done with it. Ready?"

"Let's go," Kim said as he took hold of his handle. They both lifted the footlocker and started up the steps.

"Just remember these books if she ever tells you her checking account is overdrawn by a couple dollars," Kim said with a chuckle.

"Yeah," Randy laughed. "And if she ever tells us she spent a little extra money at the grocery store we'll know we're in trouble."

Kim started laughing so hard he had to stop in the middle of the steps. "And if she ever tells you the car needs a little gas..."

They both laughed uproariously.

"I hope you two wet your pants," Joyce said as she sauntered out onto the porch. She listened as they continued to laugh between the grunts and wondered if the footlocker was going to end up in a heap at the bottom of the steps. She hoped not. The footlocker was unimportant, but she didn't want either of them getting hurt. She glanced back and checked on their progress before walking over to the porch swing.

The rhythmic creaking of the swing had a soothing, almost musical quality that accentuated the motion and seemed to beckon for her relaxation. She closed her eyes and thought about her relationship with Randy and Kim. The physical attraction she felt for Randy that morning in front of the bookstore had grown into something truly unique between the three of them. It only took a warm smile or a friendly touch for Randy to spark a flame deep within her heart, and she could listen to Kim talk for hours about writings like those of Carlos Castaneda or the Oriental teachings of Sun Tzu or Zhang Yu. They both touched her soul in a way that put her at peace with the world. She wanted to believe that she gave them back as much companionship and love as she received.

She heard someone open the screen door and walk across the porch toward her. "Sleeping?" Randy asked.

"No," she said as she opened her eyes. "Just thinking about things. Where's Kim?"

"He's on the phone ordering a pizza," he said as he walked over to the swing.

"That's silly," she said as she looked at Randy. "I could have gone to the store and picked up the ingredients. I am supposed to be cooking, you know."

"That starts tomorrow," he said as he sat down next to her. "Today we're going to kick back and enjoy the day and decide how things are going to have to run around here, now that you're part of the household."

"Oh, you mean things like toilet seats and dirty socks," she said with a smile.

Randy laughed.

"Yeah, things like that. I think having you here with Kim and I is going to make things seem more like a real family. I just hope we can make your life a little happier than it's been the last couple months."

"I've probably seemed like a basket case lately, but it's only because of the money crunch. You and Kim have really been great to me. When I started school I didn't know anyone on campus and had no family to watch out for me. It was a little like being adrift in a lifeboat. I'll always love you both for saving me from that terrible isolation."

Randy laughed as he propelled the swing backwards with a kick of his feet.

Joyce smacked him on the arm. "Don't laugh at me when I'm being serious!"

"I wasn't laughing at you," he said with a grin. "I was thinking about the way we met."

"Oh yeah, real funny," she said. "I had a bruise on my derriere for a week. All things considered, I guess it was worth it."

"As I recall you were fairly graceful going down, but I wasn't really talking about that."

"Well, I'm on pins and needles waiting on this one," she said with a hint of sarcasm. "Exactly what was it that was so damn funny?'"

"It's going to sound pretty crazy."

"Go on. I promise I'll contain myself."

"Well, the morning of the day we met, Kim got up and insisted we had to go to the library. He said he dreamed we were going to meet somebody, but didn't know who. I told him I had to stay home and study, but he wouldn't accept that. He practically dragged me out of the house. I'm telling you, I felt like an idiot standing there in front of the library, watching people go by. As far as I knew I was waiting for a stranger to walk up to me, introduce them self and admit to being in Kim's dream. Hell, I didn't know. After about an hour I got disgusted and told Kim I was leaving. I turned and started to walk away and ran right into you."

"You're kidding, right?" Joyce asked with a laugh.

"I know it sounds like a cheap line," he said as he raised his hand in the air, "but I swear to God it's true."

"I'm going to ask Kim," she said as she grabbed his raised hand. "If you're lying to me I'm going to break your fingers."

"Ask him. The whole thing was a little spooky."

Joyce kissed Randy's hand and released her grip. "I guess I should 'fess up, too," she said.

"What do you mean?" Randy asked.

"When you ran into me it was as much my fault as it was yours," she said as their eyes met.

"How's that?" he asked while holding her gaze.

Joyce smiled and looked away. "I was checking you out and got a little too close."

Randy laughed. "You mean you noticed me standing there looking stupid?"

"No," she said with a snicker. "I thought you were very attractive."

"Me?" he cried.

"Oh, don't be so modest," she said as Kim came out of the house. "Kim, where have you been?"

"I ordered a pizza, then jumped in the shower," he said as he glanced at his watch. "The delivery boy should be here in a few minutes."

"Come over here and sit down," she said as she scooted closer to Randy. "I want to ask you something."

Kim walked over to the swing. "What's up?" he asked as he took the vacant spot next to Joyce.

"You've talked a great deal about Carlos Castaneda and his writings and the subject of dreaming has always been one of the central themes. Have you ever had any remarkable episodes of dreaming?"

"Castaneda speaks of what is called lucid dreaming in which the dreamer is consciously aware of the dream state and engages in specific observations and actions. There have been a few times that I've been somewhat successful with lucid dreaming, but it's not something I'm able to do any time I want. Have you had an experience?

"No, not exactly, but...but have I ever been in one of your dreams, lucid or otherwise?" she asked.

"Well, yes and no. There was a dream in which Randy and I met someone, but I never saw them, only where we met. We went there and met you."

"Oh, my God, it's true," Joyce cried. "Randy told me and I didn't believe him. I thought he was just pulling my leg."

"I told you it was the truth," Randy said with a laugh.

"Do you remember anything about the dream?" Joyce asked.

"You never forget a dream like that," Kim said as he shook his head. "Especially when something utterly astounding happens in conjunction with it."

"Please tell me about it," Joyce begged.

"Tell us about it. I've never heard the specifics myself," Randy said.

"It's a little bit strange. There's no place in a discussion of lucid dreaming for linear thought. You have to be willing to let the linear thinker go to sleep."

"Linear thought?" Joyce questioned.

"Linear thinking. It's what I call limited thinking. Thought that's restricted within the framework of accepted scientific fact. A linear thinker will dismiss an observation or theory as flawed for no other reason than it doesn't conform to the scientific description of the world. A non linear thinker will examine the observation or theory from outside of the scientific box."

"You want us to believe what you say, regardless of how it might sound to a scientist?" Joyce asked.

"Suspend judgment based on what that scientist might say," Kim replied.

"Yeah, I can do that," Joyce responded.

"Me, too," Randy said.

"In the dream I remember seeing bolts of swirling blue energy coming toward me from two different directions. I was in a dark void at the vertex of an angle made of these bolts of energy. There was no surreal quality common to most dreams. I could feel the energy entering the palms of my hands. I could hear it crackling and I suddenly understood I was dreaming. I was dreaming and I was consciously aware of the dream. That's when it occurred to me to examine my surroundings. As I looked around the darkness of the void began to dissipate and I saw Randy at another energy vertex. A bolt of this swirling energy was connecting the palms of our hands. I continued to observe the environment in which I found myself and realized we were on campus in front of the library. Randy and I were at two of the vertexes of an energy triangle. I looked over and saw what appeared to be another person at the third point, but most of the features were hidden within a sphere of pulsating energy. I could see the palms of the hands where the energy was entering and...and there was another feature visible beyond the sphere, but I didn't recall it until after we met you. This other person had long dark red hair."

"Oh, my God," Joyce whispered as she rubbed the skin on her forearms. "I've got goose bumps all over. I think that means I'm really supposed to be here with you two," she said as she put her arms around both of them and pulled them into a hug. "I love you guys. I wish there was somebody here that could take a picture of us."

As if on cue, the pizza delivery truck pulled up in front of the house.

"Go get your camera, we'll get the pizza man to take the picture."

Joyce bolted off the swing and ran into the house. A moment later she was back with the instamatic. She handed it to the pizza man, who was just a kid, and ran back to the swing.

"Okay," the kid said as he aimed the camera. "Say pizza cheese!"

"Pizza cheese!" they yelled and broke into laughter.

Joyce clutched the picture to her chest as tears spilled from her eyes and fell onto the page of the photo album. The sorrow that gripped her was only a shadow of the anguish that had shattered her life, and still the pain pierced her heart like the thrust of a rapier.

She wiped her eyes, put the picture back in the album and closed the cover. What she wanted now was to finally come to grips with the tragedy and put it behind her, once and for all. It was something she should have done many years ago. She knew she needed to look at the rest of the pictures, but for now they could wait.

CHAPTER FOUR

The sun was just starting to break over the horizon when George turned off the highway and rolled down the long blacktop drive in front of the Aster mansion. He pulled his car into the grass next to the backhoe, shut off the engine and glanced at his watch. He didn't like conducting serious business so early in the morning, but circumstances left little choice. The issue of the artifact had to be settled quickly before someone let the cat out of the bag. He knew if anyone was likely to have a case of loose lips it was going to be Sandy. The kid was hungry for some type of recognition and fear of losing his job wouldn't keep him quiet forever.

George remembered how everyone got caught up in the excitement of the find and set out to do a good job of cleaning it up. Ned used the backhoe to lean it up against the tree before everyone went to work with brushes, rags, tools, and the garden hose. None of them were prepared for what they found under the mud. The faces carved into the logs at each side of the frame were disturbing to say the least, but the head that jutted out at the top of the frame was right out of a nightmare.

He looked over at the dark silhouette of the tarp that covered the monstrosity and felt his insides tremble. He remembered that even in the bright afternoon sun it wasn't easy to look at the thing without getting spooked. It touched that place deep inside where the childhood fears of the boogieman lurked.

George checked his watch again. He got out of the car and moved through the damp grass to the driveway. He walked along the edge of the blacktop and felt a chill run up his spine as he thought about the appalling head with its gaping jaws and jagged teeth. It was a vision that wouldn't be easily purged from his mind.

George walked up to the front door and rapped with the heavy brass knocker. He clung to the hope that Martin would be so interested in getting rid of the thing that he'd cough up money without much discussion. He felt a lump stick in his throat as he heard the deadbolt slide back and the door begin to open.

He was taken aback when the door swung open and he saw Martin standing in the foyer. Even in the dim light it was easy to see the dark circles under his eyes and the pasty cast of his complexion.

"Jesus, Martin. Were you up all night playing poker?" he asked as he stepped through the doorway.

"No," Martin said as he closed the door behind George. "I thought I got a good nights sleep until I looked in the mirror this morning," he said as they left the foyer and started into the living room. "Let's go to the study and talk over a cup of coffee."

The elegance of the living room was obvious to George, even in the dim light. The thick carpet felt like springs beneath his feet as he walked passed oil paintings hung in frames that were works of art themselves. At the far end of the room was a set of solid French doors, guarded at each side by two six foot samurai warriors crafted of fine porcelain and trimmed in gold.

George followed Martin as he opened the doors and moved into the study. The nobility of the room surprised him. The walls were trimmed with carved mahogany woodwork that accented a large walnut desk facing the doors. Behind the desk were bookcases, filled with an impressive literary collection. At the far end of the room behind a magnificent antique snooker table was a massive stone fireplace.

Martin gestured toward a pair of leather chairs on each side of a smoked glass coffee table set with cups and a sterling silver coffee service.

"Very nice room," George said as he took one of the chairs.

Martin smiled as he sat in the other chair. "I'm afraid it's an example of how I've indulged my insatiable appetite for expensive toys," he said and turned both cups upright on the saucers. He poured a cup and set it in front of George before filling his own cup. "Help yourself to the cream and sugar," he said as he set the coffee back on the tray.

George dropped two sugar cubes into his steaming cup.

"Now, what is it that you were so anxious to talk about?" Martin asked as he added some cream to his coffee.

"We've hit a little bit of a snag," he said as he stirred his coffee.

"What kind of a snag?" Martin asked.

"We dug up an artifact that was buried in the mud at the bottom of the pond," George said as he raised his cup.

Martin looked at George thoughtfully before taking a sip of his coffee. "So why is that a snag?" he asked.

"Martin, I'm going to be real frank. This thing is very unusual. It belongs in a museum, but I can't afford the publicity that will come my way if I put it there. I don't think you can either."

"What do you mean by that?" Martin asked as he leaned toward the table.

"Come on, Martin. I wasn't born yesterday. I don't know what you've got going on here, and I don't want to know, but if everything were above board I wouldn't be doing this work for you. We both know you didn't find my name in the yellow pages."

"Okay," Martin said as he leaned back in his chair. "Let's assume for a minute that you're right and neither of us want any publicity. Why can't you just get rid of this thing? Why can't you just bury the fucking thing where you found it?" he asked.

"I wish I could, but the kid that found the damn thing is really hungry for some kind of recognition or reward. I warned him to keep it quiet. I told him the publicity would shut us down and he'd be out of a job, but that's only going to work for so long."

Martin rubbed his chin thoughtfully and finally nodded his head. "We've got a problem. What the fuck is this artifact, anyway?"

George put his cup back on the saucer as he considered how to answer the question. The thought of the thing under the tarp sent chills running up his spine again.

"It would be easier if you just went out and looked at it," he finally replied.

"If I wanted to walk outside I wouldn't have asked you what it was," Martin said sharply.

"Hell, I don't know what it is! It looks like a huge goddamn mirror, except it's not glass. It's some kind of crystal that gives off a fuzzy, bluish reflection and it's framed with petrified wood. The frame has faces carved into it." He started to describe the head at the top, and then decided not to go into it any farther. "The fuckin' thing must weigh a couple tons," he said.

"And this thing is out in front of the house?" Martin asked with an excited edge to his voice.

"It's covered with a tarp."

"Let's make sure it stays that way," Martin said as he got up and walked over to the bookcases behind the desk. He pulled a book off the shelf, turned it backwards and returned it to the spot. The action released a hidden latch and let a section of the bookcase swing out, exposing the door of a safe. He opened the safe and took out two packets of bills before closing everything back up. He walked back to his chair, sat down and threw two bundles of hundreds out in the middle of the table. "I think ten thousand dollars will be enough to make this problem go away, don't you?"

George picked up the money and put it in his jacket pocket. "I'm sure of it," he said and smiled.

Joyce scanned the class, looking for a hint that someone was on the verge of grasping the essence of what had been said. The girl in the back row wearing a yellow ribbon in her hair had no idea where the discussion was headed. She was too busy whispering to the guy sitting in front of her. The kid with the greasy hair and pimples was paying attention, but the dumbfounded expression on his face betrayed his thoughts. There were others that were trying to follow her, but none of them had made the intuitive leap necessary to arrive at the point she was trying to make.

A blonde haired boy in the front row looked up at Joyce, as if to let her know he was listening, and then went back to sketching an Indian on horseback.

"Josh, what could I possibly be driving at when I say the author of our textbook did a good job of laying out Indian history, but a poor job of painting a picture of Indian life?"

Josh looked up from his picture. "I think you mean there are some things more important than simple history represented by a time line," Josh said.

"Like what?" Joyce asked.

"Well, like how they lived."

"That's right. The author tries to represent Indian life simply on the basis of times and places, and has very little to say about their society and spiritual beliefs. It's like a scientific study of an ocean based only on shorelines and wave patterns. It might produce an extensive map, but there is a boundless matrix of life that would go unnoticed." She glanced up at the clock, walked back to the chalkboard and picked up an eraser. "I would be remiss in my duties as a teacher if I let such a travesty stand," she said as she erased the board. When she was finished she picked up a piece of chalk and wrote THE TEACHINGS OF DON JUAN - A Yaqui Way of Knowledge. Below that she wrote the name Carlos Castaneda before turning back toward the class.

"This Don Juan has nothing to do with the European legend that was the basis for *The Deceiver of Seville*, by Tirso de Molina. Carlos Castaneda is an anthropologist, not a seducer of women," she said with a smile. "Sorry to disappoint some of you. There will be an essay question on the final concerning this book that will make up at least one third of your grade. I strongly suggest you read it," she said as she put down the chalk and walked back to the desk. "Most of you will read this book because it's required, and at the end of the quarter bury it away somewhere in the attic. I have no quarrel with those people, providing they come away with the understanding that Indian life was much more complex than some believe. There are, however, a few students in the class that will find this work to be a priceless treasure that touches them deeply. Those people will have received a gift that nothing can take away, and they will most certainly read Castaneda's other books. When they finish they will have had a glimpse of another description of the world, one that radiates with forces totally alien to the way we perceive our environment."

Joyce walked back to her chair and pulled it away from the desk. "That's all I have for today," she said as she sat down. "Please put your papers on the corner of my desk on your way out."

As she watched her students drop off their papers on the way out of the classroom she thought about the many nights she had sat with Kim and talked about Don Juan and the warrior's path to knowledge. He always asked if she had the time to gaze into the crystal ball. It was his way of asking if she was interested in engaging in some serious exploration of her psyche. On the occasions when there was no class the next morning or tests to study for, they would explore. It usually started with a little pot. Not enough to get stoned, but just enough to open the portals of the mind. They would plunge into conversations that were always a remarkable glimpse of a world beyond the structured scientific definition of the universe.

She pulled the stack of papers over in front of her and started skimming through the first page of the top report. She looked away from the paper as she wondered where Kim was and what he had done with his life. He could have made a good living playing the horses, or any number of games in Las Vegas, but somehow she doubted it. He could have helped Randy take the bookies for thousands of dollars while they were in college, but instead he limited it to what was needed to maintain the household. He always told her and Randy that one of the first lessons a warrior on the path to knowledge had to learn was to take only what was needed.

She let her mind drift back to the night Randy put that particular lesson to the test. It was also the night she finally found out how they made their money.

Joyce was checking on a homemade pizza when Kim walked into the kitchen and opened the refrigerator.

"Want one?" he asked as he held up a bottle of beer for her inspection.

"That sounds good," she said as she closed the oven door.

Kim set the bottles on the table as he pulled out a chair and sat down.

"Where's Randy?" she asked as she sat down next to him.

"He had to run some errands," he said as he opened one of the bottles and handed it to Joyce. "He should be back before too long."

"He better be, unless he wants to eat cold pizza," she said and took a drink from the bottle of beer.

"I doubt if it would bother him. I've seen him pick up a piece of pizza that had been sitting out all night and have it for breakfast. Of course, that was before you moved in. We don't get to leave the pizza lay around that long any more," he said with a laugh.

"Sounds like I civilized you two," she said.

"Yeah, I guess you have. Here's to being a domesticated male," he said as they clanked their bottles together.

"I just hope you guys are happy with these arrangements," Joyce said.

"It's a perfect situation in which we all get what we need. It would take a deranged person to be unhappy with it. Besides all the obvious benefits, the three of us fit very well together. I've seen real families that had to struggle to get along half as good as we do."

"So is it love or convenience that binds us together?" she asked.

He feigned a pensive look as he pretended to ponder the question. After a moment he took a drink of his beer and nodded his head. "I've formulated an equation, loaded all the values, weighed all the variables, and what I come up with is one part convenience, one part necessity, and eight parts love."

A guarded smile crossed Joyce's lips. "That's how you and I feel. I hope it's the same for Randy."

"Let me tell you something about Randy that I hope will put your mind at ease," he said as he shifted in his chair. "Before we met you Randy used to do a lot of late night partying. We passed each other in the driveway more than one morning. I'd be going to class and he'd be too tired to make it anywhere but bed. He cut a lot of classes and didn't do much studying until it was time to cram for a midterm or final. There were a few times that a brilliant grade on a final was the only thing that kept him in school. The worst part was that he was content with things that way." Kim picked up his beer, started to take a drink and stopped. "It takes someone very special to force change into a life like that," he said before putting the bottle to his lips and taking a drink.

"And you think I caused it?" Joyce asked.

"No doubt in my mind, and it takes more than just friendship to do that."

"I hope you're right," she said as she picked at the label on her beer bottle. "Because I'm starting to feel something for Randy that I've never felt before."

"I know, I can tell," Kim said.

"How can you tell?" she asked with a puzzled look.

Kim laughed. "It's written all over your face when you look at him."

"Oh God," she said as she put both hands to her cheeks. "Can he see it, too?"

"I'm a little better at picking up on non verbal communication than Randy is, but I don't think it will take him long to catch on."

Joyce took a drink of her beer and started picking at the label again. After a moment she looked at Kim. "I don't want to let something get started between Randy and I if there's a chance that it might jeopardize the relationship the three of us have."

"You're afraid I'd be jealous?" he asked in a surprised tone.

"No. This is a different kind of bond between you and I," she said. "I just worry that you might feel like you're in the way or something. You'd never be in the way, no matter what," she said as she put her hand on top of his.

Kim smiled as he picked up her hand and kissed it. "Love manifests itself in different ways. The love you and Randy share starts in the heart and fuses with the physical world. The ultimate expression of that love is found in the bedroom. The love that you and I share starts in the heart and fuses with the spiritual world. The ultimate expression of that love is found when we sit together and gaze into the crystal ball."

Joyce leaned forward and gently kissed Kim on the lips, then got up and walked to the stove. "Randy better hurry up, the pizza smells like it's about done," she said as she opened the oven door.

"He just pulled into the driveway a second ago," Kim said.

Joyce closed the oven and turned off the heat before turning around and looking at Kim. "I didn't hear anything."

"Neither did I," he said with a smile.

Joyce gave Kim a confused look and started to say something when Randy opened the back door.

"Something smells good," he said as he closed the door.

76

"You're just in time," Joyce said as she took plates out of the cupboard and set them on the counter. "I thought you were going to have to eat cold pizza."

"I told her it wouldn't have been the first time," Kim said as he leaned back in his chair and opened the refrigerator. He grabbed a beer and handed it to Randy.

"Thanks," he said as he pulled a chair out from the table and sat down.

"Did you get everything done?" Kim asked.

"Yeah," Randy said as he picked up his beer. He took a long drink before pulling a roll of money out of his jacket pocket and putting it on the table in front of Kim. "That should be enough to fill the cookie jar for awhile."

Kim picked up the money and started unrolling it as Joyce put a plate of pizza in front of him. He shuffled through the bills, stopped and looked over at Randy. "There's too much here."

Randy smiled and shrugged his shoulders. "They had a special deal. Ten good picks regardless of the point spread paid ten to one. It was like shooting fish in a barrel."

"How much extra?" Kim asked as Joyce came to the table with two more plates.

"Five hundred," Randy said as Joyce slid a plate in front of him.

Kim took a bite of pizza and chased it with a drink of beer. "We can't keep the extra," he said as he took five hundred dollars off the pile and handed it to Joyce. "Take that to the Salvation Army tomorrow."

"Why can't we keep it?" Randy demanded.

"I'm not taking this money anywhere until you guys tell me where it came from," Joyce said quietly.

"The only way we can do this safely is to walk the path of the warrior. If we get greedy and take more than we need we lose the energy that protects us. I told you when we started that there were certain rules that had to be followed. That was the point of you reading Castaneda's books. I wanted you to understand what I was talking about."

"Sorry," Randy said with a sheepish grin. "I guess I let greed overcome some of the things you've taught me."

"It's okay," Kim said as he picked up his pizza. "We'll maintain our balance as long as the extra five hundred gets into the hands of someone who needs it."

Joyce pushed the five hundred dollars out into the middle of the table.

"I think it's time you two tell me how you got this money. I've been very patient. I asked once and you said you'd tell me when the time was right. Well, the time's right. If you want me to do something with that money you better spill the beans."

Kim and Randy looked at each other.

"Want me to tell her?" Randy asked.

"I guess you better," he said and took a bite of pizza.

"We bet on football, or basketball, or whatever sport is in season. Kim picks the winners and I place the bets."

"Right," she said with a sneer. "I hope you two really don't expect me to believe you have some kind of fool proof system for picking winners."

"You mean you don't believe it?" Randy asked with a chuckle.

"No, I don't!" Joyce said obstinately. "If bookies even suspected you had a remotely successful system they wouldn't take your bets."

"I work very hard at keeping them from finding out. There are about sixty different bookies I place bets with, on a rotating basis so nobody gets suspicious. I even place an occasional losing bet just..."

"Wait a minute, Randy," Joyce said, holding up her hands. "I'm not buying into this story. If you don't want me to know for some reason, then don't tell me. I just thought you might be ready to include me."

"Don't get mad."

"I'm not mad, just a little hurt that you don't want to tell me the truth," she said.

Randy turned and looked at Kim. "I need your help, I'm not getting anywhere."

Kim nodded as he wiped his hands with a napkin before taking a drink of beer. "There was a very good reason why we didn't tell you when you first asked. You wouldn't have believed the answer. We've never lied to you about anything. Randy told you the truth. We bet on sporting events."

"But how?" Joyce demanded. "There is no system that can..."

"Joyce," Randy interrupted. "It's not a system, it's Kim. He's telepathic, with exceptional precognitive abilities. He tells me what the outcome of certain games are going to be and I place bets accordingly."

Joyce felt her frustration begin to disintegrate into confusion. She moved her lips as she tried to speak, but the words seemed frozen in her throat. A bewildered look crossed her face.

Kim smiled as he reached across the table and took her hand. "Don't burden your mind by trying to analyze it. Let the linear thinker in you go to sleep, she has no place here."

"Our only concern from the very beginning was how you were going to handle this," Randy said. "Can you imagine how I reacted the first time I heard it? I thought he was nuts. It took about three weeks of perfect predictions before my intellect started to crumble."

"I'm really struggling with this," Joyce said as she picked up the money and slipped in into her pocket.

"I know," Randy said. "It'll take a couple days."

The sound of students walking passed the classroom brought Joyce back from her memories. She glanced at her watch as she put the stack of reports with her books and got up from the desk. She was trying to figure out the best way to carry the extra papers when Jerry Lansford walked into the classroom.

"Morning, Joyce."

"Oh, hi, Jerry," she said as she looked up. "What's going on?"

"Nothing really," he said as he walked over to the desk. "I just got rid of my morning chemistry class and thought I'd stop by and see if you were still here."

"You almost missed me," she said as she picked up her purse.

"You have time for a cup of coffee?" he asked.

"I don't like to stay away from the museum too long, but I think I can squeeze it in. You still owe me an explanation about that Michigan State T-shirt you were wearing last week."

"Oh, that's right, I do," he said as he picked up the stack of reports. "If you're going to be a teacher you have to get a briefcase. It's just too hard to handle this stuff without one."

"So what about the shirt?" she asked as they walked out of the classroom.

"There's really not much to tell," he said as they headed toward the elevator. "My brother-in-law teaches at Michigan State, so naturally we have quite a rivalry going, especially during football and basketball seasons."

"You lost a bet?" she asked.

"That's very perceptive of you," he said as they stopped at the elevator.

"So when I saw you in the T-shirt you were making good on the wager?" she asked as she pushed the down button.

"Well, not exactly," he said with a chuckle. "The real payoff was the picture I had to mail him."

"Picture of what?" Joyce asked as the elevator bell dinged and the doors opened.

"I had to stand in front of Galvin Hall on the first day of the summer quarter and greet students as they arrived."

Joyce laughed as they walked into the elevator. "Did you explain the circumstances to everyone?" she asked.

"I didn't even try. But wait until this coming football season," Jerry said as he pushed the button. "There's going to be hell to pay."

Samuel was sitting at his desk reviewing the report Joyce had written for the Sheriff when Steve came into the office.

"Morning, Sam," he said as he sat on the edge of Joyce's desk. "You wanted to see me?"

Samuel nodded as he continued to read the report until he found a convenient stopping place and laid the paper aside. "I have something in the lab for you and Luther," he said as he picked up his pouch of tobacco and opened it. "But before you get it, I want something."

"Did you find a lawn mower motor?" Steve asked.

"Yes, I did," Samuel said as he scooped his pipe down into the tobacco. "It's practically new, but before you get it I want a promise you'll fix those damn double doors in the lab. Every time I turn around I'm having trouble with them and I'm sick of it."

Steve shook his head slowly. "I really don't know what to do with them, Sam. I've tried everything I can think of to keep them from binding. They're simply the wrong doors for the application. I've asked Rudy to replace them, but he just gives me the cold shoulder and says they wouldn't be a problem if I maintained them properly. Well that's a bunch of bullshit. Other than oiling the hinges and lock mechanisms there's nothing to maintain on a door that's correct for the application. The only thing I can do is continue to tighten the hinge anchor plates every couple weeks."

Samuel leaned back in his chair, lit his pipe and rubbed his chin thoughtfully. "Exactly what's wrong with them anyway?" he asked.

"They're too heavy. Those doors are designed to be hinged in a wall reinforced with steel, like a bank would have. There's not enough strength in a concrete block wall to support them, so they sag in the middle and bind against each other. It's hard to believe Rudy spent that much money when I can't get him to buy a new air conditioning unit for the security station."

"I'm not surprised. He has to take kickbacks where he can get them."

"You think that's what happened?" Steve asked.

"Of course it is," Samuel said as he sat up in the chair. "It's the only way for him to get his hands on some of his Aunt's money."

"You lost me there," Steve said as he moved to Joyce's chair.

"I forgot you don't know about the skeleton in Rudy's closet," he said with a chuckle.

"God, this sounds good," Steve said as he shifted in the chair. "I want to hear all the dirt you've got on him."

Samuel took the pipe out of his mouth, tapped the side of the bowl with his lighter and relit it. "I've said too much already. Let's talk about something else."

"Come on, Sam. I can keep a secret."

"Steve, I can't. The information could be hazardous to your employment. One slip of the tongue and that asshole would have you on the street, and I'm not joking."

Steve folded his arms across his chest and smiled. "You want your doors fixed?"

"I thought you said you couldn't?" Samuel countered as he stirred the smoldering tobacco with a small knife.

"I think you and I could develop a believable story that would force Rudy to replace the doors. I mean, if they're damaged beyond repair what choice does he have?"

"Yes, but if he replaces them with the same thing we've gained nothing," Samuel replied.

"Hey, the only way that asshole knows one set of doors from another is with the price tag. We could hang a better set of doors for the application and he'd never know it as long as he paid the premium price. We should be able to cut a side deal with the door salesman. We get the doors we want, the salesman gets premium money for less expensive doors and Rudy gets his kickback. Sounds like everybody makes out."

"I'm not sure that's the right approach, but I'll give it some thought."

"Okay, so tell me about Rudy."

"Alright, but you say nothing to anyone, especially Joyce. Agreed?"

"Promise," Steve said as he crossed his heart.

"This part of Ohio is an archaeological gold mine. When the building boom hit the area after the war, builders were digging up artifacts every time they started a new project. It wasn't long before a group of rich old widows from the area got together, formed the Allen County Historical Society and started laying claim to the artifacts as they surfaced. After twenty years these old women had a garage stacked to the ceiling with boxes of stone tools, arrow heads, pieces of pottery and bones. Rudy's Aunt was the President to the Society when she died. The will, which he expected to set him up for the rest of his life, left millions of dollars to the Historical Society for building a museum, and left him with nothing. The only thing he got out of that will was the stipulation that he be given a respectable job at the museum for as long as he wanted it."

"You're shitting me, right?" Steve asked with a shocked look on his face.

Samuel shook his head. "Not at all. That's how he came to be the Managing Director of the museum. It's also why you see such a wide range of quality in the furnishings and decor of the museum. The budget was Rudy's responsibility and he was always willing to spend a lot of money as long as a kickback was in the deal. If not, he was very frugal," he said as he dumped his pipe into the ashtray.

"You know, if I stop and look around, the story really fits. The furniture in his office must have cost thousands of dollars, but the air conditioning unit in the security station must be the cheapest model Sears sells."

"Can you imagine how much he paid to have the mural painted on the wall outside the office?" Samuel asked as he got up and walked over to the door going into the lab.

"I wonder how he's gotten away with it all these years?" Steve asked.

Samuel shrugged his shoulders. "The Directors on the Board don't want to know, so they look the other way. What could they do besides slap his hands? He's got the job for as long as he wants it." He opened the door and stepped out into the lab. "Your motor is right here in this box."

Steve got up and walked around the corner of the desk and joined Samuel in the lab. He stooped down and opened the box. "Sam, this looks like a new motor! How much did you have to pay for it?" he asked as he stood up.

"It wasn't that much. I've got friends in a lot of different occupations," he said with a sly smile.

"Is this hot?" Steve asked with a laugh.

"Don't know. I didn't ask," he said with a chuckle.

Steve stooped down, picked up the box and carried it into the office. "This is going to make Luther's day," he said as he rested it on the corner of Joyce's desk. "He was sure Rudy was going to find out about the mower before I got it fixed."

"Go give him the good news and tell him to keep the mower away from the wall."

George swore as his car hit a deep crater in the street and threw muddy water up across the windshield. He hit the washer button on the wiper switch as he continued to look for addresses on the run down houses. Most of the places were identified only by a last name painted across the side of the rural mailbox at the edge of the crumbling street.

There had been business dealings with Oscar Washington before, but always at a construction site. He had always been a reliable and inexpensive trash hauler. George had watched Oscar's old pickup pull away many times, loaded well beyond a reasonable limit, wondering if he would actually make it to his destination.

This time things were different. The job required a level of concealment, which precluded Oscar seeing the construction site, and the load was far too heavy for his truck. The deal had to be struck at his place and the load had to be delivered.

Delivery of the item was not an insurmountable problem, but finding Oscar's house was proving to be more difficult than he thought. He was about to give up and go to a pay phone when he saw Oscar's old truck sitting in a driveway next to a yard cluttered with an assortment of car parts, a couple beat up lawnmowers, and an old washing machine. As he got closer he was able to read the name painted on the side of the mailbox. It was unmistakably Washington, although the last letters were squeezed together awkwardly.

George saw Oscar sitting in a rocking chair on the porch as he pulled his car into the stone drive and shut off the engine. He opened the glove compartment and took out a bottle of Kentucky Bourbon still in the bag from the liquor store. As he got out of the car he wondered how Oscar got away with keeping so much scrap in his front yard, then laughed to himself when he remembered that almost every house on the street had at least one junker sitting somewhere on the property.

Oscar was standing next to the rocking chair when George stepped up on the porch. His weathered black face broke into a toothless grin as bony fingers clutched the front of an old tattered sweater.

"George Miller," he said in a raspy voice as they shook hands. "I thought I done seen the last of you when I up an' retired. Sit down," he said as he pulled a lawn chair over next to the rocker.

"This is for you," George said as he handed the bottle to Oscar and sat down.

Oscar chuckled. "I reckon you remembered my hankerin' for Bourbon," he said as he took the bottle out of the bag. "Thanks, George," he said with a smile. "I been cuttin' back, ya know. Retirement leaves a lot of drinkin' time. If ya want to say healthy ya got to cut back a bit. I only been havin' a couple snorts a week for the last year or so."

"I was having trouble finding your place until I saw your old truck. I'm surprised it's still running."

"It sure is," Oscar said with a laugh. "Sometimes I think it'll still be goin' when I'm pushin' up daisies. Damn thing's rolled the odometer over twice!"

"They don't make them like that any more, Oscar."

Oscar nodded in agreement. "So what's on your mind, George? I know you didn't drive out here an' look me up jus' to talk about that old truck o' mine."

"Yeah, you're right Oscar. I came out to talk you into helping me out with something."

"George, there be plenty of people out there that need your haulin' business. You don't need me."

"It's not a hauling job, Oscar. I'll explain, but can I have something to drink first?"

"Damn. I'm sorry, George. It's been so long since I had a visitor I plumb forgot how to act," he said as he got up out of the chair. "What you thirsty for?"

"Whatever you've got will be fine, just as long as it's wet."

George watched Oscar's slow, shuffling steps as he went inside and wondered if he'd be able to avoid discussing specific details about the artifact. Oscar was a product of the old South, and had a superstitious streak a mile wide. If he knew what the thing actually looked like he'd pull the shades and bolt the doors. The trick would be to get the money in his hand as soon as possible. Everybody could use some extra money, and his guess was that Oscar was barely getting by on his fixed income.

"George," Oscar called from inside the house. "I got ice tea, if that's okay."

"That's fine, Oscar. Just a little sugar."

It troubled him to have to deal with Oscar from behind a smoke screen, but there was no other way. He was glad he put half of ten grand back for him.

Oscar pushed open the screen door with his foot and walked out on the porch with two glasses of ice tea. He handed one to George before returning to the rocker. He took a drink and set the glass on the porch next to his chair.

"Okay George, what be on your mind?" Oscar asked.

George stirred his tea thoughtfully before taking a long drink. "All I really want you to do is be a middle man," he said as he set his drink next to the chair. "I'm doing a job for a man who is wealthy and somewhat eccentric. When I found out how much money he was willing to spend on the quiet elimination of what he saw as a problem, I thought of you. I can imagine how hard it is making ends meet when you're on a fixed income." George took the pack of hundred dollar bills out of his shirt pocket and handed it to Oscar.

Oscar took the pack of money and looked at it oddly. "George, I can't be doin' nothin' crooked..."

George shook his head. "There's nothing crooked about it. While we were digging on his property we found an artifact," he said as he picked up his glass. He took a drink and set it back on the porch. "He's a fair, community minded man who wants to see this artifact end up in the museum where it belongs, but, like I said, he's somewhat eccentric and doesn't want people traipsing all over his property trying to find out what else might be there."

"So you want me to pick up this thing and take it to the museum?" Oscar asked as he looked down at the money in his lap.

"It's even easier than that. We'll deliver the artifact. All you have to do is call the museum, have them pick it up and don't tell them where it came from."

Oscar laughed nervously. "That be a lot of money for doin' nothin'."

"Yeah, but he's rich, Oscar. The money doesn't mean as much to him as his privacy does."

Oscar gave George a toothless grin as he put the money in his shirt pocket. "What does this thing look like?" he asked.

George shrugged his shoulders. "It's just a piece of petrified wood with some carvings on it. It's pretty heavy. That's why we're delivering it. Your old truck wouldn't hold up under the load."

Oscar took George's hand and shook it slowly. "Thank you for thinkin' of me, George," he said and laughed. "If this fella ever wants anythin' else be sure an' let me know."

"I will," George said cheerfully, but in his heart he knew he had done Oscar a bad turn. He knew one look at the artifact would turn his taste for money sour and his insides to stone.

Steve leaned forward on the bench and pulled an orange shop rag out of his back pocket, wiped it across his chin and looked over at Luther. "These have got to be the juiciest peaches I've ever eaten," he said as he returned the rag to his pocket. "Does your brother have an orchard in Florida?"

Luther grinned as he took a cigar out of his shirt pocket and started taking off the cellophane wrapper. "Nope. He's just got a tree in his back yard. You won't be growin' peaches like that from any old tree," he said as he wadded up the cellophane and stuffed it into his pocket.

"What's so special about his tree?" Steve asked as he licked his fingers.

"He got his self a sapplin' from Georgia about ten years ago and planted it in his back yard. I reckon he really fussed over that tree 'cause that's the way he is. Some folks tinker with cars, he tinkers in his back yard with a garden an' his peach tree." He bit off the end of the cigar and spit it out into the grass. "He sent me a crate of his peaches for my birthday an' I brought a whole bag of 'em to work this mornin'. You ought to take a couple of 'em to Ralph 'fore he goes home." Luther picked up the bag at the end of the bench and handed it to Steve. "Take some down to Sam an' Joyce, too," he said as he clamped the cigar between his teeth.

Steve stood up and took the bag. "Want me to take one to Rudy, too?" he asked as he started toward the museum.

"Yeah," Luther said with a laugh as he struck a wooden match. "But I wanna piss on it first."

Steve stopped and looked back at Luther. "No, I want to," he quipped.

They both howled with laughter.

Ralph was leaning against the display case waiting for Terry Lewis when Steve came through the doors carrying the bag of peaches.

"Morning, Ralph," Steve said as he walked over to the display case. "You look like you're about ready for bed."

Ralph managed a halfhearted smile. "As soon as Terry gets here I'm going home and give it a try."

"Luther wanted me to bring you some peaches before you went home," he said as he set the bag on top of the display case.

"No, thanks," Ralph said as he shook his head.

"Go on," Steve insisted. "They're really good."

"Alright," he said as he reached for the bag with a trembling hand.

"Let me help you," Steve said as he opened the bag. He pulled out a fat peach and handed it to Ralph. "Looks like that coffee has you wired. You ought to lay off of it for awhile."

Ralph nodded his head. "I will as soon as I get back on days," he said as he opened his lunch bucket. "I just can't wean myself off of it while I'm on midnights, especially with me working twelve hours."

Steve noticed the bottle of Jack Daniels in the bottom of the lunch bucket when Ralph put away the peach. He started to say something about it, and then stopped when he heard someone rushing up the steps from the basement.

Rudy was clearly agitated when he reached the lobby. He shot a burning stare at Steve as he stomped passed. "You better find something to do besides stand around with your thumb up your ass," he yelled as he disappeared around the corner.

"Fuck you, Rudy," Steve said under his breath as he picked up the bag of peaches and started for the steps. "I hope you get out of here before he comes back."

"So do I."

"See you in the morning."

"Okay, Steve."

Samuel was sitting at his desk packing tobacco down into the bowl of his pipe when Steve walked into the office. "What the hell did you do to Rudy?" he asked as he set the bag of peaches on Joyce's desk and plopped down onto her chair. "He came flying up the steps like he had a jet strapped to his ass and gave me hell on the way past."

Samuel chuckled as he closed his tobacco pouch and set it next to the ashtray. "Did he seem a little anxious?"

"Anxious? He was lit up like a roman candle. I'll have to warn Luther to stay out of his way. What set him off?"

"Well, I'm not sure," he said as he lit the pipe. "It might have been when I told him to replace the doors or I'd go to the Board of Directors about all the kick backs."

"Oh, my God! Are you serious?"

Samuel laughed as he sent a plume of smoke toward the ceiling. "It was a bluff. I didn't have any proof, but when he stomped out of the office I knew I hit a nerve."

Steve laughed as he leaned back in the chair. "I guess that pretty much explains why he came flying up the steps like he did."

"What's in the bag?" Samuel asked.

"Some of the best peaches I've ever eaten. Luther's brother grew them in his back yard down in Florida. He wanted me to bring some in to you and Joyce."

Samuel leaned over and took a peach out of the bag. "Did Ralph get one?" he asked.

"I had to twist his arm a little. I told him to lay off the coffee, his hand was really shaking."

Samuel set his pipe aside, took a bite out of the peach and grabbed for his handkerchief as juice ran down his chin. "Juicy," he said as he leaned forward and pulled the wastebasket over in front of him.

"Sam, maybe you should have a talk with Ralph. When he put the peach in his lunch bucket I saw a bottle of Jack Daniels. Rudy would have him on the street in the blink of an eye if he found out he was drinking on the job."

"Things must be getting worse," Samuel said as he wiped the juice from his mustache. "The midnight shift has always been hard on him, but I don't think he's ever brought a bottle to work with him before." He finished the peach, threw the pit in the trash and started wiping off his hands. "I've never quite understood why his nightmares get so bad when he works midnights. I'll have a talk with him. I wish I could get him to see a doctor again."

"I've heard the stories about him being part of some kind of drug experiment when he was with the Marines. Is there a connection between the experiment and his nightmares?" Steve asked.

"I think there is, but it's impossible to know for certain. Hell, maybe Rudy causes the nightmares," he said with a laugh as he looked down at his hands. "I can't have a serious discussion with sticky fingers," he said as he got up from the desk and walked into the lab.

"Did Ralph know about the experiment, or was it one of those clandestine operations the military seems to prefer?" Steve asked over the sound of running water.

Samuel was drying his hands with a paper towel when he walked back into the office. He wadded up the towel and threw it into the wastebasket as he sat down. "Ralph volunteered, but I don't think he had any idea what he was getting himself into," Samuel replied as he pulled a small penknife out of his pocket. "Ralph probably talks more to me than anyone else. Several times he's mentioned that during the experiment the medical staff asked a lot of questions about his dreams," he said as he opened the knife and started cleaning the bowl of the pipe. "I started doing a little research. The program was classified, so there wasn't much to be found directly, but I continued to dig and started coming up with tidbits of information from different sources. I found enough that I think I have an idea of what they were doing." He dumped the pipe into the ashtray and laid it aside. "I think they were experimenting with a derivative of lysergic acid diethylamide."

"You mean LSD?" Steve asked.

"Yes, LSD. I think they were trying to develop a drug that would let the soldier see flashes of the future while dreaming."

"That's ridiculous," Steve said.

"Oh, I agree. It was a stupid concept from the very beginning and the experiment didn't last long. I'm surprised it ever got started to begin with, but I guess I can see how the notion would be attractive to the military."

"No kidding," Steve said as he took a couple peaches out of the bag and set them on Joyce's desk. "I suppose I should go find Luther and tell him Rudy's wound up."

"How's the lawn mower running?" Samuel asked.

"Great," Steve replied with a chuckle as he stood up. "Luther was a nervous wreck waiting for me to get the motor changed. Thanks again for helping us out."

"It was nothing. I was glad I could help."

"See you later," Steve said as he walked toward the door.

"Okay, Steve. Stay away from Rudy."

A gentle breeze tossed Joyce's hair as she walked along the cobblestone path with Jerry at her side. "I appreciate you taking the time to carry my papers to the car for me," Joyce said as the bright sunlight filtered through the rustling trees.

"Really, it's no problem. I couldn't just sit there and watch you make two trips, besides, I enjoy your company."

"I enjoy your company, too," she said with a smile. "You've made my transition into your academic world a little easier." She took a pair of sunglasses out of her purse and slipped them on as they walked up next to her Porsche.

"This is your car?" Jerry asked in a surprised voice. "My God, do you deal drugs on the side or something?"

"No," she said with a laugh as she unlocked the door and took the stack of papers. She set them on the passenger seat and turned back toward Jerry. "Thanks for the coffee," she said as she gently touched his forearm. "I'll go out and buy a briefcase tomorrow so you won't have to carry my papers."

"I didn't mind carrying them," he said as he leaned on the next car. "Besides, I wanted to talk to you without half of the student body trying to listen in on the conversation."

"Some dark secret about the teaching profession?" she asked.

"No, just some feelings I want to share with you," he said.

"Would you like to sit in the car?" Joyce asked. "We can talk for a few minutes, then I can drop you off at the front of the building."

"Yeah, I'd like that," he said as he started around the back of the car. "I've never been in a Porsche before."

Joyce got into the car, moved the papers to the back seat and unlocked the passenger door.

Jerry got in and closed the door as Joyce turned on the radio and put down the windows. "Oh, yeah," he said as he leaned back in the seat. "This car is really nice. Driving it to someplace like California would be a blast. Are these cars as fast as I've heard?"

"I usually baby it," she said, "but I have put my foot in it a few times. It's very fast."

Jerry looked around the interior of the car admiringly as he touched the leather upholstery. "I love this car. It's beautiful."

"Thank you," she said as she took off her sunglasses and set them on the dash. "You said you wanted to talk to me about something."

"I'm not sure how to say this," he said as their eyes locked. He held her gaze for a moment before looking away. "I'm not very good with words...God, my insides are trembling."

"You want my car?" she asked with a laugh.

"No," he said. "I want you. My soul has been on fire ever since we met."

"That's not bad, for someone who's not very good with words," she said.

"I'm so nervous... This is not like teaching," he said.

"You're a sweetheart, Jerry, but all you're seeing is the outer veneer. You don't know what I'm like on the inside. I don't do well with personal relationships. I've been told I'm a cold hearted bitch."

"I find that pretty hard to believe," he said as he reached across the console and took her hand.

"Don't misunderstand me, Jerry. We can date and have a good time, but if you try to get too close to me... That part of me died a long time ago. I don't want you to get hurt."

Jerry lifted her hand to his lips and kissed it softly. "How about if we start off real slow and see what happens?" he asked.

"Jerry, you're not listening to me," she said sternly as she pulled her hand away. "There's no seeing what happens. I'd much rather hurt you now than break your heart later. I'm attracted to you physically and it would be easy for me to go to bed with you, but there wouldn't be anything else. If you can't deal with that you should back away now, before something gets started."

"I'm sorry I made you angry," he said.

"You didn't make me angry," she whispered as she leaned across the console and kissed him on the lips. "I'm just a cold hearted bitch when it comes to love," she said softly and kissed him again.

"Okay," he said as he sat back in his seat. "How about dinner tonight?"

"That sounds good to me, as long as you remember the rules," she said as she started the car. She took a piece of paper out of her purse and wrote down her phone number and address and handed it to Jerry. "Call me later," she said as she started backing the car out of the parking place.

"One of these days I'd like to experience the performance of this piece of German engineering."

"I've got time right now, if you're serious," Joyce said as she pulled away from the parking space.

"I'm serious, but I've got a chemistry class in fifteen minutes. I want more time than that."

"There shouldn't be anything to stop us after dinner tonight," Joyce said as she stopped the car in front of Galvin Hall.

"Yeah, that sounds perfect. I'll call you," he said as he stroked her arm.

"Okay, talk to you then," she said as she watched him climb out of the car and wondered how long their relationship would last. She supposed it could last for a while, as long as he could stick to the rules. She waved as she pulled away and thought about how easy it was to have an affair with Steve. He was young and much more interested in sex and friendship than finding someone willing to settle down. It wasn't going to be as easy with Jerry, but she was willing to give it a try. She just hoped he got the message so there wouldn't be an emotional break up later, she thought as she left the campus.

During the drive back to the museum she continued to think about Jerry, their tentative relationship and all the things that could go wrong. There were definite risks involved due to the work environment, risks that were minimized with Steve because of his age. An emotional end to a tryst between two people working on the same campus could get ugly and somewhat public. There were good solid reasons why they should simply be friends, but the physical attraction she felt for him was undeniable. She wanted him and she knew if he hadn't made the first move she would have.

When she got to the museum she saw Luther trimming grass along the retaining wall. She waved at him as she turned into the drive. Steve was half way up a ladder at the front of the building working on the gutter and downspout. She gave him a quick toot on the horn when he stopped long enough to wave.

She thought about Steve as she pulled into her parking place. She had the perfect relationship with him and there was nothing in her desire for Jerry that could diminish their friendship. Given a choice between them, Jerry would lose, she thought as she climbed out of the Porsche and started across the blacktop. Steve was never inept at sex, but she taught him things about a woman's body he never knew. She spent many nights teaching him how to make love to her and she wasn't about to give that up just because somebody else caught her eye. She'd take them both, but if she could only have one she knew it would be Steve.

When she opened the door and walked into the lobby she saw Terry Lewis at the desk in the security station with the phone cradled between his head and shoulder. He was a short, stocky man, with closely cropped red hair and enough freckles to appear dark complected from across a room.

When Terry saw Joyce he motioned for her to come over.

"There shouldn't be a problem finding the address," he said into the phone as he scribbled on a message pad. "Can you tell me what it looks like?" he asked. He listened for a moment before putting the pencil down and taking the phone in his hand. "I'll make sure the curator gets the message. I'm sure they'll come out and look at whatever it is, but I can't promise they'll be interested in bringing it to the museum." He listened again, and then smiled. "Yes sir, you have a good day, too."

He hung up the phone and handed the note to Joyce. "One of the great pleasures of this job is dealing with people when nobody else is around," he said with a laugh. "I've taken some strange calls, but that one's a classic. The old man at that address has something he's sure belongs in the museum, but he doesn't know where it came from, what it is or what it looks like."

Joyce looked at the note and back to Terry. "He doesn't even know what it looks like?"

"I know," Terry said as he shook his head. "Myself, I'd trash the note, but that's up to you. He sounded like a nice old guy, but I'm thinking he might be a few cards short of a full deck."

"I won't get there tonight," she said as she slipped the paper into her purse and started walking toward the staircase. "If he calls back tell him I'll get there as soon as I can."

"Okay," Terry said as he returned to his chair, pulled open the center desk drawer and took out the Playboy he'd been looking through. He opened the magazine to the centerfold and gazed at Miss July. She was a beautiful woman, but as far as he was concerned she had nothing on Joyce Robbins.

Oscar Washington sat on his front porch and rocked slowly as the sportscaster gave his play-by-play description of the action between the Reds and Padres. The game was broadcast on one of the local television channels, but there was something special about being outside in the sunshine, listening to baseball on the radio. He usually listened closely, knew the count on the batter and who was up next, but today was different.

He heard the crack of the bat, cheers from the crowd and knew his mind had wondered again. It was an important game in the series and he didn't even know the score or who had just hit the ball. The game was nothing more than sound in the background of his thoughts, thoughts that were disrupting his concentration. His mind kept wandering back to the thing he saw George and his men unload from the flatbed truck.

He never expected anything so big, but even more of a surprise was how hard they worked at keeping it covered. It was as if they wanted to make sure nobody saw what was under the canvas and that made him uneasy. He felt the packet of bills in his pocket and wondered if it was really the blessing he thought it was. God knew he had plenty of needs for the money, but now he was afraid the deal had been too sweet and easy to be honest. It was a thought that never occurred to him until after George and his men were gone. Now he was left with nagging uneasiness about the thing in his garage, the thing that he feared might leave a terrible stain on his life.

He supposed sitting around brooding about the thing made no sense and wondered if he should go to the garage, uncover it and have a look. Maybe all he needed was a little reassurance to put his mind at ease and get back to the baseball game before it ended.

He got up from the rocking chair, moved down the steps and made his way across the yard, passing an old washing machine and two partially disassembled lawnmowers as he went. He stopped at the edge of the driveway, picked up a broom handle leaning against the tree and steadied himself with it as he started across the loose stones. He was suddenly annoyed with himself for not asking to see the thing while they unloaded it. It would have saved him a lot of worry and he wouldn't have sounded so stupid when he called the museum.

When he got to the garage he swung one of the doors open, spilling light into the dim interior. In the shadows beyond the light he could see the silhouette of the tarp covering an enormous thing leaning against one of the roof support posts. He walked over to the canvas, lifted one corner and peered under it as he reached out with his hand. There was just enough light to make out the immense size of the petrified log, but not the carved features he felt with his hand. He strained his eyes for moment, trying to make out the details before dropping the cover in frustration. He went to the other side of the garage, grabbed the trouble light dangling overhead and reeled out the cord as he walked back to the canvas. After setting the light to a nearby table he picked up the corner of the canvas again. He used the broom handle to lift it up and hook it on a nearby nail, exposing one side of the thing. After setting the broom handle aside he picked up the trouble light and turned it on. He was startled by his own fuzzy, bluish reflection from the surface of what appeared to be an enormous crystal. When he recovered from the start he stepped forward with the trouble light out in front of him. As he got closer he noticed a spot of red crisscrossing lines growing on the crystal in front of the light. He took the glasses out of his pocket and slipped them on as he watched the spot. It faded as he withdrew the light and became more pronounced as he put it closer. He moved the light from side to side and watched as the spot followed the movement, leaving a fading red trail of intersecting red lines behind it. His fascination with the spot ended abruptly when his eyes fell upon the frame, which encased the crystal.

An icy finger touched his heart as he put the light close and stared at the tormented faces carved into the strange log. He reached out with a trembling hand and ran his fingers along the features of one of the faces as he felt goose flesh creeping up his spine. The stark realization that he was in front of some kind of Godless abomination struck him like a thunderbolt. Terror raced through his body and chilled his blood as he felt the strength drain from his legs.

"Lord Jesus, help me," he whispered. That was the last sane thought Oscar Washington ever had.

In the next instant the trouble light was knocked back away from the crystal by something unseen. His sanity crumbled as his eyes beheld a sight his mind could never accept. There on the crystal was a black spot; black tinged with red and in the center a hole through which a leathery taloned finger reached, flailing the air as it searched for a purchase. As Oscar stumbled backwards away from the artifact the light fell from his hand and shattered on the ground, returning that side of the garage to shadows. In the dim light he could still see the finger reaching out and slicing the air.

Oscar turned and ran from the garage, screaming in utter madness.

94

CHAPTER FIVE

The snowy wind whipped through the man's long black hair as he inched along the sheer face of the cliff, moving from one foothold to another. His movements were like the precise steps of a dancer, moving in slow motion to some soundless rhythm. He was a stranger to the narrow stone ledge, but knew every outcropping and pocket as he knew himself.

It was only a matter of unrelenting will that kept his mind focused on his destination as the pain from his bleeding fingers radiated up his sinewy arms. He knew it was some kind of test, but his strength and inner vision had been proven years ago, before the teachings began. He journeyed to the Sacred Cave many times with his other body. Why was he summoned to come in this body?

He closed his eyes and pressed his forehead against the rock face of the cliff, then began a shallow, rhythmic breathing pattern as he projected his double. Within a heartbeat his consciousness was plunging down an inner tunnel of light toward his tenuous etheric body.

The sensations of the Sacred Cave began filtering into his awareness as his rarefied form migrated into the mouth of the cavern. He heard the chanting first, then felt the spiritual vibrations coming from the walls of the grotto. When he opened his eyes he found himself in front of the Eternal Flame facing the double of Hsuan Hsueh, the eldest of the Council of Elders.

"Samadhi," he said with a slight laugh. "Always the curious one. This is not how I asked for you to come."

"I am not far away, Master. Why is this not the way I am to see the sacred cave this time?" Samadhi asked.

"All your questions will be answered when you sit with me in your physical body. Go now, so that you can return as I have asked."

Samadhi's double withdrew toward the mouth of the cave and dissipated like a cloud of steam. A moment later he felt the coolness of the canyon wall against his forehead as his perception returned to his physical body. He immediately set upon the arduous task of completing the journey to the Sacred Cave in the unheard of fashion.

When Samadhi finally pulled himself up into the cave he was amazed as his physical eyes beheld walls ablaze with veins of gold and silver and embellished with ancient drawings of strange animals. A massive crystalline monolith jutted out of the floor of the grotto where the Eternal Flame should have been.

"Everything appears so different," he said as he looked around the cave.

"Come and sit with me and tell me what you see," Hsuan Hsueh said as he gestured toward a spot next to him.

Samadhi moved close to his master's etheric double, lowered himself to the floor and crossed his legs into the lotus position.

"The walls are filled with gold and silver, and there are strange drawings of prehistoric animals everywhere. A giant crystal protrudes from the floor where the Eternal Flame appears to my double," Samadhi said as he reached out and touched the crystal. "Did you bring me here like this so I could see how the Eternal Flame looks to these eyes?"

"You have much to understand, Samadhi. You are the one who has shown me how the Sacred Cave appears to the eyes of the physical body," the old man said as he passed his hand through the Eternal Flame. "You watched as I passed my hand through a crystal. From my perception I passed my hand through flame."

"I do not understand, Master. Have you never seen this yourself?" Samadhi asked in a confused tone.

"No, I have not. You are the first to be here like this since the great cataclysm sheared away the mountain."

"But Master, the path, I knew it well. I felt its energy," Samadhi insisted.

"You felt the energy of a path that was made for your spirit, six thousand years ago. You are the first to use it."

"How can that be?" Samadhi pleaded.

"You are one of three, Samadhi. We have nurtured three spirits throughout their many lives over the span of thousands of years. Now the destinies of these three spirits await fulfillment."

"Master, I thought my destiny was to come to Tibet and be one with the Brotherhood."

"Be patient, Samadhi. We have taken thousands of years to prepare for that which we always knew would happen. There have been many destinies to fulfill along the way. Now we must open the final book and we must read it well, because the survival of this world, as we know it, hangs in the balance. Find the quiet place in your mind and listen to my thoughts."

Samadhi closed his eyes and quieted his internal voice as he let his mind slip away toward a place where time and space lost all meaning, the place of the inner sun.

Hsuan Hsueh watched Samadhi's face until he saw the fire from within, then projected a telepathic link into his mind and released his thoughts.

In the beginning, when the Great One brought the physical universe out of blackness, a pathway between two worlds appeared that was never intended to exist. This abomination joined a world that would become populated by intelligent, passionate beings, and a world of carnivorous creatures of darkness, separated only by an electromagnetically sensitive barrier. Early humans lived in mortal terror for thousands of years until they evolved the mental capacity to understand the images we communicated to them in their dreams. They dreamed of the barrier between the two worlds, of the warning that was to be constructed around it, and of a place where the earth was soft and could swallow the horrid portal. The doorway was sealed for ten thousand years, but we knew it would return. It has now been discovered and will soon be in the hands of the other two incarnate spirits. The others knew you well during your time before The Brotherhood when you were known as Kim Lee. They have none of this enlightenment, but hold the key to the final victory in their hearts. You must journey back and join them to close the doorway forever. The first step of the journey has been completed. Your physical body has absorbed energy from the Sacred Cave. Guard this energy well, for the final battle will demand it all. Go swiftly and prepare for your quest, the price of delay will be counted in innocent lives.

Joyce thought about Jerry and their dinner together as she drove into the south end of town with its crumbling streets and dilapidated houses. The time she spent with him was relaxing and enjoyable, although most of their conversation had to do with the college and some of the more annoying people working in the administration offices. After dinner they went for a long ride through the country on some winding back roads. He seemed comfortable with her high speed driving even though she caught him reaching for something to hold onto a couple times.

When they got back to her condo it was nearly nine o'clock. She wanted him to come in, but understood when he explained he had an early class.

When he kissed her goodnight he whispered that he didn't want sex between them to be rushed and that left her wanting him all the more.

The warm morning sun was just starting to burn the dew off the grass as Joyce turned onto the unfamiliar street. After driving slowly for a few minutes she stopped the Porsche in front of the only mailbox she'd seen with a street number instead of a name. She checked the address on the note and counted houses. She was fairly sure the white house with the old truck sitting in the driveway was the place she wanted.

She drove ahead, dodging a couple potholes and stopped in front of the house. An old washing machine and a couple lawn mowers were sitting around a tree and seemed to be in different stages of repair. There was an old man sitting on the porch with his back against the house and forehead resting on drawn up knees. She could feel knots of tension building in her neck as she realized it was pretty early in the day for a nap. The last thing she wanted to do was go into an unfamiliar neighborhood alone and wake a stranger out of a drunken stupor.

As she turned the Porsche into the stone drive she noticed what seemed to be a perfectly good rocking chair turned upside down in front of the doors of a large garage. She hated it when things didn't seem to fall into place, and this picture wasn't going together quite right. She stopped the car, shut off the engine and watched the old man for any signs of waking up. After a moment she opened the car door and climbed out. "Hello," she called as she closed the door behind her. "I'm Joyce Robbins, from the museum." She wanted the old man to raise his head and give her a toothless grin, or something, but he didn't. "Hello," she repeated a little louder as she walked to the front of the car. She stepped off the driveway into the sparse grass and stopped next to the old washing machine. The breeze carried a slight odor of alcohol and something else, something unclean and disturbing.

"Hello," she yelled, but there was no response from the old man. She wanted to go back to her car, forget about whatever the old guy thought he had and leave, but something urged her on. She walked to the steps and saw a near empty bourbon bottle laying next to the old man. The reek of alcohol and another, more putrid smell had flies swarming around the porch.

She took a handkerchief out of her purse and held it to her mouth and nose as she cautiously started up the steps. She cringed at the thought of walking into the swarming flies and touching the old man, but she couldn't bring herself to return to her car without knowing his condition.

"Hello," she said one more time as she walked up next to him. She reached out, touched him on the shoulder and recoiled in horror as the stiff body fell away from her. A shiny brass key fell out of the man's hand and bounced off the bottle as his head hit the porch with a thud.

Joyce gasped as she stepped back away from the body. The stench of dead flesh and the buzzing of flies assailed her senses as the world started to spin out of control. She reached out, grabbed the screen door handle and steadied herself as her mind raced. After a moment she regained her senses, looked down at the body and knew she had to call the police.

She opened the screen door and walked into the house. There were stacks of old papers, magazines and an assortment of what appeared to be worthless junk sitting everywhere. A narrow path wound through the cluttered living room toward what she presumed was the kitchen. She found the phone in the kitchen sitting next to a stack of hubcaps on an old dilapidated desk. She picked it up and was relieved to hear a dial tone.

She called 911 rather than starting a search for the phone book in the midst of the stacks of magazines and newspapers. After a brief explanation to the operator she was connected to the Police Department. The officer who answered the phone was polite, asked a few questions and then assured her a police car would be dispatched promptly. She broke the connection and dialed Samuel's number as she glanced around the cluttered room.

"Hello," Martha answered.

"Martha, this is Joyce. Has Sam left yet?"

"He's right here, just a second."

"Morning, Joyce. What's up?"

"Sam," she said with a trembling voice as she fought back tears. "I'm going to be late getting to the museum this morning."

"Joyce, what's wrong," he asked in an alarmed tone.

"I'm alright," she said. "I was following up on a phone call from yesterday on a possible acquisition when I found a body."

"Oh, my God! Do you want me to come?" he asked.

"I would have preferred that you found the guy, but I think things are under control now. There's no sense in you getting involved."

"Are you sure?" he asked.

"Yes, I'm fine, but I'll be tied up here until the police are finished with me."

"Don't be worrying about a damn acquisition, just take care of business and get out of there."

"I don't have a clue about why I'm here. I certainly haven't seen anything we want," she said as she looked around the disorder of the room. "I'm sure I'll be coming back empty handed."

"Alright, you take care of yourself. I'll see you at the museum."

"Bye," she said and hung up.

She stood by the phone for a moment longer and wished she knew more about whatever it was the old man thought belonged in the museum. After a moment she returned to the living room and took another quick look at the mess. She wasn't in the mood for a scavenger hunt, she thought as she walked to the door. She turned for one last look and saw nothing but junk.

She pushed the screen door open, stepped out on the porch with the swarming flies and nauseating malodor, and went down the steps without looking back at the body. She didn't need to be reminded of how the rigid body felt to her touch, or the way the corpse retained its position as it rolled to the side. And she certainly didn't want to see flies crawling up into the old man's nose and mouth, searching for a suitable place to lay eggs.

As she walked back to her car she remembered how Terry described the phone call that brought her to this deteriorating neighborhood. The old guy, whose body was now drawing flies and Lord only knew what else, had absolutely no idea what the thing was that he wanted the museum to take. That ruled out a lot of stuff. Actually, it ruled out just about everything that came to her mind.

She got into the car, closed the door and turned on the radio. There was no way of asking the old man what in the hell he'd been talking about, and beyond that, the acquisition was a dead end, no pun intended. There was nothing else to do but wait for the police and take care of some distasteful business, she thought as she stared through the windshield at the upside down rocker in front of the garage.

For lack of anything else to do while she waited, she got back out of the car and walked toward the garage. Maybe the rocking chair only looked like it was in good shape. Maybe it was really broken. That, at least, would explain why the old man had been sitting on the floor of the porch instead of in the chair.

When she got to the garage she realized the end of the rockers had been driven into the ground, securing the chair in place wedged tightly against the doors. The ends of the rockers that were pointing upward were mushroomed like the ends of stakes and a hammer was lying on the ground nearby.

"A mystery at every turn," she said to herself. She was tired of this place. She should have known better than to follow up on such a questionable call, she thought as she turned away. She took one step and stopped. Something on the garage door had caught her eye just as she had turned and it sparked something in her mind. She turned back toward the garage and looked again. Hanging in the hasp was a shiny new padlock securing the door. Suddenly she remembered the shiny brass key that had fallen out of the old man's hand. Her interest in what might be in the garage unexpectedly blazed to life.

She hurried back to the front of the house and looked. The key was lying next to the bottle where it had fallen. She took a deep breath, ran up the steps, fanning away flies as she went and grabbed the key. She hurried back down the steps, certain that the old man had died with the key in his hand while waiting for someone from the museum.

She walked back to the garage, slipped the key into the lock, grasped the rocking chair and pulled. She was surprised how firmly the rockers were embedded in the ground. On the third attempt she finally freed the chair out of the stony soil of the driveway. After setting it aside she grabbed the padlock and turned the key. The lock popped open with ease, which seemed to indicate it hadn't been exposed to the weather for long. She removed the lock from the hasp, swung the doors open and peered into the dim light of the garage with no idea of what she expected to find.

Her eyes adjusted slowly. At first she saw an area much like the living room with stacks of papers and magazines, but then she noticed bigger things lying around, too. She recognized a car engine and rear axle lying together in the corner near the door and there were others things that were unfamiliar to her, but certainly nothing unknown to a master junk guru. On the ground in front of her was a trouble light, with shards of glass from a shattered light bulb scattered about. Beyond the shattered light in the shadows was something partially covered with a large canvas tarp. She stepped forward and strained her eyes, looking for some clue that would identify the object, but there simply wasn't enough light. After scanning the shadows for anything obvious she went back to her car, grabbed a flashlight from the glove box and returned to the garage.

She turned on the light and directed it toward the tarp. When the light beam reflected back toward her she immediately thought of an old mirror. She shined the light toward the top of the canvas as she moved forward and at once realized the thing was huge. She swept the beam back to the bottom where the corner of the tarp was raised and hooked on a nail. Her pulse quickened when she realized the exposed section of frame appeared to be petrified wood. She moved in for a closer look and was astonished by the sight of a massive petrified log. Her astonishment turned to shock when she saw a face carved into the log. "Oh, my God," she whispered as she lifted the corner of the canvas, exposing more of the log and more carved faces.

She threw the cover up over the top corner of the frame, uncovering the entire side member and stepped back. Her heart pounded in her chest as she looked at her own fuzzy, bluish reflection on the surface of an enormous crystal protruding from a bed of black slate encased within the frame. Her insides were trembling with excitement as she reached out and ran her fingers across the face of the crystal. She felt a rough texture created by thousands of tiny protrusions rising from the surface.

Nowhere in any archaeological literature had she ever seen reference to anything remotely similar and it had her mind racing. It was no longer surprising that the old man didn't know what it was, because she didn't either. Discovery of an undocumented artifact this day and age was the stuff of dreams. It simply didn't happen.

She took hold of the other side of the canvas and tossed it up over the top, exposing another massive petrified log with carved faces. The cover was completely off the artifact except in the center at the top where it was caught on some kind of large protruding feature. She looked around for something long enough to reach the bunched up material and found a broom handle lying on the ground nearby. She picked up the handle, extended it upward and tried to dislodge the material. After a brief struggle it became apparent that the material was pulled tight and she needed to grasp it with her hands to release it.

She threw the broom handle aside, grabbed a barrel of rags and dragged it over in front of the artifact. She dumped the rags into a pile, turned the barrel upside down and climbed up on top of it, putting her eye level with the tarp covered protrusion. After making sure her footing was stable she put her fingers under the canvas, pulled it free and let it drop behind the artifact. A sudden chill ran up her spine when she found herself face to face with the likeness of a bizarre looking creature with gaping jaws and rows of carnivorous teeth. The stony effigy had a ghastly cast that sent chills radiating throughout her body. She eased herself down off the barrel as she kept her eyes on the jutting head.

After a moment she looked over at details of the faces carved into the side logs. Each of the faces bore similar expressions of panic and horror. She was deeply absorbed in studying the faces when something touched her shoulder. Terror leaped into her mind as she yelled and spun around.

"I'm sorry," the officer said with an awkward smile, "I didn't mean to scare you."

"Oh, Jesus," Joyce cried, as she cupped one hand over her mouth and held the other to her chest.

"Are you Joyce Robbins?" the officer asked.

Joyce nodded her head as she waited for her heart to come down from her throat.

"I'm Officer Liemer, my partner's out front with the corpse. We'd like to get some information for our report, if you don't mind," he said as he turned and left the garage.

Joyce caught her breath and waited for her trembling insides to stop their jittery dancing, but they didn't even slow down. She walked out of the garage and shaded her eyes from the bright sunlight.

A police car was pulled across the mouth of the driveway, behind her Porsche, with its lights flashing slowly. The officer was standing at the front of her car writing on a form attached to his clipboard.

"Is this your car?" he asked.

"Yes," she responded.

"Did you touch anything, or move anything around?" he asked as an ambulance, followed by another car, pulled off the street and into the front yard.

As she started explaining everything to the officer, two men in white uniforms got out of the ambulance and talked with the man in a white lab coat, who had gotten out of the car. After a moment the men in white uniforms went to the back of the ambulance and got the stretcher. The other man walked up to the house where the officer was crouched down, looking at the body.

"Hello, Riggs," he said as he stepped up on the porch.

"Hi, Doc," the officer said as he looked up. "Don't see any bullet holes. Pretty unusual to find a body in this part of town without them."

The doctor wrinkled his nose as he looked around.

"It smells like that's what killed him," he said as he pointed to the nearly empty bottle lying on its side.

"Well, I'll be dipped in shit," Riggs said as he stood up, holding a fat church envelope that he found on the body. "There must be three or four thousand dollars here," he said, as he held the envelope open and showed the doctor. "Guess he was trying to get right with God or something."

"I wonder if God accepts payments postmarked, but not delivered?" the Doctor asked with a chuckle.

"Well, Doc, the customer's yours now," the officer said as the ambulance men rolled the stretcher up to the porch. "Lieutenant Morgan will have the report," he said as he went down the steps. "You can call him with a positive identification."

"Okay, Riggs. We'll take good care of him," the doctor said with a grin as he turned to help the other men with the body.

Joyce was standing beside her car, with the door open, talking with Liemer when Riggs walked up next to him.

"The house is secured. We ready to roll?" Riggs asked.

"I need to lock up the garage. If you move the car Miss Robbins can leave." He started toward the garage, then stopped and turned back to Joyce. "Call Lieutenant Morgan after lunch, he'll tell you what you have to do to move the artifact."

Joyce got in her car and started the engine as she waited for Riggs to move the cruiser. When the patrol car was out of the way she backed the Porsche out of the driveway and started down the decaying street, her mind aflame with the discovery of the artifact and the endless succession of questions it spawned. She drove out of the neighborhood with a mental list of things that had to be done running through her head. She felt a surprising surge of energy as she realized the business of archaeology had just been thrust into high gear.

Ralph did his best to hold his trembling hand steady as he filled his coffee cup, but it did little good. It seemed as though the jitters were beginning to consume his life. Sometimes he wished it was the onset of Parkinson's disease, or Cerebral Palsy, but he knew better. He knew it was the nightmares. If he could stop them things would get better, but the way it was going he knew he'd have a better chance of stopping a runaway train. He could remember the time when his sleep was disrupted only once or twice a month. It was only a few months ago, but seemed like a previous life. Now, without fail, the dreams were creeping into his mind every time he tried to sleep without being stone drunk. Sometimes they came anyway. Even his naps, which had been his salvation for the last few weeks were beginning to collapse into the same horrid vision.

He set his coffee on the desk next to his lunch bucket, pulled out the chair and sat down. For a moment he thought about drinking the coffee straight, but then dismissed the notion. He took a quick look around the lobby as he opened his lunch bucket and grabbed the pint bottle of whiskey. He quickly dumped a healthy shot into the steaming coffee and returned the bottle to its hiding place.

His life was changing. The nightmares weren't simply more frequent, they were becoming more intense, something he would never have believed possible. To compensate he was drinking more and more. He knew he was losing control and there was nothing he could do. There was no way to stop the torment and he was becoming increasingly bitter about the experimental drug he knew had ruined his life. His attitude toward the Marines and the Government was degenerating into something venomous and far removed from patriotism.

He thought he understood how people like Ted Bundy got their start. They probably got screwed once too often and decided to even the score. As God was his witness, he had a score to settle and maybe wrapping his body in plastic explosives and paying the Pentagon a visit wasn't such a bad idea. His dress blues fit him loose enough now that nobody would notice the extra baggage. There was no doubt in his mind that he could pull the switch, but he'd want to talk with the Washington Post first. Oh yeah, that would be one eye opening conversation, with him sitting in the middle of the Pentagon, one hand on the switch and the other holding the phone. The conversation would be blunt.

The name's Ralph Mason, he imagined himself saying into the phone. I used to be Lance Corporal Mason of the Third Marine Battalion. I'm at the Pentagon with several pounds of plastic explosives strapped to my body. Thirty-five years ago the Marines injected me with an experimental drug, which had something to do with dreams. Now I have repeating nightmares about horrendous flying creatures and it's ruined my life. You might want to step away from the windows, because I'm about to end my nightmares forever.

When he tried to steer his thoughts away from the death fantasy, he was surprised to find that part of his mind wanted to cling to it. It felt good to think about revenge, but it felt even better to think about ending the nightmares. The realization that part of him wanted to embrace the notion frightened him a little, but he also found it invigorating.

Ralph looked up at the convex security mirror when he heard the lobby doors open and saw Samuel coming in. He was glad he'd have someone to talk to, even if it was only going to be for a couple minutes. He pushed himself away from the desk and stood up just as Samuel looked around the corner.

"Morning, Ralph."

"Hi, Sam," Ralph said as he walked over to the display case.

"You have any coffee made?" Samuel asked.

"I made a fresh pot a couple hours ago. Have a seat, I'll get you a cup," he said as he walked back to the coffee maker.

Samuel walked around the end of the display case and pulled the extra chair over next to the desk as he watched Ralph fumbling with a stack of paper cups and wondered how to approach the subject of his drinking. He was concerned mostly about the state of his health, but his employment was also an issue. He wanted to have a talk with him without putting him on the defensive. He watched Ralph walk back to the desk and set the cup in front of him with a trembling hand and wondered if his health was already gone.

He picked up the cup and blew the steam off the top of the dark brew before taking a sip. "That's good coffee, Ralph. You've definitely got the touch," he said as he set the cup back on the desk. "I talked to Joyce before I left home. She was following up on an acquisition this morning and found a dead body."

"Oh, God," Ralph said sympathetically. "I bet she was a basket case. I don't imagine anything like that ever happened to her before."

"At first she sounded pretty shook up, but I think she was okay," he said as he took his pipe and tobacco pouch out of his jacket pocket. "She was waiting for the police, so I don't know when to expect her."

"She's a good kid," Ralph said with a smile. "I hope she doesn't suffer any long term affects because of the experience."

"You mean like nightmares?" Samuel asked as he opened the pouch and started filling the pipe.

The smile faded from Ralph's face as he looked down at his coffee. "Yeah, like nightmares," he said with little more than a whisper.

Samuel finished filling his pipe, closed the pouch and returned it to his jacket pocket. "Ralph, I think you and I need to have a heart to heart talk," he said as he set the pipe on the desk.

"About what?" Ralph asked in a subdued tone without looking up.

"Your health. It's not all that difficult to tell you're in trouble, and I understand what the root cause is, but that doesn't mean I should stand by and watch you kill yourself. That's exactly what you're doing; you're killing yourself. Rudy must be the only one that doesn't know you've got a bottle in your lunch bucket right now. If he finds out he'll have you on the street before you can blink and I won't be able to help you."

Ralph raised his eyes and cast a hopeless stare at Samuel. "Sam, you don't know what it's like," he said as tears welled up in his eyes. "It's always the same, it never changes. For Christ's sake I'd rather be dead than see those damn creatures again!" he shrieked. He pulled a handkerchief out of his pocket, wiped his eyes and blew his nose. "I'm sorry, Sam. I know you're only trying to help, but you don't understand what it's like. I know, you're thinking it's only a dream, but when you have the same dream so many times over and over it starts taking on a reality of its own." He wiped his nose again before returning the handkerchief to his pocket. "Years ago, when I first started having the dreams I only saw those hideous things from a distance. Over the years they've gotten closer, a lot closer. Now they're on me, ripping my flesh open and...and eating me alive. I smell their putrid breath, I feel their teeth ripping into me and I feel myself dying. So, you see, the thought of dying for real doesn't scare me much. At least this torment would be over forever."

"Ralph, I understand, but I also know there's medicine out there that can help you. Killing yourself with alcohol isn't an answer," he said as he picked up the pipe and lit it. "Let me help you."

"Sam, the help I need begins with the Government being held accountable for what they've done to me. I don't think you're up to it. There's only one thing you could do. Get me off this shift. If you could do that it would help, but Rudy seems to be set on having me on midnights for some reason."

"I can't promise anything. Rudy's pretty hard to deal with when he feels he's on his own turf, but I'm willing to try. If I can get him to change your schedule I want you to promise me something."

"I think I'd probably do just about anything to get off this shift. What do you want?" Ralph asked.

"I want you to see a doctor again. You've got to get some help. These nightmares have obviously gotten a lot worse."

Ralph drank the last of the coffee and crumpled the cup. "Sam, I don't think it will do any good, but I promise I'll try it again," he said as he threw the cup into the trash.

"I'll talk to him today," Samuel said as he stood up and pushed the chair back against the wall. "I hope I can say something to him that will bring him around."

"So do I," Ralph said wearily.

Samuel picked up his coffee and walked around the end of the display case and stopped. "I'm expecting somebody from Wilson Security Doors this morning. Send him down to the office when he shows up."

"Okay, Sam."

The small boat crested over a breaking wave as Martin Aster watched a pelican flying over the deserted beach and wondered how he could have been so stupid. Pouring out all the liquor in the house would have been such a simple thing. He could have wrapped up the whole mess with Grady very neatly, but he let his need for revenge cloud his vision. He got careless and now he was a dead man waiting to fall over.

He wished everything could have turned out differently. He loved Ruth and would have traded all the diamonds in South Africa for the loyal companionship he mistakenly thought was his. They could have had a grand life together, if only her love for him had been real. Instead of love he had gotten deceit and treachery. In the end, as angry as he was, killing her hadn't been easy.

Killing Grady was going to be a different story, he thought as he looked toward the front of the boat where he was laying in a drug-induced coma. A tall man with long brown hair pulled back into a ponytail was straddling him. There was another man with stringy black hair in the back of the boat running the motor. He didn't even know the men. They were just loaners sent by their boss to help fulfill a dying man's request. He knew he didn't have the strength left to do the job himself, not the way he wanted it done.

He had wanted to hear Grady scream as the concrete poured slowly in on him, but the poison had robbed him of the time required to complete the pool. He had been forced into acting quickly while a stalemate was still possible. It had taken some effort to come up with a replacement plan and for a while he had been disappointed until he realized Grady would experience unbearable pain and suffering.

With the pain as a constant reminder of the toxin inexorably advancing through his system it was difficult to find anything amusing, but the thought of Grady's impending torment made him smile. During the last minutes of his life he wanted Grady to suffer a lifetime of agony. He smiled again as he thought of the strange twist Grady's fate was about to take. Given the choice, he was sure he would have wanted to be buried alive in concrete.

The man behind Martin killed the motor as the front of the boat plowed into the sandy beach. The man in the front jumped out and pulled the boat farther up on the sand as hundreds of small crabs scurried away.

"Fuck you, Ronnie!" the man at the back of the dingy screamed. "I'm not getting out there with those fucking things. No fucking way. They look like a bunch of goddamn spiders."

Ronnie stared at him coldly as he reached down into the front of the boat and picked up a cattle prod and a shovel. "Jack, you get the fuck out here or I'll run this thing up your ass," Ronnie said as he gestured with the prod.

"Ronnie, I'm afraid of spiders," he said as he watched Martin climb over the side of the boat.

"Jack, you listen to me. They're crabs, not spiders, and they'll run from you. You can hold the cattle prod if it makes you feel better, but if you don't get out of that boat I'm gonna drag you out. There are enough of these crabs to eat two people, you know. Now hand me that chair and get your ass out here."

Jack hesitated before reaching down and grabbing the small kitchen chair lying in the middle of the boat.

"Come on. Singe a couple of the little bastards and you'll feel better," he said as he took the chair and threw it down in the sand.

Jack climbed over the side of the boat carefully while he kept a close eye on the crabs that had massed about fifteen feet away. He took the prod from Ronnie and held it out in front of him like a poised weapon.

"You keep an eye on our friend in the boat while I get things ready for him," he said as he picked up the chair.

Martin sat on a large rock near the water and watched the two men. Jack paced back and forth in front of the boat and kept his eyes on the crabs while Ronnie looked for a suitable spot for the chair.

After a couple minutes Ronnie found a spot that looked right. He put the chair down and went to work with the shovel. When he finished digging he set the chair in the hole and scooped the sand back in until the chair was buried up to the seat. When he was finished he walked back to the boat where Jack was still pacing.

"You ready?" he asked as he threw the shovel into the boat.

"Who's gonna watch those fucking things?" Jack asked as his eyes danced nervously between Ronnie and the crabs.

"Jack, you don't have to worry about the crabs," he said as he took a long bamboo pole out of the boat and threw it toward the chair. "They won't bother you as long as you keep moving, now grab an arm and help me drag this guy out of the boat."

Martin was watching the two men pull Grady from the boat when he was hit with a particularly punishing spasm of coughing that doubled him over. When the coughing subsided he tried to stand, but sat back down when he felt like he was going to pass out. It suddenly occurred to him that he might not live to enjoy Grady's torment. He took some deep breaths as he pulled a handkerchief out of his back pocket and wiped his mouth. Lately, coughing that left the taste of blood in his mouth was nothing unusual, but the bright red blood he found on the handkerchief was new. He took another deep breath and pushed himself off the rock. He felt washed out, but determined as he stood up. He watched as the two men started removing Grady's clothes and wondered how closely they would have followed the game plan if he died before the deed was done. He suspected they'd simply put a bullet in Grady's head and leave both of the bodies for the crabs. He felt some of his strength return as he started walking slowly toward the execution site.

Ronnie stuffed all of Grady's money in his pocket and threw the empty wallet on top of the pile of clothes.

"Take that stuff back to the boat, then come back and help me get him positioned," he said as he picked up the bamboo pole and tossed it behind the chair.

When Jack returned they picked up Grady and laid him face down on the sand, with the chair between his spread legs. Ronnie went behind the chair and positioned the pole under Grady's legs just above the ankles. He took two pair of handcuffs out of his pocket and hung them over the back of the chair.

"Martin, you want to cuff him?" Ronnie asked as he walked back to where Grady's upper body lay in the sand.

"Yeah," Martin replied as he slowly walked to the back of the chair and picked up the handcuffs.

"Wait until we get him positioned and I'll help you with the pole," he said.

They each took an arm; raised Grady to his knees and sat him in the chair with his legs bent back behind him. Jack put a hand in the middle of his chest and kept him from falling forward while Ronnie went back to help Martin.

Martin put a pair of cuffs on each of Grady's wrists and waited for Ronnie to raise the bamboo pole.

"Jack, hold him tight," Ronnie said as he grabbed the center of the bamboo pole and lifted.

Martin crossed Grady's arms behind the chair, locked the cuffs on the pole and sat down in the sand to catch his breath. After a moment he stood up and walked around to the front of the chair. "You sure he can't get out of that?" Martin asked as he grabbed a handful of Grady's hair and lifted his head.

"He's not going anywhere," Ronnie said as he shook his head. "That's the New York version of hog tying. There's no way he's going to escape."

"Bring him around," Martin said as he let Grady's head fall and stepped back.

"Jack, go get that roll of duct tape out of the boat," Ronnie said as he took a small oblong box out of his shirt pocket.

"I want him to have a chance to talk before his mouth gets taped shut," Martin said as he looked past the chair and watched the crabs.

"He's not in a very comfortable position, he'll be doing more screaming than anything else," Ronnie said as he opened the box and took out a loaded syringe.

"Here's the tape," Jack said as he walked up next to Ronnie.

"Hold his head for a minute," Ronnie said as he pushed Grady's head to the side and felt for his pulse. When he located the carotid artery he inserted the needle, pushed the plunger and backed away.

As Martin stood there watching Grady, waiting for him to lift his head, he felt a disquieting emotion wash over him. Remorse was something he purged from his life many years ago when he recognized it as a threat to his career. Now, as he waited to send Grady to a torturous death he acknowledged the remorse in his heart. It was for Ruth, it was for a life riddled with brutality, and it was for the cold-hearted act he was about to commit. He allowed the emotion to tear at his heart for a moment before turning it away as Grady slowly raised his head.

He stared incoherently at Martin through partially opened eyes as the sounds and smells of the new environment began sifting into his consciousness. His head bobbed and swayed as he tried to move. The efforts became more urgent until his entire body was trembling with tension. His eyelids suddenly snapped open wide as he screamed out in agony.

Martin put a hand over his mouth and looked into his panic stricken eyes.

"Grady, you have to relax a little. You're making it worse. You have to be quiet when I take my hand away or they'll tape your mouth shut. I want us to be able to talk," he said and pulled his hand away.

"You motherfucker!" he screamed as his body jerked forward violently. "Untie me you worthless fucking bastard! You're a fucking dead man, you son of a bitch!"

He continued to scream until Martin delivered a bruising backhand slap across his face that snapped his head back against the chair.

"I wanted to have a civilized conversation before we proceeded with this distasteful task," Martin said as he took the roll of tape from Jack. He tore a piece from the roll and handed it back. "But you're making that impossible."

Grady looked up at him with blood dripping from a cut on his lip. "Fuck you, Martin!" he screamed and spit at him.

"No, fuck you," Martin said calmly as he stretched the tape across his mouth. "Ruth died a lot easier than you will. It's a real shame you can't see all the crabs behind you, waiting for us to leave," he said as he pulled a switchblade out of his pocket.

Grady's eyes were wide with panic as he jerked forward in the chair, trying desperately to free himself.

"Before this is over you'll wish I had cut your throat with this knife," Martin said as the blade flashed open with a snap.

Grady tried to scream through the tape as Martin slashed the blade across the inside of his thigh, leaving a bleeding wound. "That should serve as an appetizer for my friends back there," Martin said as he looked down at the flowing blood. He looked into Grady's wide eyes and smiled. "Did you really think you'd get away with it? Yeah, you probably did. Well, Grady, I'll see you in hell," he said as he turned toward Ronnie and handed him the knife. "I'm going back to the boat. Cut the head of his dick off and stick it in his mouth," he said as he walked away.

Jack waited until Martin was out of earshot before turning to Ronnie. "Finish him off, Ronnie. We don't need to do anything else to this poor fucker."

"Don't be stupid, Jack. The Boss told us to follow Martin's orders. I don't know about you, but I don't want to end up like this. I'll do the cuttin', you peel back the tape and hold his mouth open."

The muffled screams were bad, but Jack had never heard wailing like he did when he removed the tape. He expected a struggle when he held Grady's mouth open, but most of his fight was gone.

No one spoke on the way back to the yacht.

Martin was too exhausted, Jack was trying to keep his breakfast down, and Ronnie was trying to forget how it felt in the palm of his hand.

A few minutes later Martin was standing on the bridge of the yacht with a pair of binoculars. At that distance the crabs looked like a dark blob moving across the beach and surrounding Grady. Grady's head was jerking wildly from side to side as the intensity of the feeding frenzy started building.

Martin watched Grady's agony for a few more minutes, and then handed the field glasses back to his friend.

"I've seen enough. I'm going below," he said without emotion.

As he left the bridge the sudden emptiness of his life hit him like a tidal wave. Ruth and Grady were gone and all that was left was his own suffering, and the remorse that was waiting to rip open his heart.

He could feel tears stinging his eyes as he opened the door to his cabin. He wanted to wake up in his own bed and breathe a sigh of relief as he realized it had all been a nightmare. He wanted to roll over and put his arm around Ruth and tell her how much he loved her. He wanted the world to be a delightful place again.

Tears were running down his face as he sat down on the bed and picked up the gun. He looked at it for a moment, and then put the barrel in his mouth. In the last instant of his life he felt the recoil of the gun and tasted gunpowder. A millisecond later his brains splattered over the inside of the cabin.

Steve was on the roof replacing a shingle lost to the wind when he heard the throaty rumble of the Porsche and wondered about Joyce's emotional state. He knew she wasn't easily shaken, but discovering a dead body in a strange part of town wasn't the kind of thing that happened to her every day.

He put his tools aside, carefully scooted over to the ladder and started down. Joyce was just turning into the drive when he got to the ground. He pulled a bandanna out of his back pocket and wiped the sweat from his forehead as he watched the car come up the hill. He wasn't sure how to react if she was a basket case. Normally, it was a hands off policy around the museum, but under the circumstances she might need a hug. He'd try to play it by ear, he thought as he watched her back the Porsche into her parking place. He returned the bandanna to his pocket as he walked over to the car. "You okay?" he asked as he opened the car door. "Sam told everybody about the body."

"I'm alright," she said as she shut off the engine.

"Had he been dead very long, I mean, was he stiff?" Steve asked in a grim tone.

"Steve, forget about the dead body," she said as she climbed out of the car. "It was nothing compared to the artifact I found in the old guy's garage," she said with an anxious edge to her voice. She closed the car door and looked over at Steve with eager eyes. "Wait until you see this thing. It's unbelievable," she said as she leaned against the car.

He was relieved that she didn't seem stressed out, but confused by the reference to an artifact. "Sam didn't say anything about an artifact."

"I didn't find the thing until after I talked to him on the phone."

"What is it?" he asked as he felt himself being swept up by her excitement.

"Steve, I honestly don't know," she said as she shook her head. "I've never seen anything like it. I've never even heard of anything like this. I think it's a totally unique discovery."

"Joyce, you're making me crazy. What does it look like?"

"It's a huge frame of petrified logs holding an enormous crystal. I've never seen a crystal like it before, but the frame...it's carved. These petrified logs that make up the frame have faces carved into them like totems. The faces are really gruesome. The thing is really scary looking," she said anxiously.

"Jesus, Joyce," Steve whispered as he rubbed at the goose flesh that had risen on his arms. "You're giving me the heebie-jeebies." He was shocked when she reached out and combed her fingers through his hair tenderly.

"Sweetie, if you've got the heebie-jeebies now, wait until you see this thing. We'll have to call 911 for you. I've got to find Sam," she said as she pushed herself away from the car. "I'll see you later."

"I'm going back up on the roof and let the sun burn away my goose bumps," he said as he watched Joyce walk away.

Terry heard the Porsche come up the drive and was standing at the display case when Joyce came into the museum. "Well, hello," he said with a grin. "I understand you've had a pretty tough morning already."

Joyce smiled and shook her head as she walked over to the security station. "Does everybody know about it?" she asked.

"Well, Sam told me first, then Steve told me, then Luther told me. I guess Rudy's the only one I haven't heard it from."

"That's because nobody wants to talk to him unless they have to," she said with a snicker. "Is Sam downstairs?"

"Yeah, as far as I know he is," Terry said.

"I've got to talk to him. I'll see you later, Terry," she said as she turned away.

"Okay," Terry said.

When Joyce got to the office she found Samuel at his desk sorting through a pile of neglected mail. "I finally made it," she said, her voice suddenly trembling.

"Are you alright?" Samuel asked as he jumped to his feet.

"Yes, I'm fine," she said as she set her purse down, but her voice betrayed a swell of emotions that she had been holding back. She turned and looked at Samuel as she felt herself losing control. "Maybe not..." she managed to choke out, and then began to cry. At first the tears were from the stress of the morning, but as Samuel held her she began to sob and suddenly realized she was releasing emotions that had been pent up longer than a few hours. There were old memories driving her tears now. The pain of watching Randy read his induction notice, the agony of holding his hand for the last time as he boarded the bus, and the all consuming anguish of hearing Kim tell her Randy was dead. Samuel held her tightly until the tears began to subside.

"I think that was a lot more than just this morning," Samuel said softly as he took a handkerchief out of his pocket and slipped it into her hand.

Joyce nodded her head as she pulled herself away. "I've needed that for a very long time," she said as she wiped her eyes. "I don't know whether it's over or not."

"You've always got my shoulder to cry on, if you need it," Samuel said compassionately.

"Sam, I found something at that old man's place this morning, but I can't talk with my face looking like this. I'll be back in a minute."

"I'll be here," he said as she opened the door and walked out into the lab.

A few minutes later Joyce returned, looking emotionally drained, but eager to talk.

"Sam, I'm sorry for breaking down like that," she said as she pulled the chair out from her desk and sat down. "I lost a very close friend in Vietnam. Randy and I were in love and he was a dear friend. I've tried to close myself off from the memories for a very long time and now they're coming back to me for some reason."

"There's no reason to apologize," he said with a gentle smile. "You need to deal with those memories or they'll haunt you the rest of your life."

Joyce nodded as she pressed the handkerchief to the corner of her eye. "I think, after all these years, I'm beginning to understand that."

"Now, tell me what you found," Samuel said as he picked up his pipe and dumped the charred remains of the last bowl into the ashtray.

Joyce started to say something, then stopped and shook her head. "Sam, it's hard to talk about because I don't know what the hell it is. I don't even remember hearing about anything remotely like it before."

"Well, then tell me about your morning, and when you get to the part about this thing you can just tell me what it looks like," he said as he opened a new pouch of cherry blend tobacco and started filling his pipe.

He listened intently as Joyce began relating her experience, beginning with finding the old man's body. He became intrigued and leaned forward in his chair as she described how the ends of the rockers had been driven into the ground in front of the garage doors. His fascination soon turned to professional inquisitiveness and a mild sense of aversion, as she verbally conveyed the image of the artifact.

"It's not a real pleasant thing to look at," she said grimly.

Samuel picked up his lighter and toyed with it thoughtfully, then looked at Joyce. "What are the chances that it's some kind of hoax?" he asked tentatively.

"Sam, I don't know what the hell this thing is, but it's not a hoax. When you see it you'll know exactly what I mean."

He leaned back in his chair, lit his pipe and sent a plume of aromatic smoke toward the ceiling. He watched thoughtfully as it drifted toward the lab. "I'm fighting the temptation of going to see this thing for myself right now, you know. On one hand it's hard for me to believe it's not a hoax, but on the other hand I have an enormous amount of respect for your abilities as an archeologist. If you're correct, I believe you have stumbled upon a totally unique find," he said with an edge of exhilaration in his voice.

The phone rang before Joyce had a chance to reassert herself on the question of authenticity.

Samuel answered the phone and listened for a moment. "Send him down. Oh, Terry, find Steve and send him down, too. Thanks," he said and hung up the phone. He looked at Joyce and smiled. "Yesterday that call would have been a great triumph, but today it's just an annoyance that keeps me from going to see this artifact of yours."

"What's going on?" she asked.

"I'm getting those double doors replaced," he said with a grin. "There's a company rep on his way down."

"I'd like to hear how you pulled that one off, but I've got to go to the police station and see about getting the artifact released to the museum," she said as she stood up. "I'll be back after lunch."

"Okay, I'll see you then."

Rudy pushed his glasses back up on the bridge of his nose as he started reading the Pinkerton brochure on contract security staffing. He never thought much about contracting the security positions, but he found the prospectus informative and quite impressive. The hourly rate was somewhat higher than he paid his own people, but that was easily justified due to the cost of benefits. The use of Pinkerton personnel could eliminate all worry about vacations, sickness and overtime, not to mention medical insurance and Social Security taxes. The loss of complete control was the only thing he found troubling. There would be personnel on duty around the clock, but he wouldn't be in a position to assign any special duties to keep them busy. There was a lot of personal satisfaction in having dominion over employees, but he had to be practical. He had one guard using up vacation before retirement and another in the hospital. Even if Bill came back to work, which he thought unlikely, he still needed to hire somebody and that made the argument for Pinkerton somewhat compelling.

Rudy looked up from the brochure when he heard a knock and saw Samuel standing in the doorway.

"I hope you can spare a few minutes," Samuel said as he stepped into Rudy's office.

"More extortion?" Rudy asked in a surly tone as he turned the pamphlet face down on the desk. "After yesterday I'm surprised we have anything to talk about," Rudy said as he gestured toward one of the chairs in front of his desk.

"I want this to be communication, not confrontation," he said as he walked in, "but if you had listened to me in the first place I wouldn't have had to stoop to what you call extortion. Frankly, I could care less about how you budget money and the secret deals you make, unless you step on my toes," he said as he lowered himself into the chair.

"Fine," Rudy said harshly. "We'll leave it at that. Now what do you want?"

"I want to talk to you about the schedule you have Ralph working," Samuel replied.

Rudy sneered contemptuously. "Samuel, I think his schedule is just a little beyond what you have a right to be concerned with around here. Why do you insist on meddling in my business? I don't appreciate it. Ralph will continue to work the schedule I set up for him until I decide otherwise."

"Rudy, I can't just sit by and watch you drive him into a physical and mental breakdown. The man isn't going to last much longer under these conditions, a fact that you're either blind to or don't care about. You're heading down a morally irresponsible path, and that is my business, whether you like it or not. You don't talk with Ralph, but I do, and I'm telling you that he's at the breaking point. He has some very deep psychological problems that are aggravated by the midnight shift. Normally it's all he can do to make it through a month. Now, not only have you extended the normal cycle, you've got him working seven days a week and twelve hours a day."

Rudy removed his glasses, set them on the desk and rubbed his temples thoughtfully as he leaned back in his leather chair. Every fiber of his being wanted to resist Samuel at every turn, but if his assessment of Ralph's state of mind was correct he was facing more manpower issues. It suddenly occurred to him that he could bring in Pinkerton and hang the blame on Samuel. A layoff notice for two guards would be a real slap in the face for the resident working class hero.

"Look, Samuel, I've got a museum to run here. If I don't have around the clock security the insurance rates will go right through the ceiling," he said as he picked up his glasses and slipped them back on. "I don't really care to pay the overtime, but right now I don't have any choice. If I figure out how to address your concern while fulfilling my obligation to control costs, you'll be the first to know. Now, if there's nothing else, I'm busy."

Samuel stood up without saying anything, walked to the door and stopped. "I want to believe you have enough compassion to do the right thing for Ralph. If you don't he'll end up in the hospital in the psychiatric ward and you'll be responsible."

Rudy watched Samuel turn and walk out of the office. "I'll do what I can," he said as he picked up the Pinkerton brochure.

Joyce walked into the police station and was surprised to find that the level of activity was nothing like Hill Street Blues. There were no police officers struggling to control combative prisoners or less active detainees waiting to be processed through the legal system and there were no crime victims trying to relate the circumstances of their recent ordeal to the desk sergeant. The place reminded her more of a library than the gearbox of the judicial system. She wondered if there really were police stations where the action was non-stop or if her expectations had been tuned by the poetic license of television writers.

There was a blonde haired officer sitting at the dispatch desk in the center of the lobby. He turned and looked at Joyce as she walked up to the low wooden enclosure surrounding the area. "Can I help you?" he asked.

Joyce smiled as she looked into his deep blue eyes and felt a sudden rush of passion that caught her off guard. She was fighting the intense desire to talk about anything except the business at hand when she realized the officer reminded her of Randy. Her smile faded as the sensuous craving collapsed into blackness as suddenly as it had surfaced.

"I'm Joyce Robbins from the museum. I need to see Lieutenant Morgan."

"Can I tell him what it's in reference to?" he asked as he picked up phone and started punching numbers into the keypad.

"It's concerning an artifact that I found this morning, along with a body."

"There's a body?" the officer asked urgently as his head snapped around and his eyes locked on her face.

"No, no," Joyce said with a laugh. "You people already know about the body. I need to see the Lieutenant about the artifact."

The officer relaxed and finished punching in the numbers, then waited for an answer.

"Lieutenant, there's a Joyce Robbins from the museum to see you. It's in reference to an artifact she found this morning. Yes, sir," he said and broke the connection. "The Lieutenant will be with you in a few minutes," he said as he turned back toward Joyce. "You can have a seat if you like," he said as he gestured toward a waiting area. "There's vending machines through the green doors if you want a cup of coffee or something."

"Thank you," Joyce said as she turned away. She walked across the lobby to the small waiting area, sat down in one of the rigid wooden chairs and glanced at her watch. After a moment she picked up one of the news magazines and started leafing through it absently.

There were plenty of articles in the publication that were short enough to read in a few minutes, but she was having trouble focusing her concentration on anything but the artifact. A single perplexing issue kept raising its head and refused to go away, an issue that seemed to suggest a paradox. All you had to do was entertain the thought of time travel and a paradox was bound to fall in your lap, but it didn't happen in scientific disciplines. She wondered why it had taken her mind several hours to come to the realization that the artifact was an enigma. Carved faces and petrified wood simply didn't go together. The age of petrified wood was usually placed at about one hundred and fifty million years, making the trees that went through the agatization process somewhat older, given the reaction time. And that was the rub, wasn't it. Who in the hell was around that long ago to carve the logs? Certainly no one she had ever heard about, and yet the artifact did exist.

Now that the issue was clearly defined in her own mind she was surprised that Sam hadn't picked up on it right away. She supposed there was a big difference between hearing somebody describe a thing that shouldn't exist and seeing it for yourself. A thousand words of descriptive prose would not have prepared her for the sight of the artifact, she thought. Suddenly she was aware that her insides had started trembling again. She knew the excitement of the find was beginning to really hit home, but there was something else, too. Something just beyond her grasp and understanding, like the fading memories of a dream.

Joyce returned the magazine to the table when she noticed an officer wearing a gold shield step out of the elevator and start walking toward her. He was a stout looking man with closely cropped salt and pepper hair.

"Joyce?" he asked warmly as he walked into the waiting area.

"Yes," Joyce said as she stood up.

"Lieutenant Morgan," he said as he shook her hand. "Please, sit down. I understand that you're the one who found Oscar Washington this morning," he said as he took a seat across the table from her.

Joyce nodded her head. "I don't think I've fully recovered yet."

"It's a stressful situation for someone not used to those kinds of things. I talked with the officers that were on the scene. They said they told you to contact me about the artifact," he said as he handed Joyce the key. "I apologize for making you come up here to the station. I would have let you keep the key until you moved the thing, but it was a new situation for the officers."

"No harm," Joyce said with a smile. "It really hasn't delayed anything since I have to make arrangements to get it delivered to the museum. Besides, it gave me a chance to see the inside of the police station. I'm surprised at how quiet it is."

"It only seems quiet. There's actually a lot going on. It's been a real crazy week, so far," he said as he shook his head.

"Have I missed something on the news?" she asked.

"It's not unusual for us to find a body once in a while, but it's usually a drug dealer full of bullet holes. Counting Oscar Washington we've got three this week, and judging by a note that led us to a woman's body, there's two more somewhere. So, like I said, it only seems quiet," he said as he stood up. "I'd appreciate it if you'd return the key to me when you've finished with it."

"I will," she said as she stood up and shook his hand again. "Nice meeting you."

"You too, Joyce. I hope you don't find any more bodies for awhile."

"Me too," she said with a smile as she turned and walked away.

She left the police station and walked back to her car in an enthusiastic mood, tempered with the uneasiness of knowing her next stop would be to see a friend and former lover. Lover was certainly an awkward term to apply to the relationship between her and Mark, she thought. They were friends and had been sexual partners, but to say they had been lovers seemed to suggest some emotional link beyond friendship. Mark was one of the few men who actually respected her need to maintain her own, unviolated space. He respected her need, but wanted more out of the relationship than she had to give, and it had broken his heart.

She started the sports car and pulled away from the police station wondering if a year had been enough time to heal the wound from their broken relationship.

A few minutes later she parked in front of the old brick building that housed the administrative office for the company Mark's father named Pyramid Movers. After a moment of fighting the urge to simply drive away she climbed out of the Porsche. From the curb she could see Mark sitting at his desk just beyond the large plate glass window. He looked well, she thought as she reluctantly pushed herself away from the car.

Mark looked up from his desk when he heard the door open. His dark hair and olive complexion were bold declarations of his Greek heritage.

"Joyce," he said in a surprised tone as he pushed his chair back and stood up. "My God, you're the last person I expected to see. How have you been?" he asked as he took her hand.

"I'm fine," she replied with a warm smile. "You look like you've been taking good care of yourself. How are your Mom and Dad?"

"They're doing pretty good, I guess. They moved to Key West about six months ago and opened a bar."

"You're kidding," Joyce said with a laugh.

"Nope. Dad said they were going down there to fish and get permanent suntans. I think he was planning on making Mom run the bar. I'm not sure how that part of his plan worked out. Have a seat," he said as he released her hand and gestured toward a chair in front of his desk. "You still driving that old Corvette?" he asked as he returned to his chair.

"No, I traded it off early in March. That's my red 911 parked out front. I still have the Jeep for winter."

Mark rose up in his seat and looked out the front window. "Wow!" he said as he leaned back. "Pretty car. I've heard they're real fast."

"So have I," Joyce said, and then laughed.

"God, you look good. It's really great seeing you again. I wish this was a social visit, but I know it's not, and the only thing that leaves is business.

What can I do for you?"

"I discovered an artifact this morning, and it's a little too large for me to deal with. I know your business is moving heavy machinery, but I figured moving this thing probably wasn't all that far removed from what you do every day, so here I am."

"What is it that you've found?" Mark asked inquisitively.

"That's the question I've been asking myself all morning, and I still don't have an answer. Whatever it is has the potential to force archaeologists to develop new theories to deal with the reality of its existence," she said with an edge of excitement in her voice. "What I need you to do is crate it up, just like you do with expensive machinery, and move it to the museum. I know I'm really pressing my luck when I walk into your office and tell you I need something right away, but that's what I need."

"New theories? What the hell does this thing look like?"

"You need to see it anyway, why don't we take a ride."

"In that?" Mark asked with a grin as he looked out the window.

"Yeah. We can even take the interstate and find out if it's really fast," she replied with a teasing smile.

Joyce expected the drive to be punctuated with uncomfortable moments of silence, but the conversation continued to come as easily as it had in Mark's office. They talked about the last year and what had happened to each of them, but gave the subject of their relationship a wide berth. The only time the dialogue came to a complete halt was when Joyce used the interstate to prove that she was capable of putting the Porsche through its paces, and that its zero to sixty acceleration claim was more than just advertising hype. After that they talked about cars and little else until they took the exit ramp into a run down neighborhood Mark had never seen.

Joyce felt her insides start to quiver as she turned onto Oscar Washington's street, and again her mind was touched by something that seemed just beyond her understanding. It was like trying to recall a dream that had already slipped away from the grasp of her conscious mind. It had been there, and had meant something, but was gone in a fleeting moment.

Her shoulders began to tense up as she turned into the driveway and stopped behind the old pickup. Her hands trembled noticeably as she reached for the keys and shut off the engine.

"Joyce, you're shaking. Is something wrong?" he asked in a concerned tone.

"I'm okay, just having a little nervous flashback, I guess," she said as she turned toward Mark. "I found a body here this morning. I guess I haven't quite recovered yet."

"A body? Whose body?" Mark asked.

"The old man who used to live here," she said as she opened the car door. She climbed out of the car, and then looked back at Mark, who was trying to get out gracefully.

"It takes a little practice to get out smoothly," she said in a jittery voice.

"You're really shook up," Mark said when he finally got to his feet. "Will you feel better if I hold your hand?" he asked as he walked around the front of the car. To his surprise she took his hand as he walked up next to her.

"I should warn you that you're about to see something that's going to look pretty gruesome," she said as they walked to the garage. She fished the key out of her pocket and tried to insert it into the padlock with trembling hands.

"Let me have that," Mark said as he took the key from her and opened the padlock. He hooked it in the hasp, and then pulled the door open. Joyce took Mark's hand again as they both stood in the doorway, waiting for their eyes to adjust to the shadows.

"Oh, my God," Mark whispered, as his eyes found the artifact.

"You need a closer look," Joyce said as she took a step into the garage.

"I can see fine from right here," Mark said as he stood firm.

"Come on," Joyce said as she pulled him into the garage. "I have to show you something." Mark reluctantly followed her as she walked toward the thing.

"It doesn't look like it was intended to stand upright," she said as she pointed toward the bottom member of the frame, "but for examination and display purposes we need it that way. So I want you to build a base for it. Something that it can sit down into, but not attached to it. You have to avoid damaging any of the features, so drilling holes into the petrified wood is out, absolutely," she said firmly and looked over at Mark.

Mark nodded silently as he looked up at the head at the top of the artifact, with its gaping carnivorous jaws. "Can we go now?" he asked nervously.

"How soon can you get it crated up and moved to the museum?"

"Tomorrow afternoon," he muttered as he stepped backward out of the garage.

"Let's go," she said as she turned away.

Mark moved quickly to stay beside her.

Joyce closed the garage door, locked it and handed the key to Mark.

"I have to return that to the police, so make sure I get it back.

Mark put the key in his pocket, then shaded his eyes as he looked up at the sky. "It feels good to be back out in the sunlight," he said.

Joyce nodded. "I know what you mean. The artifact seems to act on the psyche at some subliminal level," she said as they walked back toward the car.

A silent procession of figures clad in hooded black robes descended the circular stone staircase. At the bottom of the steps was a twelve sided chamber illuminated by hundreds of candles. Thousands of golden stars, each with a diamond at its center, were inlaid in the walls forming twelve different star charts. The diamonds refracted the flickering candlelight and cast a dynamic ocean of color across the high ceiling. Each member in the ritual stepped away from the staircase and moved to a golden sunburst set in the center of the marble floor. They stood upon the sunburst for a moment before taking up position in a wide circle near the bejeweled walls. They were followed into the chamber by a smaller group in gray robes who repeated the actions, then positioned themselves in a tighter circle. The next group to descend the staircase and move into the chamber were four in white robes. They stepped to the center of the sunburst and back out onto its circumference. Samadhi was the last one to come down into the chamber of dancing candlelight. He wore jeans, a heavy denim jacket and carried a small backpack slung over one shoulder. His long black hair was tied back into a braid that hung to the center of his back. While the four in white robes waited around the sunburst, Samadhi moved to the outer circle and embraced each one as he slowly made his way around the room. He did the same with the ones in the inner circle, then went to the final group and stood in the center of the sunburst.

Dhyana was the first to step forward and throw back the hood of his robe. He was a tall man of Norse descent with long blonde hair and beard, streaked with gray. His blue eyes sparkled in the candlelight as he looked at Samadhi with great affection. "Our spirits have shared much, Samadhi. Go with strength and courage, for I will be with you. Use all the crafts that I have taught you to protect yourself and avoid delays, for the future of humanity hangs in the balance." He embraced Samadhi tightly before stepping back to his position.

Rishi was the next to step forward and remove her hood. She had the reddish brown complexion of the American Indian, with long black hair and dark eyes. "I remember when you first came to us, Samadhi. You have learned much and are no longer the child of mind that you once were. Go without fear, for I will also be with you. Reach out with your mind so that the vision of the path you must follow is always lucid." She embraced Samadhi and held him for a moment, then stepped back as she wiped a tear away from her cheek.

The next one to step forward was Moksha. He was a short, thin man of Japanese heritage. His long black hair had a single ribbon of silver running back away from one side of a widow's peak. "Samadhi, we have walked along many paths together and you have learned your lessons well. Heed my teaching on air travel. It will dissipate your energy and you will require three full days to replenish it. Let the heart of the lion beat within your chest, for I too, will be with you." Moksha embraced Samadhi and stepped back.

The last one to move upon the sunburst and pull back his hood was Hsuan Hsueh. He was a small, almost frail looking man with long white hair and dark, weathered skin. "Samadhi, the outside world holds many temptations that could blind you to the path you must follow. Should you falter, the sun will set on humanity and all that to which it aspires. Go now, back into the world of tribulation and be known again as Kim Lee. Speak not of your spiritual name once you are beyond the circle of Yu Wu." He embraced Samadhi tightly, then released him and grasped him firmly by the shoulders. "Destroy the crystal and seal the rift between the worlds. If the others survive you must bring them back with you, for only here can they be made whole again."

The two circles parted as Dhyana and Samadhi walked across the chamber to a massive wooden door. Dhyana slid back a heavy iron bolt and pulled open the door.

"May God light your way and give you the inner strength and wisdom you will need to save humanity," he said as they clasped hands.

One last look passed between them before Samadhi stepped out into the moonlit night. Darkness engulfed him as the door closed and dark clouds eclipsed the full moon.

CHAPTER SIX

The nightmare ended abruptly as Joyce bolted upright in bed with the sheets clinging to her damp body. She wiped her eyes as she looked over at the clock and realized she had only been asleep for a short time. Given the stress of the day she wasn't surprised by the nightmare about Oscar Washington's place, but Randy and Kim had been there, and that part of it left her trembling with emotion.

Most of the dream was already beyond the grasp of her recall, but certain parts of it lingered like ghostly apparitions. She remembered finding Oscar on the porch, but when she touched him things changed and Randy was suddenly standing next to her. The feeling of overpowering joy was still struggling against the truth that was slowly creeping into her heart. She remembered Kim standing in front of the garage blocking their way and shaking his head as she took Randy to see the artifact. And she remembered something else. It was the image that shattered the dream and left her with a strange, undefined anxiety. In that vision she was standing in front of the artifact with Randy. At first she saw only their fuzzy bluish reflections in the mirror, then she saw the eyes. Large red, cat like eyes that seemed to come at them out of a dense fog bank. Terrifying eyes, and for just an instant there was the heart stopping face of the hideous creature that went with those eyes.

Too shaken to sleep, she lay back on the bed and thought about the last summer she had with Randy.

Joyce's relationship with Randy and Kim grew into something truly unique. She loved them both, but not in quite the same way.

She and Kim shared a love that was driven by a spiritual kinship that, at times, strained the limits of her comprehension. It was as if their love had transcended time by leaping into the present from some previous life.

Her love for Randy was more traditional. An emotional bond that was rarely seen, even in couples that had been happily married for years joined them. It was the kind of love that many sought, but few found.

There was no jealousy and no rivalry for affection, only a deep love that bound the three of them together in a kind of ménage à trois. Together they were like a small clan that was much greater than the sum of its parts, and none of them wanted it to ever change.

Despite their happiness there were deep concerns over Randy's approaching graduation. They always knew it would trigger a change in his draft classification, but it was something they simply didn't discuss. Instead they chose to believe the war in Vietnam would end before it became a problem, but as Randy's graduation approached the war raged on. Their neglect of the subject ended a few days before Randy received his sheepskin.

They were sitting in a circle on the porch with their legs crossed, facing each other. Behind them were the remains of two pizzas and five empty beer cans. The last can sat on the floor between them as community property. Kim put the finishing touches on the joint he was rolling and handed it to Randy.

Randy lit the twisted cigarette, inhaled deeply and passed it to Joyce. "Five years ago when I was graduating from high school I was certain the war would be over long before I finished college," he said as he slowly exhaled smoke. "But, here I am, getting ready to graduate and guys are still dying over there."

Joyce hit the joint, and then passed it to Kim. "I've never really wanted to talk about the war and the affect it could have on us. I always believed everything would turn out okay, but now...now I'm beginning to worry. I love you both and I don't want either of you to have to go over there," she said as she looked at Randy. "I want you here while Kim and I finish school, and I want you at our graduation, but most of all, I always want us to be together."

"We all feel the same way," Kim said as he passed the smoke back to Randy, "but we need to talk about what we do if Randy gets drafted. We can't just continue ignoring the possibility and hope it doesn't happen."

"If I get drafted it has to be business as usual for you two. You both have to get through school, Joyce has to take my place running the bets, and you have to keep the home fires burning for me. The up side in all this is the birthday lottery. They'll only be drafting a few people this summer under the old system, and then in September they start the lottery. As long as my birthday doesn't get drawn right away everything will be okay."

"If you get drafted, running bets will be the last thing on my mind. I won't even be able to study," Joyce said morosely as she picked up the can of beer.

Randy shook his head slowly. "Sweetheart, I hope it doesn't happen. I don't want to leave you and Kim, but if it comes to that you've got to deal with it. We've got a year to put the finishing touches on our bankroll. If I'm not here to do it you've got to take over for me so we have money to buy a house after you guys graduate," he said as he took the can of beer from her.

"He's right, Joyce," Kim said. "Not having him here will be emotionally painful, but our plans have to go forward. We have to have our financial ducks in a row when he comes home."

"I don't think I can stand to talk about this anymore tonight," Joyce said as she took the empty can from Randy and put it with the rest of the trash. "It makes me feel so helpless. I know you guys would never let anything happen to me, and there's no way I can return that comfort. Marriage isn't even a damn draft deferment anymore."

"It's okay," Randy said as he scooted around and put his arm around her. "I know you love me, and that will keep me going, no matter what."

Joyce reached out and took Kim's hand as Randy held her. "I love you guys," she said as she felt a lump in her throat and tears welled up in her eyes.

Randy's graduation marked the unofficial start of summer and awakened the impulse in all of them to travel. The following Monday began with a frantic search for the appropriate vehicle, and on Tuesday they traded Randy's old beat up 1954 Chevy for a 1962 red Cadillac convertible that was in remarkable condition. The next morning they were on the road, headed for California with the sun at their back and the wind in their hair. Before the summer was over they racked up over ten thousand miles on the Cadillac. During their excursions they learned to surf in Long Beach, scuba dive in Key West, and sail in Boston, but during that summer they never talked about the draft and Vietnam again.

With September came cooler nighttime temperatures and the haunting realization that the moment of truth was only a few days away. No one spoke of it, but they all knew that soon they would either be relieved of the dark burden or know their greatest fear. It all hinged on a game of chance.

The odds were comforting, right up until the bottom fell out of their world. They were all sitting around the television when the news came, and it hit them all like a brutal punch to the stomach. Randy's birthday, a date that he had celebrated all his life, had just been drawn for the first lottery spot and had sealed his fate for the next two years. They were all stunned.

"I don't believe it," Randy said as he stood up and turned off the television. "Lady luck certainly didn't smile on us today."

Kim stared at the dark television screen and shook his head. "I never wanted to be wrong so badly in my life," he said bitterly.

"You knew, didn't you," Randy said pensively.

Kim nodded his head slowly. "I just couldn't bring myself to tell you. Are you angry with me?"

"No, of course not," Randy said and managed a warm smile. "You did the right thing. We've had a damn good summer together. It wouldn't have been the same if we'd known."

Joyce was unable to hold back the tears and began to cry. "I'll remember this summer for the rest of my life," she said, choking on the words. She stood up and put her arms around Randy and began to sob.

There was little certainty about how long they had before Uncle Sam came knocking, but no one believed there would be much of a delay. They did their best to avoid the dark emotions that closed in on them as the days passed. They went to football games, watched movies, played Monopoly and went for long walks, but the best diversion was when the three of them simply snuggled up under blankets together and talked about their plans for the future.

Classes started for Joyce and Kim the last week of September and at the end of the next week Randy received his letter. The date for his pre-induction physical was set, and if everything went well he was scheduled to leave for boot camp on the twenty-ninth of October.

For Randy, passing the physical was a snap. He was in excellent physical condition, had no flaws in his eyesight or hearing, and had all his fingers and toes. Later when he returned home he told the others that the examination was so superficial that a dead man could have passed.

Randy spent his last week teaching Joyce everything he knew about running bets. He taught her how to stagger bets by rotating bookies, when to wager a lot of money, when to lie low, and why a sprinkle of bad bets across the board helped cover their tracks. He stressed their tracks had to be covered because she would be walking a fine line between the police, who were always trying to shut down illegal betting activities, and men who made their living by feeding off people that were addicted to gambling.

Randy's last night at home was a struggle for everyone. Every time Joyce looked at Randy she had to fight back tears. Throughout dinner everyone tried to keep things light, but it seemed as though every conversation had an emotional trip wire that had to be carefully negotiated. After dinner Joyce set three shot glasses, a bottle of tequila, a dish of lemon wedges, and a saltshaker in the center of the table while Kim rolled a joint. Only after the doobie made several trips around the table and everyone hoisted a number of shots did the stress begin to subside.

Randy refilled all three shot glasses and set the bottle aside. "Right now the worst part is not knowing what to expect," he said, slurring the words a bit. "I don't mean boot camp. I've seen enough movies that I think I know what it'll be like, but Vietnam, that's a little different," he said as he poured salt on his hand. "I can't even imagine being shot at, or shooting at anybody else, for that matter." He licked the salt off his hand and slammed back the tequila. After a moment he picked up a lemon wedge and bit down on it. "Oh God, that's sour," he said as he made a face. "Sometimes I think the lemon is the worst part."

Kim picked up his shot glass and threw the tequila into his mouth. "I don't know about that," Kim said with a grimace. He studied the empty shot glass as he rolled it between his fingers. "The three of us are a family," he said as he set the glass on the table. "And we've all got jobs to do," he said as he picked up the bottle of tequila and gestured to Joyce to drink up. He watched her pick up the glass, and then looked back at Randy. "Joyce and I have to each write you at least a letter a week. We'll be your anchors." He poured tequila into all three glasses. "Your job is to stay alive and hold on to that anchor line."

Joyce was trying to be strong, but her trembling lip betrayed her emotions. "If something happened to you I don't think I could ever get over it," she said as tears welled up in her eyes. "I pray that God brings you back to us safely." A single tear crested over her bottom eyelid and plummeted to the table. "Damn it. I swore I wouldn't do that," she said, then picked up her glass and slammed back the shot.

They continued their assault on the bottle until the clock slipped well beyond midnight. Finally they tried to help each other to bed. As they stumbled through the house with their arms around each other they sang their way through Walk Like A Man by The Hollies. They made it as far as Joyce's room before they crashed on the bed laughing and fell asleep together.

The next morning the drug-induced euphoria was gone, replaced by three tequila hangovers, done up in grand style.

Joyce cooked breakfast, but nobody was very interested in eating. Besides the hangovers, they were faced with the stark realization that Randy had just spent his last night in the house and it would be some time before they were all together again.

The ride to the awaiting bus was mostly silent except for a couple passing comments about the fog that had rolled in overnight. When they got to the post office most of the draftees were milling around the outside of the greyhound bus, talking to girl friends or smoking cigarettes.

Kim took Randy's duffle bag out of the trunk and set it on the sidewalk next to the car.

Randy looked at his friends and shrugged his shoulders.

"I guess this is it," he said in a shaky voice as he reached out and put his arms around both of them. "You guys have to take care of each other. Don't forget the letters, and I swear, no matter what it takes, I'll come back to you. I love you guys," he said and hugged them.

"I love you, too, man. Take care of yourself," Kim said as he hugged him back.

Joyce was crying as she hugged him and kissed him on the ear. "I love you, too, baby. Promise me you'll take care of yourself."

"I promise," Randy said, then kissed her on the lips. He broke the hug, picked up his duffle bag and threw it over his shoulder. "I love you both," he said as he turned and walked away.

They watched him board the bus, and then Kim put his arm around Joyce and walked her around to the passenger side of the Cadillac.

Randy's absence was more difficult to deal with than either of them thought. There was emptiness in their lives that wouldn't go away no matter how busy they kept themselves with school and building the nest egg. It was a void that remained despite their efforts to invent diversions. Even their close dedication to each other failed to heal the wound.

As the weeks stretched into months they kept up with their promised letters and eagerly awaited the mail delivery when a letter from Vietnam was due. The return letters came as regularly as clockwork, and gave them a much-needed feeling of unity with Randy, but nothing like the phone calls. They didn't come often and never lasted long, but the sound of his voice was magic for both of them.

Winter passed and spring brought new life and the hope that they had gone through the worst of it. Randy's tour in Vietnam was almost half over, graduation was approaching, and the nest egg they had been building for two years was nearly complete. Another six months and everything would start coming together. Randy would be left with another year of military service in the states, their bank account would be something close to sixty thousand dollars and the three of them could begin serious work on their house plans.

Finals lasted throughout the last week in May and marked the end of a grueling year, with graduation only two weeks away. Those two weeks were heavily scheduled with parties celebrating the culmination of academic careers. Joyce and Kim both were relieved that school was finished, but weren't sure they were emotionally fit for revelry. After discussing the mood they had fallen into they realized they were in need of the kind of therapy a party had to offer.

They made some quick plans, and then Kim started calling a few people while Joyce went to the store for party supplies.

Nearly an hour later Joyce returned from the store with a back seat full of groceries and a trunk full of beer. She pushed the trunk release button and grabbed a couple bags of groceries.

"Kim," Joyce called as she pushed open the back door. "There's beer in the trunk." She heard a strange beeping signal coming from the other side of the kitchen as she walked in and set the groceries on the counter. She turned around and saw the wall phone dangling from the cord and realized she was hearing something like a loud busy signal.

"Kim," she called again as she walked over to the phone and cradled the receiver. She walked into the living room and found Kim sitting in the platform rocker, staring out the front window. "There's beer in the trunk," she said as she walked over and put her hands on his shoulders.

Kim put his hand on top of hers and held it, but didn't turn around.

"You okay?" Joyce asked in a concerned tone.

Kim shook his head.

"You better sit down," he said in a trembling voice.

"What the hell's wrong," Joyce demanded as she turned the chair around. Her heart sunk as she saw the tears running down Kim's cheeks. "Oh. God, no!" she screamed and raised trembling hands to her mouth.

Kim stood up and pulled her to him as she began to cry.

"Randy's dead," he said in a weak voice.

The words struck her heart like a hammer.

"No!" she screamed and began to sob.

The party was cancelled and for the next few days they tried to comfort each other, but it did little good. They were like zombies. They didn't eat, they talked very little, and they wondered over the campus aimlessly. Sleep was their only solace.

Three days before graduation Joyce walked into the kitchen and sat down at the table next to Kim as he poured the remains of a bottle of tequila into a water glass, filling it half way. He hadn't shaved in several days, his eyes were red from crying, and he was drunk.

"I can't stop thinking of our last night together," he said dully.

"I know," Joyce said, as she laid an unopened letter on the table. "It was in the mail," she said, choking on the words. Her hand trembled as she slid the envelope over to him. "I can't open it," she whispered.

Kim picked up the letter and examined it for a moment. "You might feel differently in a few months," he said as he tossed it over to the other side of the table.

"Kim, we need to talk," she said as she laid her hand on top of his.

"Sounds like I need a drink for this," he said as he raised the glass to his lips. When he put it down it was empty.

"I can't stay here any longer," she said as she fought back tears. "There are too many memories. I'm leaving in the morning."

"We still have each other," Kim demanded.

"I'll always love you, but it will never be the same. Part of me died with Randy," Joyce said as tears ran down her cheeks. "I just want to get away."

"What about graduation?" Kim asked.

"I just don't care anymore," she said as she wiped away the tears. "I want you to take me to the bus station in the morning."

"Where are you going?"

Joyce shrugged her shoulders. "I don't know. I've been saving my trust allowance, I'll probably just travel around for awhile."

"Is there any way I can talk you out of this?" Kim asked.

Joyce shook her head as the tears started again. "I can't go on like this, and you can't either."

Kim nodded his head dolefully as he pulled his wallet out of his back pocket. He took out a bankbook and set the wallet aside.

"You've got some money coming. I'll take you to the bank in the morning," he said as he opened the book. "Looks like your half is about twenty thousand."

"I don't want any of that money."

"Don't argue with me on this," Kim said sternly. "I don't want you to

133

leave, so if you're going you go on my terms. You take the Cadillac, too. It's in your name anyway."

"I'll sign it over to you. It's just more memories."

"I've got my own memories to deal with," Kim said as tears welled up in his eyes. "Take the car and trade it in on something else when it feels right."

The next morning after going to the bank Joyce drove Kim back home. They said a tearful goodbye in the driveway, and then Joyce left and never looked back.

The flood of memories was like a drug, taking her closer and closer to sleep until she drifted off. There were no dreams or nightmares this time, only deep tranquil repose.

Kim listened to the drone of the battered outboard and watched absently as the old fisherman piloted the small craft through the muddy river water. He picked up a lead fishing sinker that was lying in the bottom of the boat and pressed it into the palm of his hand as he thought about the visions he was given before he passed beyond the circle of Yu Wu. The horror to be faced was unspeakable, but his mind was consumed by the revelation that Randy was alive. The joy in his heart was diminished only by the mortal danger he knew Randy and Joyce would be facing.

He had projected bits of his newly acquired knowledge into Joyce's dreams but was unsuccessful in penetrating to her conscious mind. In her heart Randy had been dead for nearly thirty years, and the message that he was alive was simply too much of a disconnect for her to retain. It was even less likely that she was able to grasp his warning about the artifact.

He focused a part of his mind on the piece of lead in his hand as he thought about Joyce. After so many years the memory of the anguish she suffered still haunted him and tore at his heart. Back then he understood the agony that gnawed at her, forcing her to leave. He understood, but their last goodbye sent his life spinning out of control just the same.

After Joyce left, his existence became a blur of alcohol, drugs, and one night flings with a number of women. The reckless use of alcohol nearly ruined his health, the drugs he always warned others about came close to draining his bank account and none of the women even came close to healing his broken heart. His wake up call came one morning about three months later when he found himself on the bathroom floor in a puddle of bloody vomit.

He closed his eyes and let the sun warm his face as he let his mind drift back to the day when he first started putting his life back together again.

There was just enough money left in the bank account to buy a sixty-two Falcon with a crumpled trunk lid and to put a little working capital in his pocket. When he walked out of the house for the last time he left behind the memories of a lost dream and everything that wouldn't fit in the back seat of the Falcon.

His plans were simple, get to Las Vegas as quickly as possible and correct the financial trouble in which he found himself. The spiritual values he always tried to distill in Joyce and Randy were far from his mind. He was no longer concerned about the moral use of his abilities and he didn't care who got hurt. A society consumed with its own self importance took something precious and irreplaceable from him, and Vegas was going to pay the price. He was going to bleed the casinos until they were anemic.

The old beat up Ford made it as far as the outskirts of St. Louis on Interstate Forty before the head gasket gave up the ghost and sent high temperature exhaust gas into the water jacket. Within minutes the top radiator hose burst under the pressure and engulfed the chugging engine in a cloud of steam.

Kim cursed the man who sold him the car as it rolled to a stop on the edge of the highway. He felt hopelessly lost as he watched the speeding traffic moving passed him in an endless motorcade. After doing a mental review of his options he got out of the car and pulled his duffle bag out of the back. He took one last look at his stereo and other assorted belongings, then threw the bag over his shoulder, slammed the door and started walking along the side of the interstate with his thumb in the air.

He walked a couple miles before a semi pulled off the side of the road and stopped ahead of him. As he ran for the truck the passenger door of the cab popped open. When he got to the open door he lifted his duffle bag up to the waiting hands of the driver. "Thanks for the ride," Kim said as he climbed up into the cab.

The driver was a big man with a round belly, thinning blonde hair and scraggly beard. He grinned from behind the unlit cigar he had clamped between his back teeth. "Glad to have the company. Driving this rig gets pretty lonely without somebody to talk to," he said as he checked the side mirror. The truck lurched forward and shuddered under the load as he released the clutch. "Was that your old Falcon off the side of the road a couple miles back?" he asked as he changed gears.

"Yeah," Kim said absently as he looked around the inside of the cab. "I've never been inside of one of these before. You can see a lot of the road."

"Name's Greg," the driver said as he changed gears and eased the eighteen-wheeler onto the highway. "Make yourself at home. Where you heading?"

"Glad to meet you, Greg. My name's Kim and I'm on the way to Vegas."

Greg revved the engine and shifted as he looked over at Kim. "I can take you as far as Salt Lake City. That's where I have to pick up Ninety-One north into Idaho. Ninety-One south will take you right into Vegas. After ten years on the road I've had the chance to meet a lot of people. Some of them were going places, and others were just wandering. What's your story? You don't look like a gambler," he said as he pulled the shift lever back and locked in high gear.

"Honestly, I don't know what my story is right now. A couple days ago I walked away from a life that was in shambles. I guess I'd have to say I'm adrift."

"How'd your life get to be in such a mess?"

Kim shook his head, but didn't answer.

"I don't mean to pry, I just like to keep the conversation going when I have company," Greg said as he started maneuvering around a slower moving truck.

"There wasn't anything wrong with the question, I was just trying to figure out a good answer," Kim said as he leaned over and pulled his wallet out of the back pocket of his jeans. He took out a snapshot and handed it to Greg. It was a picture of the three of them sitting together on the porch swing. "That was taken about three years ago."

"Pretty girl," Greg said as he held the picture up in front of him. "Looks like a happy group," he said as he handed the photo back to Kim.

"The three of us lived together while we were in college and we were very happy," he said as he returned the photograph to his wallet. "Randy's dead, killed in Vietnam, and Joyce is...Joyce is gone. She just couldn't handle the pain of losing Randy...not that I did any better."

"Why didn't you go with her?" Greg asked.

"It wasn't what she wanted and I had my own pain to deal with. If we'd stayed together it would have been a constant reminder that we were no longer complete."

"Now you're on your way to Vegas to start a new life?"

"Yeah, pick up the pieces and start over," Kim said as he glanced over at the speedometer. "You might want to watch your speed, there's a cop on the other side of the hill."

"Now how could you possibly know that?" Greg scoffed.

"I just do."

When the truck crested over the hill they both saw the Missouri State Patrol car sitting in the emergency turnaround about a quarter of a mile away. Greg hit the brakes, bringing the rig back into the tolerable speed zone.

"Hey, how'd you do that?" Greg demanded.

"I can't explain it. It's just something that happens."

"That's pretty hard to swallow. I suppose next you're going to tell me you know how the dice are going to roll or what number will hit in roulette," Greg said with a chuckle.

Kim reached into his pocket and pulled out a small wad of money. "I've got three hundred dollars here," he said as he held it up for examination. "It's all I have. You find a race track and I'll show you how to make money."

Greg clamped down on his cigar as he looked over at Kim. "I'll tell you what I'm gonna do, sonny boy. I know a bookie in Springfield. We'll stop there and you can place whatever trifecta bet you want. Win the bet and I'll drive you to Vegas myself."

Kim let go of his memories as he heard the fisherman shut down the outboard. He watched as the old man tilted the motor up before easing himself over the side of the boat with the bowline in his hand. He moved through the shallow water, stepped up on the muddy riverbank and helped Kim out of the boat. "They land their planes in a clearing on the other side of the woods," he said in Chinese as he pointed a bony finger toward a small stand of pine trees. "You must be careful, they will not be happy to see a stranger."

"Thank you," Kim said as he handed the old man the sinker he had been holding in his hand.

The old man looked at the piece of gold in his hand and broke into a wide toothless grin. "May Buddha walk with you," he said as he waded back into the river.

Mark watched the girl behind the counter as she went about filling his order. She was an attractive girl with a pleasant smile and long auburn hair that reminded him of Joyce Robbins.

Seeing Joyce walk into his office again was a surprise that left him feeling emotionally confused. The sudden ache in his heart told him he still wanted her, but the memories of their breakup remained painfully vivid. On the surface she was a warm and strikingly beautiful woman, but beneath the beauty was an impenetrable wall. She was comfortable with their sexual friendship, but the prospect of it growing into love turned her heart to stone.

"Enjoy your breakfast, sir," the girl said as she set three large cups of coffee on the tray next to the pile of breakfast sandwiches and hash browns.

"Thanks," Mark said as he picked up the tray. He stopped for some napkins before walking to the round table where his two workmen waited.

"Dig in, you guys," he said as he put the tray in the middle of the table. He pulled out a chair and sat down as the two men started sorting out their breakfasts.

Jack was the older of the two brothers, but the family resemblance was more obvious than the three years that separated them. They both had sandy blonde hair and the same blue color in their eyes, but Lonny sported a bushy mustache that covered most of his mouth.

"Lonny, when the boss buys you breakfast at McDonald's instead of a bag of Dunkin' Doughnuts, you know you're in for a tough day's work," Jack said and took a bite out of his sandwich.

"Yeah, Mark. What gives?" Lonny asked as he dumped cream and sugar into his coffee.

Mark took a drink of his coffee before setting it aside and picking up a sandwich. "Remember Joyce? She drove a black sixty-two Vette," he said as he started unwrapping the sandwich.

"Oh, yeah," Lonny said as he broke off a piece of his hash browns and popped it in his mouth. "Great looking legs and nice ass."

Jack laughed and shook his head. "I think that's all he ever looks at."

"Well, then he probably doesn't remember she worked for the museum," Mark said.

"I do," Jack said. "But then I remember what she looks like, too."

Mark laughed as he took a bite of his sandwich. "She found an artifact. We're going to crate it up and move it to the museum for her."

"That doesn't sound too tough," Lonny said.

"What kind of artifact?" Jack asked.

"I've never seen anything like it," Mark said as he added more sugar to his coffee. "There's a huge crystal inside this massive frame, and I'm here to tell you that it's a grotesque looking son of a bitch. It's covered with carvings that are enough to scare the heebie jeebies out of Stephen King himself," he said as he stirred the coffee.

"So we're just picking it up and moving it?" Lonny asked.

"It's going to be a little more involved than that. We have to custom build a display stand for it and build a shipping crate around it so it doesn't get damaged. The lumber was delivered to the site last night. Four by eight beams, pine for the crate and oak for the stand. I've got a sketch of what I think the display stand should look like, but I'm depending on you guys to make it work, so you'll get to be creative."

"Oh, man," Lonny said. "I hate working with four by eight beams. Everything has to be bolted together. This is starting to sound like a pain in the ass."

"Working with the lumber may end up being the easy part. You're going to have to drag it out of the garage with the cherry picker and hold it upright while you build the stand under it."

"This doesn't sound like a one day job," Jack said.

Mark shrugged his shoulders. "It's hard to say. It probably depends on how much trouble you have moving the artifact around."

"Hell, we have a machine for that, the two of us moving those oak beams around is going to be a bitch," Lonny grumbled.

"Oh, quit complaining," Jack said with a chuckle. "You're just afraid you won't have enough energy to take care of Sherri. Let her get on top."

"Who's Sherri?" Mark asked.

"Oh, you haven't heard. Lonny's got a steady girl friend."

"Lonny has given up his wild ways for one woman?" Mark asked in a surprised tone.

"I guess so," Jack said with a grin. "For two years he's been eating dinner with Betty and I on Fridays, then playing a couple games of chess with me before heading for the night spots. A couple weeks ago he asked if he could bring a friend, and showed up with this cute blonde on his arm. Hell, he was so busy talking to her that we didn't even get to play chess."

"Did it look serious?"

"Serious? My God, they couldn't keep their hands off of each other. It was down right disgusting," Jack said with a wink.

"I suppose she has great legs and a nice ass, too," Mark said with a laugh.

"I couldn't see her legs, she had on jeans, but the boy definitely has an eye for a nice derriere," Jack said.

"Lonny, is it love?" Mark asked with a grin.

"I don't know," he said as he took the last bite of his sandwich. "I've never been in love before, but it's different. When I'm with her I don't want to leave, and when I'm not with her I can't get her out of my mind."

"He lets her drive his car," Jack said with a smile.

"His car? Hell, it's love for certain," Mark said with a grin. "I'll start shopping for a wedding present."

"Yeah, me too," Jack said as he started wadding up his sandwich wrappers.

Mark was the last one to finish eating. He wiped his mouth with a napkin and crammed all of his trash into the empty coffee cup as he stood up.

"You guys stay close behind me," he said as he pulled the car keys out of his pocket. "We're going to a part of town I didn't know existed until yesterday. I don't want you two getting lost."

"Right behind you, boss," Jack said as he and Lonny stood up.

Mark was relieved when he saw the red cherry picker sitting in the front yard next to the stripped washing machine. It was a welcomed landmark in a strange part of town he'd only seen once before. As he pulled his Jeep into the yard next to the small crane he wondered if the delivery crew had any problems finding the place.

Jack and Lonny pulled their truck into the stone driveway next to the old pickup and the pile of beams stacked behind it.

Jack shut off the truck and looked over at his brother. "Some neighborhood."

"Yeah, and the neighbors probably complain about this place," Lonny said as he looked at the assortment of junk scattered across the front yard. He pushed his door open and got out.

"Welcome to the country club," Mark said as he walked up to the driveway.

"This looks like some prime investment property," Jack said as he got out of the pickup.

"Yeah, and I see a lot of valuable artifacts lying around, too," Lonny said with a laugh as he walked around the front of the truck. "I can't wait to see the jewel we're shipping to the museum," he said with a snicker.

"It's in the garage," Mark said as he took a key out of his pocket and handed it to Lonny. "I hope you're not prone to nightmares."

"I like nightmares," Lonny said with a smile. "Jack always took me to see spooky movies when I was a kid. I think he warped me," he said as he turned and walked toward the garage.

"You were the one who always hid behind the seat when things got scary," Jack said with a laugh.

"Here's the sketch of the display stand," Mark said as he pulled a piece of paper out of his shirt pocket and unfolded it.

Jack took the paper, studied it for a moment and nodded his head. "Oak is hard to work with. We could save some time by using pine," he said.

Mark shook his head. "Pine won't work. The artifact is too heavy. We need a lot of weight in the base. I hope the cherry picker has enough ass to pick it up. You remember how to run it, don't you?" Mark asked as they started walking toward the garage.

"I'm probably a little rusty, but it's not too complicated. We'll get it figured out," Jack said.

They both stopped next to the old pickup when they saw Lonny backing out of the garage. He jumped involuntarily and cried out as he backed into the front of the old pickup.

"He spooks pretty easy for somebody that was warped by scary movies when he was little," Jack said laughing.

"God damn it, Jack, you haven't seen that fucking thing," Lonny shrieked as he pointed into the garage.

"It is a little frightening," Mark said sympathetically.

"I'm sure it'll be a lot less intimidating when we get it out here in the sunlight," Jack said as he walked toward the garage.

"Yeah, right, Jack. It'll probably be worse," Lonny said nervously.

Jack walked up to the open door and peered into the garage. He saw his own fuzzy, bluish reflection in the crystal, and then, as his eyes adjusted, he made out the carved features of the frame. "Shit," he cried out in a startled voice as he flinched and took a quick step backward.

"Well, I'm going to take off and let you guys get to work," Mark said with a grin. "You've got the mobile phone, call me if you need anything."

"You mean like an exorcist?" Jack asked as he turned away from the garage.

"Yeah, or a crucifix and a wooden stake," Mark said with a laugh as he walked across the yard to his Jeep.

Luther sat on the bench next to Steve and watched as he oiled a control cable from the disassembled snow blower that was spread out on the grass.

"Sure is funny, seein' you workin' on that snow blower in this heat," Luther said as he wiped the sweat from his forehead with the back of his hand.

"You can't wait until winter to work on a snow blower," Steve said as he set the oilcan aside and pulled an orange shop rag out of his pocket. "If this thing broke down in the middle of January Rudy would be camped out on my ass until I got it fixed." He wiped the oil off the outside of the cable and laid it on a piece of cardboard in front of him on the grass. "I can do without that kind of attention."

"I know whatcha mean," Luther said as he bit off the end of the cigar and spit it in the grass.

"You thirsty?" Steve asked as he wiped the sweat out of his eyes.

"Yeah, I am," Luther said as he pulled a dollar bill out of his pocket, "but you gotta give me some change."

"That's no problem," Steve said as he pulled a handful of quarters out of his pocket. "You think you're gonna break my streak?"

"Yeah, I think you gonna be takin' the big fall today," Luther said as he exchanged the money with Steve.

"Your call," Steve said as he positioned a quarter on his thumb.

Luther thought for a moment, and then grinned.

"You match me," he said defiantly.

"On the cardboard," Steve said as he flipped his coin.

Both quarters landed heads up on the cardboard.

"Shit, you be the luckiest damn white boy I know," Luther grumbled as he pulled another dollar out of his pocket. "Root beer?" he asked sourly.

"Yeah," Steve said with a laugh as he gave Luther four more quarters.

"You gettin' pretty close to bein' a income tax deduction," Luther said with a sigh as he got up off the bench and started walking toward the museum.

Before Steve could pick up another piece of the snow blower he saw a red van turn in from the street. Atlas Security Doors was stenciled on the side of the vehicle with flowing white letters. The van rolled to a stop at the top of the hill as the driver opened the window.

"Looking for Samuel Prince," the driver said.

"I bet you're here to fix his door problem," Steve said as he stood up and walked over to the edge of the driveway. "I was talking with one of your salesmen about the problem yesterday. He'll be glad to see you. Park the van and I'll take you to his office."

"Thanks," the driver said as he pulled away.

Steve walked over to the museum and waited for the driver. He wondered how much money Rudy skimmed off the deal on the doors and how many other kickbacks there had been. He started looking at the museum a little differently since Sam told him about Rudy and the money his aunt left the historical society. There were plenty of extravagant items like Rudy's desk, or the mural above the door to Sam's office, but there was a lot of junk, too, like the cheap air conditioning unit in the security station that had been run to death, or the cheesy, second rate lawn equipment Luther had to use. He supposed when a kickback was available Rudy went for the most expensive, and when it wasn't he became a miser.

The driver walked up next to Steve and extended his hand.

"Bill Bruster from Atlas Security Doors."

Steve smiled and shook his hand.

"Glad to meet you, Bill," Steve said as they shook hands. "I'm Steve, the resident maintenance man," he said as he opened the door. "I've got a real frustrating relationship with the doors you're here to look at."

"What seems to be the problem with them?" Bill asked as he stepped into the air-conditioned environment.

"Well, I'm not in the business, but I think it's simply too much door for the application," Steve said as he stopped at the top of the steps. "I wish I had five bucks for every time I've tightened them up. They pull away from the frame and bind in the center."

"Definitely sounds like an application problem," Bill said as he followed Steve down the steps.

When Steve walked into the office Samuel was sorting through a stack of old National Geographic magazines.

"Morning, Sam. I've got a guy here who wants to take a look at the double doors in the lab."

"You just got my attention," Samuel said as he got up and laid the magazine aside.

Bill extended his hand. "Bill Bruster from Atlas Security doors."

"Glad to meet you, Bill," Samuel said as he shook his hand.

"Our salesman says you've got a problem with a set of our doors."

"Yeah, I do," Samuel said as he opened the door to the lab. "Come on, I'll let you take a look."

"Sam, I'll see you later, I've got a cold root beer waiting for me."

Samuel gave him an acknowledging wave as he disappeared into the lab.

"Thanks, Steve," Bill said as he turned and followed Samuel.

Jerry was in the hall waiting for Joyce as she followed the last student out of the classroom.

"Hi," Jerry said as he pushed himself away from the wall and started walking beside Joyce.

"Morning, Jerry. I took your suggestion," she said as she raised a black leather attaché case for his inspection.

"Looks expensive," he said as he touched the case.

"Yeah, it is. I really spoil myself sometimes," Joyce said with a smile. "I was hoping to run into you. You've got to hear my story."

"Story about what?" Jerry asked as they stopped in front of the elevator.

"Oh, you're not hearing this without buying me a cup of coffee," she said as she pushed the elevator button. "Yesterday was one hell of a day for me."

"Well, you didn't have class yesterday, so you must have been arrested for speeding after a cross county chase," Jerry said with a chuckle as the elevator bell rang and the doors opened.

"I'm shocked that you could even suggest such a thing," she said with a laugh as they stepped aboard the elevator.

"Yeah, right," Jerry said as he pushed the button for the basement. "You scared the shit out of me the other night."

"You're the one who wanted to see how fast the car was."

"Yeah, but I didn't think you'd really show me," Jerry said as the elevator stopped and the doors opened.

The hall was filled with students. The ones that weren't piling into the elevator were either standing in line at the bookstore or going into the commons for a break between classes.

"This is crazy," Jerry said as he grabbed Joyce's hand and worked through the crush of students. Once they were across the hall and into the commons the traffic thinned out.

"I'll get the coffee," Jerry said as he turned toward the line of vending machines.

"Cream and sugar," Joyce said as she put her purse on the table and set the attaché case on the floor next to her chair. She looked around at the empty tables in the sparsely occupied break area and wondered if it became a student hangout when the fall quarter started. She could imagine the place being some sort of cultural center between classes. It was probably too noisy for serious studying, but just right for impromptu meetings and socializing.

Jerry came back from the vending machines carrying two cups of coffee and a package of small powered doughnuts. He set everything on the table and pulled out his chair.

"I need to shed a couple pounds, but I just can't resist these little doughnuts," he said as he sat down. "If you eat half of them I'll be okay."

"I've got my own waistline to worry about, thank you," Joyce said with a smile.

"You look like the type who can eat anything without worrying about your weight," Jerry said as he opened the package and took out a doughnut.

"It used to be like that when I was younger, but anymore I have to be careful," she said.

"Okay, you've got your coffee, tell me your story," Jerry said as he broke the doughnut in two pieces and offered half of it to Joyce.

Joyce took the cruller and knocked the excess powdered sugar off into an empty ashtray.

"Yesterday morning on the way to work I took some time and followed up on a call from the day before. The caller that left the message thought he had something that belonged in the museum. You'd be surprised at the number of calls we receive. Most of the stuff turns out to be junk, but I always like to follow up on everything I possibly can," she said, then popped the small piece of doughnut into her mouth and dusted off her hands as she continued. "So, after about twenty minutes I finally found the address in the middle of this run down neighborhood. I mean this part of town was bad, junk cars and the whole nine yards. The address I was looking for turned out to be the worst place on the block. There was all kinds of junk laying around in the front yard. I'm talking about an old washing machine and disassembled lawnmowers. The place reminded me of that old television series with Redd Foxx..."

"You mean 'Sanford and Son'?" Jerry asked.

"Yeah, that's what the place was like, and there was even an old black man sitting on the porch with his back against the wall. I kept calling to him, but he didn't answer. My God, Jerry, the old guy was dead!"

Jerry stopped suddenly with a doughnut half way to his mouth. "Dead?" he asked in a surprised tone.

"Yes. I touched him," she said with revulsion in her voice. "He just fell over."

"Oh, God," Jerry said as he put the doughnut down. "Did you figure out why he called?"

"Well, this is where the story takes a real weird turn."

"You mean there's more to this story?"

Joyce picked up her coffee and took a drink. "When the old guy rolled over a key fell out of his hand. It didn't really register at the time, but a few minutes later I found a new pad lock on the garage door. The key fit the lock, but before I could open the garage doors I had to pull a rocking chair out of the ground."

"Wait a minute, I'm having a little trouble here. There was a rocking chair buried in front of the garage doors?"

"The ends of the rockers were driven into the ground like stakes, so the doors couldn't be opened."

Jerry picked up the doughnut he'd set aside and took a bite out of it. "So, after all this, what kind of junk did you find in the garage."

Joyce smiled and shook her head slowly as she set the cup on the table. "An archaeologist's dream is to discover that once in a lifetime artifact that brings fame and recognition," Joyce said.

"Joyce, you're making me crazy. What was in the garage?" he pleaded.

"I don't have the foggiest notion," she said with a nervous laugh. "I've never seen or heard of anything like it before and neither has my boss. The inside of the garage was dark, so I didn't see it right away. When I got my first glimpse I thought it was a huge antique mirror, but when I took a closer look I was absolutely stunned. It was actually an immense crystal, but it was different. Every crystal I've ever seen has had smooth surfaces. This one was rough to my touch."

"I've never heard of a crystal that wasn't smooth," Jerry said thoughtfully. "Are you sure it was a crystal?"

"Jerry, don't get hung up on the crystal, there's more. This crystal is framed by logs of petrified wood." She paused long enough to take a drink of her coffee. "Jerry, these petrified logs are covered with carvings."

"Carvings?" Jerry asked in an uncertain tone.

"Yes, horrible looking faces, and there's some kind of animal head at the top of the frame. This thing is more than just a little frightening."

"Wait," Jerry said as he rubbed at his temple. "I'm having some trouble with these carvings. I had some geology in college..."

"I already know what you're going to say," Joyce interrupted. "Petrified wood is usually aged at around one hundred and fifty million years, and you want to know who in the hell was around that long ago to do the carvings."

"Well, yeah. That was my point," Jerry said.

"I've already considered the possibility of some type of hoax, and it can't be totally ruled out until a complete examination has been performed, but I don't buy it. I'll stake my reputation on the authenticity of this artifact. Maybe there's some factor that we're unaware of that can accelerate the agatization process. I think one look at it and you'll be as convinced as I am."

"Let's go," Jerry said as he glanced at his watch. "I don't have another class until one o'clock. I'll buy you lunch."

"Great idea, but the artifact hasn't been delivered yet. How about a rain check?" she asked.

"Certainly," Jerry said with a smile. "I can't wait to see this thing. I have a definite weakness for creepy stuff."

"Yeah, well I'm betting this artifact is the creepiest thing you've ever seen," Joyce said darkly.

Jack steadied the hammer, and then drove the last wedge, securing the artifact in the display stand. He backed away and looked over at Lonny.

"Hope it's in there straight. That's a lot of weight to be leaning."

"It hasn't fallen over yet," Lonny said as he held a plumb line next to the artifact. He studied it for a moment before winding the line around the brass plumb bob. "It looks pretty good to me," he said as he returned the tool to its plastic box.

"I'm getting hungry," Jack said as he glanced at his watch. "That McDonald's breakfast didn't hold me very long."

"I'm a little hungry myself. I guess we're not use to working this hard," Lonny said as he walked over to the truck and set the plastic box on the seat. "How long do you think it'll take us to finish up?"

"Well, we've got to cut and drill the beams, then bolt everything together. We're probably looking at another three hours, maybe a little more. You want to finish up tomorrow?" Jack asked.

"Hell, no! That fuckin' thing gives me the creeps," Lonny said as he crossed his arms and leaned against the truck. "When I go home tonight I want to know I'm done with it."

"Let's go get something to eat. We'll come back after lunch and finish."

"Help me put some of the beams up on the saw horses and I'll start working them while you go pick up something for us," Lonny said as he walked over and picked up one end of a four by eight. Jack picked up the other end and helped Lonny hoist it up onto the sawhorses.

"Aren't you afraid to be here alone?" Jack taunted.

"Don't be ridiculous," Lonny said as they grabbed another beam. "It doesn't scare me, it gives me the willies."

"What the hell's the difference?" Jack asked with a laugh as they set the timber on the horses.

"God, you ask stupid questions sometimes."

"Well, is there a difference?" Jack prodded.

"Hell yes, there's a difference," Lonny insisted as they walked over to another beam. "You get the willies when something makes you uneasy and works on you at a subliminal level, like a spooky movie, for instance. Rabid dogs, on the other hand, scare the hell out of me."

Jack shook his head and laughed as they lifted the beam. "Mom was right. You're so full of shit it's a wonder your eyes aren't brown."

"Hey, I don't ever remember Mom saying anything like that."

"Every time you told one of your wild stories," Jack said with a snicker.

"I never told wild stories," Lonny said as he walked over to another piece of lumber.

"Bull shit! What about the time you came home dripping wet and told everybody the wind blew you in the creek."

"Hey, damnit, that was true," Lonny said as he bent down and picked up his end of the beam.

"Yeah, right. You still believe there were little people living in our basement?" Jack asked as he lifted his end of the beam.

"Well, I don't...son of a bitch!" Lonny yelled as he dropped his end of the four by eight and jumped back.

"What the hell's wrong with you?" Jack asked as he struggled to hold onto the beam.

"Fuckin' centipedes! I hate those goddamn things," Lonny screamed.

"All that jumping around over a bug?"

"Those damn things bite," Lonny retorted.

"How about some help before I drop this thing on my foot," Jack said as he shifted his grip on the wood.

Lonny did a quick bug inspection before grabbing his end of the timber and lifting it up onto the sawhorses.

Jack unclipped a tape measure from his belt and hooked it to the end of one of the beams.

"What do you want to eat?" he asked as he reeled out the tape.

"I don't know," Lonny said as he pulled a pencil out from behind his ear and put a hash mark on the wood. "A steak sandwich and a beer from the Avenue Cafe sounds kinda good to me."

"Yeah, a cold beer would go down good," Jack said as he rolled up the tape. He clipped the tool back on his belt and pulled a bandanna out of his pocket. "You want fries or anything like that?" he asked as he wiped the sweat from his forehead.

"No, just a sandwich and a couple beers."

"I guess I may as well call in the order," Jack said as he walked back to the truck.

While Jack called in the order Lonny lined up the ends of the beams, laid a square across them and scribed a cut line with his pencil.

"I'll be back as soon as I can," Jack said as he hung up the phone and took the keys out of his pocket.

"Okay," Lonny said as he put safety goggles over his eyes. He picked up the saber saw, lined it up on the pencil mark and pulled the trigger. Nothing happened. He clicked the trigger again before checking the power cord. The connection seemed fine, but he noticed a section of the extension cord that had been driven into the soft ground by the end of the beam he dropped.

"Hey, Jack," Lonny yelled as he pulled the goggles down around his neck.

"What?" Jack asked as he stuck his head out the window.

"Hold up for a minute. I fucked up the extension cord when I dropped the beam," Lonny said as he walked to the truck. He reached in the back and pulled out a coiled extension cord. "You know, that centipede didn't give me the willies, it scared me," he said with a smile. He started to walk away, then turned back. "Remember, cold beer and hot food," Lonny said as he took the receptacle in one hand and the coil in the other. "If you play that damn pinball machine it'll be the other way around."

"Yes sir," Jack said mockingly as he backed the truck out of the driveway.

Lonny walked back to the sawhorses and tossed the coil toward the garage while holding onto the receptacle. Part of the uncoiling cord draped over the top of the artifact and hung down the front of the crystal. The rest of it landed in the driveway next to the garage. After unplugging the power tools he hooked them up to the new extension cord and walked back to the garage to complete the circuit. When he got back to the sawhorses he pulled the safety goggles up over his eyes, lined the saw up on the pencil mark and started cutting the beams.

After taking the first cut he stopped, rolled each of the timbers over and finished lobbing off the ends. He stepped back, pulled the goggles down around his neck and brushed the sawdust out of his mustache as he picked up a plywood hole template. He set the template on the end of the first beam and marked the hole location as he wondered if Jack had managed to avoid the pinball machine. He laughed to himself as he thought about what his brother referred to as his addiction. Jack was compelled to play a machine until he learned all its secrets. When he was able to win free games on a regular basis the conquest was complete and his compulsion tempered. His craving would then be manageable until he happened upon the next challenge. The machine at the Avenue was new, and so far unbeaten.

He supposed Jack's weakness wasn't all that different from his own obsession, except pinball machines were cheaper to chase than women. Women made him crazy, it was as simple as that. The lure of enticing a new woman into bed was as irresistible to him as a new pinball machine was to Jack. He laughed aloud when he realized his conquest of a woman and Jack's conquest of a pinball machine always ended the same way. When he knew all her secrets and was able to make love to her whenever he wanted the challenge was over.

He set the template aside and picked up the drill as he thought about the one woman that was changing his life. His relationship with her was more rewarding than all the one-night stands and meaningless affairs that had come before. It felt as if they were made for each other. He never even suspected that love could bring such contentment. He smiled as he placed the drill bit at the first hole location and pulled the trigger.

Rational thought came to an abrupt end for Lonny as the drill was yanked from his hand and pulled toward the artifact with a jerky motion. He watched in utter disbelief as the drill and saw bounced down the driveway and disappeared through a vertical fissure in the crystal.

There was a part of him that wanted to turn and run, yet he was held in place by the need to understand what he had just seen. He stepped toward the artifact hesitantly as his heart pounded in his chest and his mind raced. The world around him seemed to shift into slow motion and fade to white as he moved cautiously. He felt apprehension gripping his heart, but was only vaguely aware of the paralyzing affect on his intellect as he took his last tentative steps and stopped in front of the artifact. The impossibility of what he saw drove him toward sheer madness.

In the center of the now strangely discolored crystal was a shoulder width vertical crevice opening onto an alien landscape with jagged mountain peaks and a cloudless crimson sky. At the bottom of the fissure was what appeared to be a dune of coarse white sand.

The part of his mind that was still capable of rudimentary thought commanded his body to move away from the abomination but his muscles were ridged with terror. He flinched involuntarily as something dropped out of the air and onto the dune with a crunching sound. When he saw the yellow, cat like eyes and gaping carnivorous jaws he mustered one debilitated step backward, but it was too late. He managed to scream out as the leathery arm struck out from the other side of the fissure and drove hooked talons deep into his shoulder. One swift, powerful jerk took him off his feet and pulled him through the opening. The horrid beast released him as he tumbled through the air. He felt searing pain in his shoulder as he crashed down on his back in the center of the dune. He screamed in terror as he kicked and slapped at the winged creature. The thing dodged his blows, then leaped in the air and came down on his chest with talons slashing into his body. Lonny screamed out in agony as the thing began ripping bloody chunks of flesh from his body with its jaws. He screamed one last time, and then fell silent as other creatures began dropping out of the air to share in the prize.

The edges of the fissure cast a ghostly light as the rift between the worlds began to close. The dark coloration of the crystal began to dissipate as the crevice grew smaller. Once the opening sealed the crystal returned to its bluish hue.

CHAPTER SEVEN

Kim sat with his back against a tall pine tree near the clandestine landing field and watched the last light of day fade into twilight. He chewed on a small piece of wild root and listened to the breeze moving through the trees as he thought about his journey that started in Las Vegas so long ago.

Kim saw the lights of Las Vegas for the first time as he awoke to the sound of air brakes.

"We're here," Greg said as he maneuvered the rig into a parking place at a truck stop on the edge of town.

"What time is it?" Kim asked as he gazed at the lights illuminating the dark sky.

"It's almost five o'clock, but it doesn't matter, this is the town that never sleeps," Greg said as he killed the engine, rolled down the window and tossed out the stub of his chewed up cigar. "I've got to be back on the road tomorrow morning by six. Whatever plan you come up with has to fit into that twenty-four hour slot."

"Well, I need a shower and some breakfast," Kim said as he rubbed his eyes. "You've been driving all night, you want to get some sleep before we hit the casinos?"

"I'll get some shuteye tonight," he said as he pulled a plastic bag out of his pocket. He took two of the black capsules out of the bag and returned it to his pocket. "These babies will keep me going for about twelve hours," he said. He threw them into his mouth and swallowed. "I might talk your leg off, but I won't fall asleep," he said as he took a fresh cigar out of his shirt pocket and removed the cellophane.

"How much money do you have?" Kim asked as he pulled a wad of bills out of his pocket and started counting.

Greg clamped the cigar between his teeth and pulled a long chained wallet out of his back pocket. He opened the zipper and counted. "I've got almost seven hundred dollars," he said.

"Thanks to your buddy in Springfield I've got a little over five thousand," Kim said as he returned the money to his pocket.

"Hell, that sounds like a fortune. All we gotta do is put down our first bet," Greg said with a grin.

"We've got enough money, but it's not quite that simple. We can't just walk in and hit a bundle on the first bet; it'll draw too much attention. We need to lose some money first, and then hit them a couple times before moving on to another casino. We don't want to leave any footprints."

"Okay, kid. You're calling the shots, I'm just along for the ride," Greg said as he rolled up his window. "My wife and I spent our honeymoon at the Sands Hotel. They've got a great restaurant and casino. You got any objections to getting our rooms there?"

"We've got to start somewhere," Kim said as he grabbed his duffel bag and set it up on his lap.

"The Sands it is," Greg said as he pulled a satchel out of the sleeper and opened his door. "I can't wait to see if anything has changed."

"I can't wait to take a shower and get into some clean clothes," Kim said with a laugh as he opened his door.

They flagged down a taxi in front of the truck stop and directed the driver to the Sands Hotel, where they checked into adjacent rooms on the tenth floor.

After getting cleaned up they went to the restaurant and each ordered the Texas steak and egg breakfast. During the meal Kim developed a series of subtle hand signals as he explained that they would enter the casino separately and meet at one of the roulette tables. He stressed that they had to give the appearance of being strangers.

Two hours after rolling into town Kim walked into the casino at the Sands Hotel and went about the business of losing some money while he waited for Greg.

Kim had already lost fifty dollars when Greg walked up to the opposite side of the table and placed his bets. They both played for a while, then Kim signaled Greg and placed a bet on twenty-two. When the white ball fell into a losing slot he walked away from the table. Greg placed a hundred dollar chip on twenty-two for the next spin of the wheel and won ten times their combined losses.

They were even bigger winners at the craps table. Greg rolled the dice or passed, depending on the signal, while Kim milked the other players with side bets. When they left the dice game they cashed in their chips and walked out of the casino with nearly sixteen thousand dollars between them.

Throughout the morning and afternoon they moved between casinos playing blackjack, poker or roulette, but never straying far from a craps table where they did their best work. They paid a visit to every casino on the strip, then made their way back to The Sands for a last tour of the casino and dinner.

By seven o'clock Greg was sitting at the desk in Kim's room watching him count hundred dollars bills and place them into neat five thousand dollar stacks. When he was finished there were twelve stacks and a pile of fifties and twenties.

"We did okay. You get six stacks and as much change as you want," Kim said with a laugh as he threw the twenties and fifties on the bed.

"I'm gonna leave all that change for you," Greg said with a smile. "If it wasn't for you I'd have almost seven hundred instead of thirty grand."

Kim shrugged his shoulders.

"If it wasn't for you I might still be walking," he said as he gathered Greg's money and handed it to him. "Put it to good use."

"I'll look for some real sound investments," Greg said as he stuffed a roll of hundreds into each pants pocket. "You gonna hit the casinos again tomorrow?"

"No. I don't want anybody to remember me when I go back. I'll buy a set of wheels tomorrow and try to find an apartment, then just relax for awhile."

"I better head back to my room and get some sleep," Greg said through a yawn. He extended his hand to Kim. "All this is going to make one hell of a story for my grand kids," he said as they shook hands.

"I've really enjoyed your company and expanding your horizons," Kim said as they walked to the door. "Take care of yourself."

"You do the same," Greg said as he opened the door. "I hope you run into that girl again some day."

"Thanks," Kim said, and then closed the door behind him.

The next day was busy for Kim. After breakfast he took a taxi to the largest car dealer in the area and started searching for a vehicle suitable for his needs. After looking at dozens of cars he found an immaculate yellow 1964 MG that sparked his interest. He took the car for a test drive and fell in love with the tight response of the rack and pinion steering and quick revving engine. Twenty minutes later he drove the sports car off the lot with the top down and a clear title in his pocket.

His first stop after the gas station was a real estate office, where he picked up a map and a rental property listing. He spent the rest of the morning and afternoon driving through the area looking at apartments and houses.

Everything he looked at seemed cold and impersonal until he found a small house of Spanish architecture a few miles from route 93, half way between Whitney and Lake Mead. He looked at a few more places, but his heart kept taking him back to the hacienda with the view of the Virgin Mountains.

The next morning he met the landlord, went through the house, signed the lease and paid the rent through the first year in cash. The rest of the morning was spent in Whitney going through the drudgery of putting the utilities in his name and opening bank accounts.

He continued to stay at the hotel at night while he went about the task of buying everything from a television and stereo system to furniture, bedding linen, and towels. When he wasn't shopping he was at the house waiting for delivery trucks or just enjoying the tranquility of the desert.

He moved in after everything was delivered and spent most of his time relaxing and getting used to the idea of sharing his small piece of the desert with a seemingly endless variety of bugs and spiders. It only took one near miss with a scorpion to learn that the creatures of the desert were opportunists looking for any cover, including shoes and clothing left unprotected.

A few weeks after moving in he started taking road trips in the sports car. At first the excursions were only a few hours in length, then, as he became more familiar with the highways and back roads, the journeys became longer and more than simple wandering. They became systematic searches for gambling establishments such as horse or dog tracks. The sojourns took him west into southern California, and south through Arizona, and into Mexico.

After three months of exploring the Southwest he had a comprehensive list of horse and dog tracks to supplement the casinos in Las Vegas and provide a broad base for his craft. There would be no footprints, only a silent flow of cash from his collective prey.

He methodically tracked his movements and maintained a journal with dates and times associated with racetracks and casinos to insure there were no patterns to his activities. He planned at least one month between visits to any one establishment, and subsequent visits were never during the same time of day. His itinerary usually put him at two locations every day, and gave him a substantial weekly take.

Within a year his bank accounts were swollen and what he called petty cash was stuffed into a pair of coffee cans on the top shelf of a kitchen cupboard. He was compelled to augment his burgeoning fortune regardless of his needs. The wealth provided a bounty of material possessions, including the house he had been leasing, a twenty-four foot sail boat and a new Mercedes, but the contentment he'd known while living with Joyce and Randy eluded him. There was no real happiness in his life, only the lure of easy money and an empty existence that seemed to have less meaning every day.

After nearly three years of sucking the lifeblood from unsuspecting casinos and race tracks throughout the Southwest his life took a sudden, mind-boggling turn.

He was counting a handful of hundred dollar bills as he walked away from a pay window at a dog track in El Cajon when he saw an old Indian sitting in a corner near the entrance. He was wrapped in a tattered blanket and held a tin cup filled with pencils. A small card taped to the side of the cup simply said "blind". As Kim got closer he could see the old man's weathered face and deeply scarred craters where his eyes should have been.

Kim knelt down next to the Indian. "Here's some money for you, Chief," Kim said as he peeled a bill from the roll. "It's a hundred dollar bill, put it someplace safe."

The old man gave Kim a toothless grin as a bony hand came out from under the blanket and groped for the money.

Kim took hold of the Indian's hand and closed his fingers around the bill. "I hope that helps you out," Kim said as he watched the hand disappear under the blanket with the money.

"Hope pencil help you," the Indian whispered, and then cackled with crazed laughter.

"You keep the pencil," Kim said as he patted the old man's shoulder and stood up. He was caught off guard when the Indian's bony hand came out from under the blanket with one swift motion and grasped his wrist firmly.

The Indian shook the tin cup and rattled the pencils as he held his grip tightly.

"I guess I'll have one after all," Kim said with a nervous laugh as he took a pencil from the cup.

The old man immediately released his grip and drew his hand back under the blanket.

Kim stepped away, still a little shaken by the encounter and looked at the unsharpened yellow writing instrument. What he saw stopped him dead in his tracks. There was a message in flashing red letters along the side of the pencil: "we know who you are and we know what you're doing," followed by a phone number in fixed black numbers.

Kim's legs were suddenly wobbly as he turned around to look at the Indian, but he had vanished. He snapped his attention back to the pencil and found a new message flashing: "call us, we're waiting."

Whispering voices and the sound of men moving through the thicket brought Kim back from his thoughts. He watched silently as the silhouette of four men and four burdened packhorses moved through the brush a few yards beyond his position. He could hear the drone of a single engine aircraft approaching in the distance as two of the men ignited flares, ran out into the moonlit clearing and speared them into the ground at the edges of the landing field.

A few minutes later a small plane came in just above the trees and dropped into the clearing like a crop duster. The plane glided downward and bounced in a cloud of dust as the wheels hit the ground. The pilot taxied the aircraft to the end of the field and pivoted around into takeoff position before killing the lights and engine.

A black man wearing a ball cap and leather flight jacket popped open the door and climbed down out of the plane as the four men approached with the packhorses.

"Let's go!" he yelled as he opened a cargo hatch behind the door. "I've got to be off the ground in fifteen minutes," he said as he pulled the first long wooden box out of the compartment and set it on the ground.

The men led the horses along side of the plane as the pilot pulled another box out of the cargo hold.

"Albert, you have something for me?" the leader asked with a heavy Chinese accent as he handed one of the other men the reins to his horse.

"I've got eight boxes of government issue M16's for the General, and I've got something real special for my friend, Yuan," Albert said as he pulled another box from the plane and set it on the ground. The men shook hands, and then Albert pulled a large frame, pearl handled automatic from inside his jacket and handed it to Yuan.

"What is it?" Yuan asked as he admired the gun.

"That's a CIA issue ten millimeter auto with a ten shot clip. The clip's loaded, and there are four hundred rounds in one of the boxes. I'll bring you more next trip."

Yuan barked orders in Chinese as he turned the gun over in his hand and studied its features in the moonlight.

The other men started unloading the packhorses and throwing the heavy burlap sacks on the ground next to the plane.

Albert stooped down, opened the top of one of the sacks with a small knife and pulled out a rectangular package wrapped in heavy paper as Yuan took more boxes out of the plane.

"God, I hate doing this," he said as he opened the package and cut a small sliver from the block of pressed heroin. "You don't insist on firing the guns, why should I have to test this stuff?" he said as he pulled a test tube of clear liquid out of his jacket pocket.

"We are only pawns in a game of chess," Yuan said as he sighted down the barrel of the gun. "Do what you must, it does not offend me."

Albert uncapped the test tube, added the sliver of heroin, replaced the cap and shook it.

"Good stuff," he said as he examined the liquid that had turned a dark red color.

Albert and Yuan both dropped to the ground as the still night was pierced by a terrified scream, followed by two gunshots.

"What the hell's going on, Yuan?" Albert demanded as he pulled a small gun out of his jacket pocket.

Yuan barked out a similar question in Chinese as two of the men struggled to hold the horses.

A troubled response came from the third man near the back of the plane.

"Tiger," Yuan said as he pulled back the slide on the ten-millimeter and chambered a round.

Both men scanned the area for a few minutes, and then stood up cautiously.

"I hope the cat took those two slugs and crawled off to die," Albert said as he put his gun away and brushed off his pants. "Stay alert going back through the brush, good friends are hard to come by."

"I will test my gift on him if he returns," Yuan said as he brandished the ten millimeter.

"I've got the perfect place for a tiger skin rug," Albert said as he turned back toward the plane and pulled out the last box.

"Next trip it will be my gift to you," Yuan said. He picked up a burlap bag and slid it into the cargo hold as the other men started cinching the boxes onto the animals.

When the belly of the plane was filled Albert secured the cargo door, then turned toward his friend who was holding the reins of his loaded horse.

"Don't put yourself at risk for that tiger skin," Albert said as they shook hands.

"Life is full of risks. I will be cautious," Yuan said with a smile. "I will see you next trip."

Albert gave him a wave and stepped up into the plane.

He started the engine and taxied slowly for a few feet, then accelerated, leaving a lingering trail of dust hanging in the air. As soon as the craft became airborne he pushed the throttle all the way forward and pulled into a steep climb. He brought it up out of the clearing and leveled off a couple hundred feet above the trees, then relaxed back into the seat and pushed a cassette into the tape player mounted below the instrumentation panel. A moment later he started singing the blues with B. B. King as he piloted the aircraft in the narrow band between the tree tops and the radar threshold.

Albert had been in the air for about twenty minutes when he was startled by the sudden appearance of a strange light formation off the port wing. He watched in astonishment as orbs of red light danced along the end of the wing in irregular movements. Except for occasional glances at the altimeter and compass he kept his eyes fixed on the glowing spheres, trying to gain insight into the phenomenon. He dipped the wing twice, and both times the lights held their position. After a few minutes the lights grew dim and faded away, leaving a slight afterglow. He scanned his field of view from the side window, and then turned to look out the other window. He flinched and cried out at the sight of a passenger in the seat next to him. "What the fuck! Where the hell did you come from?"

"Back there," Kim said placidly as he gestured toward the back of the plane. "You have a very pleasant singing voice."

"Don't try to be funny, asshole. What the hell are you doing on this plane?" Albert demanded.

"I guess you could call me a stowaway. I needed a ride. I'll make it worth your while," Kim said with a smile.

"How the hell did you get on board?"

"Oh, you and your friends were distracted for a couple minutes."

Albert recoiled violently as Kim's head metamorphosed into that of a tiger.

"Neat trick, huh," Kim said through his tiger mouth. "Those lights out there at the end of the wing were my handiwork, too," he said as he changed back. "I had to distract you so I could come up here and get comfortable. Now here's the deal. You can help me get to the United States, or you can try to throw me out of the plane, just like you were thinking," he said as he raised his hands in front of him, palms facing. "If you try to kill me, you'll die, and I'll learn to fly this plane," he said as an electrical discharge jumped between his hands. "I know all about you and this smuggling ring. You fly guns from the United States to a little island off the Chinese coast using a small jet, and then transfer the cargo to this plane for the trip inland. The guns are traded to the Tibetan resistance for heroine, which makes the return trip to the United States. I know how big the operation is, and I know how many operatives are smuggling contraband in and out of China. I don't care about all that. It's of the utmost importance that I get to the United States. You will be compensated for your help."

"How?" Albert asked in a shaky voice.

"I know about the high stakes poker game played on the island. It never ends. The players change as the air traffic ebbs and flows, but there's always somebody at that table. That's where you'll find your reward." He winked at Albert as his body shimmered, then disassociated and dispersed like a cloud of vapor.

"Oh, Jesus," Albert cried as he cowered away. "I'm going fuckin' loony tunes."

"No you're not," Kim said with a laugh as he made his way from the back of the plane and climbed up into the passenger seat.

"What the hell's going on?" Albert asked in a confused tone.

"That was my other body. It's something like an illusion. This is the real me."

"You gonna change again?" Albert whined.

"No, I can only shape shift in my other body, but I can still read your thoughts and do the electricity thing," Kim said with a smile. "So, are you going to help me?"

"Do I have a choice?" Albert asked.

"No, not really. You can get me to the United States and be rewarded, or I can go as you."

"I'm a dead man if anything goes wrong."

"Believe me, the fate that awaits mankind if I don't get to the United States is far worse than anything your employers could dream up for you."

Steve leaned forward on the bench and watched as Luther peeled an apple with surprising dexterity. His steady hand guided the blade with surgical precision as it separated the skin from the fruit and left it dangling in a thin spiraling strip. "I've never seen Ralph mad before," Steve said absently as he watched the strip of peel sway in the breeze. "Guess everybody's got a boiling point, I just never expected to see him like that."

"Ralph got a lotta bottled up rage inside, just like some black folks," Luther said without looking up from the apple. "He need to let it go, but he can't. Hope he made it home okay."

"I still can't believe that asshole Rudy had the balls to do it," Steve said as he pulled a bandanna out of his back pocket and wiped the sweat from his forehead. "You know, either one of us could be next. I mean, it could happen the same damn way. Who knows, maybe it already has and we just don't know it yet."

"I'd miss you an' the others, but it'd be a blessin' to get away from him."

"I know. Sometimes I just want to tell him to get fucked."

"Best thing you can do is stay outa his way," Luther said as he cut a slice from the fruit and handed it to Steve.

Steve heard the familiar throaty sound of Joyce downshifting her Porsche as he took a bite of the apple slice. A moment later the sports car turned off the street and started up the drive.

"I've got to talk to her," Steve said as he stood up and shoved the rest of the apple slice into his mouth. "She needs to know what happened this morning."

As he walked across the lawn toward her parking spot he caught himself thinking about her legs instead of the news he had to share. Between her new teaching position and discovery of the artifact he hadn't seen much of her the last few days and he was feeling a little tense, not that sex was the only thing he missed. Things just felt wrong when he knew he couldn't go to her office or the lab and share a funny story or simply say hi. He wondered if that was a sign he was letting himself get too close.

Joyce turned into her parking place and shut off the engine as Steve walked over and stopped at the edge of the blacktop. "Morning, Steve," she said as she opened the car door.

"Hi, sweetie," he said as he watched her climb out of the Porsche. The fleeting glimpse of her black garter belt and panties left his manhood twitching.

"Is the artifact here yet?" she asked eagerly.

"No deliveries, just those guys from the door company working in the lab."

"That probably makes Sam happy," Joyce said as she closed the car door.

"If he's happy it's because he doesn't know what happened this morning,"

Steve said as he leaned against the Porsche.

"What are you talking about?" Joyce asked.

Steve hesitated. He didn't want to be the bearer of bad news; he wanted to make love to her. There was just no way to breach both subjects in the same conversation.

"Rudy gave Ralph and Terry two week notices today," Steve said grimly.

"Layoff notices?" Joyce asked in a shocked voice.

"Yeah," Steve said as he pushed himself away from the car. "That fat fuck is bringing in Pinkerton rent a bodies to replace them."

"That bastard. Does Sam know about this?"

Steve shrugged his shoulders. "Luther and I have been laying low ever since we talked to Ralph. We figure we might be next."

"God, this is going to be a stressful day. You and I better schedule an attitude adjustment after work. I hope you're free," she said as she stepped away from the car and walked toward the museum.

"I'll check my calendar," Steve said with a laugh as he watched her body move under the silky dress.

Samuel was sitting at his desk studying pictures in an archaeological reference book when Joyce walked into the office. "Morning, Sam," she said as she pulled the chair out from her desk and sat down.

"Morning," he said loudly without looking up from the book.

"What are you yelling about?" she asked.

"Sorry about that," he said in a more subdued voice as he pulled cotton out of his ears and threw it into the trash. "It was pretty noisy when they were in the lab cutting the door frame out of the wall. I thought you were staying at school until this afternoon."

"I couldn't concentrate, something like opening night jitters, I guess. I was hoping the artifact would be here already."

"I was just looking through a reference book on unique archaeological discoveries of this century. A lot of interesting stuff, but nothing like you found," he said as he scooped his pipe down into the pouch of tobacco. "Judging from the book, we need to do a lot of photographic documentation," he said, and then chuckled. "I think I've got a slight case of jitters myself."

She watched Samuel light his pipe and wondered how she was going to keep a lid on things when he found out about Ralph and Terry. She knew he would be furious.

"We need to talk," Joyce said as she watched a small plume of smoke drift toward the ceiling.

"About the artifact?"

"No, about Ralph and Terry. They have a problem," Joyce said.

"What kind of problem?" Samuel asked as he leaned forward in his chair.

"Steve said Rudy gave them both a two week notice this morning. He's bringing in Pinkerton security to replace them."

"That son of a bitch!" Samuel snarled as he banged his pipe down in the ashtray. "That bastard isn't going to get away with this," he shrieked as he leaped to his feet and started toward the door.

Joyce vaulted out of her chair and put herself in front of him. "Sam, there's nothing you can do about it," she said as she put her hands on his shoulders. "As unsettling as it is, Rudy has the authority to make those kind of decisions. If you go charging up there and rip into him you'll be giving him exactly what he wants. All we can do now is help Ralph and Terry find new jobs," she said as her phone rang. "I can't answer that unless you sit down." For a moment she wasn't sure what was going to happen. She knew she could never hold him if he was determined to get past her. The phone rang twice more before Samuel returned to his desk. Joyce kept her eyes on him as she picked up the phone.

"Hello," she said as she put the receiver to her ear.

"Joyce, this is Mark. I just wanted to touch base with you. There's going to be a delay in getting the artifact delivered."

"A delay? What's the problem? I expected it this morning," Joyce said with disappointment in her voice.

"I'm sorry. I expected to have it delivered by now, but there's been complications," he said apologetically.

"Complications with the artifact?" she asked.

"No, complications with my crew. One of the guys I had working the project is missing. It's not like him to walk away from a job site without telling somebody. His girlfriend doesn't know where he is either. I just don't understand. Some of my power tools are gone, too. And you should see what's left of the power cord. It's...it's not your problem. Listen, I'll deliver the artifact to the museum no later than noon tomorrow. Okay?"

"I'm holding you to it. Hope you find your guy."

"Thanks for understanding. See you tomorrow."

"Tomorrow," Joyce said and hung up the phone.

"This is my fault," Samuel said as he shook his head. "I backed that son of a bitch into a corner and got my way with the lab doors and he repaid me by doing this. I bet Ralph is real happy with the way I got him off third shift."

"Sam, you can't blame yourself. Rudy is a shameless bastard who did this of his own volition. You may have pissed him off, but you certainly didn't force him to react this way. I think Ralph and Terry know who to blame."

"I hope so," Samuel said as he picked up his pipe and dumped the partially burned tobacco into the ashtray. "Do you have any Tums?"

Joyce took a roll of generic antacid tablets out of her desk drawer and threw them to Samuel.

"What's going on with your artifact?" he asked as he peeled back the roll and removed two tablets.

"There's been a delay. One of the men Mark had working on the project is missing. He promised to have it here tomorrow by noon."

"I'm disappointed, but probably not like you are," Samuel said as he threw the tablets into his mouth.

"Oh, I'll live. It's just that this is my first shot at something as big as the first Egyptian tomb you discovered. I'm sure you remember what that was like," Joyce said.

"Yeah, I do," Samuel said with a smile. "We discovered the entrance late in the day and had to wait until morning to open it up. I didn't sleep a wink. I was like a little boy waiting for Christmas morning to come."

They were both surprised when the door to the lab opened and Bill Bruster stuck his head in.

"Sam, can I see you for a minute?" Bill asked.

"Sure, come on in," Samuel said as he stood up.

"Sorry to disturb you," Bill said as he stepped into the office.

"No problem. Bill, I don't think you've met my assistant, Joyce Robbins. Joyce, this is Bill Bruster from Atlas Security Doors."

"Glad to meet you, Bill," Joyce said as she stood up and shook his hand.

"The pleasure's mine," Bill said with a big smile, then turned his attention back to Samuel. "Sam, we've got a little problem. We thought we had the door you needed in St. Louis, but it was a computer input error. We've got to build one, and that's going to cause a delay of about a week," he said.

"What about the hole in my wall?" Samuel asked.

"We can cover the opening with a sheet of plastic to keep out the weather, but you won't be able to go in and out."

"You need to do something temporary just for tonight. We've got a delivery tomorrow about noon that has to come in that way. After that you can seal it up until the doors are ready," Samuel responded.

"Okay. We'll do something quick tonight. We'll come back tomorrow afternoon. I apologize for the delay," Bill said.

"Things happen," Samuel said as he shrugged his shoulders. "We'll have to deal with it."

"Thanks, Sam. I'll get my crew back here to close up the doorway. See you later. Nice meeting you, Joyce."

"You too, Bill," Joyce said as he left the office.

Samuel sat back in his chair and let out a weary sigh.

"There hasn't been much good news yet today," he said.

"I know," Joyce said. "Steve and I are stopping after work for an attitude adjustment. You can join us if you want."

"I might do that," Samuel said somberly.

Ralph sat at his kitchen table and stared at the nickel-plated Colt automatic laying in front of him in its mahogany presentation case. The Marines called it a special duty service award, but he knew it was nothing more than a tool to be used if the nightmares became unbearable. Next to the gun was an open box of ammunition and a half empty bottle of Jack Daniels.

The nightmares had definitely become unbearable. What was once a hellish vision of winged creatures dropping out of the sky had evolved into a study of anguish and torment. A dream that could conjure up the pain and suffering of being eaten alive was, at one time, unimaginable, but no longer. Now the nightmares were replete with the agony of talons shredding his flesh and jaws ripping chunks of meat from his body.

Now he was losing his job. He never missed a single day of work and always followed Rudy's instructions, no matter how much he despised him. He was being fired and Rudy expected him to believe it was nothing more than costs driving the change to Pinkerton. Regardless of what Rudy thought, he wasn't stupid. He knew all about the fight he and Sam had over the doors in the lab. Bringing Pinkerton in to take over the security function was simply Rudy's way of striking back.

Between the nightmares and being fired, his life, or what was left of it, was crumbling down around him. There was nothing left except the nightmares, the whiskey and the black pit of depression from which he couldn't escape. There was no savings to fall back on, he was too old to find another job, he was still three years away from collecting Social Security and the unemployment benefits he could draw were shamefully meager.

It seemed there was only one thing left to do, he thought as he picked up the gun and rolled it over in his hands. He released the clip from the handle and laid the gun on the table as he gazed at the box of ammunition. The bullets looked like a platoon of tiny soldiers standing at attention, awaiting orders. One of them would end his nightmares forever.

He took a bullet out of the box, kissed the tip of the steel jacketed slug and loaded it into the clip. He wondered if he'd taste gunpowder in his last instant of awareness. His hands trembled as he picked up the bottle of whiskey and took one final swig before picking up the gun and loading the clip into the handle. "God forgive me," he whispered as he pulled back the slide on the Colt and chambered the round. He bowed his head and put the barrel of the gun in his mouth. In his heart he knew God understood. He put his finger on the trigger and...hesitated.

Not yet, he thought as he took the gun out of his mouth and laid it on the table. He had to write a letter to the Washington Post. A letter that would explain the horrible torment he'd suffered because of the drug experiment. They couldn't prosecute him for writing about classified information when he was dead. On the heels of that assessment came another, more murderous thought. They couldn't charge a dead man with homicide either.

He ejected the live round from the automatic and released the clip from the handle as he made room in his thoughts for Rudy VanBurg. First one in, last one out, he thought as he picked up his bullet and reloaded it into the magazine. He continued to load rounds into the clip as he played out in his mind the way it would end.

In the clip just ahead of the bullet that would end his own life was the one that would blow Rudy's head apart like an over ripe watermelon, but he wouldn't rush. There were five rounds in the clip before that one. Five rounds for five body parts. Rudy's death would come only after an acceptable level of suffering. He would beg for an end to the pain.

As he stood up to get a pen and paper he wondered how long it would take him to compose a rational letter. He knew it might take several days, but it didn't matter. When the editor of the Washington Post read it his nightmare would be over, the Marines' drug experiment would be exposed, and Rudy would be dead. It all gave him a sense of justice.

The poker room was nothing more than an old storeroom appropriated by the smugglers. The table was a round piece of plywood bolted to the top of a barrel and covered with an army blanket. Seven folding chairs sat around the table with more positioned atop empty shipping crates for spectators or waiting players.

Kim sat in the elevated chairs with two other onlookers watching the table. After six hours the game was down to four players: Albert, Bill "Crabby" Higgins, John "Iceman" Washakie, and Tony "Skiver" Masterson.

Bill Higgins, sitting to Albert's right, was an old Navy man with saltwater in his veins and tattoos covering both forearms. Except for his eyebrows the only hair on his head was a bushy, unkempt gray beard. Bill was notorious for frequenting prostitutes and earned the nickname "Crabby" after a particularly voracious and defiant family of crabs set up housekeeping in his beard.

John Washakie, sitting on Albert's left, was a full-blooded Iroquois. His steady, unshakable concentration and peerless hand-to-hand combat skills won the respect and admiration of his fellow Green Beret, who nicknamed him "Iceman." It was a name that also suited him well as a poker player.

Tony Masterson, sitting across the table from Albert, was the youngest and smallest of the group. He was the one that everybody watched cautiously. He grew up on the streets of Harlem and learned early in life to compensate for his small stature with a knife, earning the nickname "Skiver". He was considered by most to be dangerously unpredictable.

Most of the money had slowly migrated to Albert's side of the table. Three players had gone belly up, Crabby had managed to hold his losses to a few hundred dollars, Iceman had played a nearly flawless game and had maintained a strong bank, and Skiver had been on the verge of financial collapse for an hour.

Albert watched Skiver closely as he shuffled the cards. He was down several thousand dollars and just about stupid enough to try a crooked deal. If Iceman caught him stacking the deck there would be the kind of serious trouble Albert preferred to avoid.

"Ante twenty dollars for seven card stud," Skiver announced as he threw a twenty out into the middle of the table, and then offered a cut. Iceman threw his money into the pot and declined the cut as the others anted up. Skiver started dealing. One card down, a second card down, then a six of spades to Crabby, ten of diamonds to Albert, queen of diamonds to Iceman, and finally a seven of clubs to himself.

Albert checked his hole cards and found a pair of kings. He didn't need any help playing the concealed royalty, but Kim was in his thoughts just the same. The telepathic advice was always simple and clear, telling him to fold, bet, or raise. The message this time was bet.

"Forty on the queen," Iceman said as he threw a hundred dollar bill out into the center of the table and pulled three twenties back out.

Skiver glanced at his hole cards again, and then looked at the dwindling stack of money in front of him.

"Call," he said as he tossed a pair of twenties into the pot.

"It's just plain fuckin' stupid, but I gotta buy one more card," Crabby said as he called the bet.

"Pot's right," Albert said as he threw his money into the center of the table.

Skiver dealt the cards. The five of hearts went to Crabby, king of hearts to Albert, ten of hearts to Iceman, and seven of diamonds to the dealer.

"Fifty on the pair of sevens," Skiver said with a grin.

Crabby shook his head as he folded his cards.

Albert wanted to build Skiver's confidence in his pair of sevens, but Kim was in his head telling him to raise.

"Make it a hundred," he said as he threw a single bill into the pot.

"You must be proud of those kings," Iceman said quietly as he called the bet.

Skiver grumbled and threw another fifty into the pot just as the door opened and a stocky man with black hair stepped into the room carrying a rosewood cane with a brass lion head grip the size of a baseball.

"Rocko! How's it hangin'?" Crabby asked with a grin.

"Down to about my knees," Rocko said with a laugh as he walked up to the table and pulled out the chair between Skiver and Crabby. "Got something for you, Skiver," Rocko said as he handed him the cane. "It has a spring loaded blade in the tip. The lion's lower jaw is the trigger. Deal me in next hand," he said as he sat down.

Skiver held the cane up in front of him and admired the workmanship, then pointed it toward the floor and squeezed the trigger. With a flash of polished steel an eighteen-inch stiletto blade shot from the end of the walking stick and locked into place.

"Holy shit!" Skiver squealed.

"Quit playing with that fuckin' toad sticker and deal the cards," Iceman demanded.

"Didn't your daddy ever teach you not to be rude to a man with a knife?" Skiver asked as he pulled the trigger again and retracted the blade back into the tip of the cane.

"Nope, he only taught me how to take knives from fools that wave them around," Iceman said coldly.

"Maybe someday I'll put you to the test," Skiver said arrogantly.

"I'll be ready," Iceman replied quietly.

"Come on, Skiver, deal. We're not here to test anybody's manhood," Crabby said gruffly.

Skiver laid the cane on the floor next to his chair and started dealing again. The nine of hearts went to Albert, the two of spades went to Iceman, and the dealer received the queen of hearts.

"Same bet," Skiver said as he threw a pair of twenties into the pot.

Years of experience at a poker table told Albert he had the best hand and was supposed to raise. He could cripple Skiver and probably put him out of the game, but Kim was in his head telling him to fold his cards. The longer he deliberated the more intense the message became. His skull felt like it was about to explode when he finally succumbed to Kim's demand and folded his hand.

"Deal me out next hand. I gotta piss and get something to drink," he said as he pushed himself away from the table. As he stood up he looked at Kim and gestured toward the door, then walked out of the room.

Kim watched the hand play out, then jumped down from his perch and walked out the door. Albert was outside leaning against the pop machine, drinking from a can of Pepsi.

"What the hell's wrong with you?" Albert asked in a low voice. "I could have won that hand and put that little cocksucker out of the game."

"I don't want him out of the game yet," Kim said as he put his hand on the side of the pop machine. A second later the machine made a strange groaning noise and a can of Pepsi rolled out into the delivery tray.

"Why are you protecting him? You've seen him in action. He's a little prick!"

"I'm not protecting him," Kim said as he picked up the can of Pepsi and popped the tab. "I want that cane of his."

"What the hell do you want with that?" Albert asked.

"I'm doing all I can to protect a couple friends that are going to be in extreme danger. Skiver won the last hand and he's winning this one. He thinks he's making a comeback. You get him to put up the cane to cover a short bet, I'll do everything else."

"What if he folds instead of covering his short bet?"

"He won't," Kim said with certainty as they moved toward the door.

"I hope this doesn't take long, it's getting late."

"Just one more hand," Kim said.

Iceman had just finished shuffling the cards when Albert and Kim walked back into the room.

"You lost your deal, and you almost missed the hand. Ante twenty for seven card stud," Iceman said.

Albert took a twenty from his stack and threw it into the kitty as he sat down.

After the fifth card Iceman and Crabby both folded. After the sixth card Skiver held four jacks, two of them in the hole, Rocko had a pair of queens showing, and Albert held four diamonds with a gut shot to hit a straight flush.

"Pair of jacks bet five hundred dollars," Skiver announced as he threw five one hundred bills onto the pile of money in the center of the table.

"Too rich for my blood," Rocko said as he turned over his cards.

"Call," Albert said as he made the pot right.

"Last card down and dirty," Iceman said as he took the top card off the deck and slid it in front of Skiver, face down. He did the same for Albert.

"Same bet," Skiver said as he threw his money into the pot without looking at his last hole card.

Albert looked at the last hole card and found his gut shot, much to his expectation. He picked up a handful of hundreds and threw five into the pot.

"There's your five and I'll bump it two thousand," Albert said as he spread more hundred-dollar bills across the top of the pile of money.

"You son of a bitch," Skiver growled. "You're trying to buy the fucking pot. Rocko, loan me six hundred dollars. I'll pay you right back."

"Can't do it Skiver. Only a fool loans money during a poker game," Rocko replied.

Skiver looked at Crabby, then Iceman and got negative gestures.

"Tell you what I'll do, Skiver. I'll let you cover your bet with that toad sticker Rocko just gave you," Albert said.

A triumphant grin spread across Skiver's face as he reached down beside his chair and picked up the walking stick.

"Call," he said defiantly as he laid the cane on the table beside the pile of money. He turned his first two hole cards over, not bothering with the last one. "Four jacks," he said with a wide grin.

"Ten high straight flush," Albert said as he turned over his cards.

"You motherfucker!" Skiver screamed as he grabbed for the walking stick.

Iceman caught his hand and slammed it down on the table.

"You lost, Skiver. The pot, including that toad sticker goes to Albert."

"Fuck you, Washakie!"

In a blur of movement Iceman let go of Skiver's hand and cracked him across the forehead with a back fist that sent Skiver sprawling to the floor.

"No, fuck you. And it's Iceman, or Mister Washakie to you, prick."

Skiver was out cold and never heard Iceman's rebuke.

CHAPTER EIGHT

Ralph paced nervously between the desk and the display case while he waited for Sam to return as he'd promised just minutes before. He came in, waved as he started down the steps and said he'd be back to talk, and that made him uneasy. He knew the conversation was going to be more than a little painful. They'd talk about Rudy's deception and plans for a job search, while he maintained the facade of normality, concealing his deadly plans for revenge and suicide. Knowing he could have no last good-bye with his friend hurt more than anything else, but it was the way it had to be. He didn't want any interference and he didn't want anyone else getting hurt. Ralph stopped pacing and dropped into his chair as he heard Samuel coming up the steps.

He came around the display case, took the chair on the other side of the desk and gave Ralph a troubled look. "I'm sorry, Ralph. I didn't find out about what happened until after you'd already gone home."

"Sam, there's no reason for you to be sorry. Yeah, Rudy did a real screw job on me, but it wasn't your fault. He said he was driven by your concern for my health, but I'm not stupid. I know he was trying to get to you. He's probably waiting for you to bust into his office screaming. Don't do it. Someday he'll get what he's got coming."

"Joyce and I are going to do everything we can to find you and Terry new jobs."

"Sam, I want you and Joyce to help Terry, but there's not much you can do for me. Take a good look. Nobody's going to hire me. My nerves are shot, I can't sleep, and I look like death warmed over. Hell, I wouldn't hire me. I think my life has pretty much run its course," he said as tears of despair welled up in his eyes.

"Ralph, you need to get some help. You've let this thing with the nightmares go on way too long."

"We haven't talked about them for awhile. They've gotten a lot worse. I think my time's up."

"There's always time to get help. You can't give in to it. Let me make you an appointment with somebody."

"We've been over this ground before. If these were ordinary nightmares a doctor might help, but we both know that's not the case. The Marines fucked my brain up with those drugs, and all the psychological counseling in the world won't help."

Samuel was ready to press the issue further when Steve pushed open the door and came running into the lobby.

"Sam! There's a flatbed truck out front loaded with a huge wooden crate. It must be Joyce's artifact."

"Back in a minute, Ralph," Samuel said as he raised himself out of the chair and moved around the end of the display case to join Steve. They both walked outside and found the truck coming slowly up the drive.

"My God," Samuel muttered when he saw the crate. Fettered to the flatbed behind it was a forklift that looked too small for the job. Following the truck up the drive was a pickup with two men in the front and two others in the back.

The air brakes hissed as the truck came to a stop at the crest of the hill in front of Samuel. The passenger door opened and Mark climbed down out of the cab.

"Samuel," he said as he extended his hand. "Good to see you again."

"Hello, Mark," Samuel said with a smile as they shook hands. "Joyce told me about the artifact, but I had no idea it was so big."

"Sam, I've seen it," Mark said as he looked back at the load. "It gives me the willies. I'm glad to get rid of it."

"How heavy is it?" Steve asked as he walked back for a closer look at the box.

"We figure about eight thousand pounds," Mark said as he pulled a handkerchief out of his pocket and wiped sweat from his brow. "Joyce didn't ask for wheels, but I figured you might not want to keep it in one place forever, so we built a dolly to go under it. We'll attach it to the stand when we set it up."

"Good thinking. Eight thousand pounds and no wheels would have been a definite problem," Samuel said with a laugh as he slapped Mark on the back.

"Well, where's it going?" Mark asked as he took a pair of leather gloves out of his back pocket.

"Go around the back. At the bottom of the hill on the other side of the building you'll find a wide doorway that goes into the lab. Steve, how about tearing down that sheet of plastic and getting it out of the way."

"Okay," Steve said and took another look at the box as he walked past.

Mark climbed up on the side of the truck and opened the door. "Pull it around back and give us plenty of room to work." He closed the door and jumped back down to the pavement. "We'll have it in the lab in about half an hour, Sam."

"Okay. See you inside," Samuel said as he turned and walked back to the museum. He opened the door and moved into the lobby wondering if there was any way to get through to Ralph.

When he got back to the security station Ralph was bent over holding his head with both hands. "Ralph, what's wrong? Are you okay?" he asked as he walked around the end of the display case.

Ralph raised his head and looked at Samuel with a dazed expression. "I was sitting here, waiting for you to come back, and it...it was like somebody changed television stations. I flashed into the nightmare, then flashed back."

"You probably fell asleep without realizing it," Samuel said as he returned to his chair. "You could have been behind the wheel of your car, you know. How would you feel if that happened and you killed somebody?"

"Sam, I didn't fall asleep."

"Ralph, whether you did or not really isn't the point. You need to be under the care of a doctor. If nothing else he could get you on some drugs to help you sleep. Please, let me put you in touch with somebody. Why are you so afraid of dealing with this thing?"

"Sam, maybe I'm dying," Ralph said in little more than a whisper. "I don't want to spend my last days tied to a bed in the hospital nut ward."

After a long, awkward moment Samuel raised himself out of the chair. "Ralph, we've been friends for a long time. I wish to God you'd let me help you, but I can't force it on you. If you need anything, anything at all, you know where I am," he said and walked out of the security station. When he got to the top of the steps he looked back at Ralph. Sitting there with his shoulders slumped and head dropped he seemed to be broken, both physically and spiritually. He was afraid Ralph was right about his approaching death, and that left him frustrated and angry because there was apparently no way to stop it.

He started down the steps and thought about the way Rudy had twisted the motive for his handiwork. He wondered if Terry was smart enough to see through his ruse. Deceit masquerading as concern was often successful, and Rudy was a master at that type of game.

When he got to the bottom of the steps he heard his phone ringing. He trotted around a display case and across the room to his office.

"Hello," he said as he put the phone to his ear.

"Hi, sweetheart," Martha said.

"Hi, honey," Samuel said with a smile. "Taking a break, or haven't started yet?"

"I'll have you know I was at the typewriter before my first cup of coffee was finished. I took a break to see if you were free for lunch," she said.

"I'll make time," Samuel replied cheerfully.

"If you're busy we can have lunch tomorrow, or something."

"Today is probably best. They're delivering Joyce's artifact right now, and I may be up to my elbows in work tomorrow."

"Will I be able to see it while I'm there?" Martha asked eagerly.

"I guess that depends on how long it takes Steve to disassemble the shipping crate. We could plan a late lunch, say twelve-thirty. He should be finished when we return. How's that sound?"

"It works for me," Martha said. "I'll see you then. Love you."

"Love you, too," Samuel responded and broke the connection while still holding the receiver. He pulled the chair out from his desk and sat down as he started making a call. The phone rang twice and was answered.

"Good morning, Atlas Security Doors," a pleasant female voice said.

"Could I speak with Bill Bruster, please?"

"One moment, sir," the girl said and put the call on hold.

Samuel cradled the receiver on his shoulder as he took his pipe and tobacco pouch out of his jacket pocket. He started filling his pipe as he tried to remember exactly what Joyce had told him about the artifact. His mind unexpectedly spewed forth a single perplexing image of a rocking chair with its rockers driven into the ground like stakes. He wondered if the old man was having hallucinations before he died.

"Hello, this is Bill Bruster."

"Bill, this is Samuel Prince from the museum. The delivery we were waiting for is being moved into the lab right now. You can reseal the doorway this afternoon."

"Okay, Sam. I'll get a man over there right after lunch. I spoke with St. Louis this morning. Your doors should arrive here by the end of next week. I apologize again for the delay."

"It's no big deal, Bill," Samuel said reassuringly.

"Thanks for understanding. See you in a week or so."

"See you then," Samuel said and hung up the phone.

He leaned back in his chair and lit his pipe as his mind went back to what Joyce had told him about the artifact. She said it was an enormous crystal framed with logs that had been carved into totems. Petrified logs. Suddenly his mind was aflame with a paradox so absurd that it defied any measure of logic. Given the normal reaction time for agatization, carvings on petrified logs would predate primitive man by millions of years. Modern tools in the hands of the right sculptor could chisel petrified wood or stone easily, but the process exhibited distinct characteristics. It might be easy for a layman to confuse the two methods, but not a professional, and that was the rub. Joyce was a professional whom he held in the highest regard. He found it extremely difficult to believe that she made an incorrect assessment of the artifact. If the petrified logs proved to be carved it was going to upset the archaeological apple cart.

He doodled aimlessly as his mind continued to grapple with the problem. There had to be a reasonable solution to what seemed to be a scientific bogeyman. The logical answer was that Joyce had made a mistake, yet every nerve in his body was fighting against that judgment.

After filling a complete page with intricate doodling he finally gave up with no probable resolution to the riddle. Only his own examination would sort out things. Either Joyce was wrong, or the scientific community was about to be knocked for a loop.

Kim looked out the side window of the Lear jet and saw nothing but blue ocean to the horizon. Hawaii might have been visible if they were still at thirty thousand feet, but Albert had the plane below the radar threshold for the approach to the refueling station on Necker Island. He was glad the eleven-hour trip was almost over. The flight was a grueling combination of boredom and stress, even for him. He was surprised that Albert's body was still standing up to the punishment of the weekly trips.

Necker Island was nothing but a forty-acre dot in the middle of the Pacific with a runway, fuel depot, and underground living quarters. It was one of several forgotten islands that were still considered part of the Hawaiian chain on some maps. It was small, out of the way, and on a nearly direct route between the United States and China, making it an ideal way station for the smugglers. For Albert the island meant a hot shower, warm food, and a few hours sleep. For Kim it was simply a mile marker putting him one step closer to Joyce, Randy, and the nightmarish confrontation for which he had been prepared.

Kim's eyes scanned the rippling waves moving across the water as his mind drifted back to what he remembered as the great upheaval in his life.

He tried to forget his encounter with the old blind Indian and continue business as usual, but it was impossible. He found his precognitive vision blurred and concentration broken, but the most devastating blow to his lifestyle was the sudden return of an inner wisdom and prescience that began fading from his life the day Joyce left. It was as if he had abruptly awakened to find himself surrounded by a depraved world of greed and self-indulgence. After a few days of spiritual introspection and contemplation he called the number that was now burned into the side of the pencil. The phone was answered by a voice that reverberated in the depths of his soul.

"I have been awaiting your call. You must travel into the Tehachapi Mountains of southern California and seek me out. Use your inner vision to find the path upon which I have cast the light."

The connection terminated before Kim could say a word, but the voice had filled his being with a wondrous joy and harmony, which he had never before experienced. It was as if the vessel of his spirit was suddenly overflowing with the spiritual essence of the universe.

The next morning he drove away in his yellow MG, abandoning a life devoid of inner light and embarking on a path of spiritual healing. He departed Nevada leaving behind a house, Mercedes, sailboat, and thousands of dollars in cash and bank accounts.

It was early afternoon before he got into the Tehachapi Mountains. After wandering for a couple hours he found a small-unmarked road that branched off from route sixty-six. To his innate senses it was as if gleaming jewels had been scattered along the way. The crumbling secondary road wound upward into the mountains and slowly degraded into a stone trail, and finally into a path too narrow to drive. He got out of the car and began walking the footpath as it ascended into the rocky terrain.

He followed the path upward as it cut through sparse stands of pine trees and around outcroppings of rock, driven by the need to hear that voice again. His heart longed to connect with the energy he felt come through the phone and to know more of the overpowering joy. He would find the way, and it no longer mattered how far, difficult or dangerous the pilgrimage.

The daylight was beginning to fade when he stopped to rest next to a lone pine tree. He wanted to continue, but he was exhausted from the climb, his hands were cut and bleeding, and hunger pangs spoke of an ill planned journey. He sat near the edge of a cliff and wrapped a handkerchief around his hand as he looked out at the surrounding mountain peaks. A cool wind cut through his sweatshirt and reminded him that his jacket was in the car hundreds of feet below. He huddled against the wind and wondered if he was going to die on the mountain because of his own stupidity. Better to die on the mountain seeking spiritual truth than to live a life of debauchery, he thought as his body began shivering. He scooted back away from the edge of the rock, leaned against the tree, and drifted off into a deep dreamless sleep.

The next morning he found himself inside a cave on a bed of pine needles with his jacket covering his upper body. He sat up and looked around, unsure of his surroundings. Outside the mouth of the cave he saw the tree against which he had fallen asleep.

"You're awake," someone said from behind him.

The sound of the voice charged Kim's inner being with spiritual energy as he turned and saw a small man with dark, weathered skin and long white hair.

"It was your voice on the phone," Kim said as he tried to stand.

"Sit, you are still weak. You did not plan your trip very well. I went back to the car and got your jacket. I hope it kept you warm during the night. If you forget the needs of the physical body your search for spiritual truth will be short," the old man said with a gentle laugh. He stepped forward with a burlap bag and lowered himself down onto the pine bed. He crossed his legs as he took a small apple from the bag and handed it to him. "We must rebuild your strength before we can do anything else."

Kim took the fruit and started eating ravenously. "Who are you? Why have you brought me here?" he asked between bites.

"Hsuan Hsueh is my spiritual name. You may call me Teacher for now," he said as he pulled a banana from the bag. "When we leave this mountain we will begin a journey to our spiritual home within the circle of Yu Wu. Before we depart you must remember who you are," he said as he started peeling the fruit.

"I don't understand," Kim said as he held the apple core in his hand and looked around the cave for a place to put it.

"Of course you do not understand. If you did there would be no need for a teacher," he said as he took the remains of the apple and threw it out the cave entrance. "To be one with nature we must share our bounty. That which is refuse to us is a banquet to another. That which we shed at our death must be returned to the earth. Western man has so many things backwards. They wrap their garbage in plastic bags and seal the bodies of the dead in concrete tombs. How utterly self-indulgent," he said as he took an orange out of the burlap bag and handed it to Kim.

"But I know who I am," Kim said as he started tearing the rind from the orange. "It was a hard climb, but I didn't fall and knock myself unconscious."

"Life knocked you unconscious a long time ago. You only think you know who you are," he said as he picked up a pine needle and held it out in front of him. "The pine needle lives, dies, and returns to the earth, just as you do. The end of one cycle is but the beginning of another. This is a truth for all things. Daylight fades into twilight so that the darkness may give birth to the dawn."

"You speak as though you intend to obscure the meaning of your words. It's very confusing," Kim said as he split off a section of the orange and put it in his mouth. "You answer my questions with vague concepts that raise more questions. I don't even understand why you fill my inner being with such wondrous energy."

"You must not be impatient. Learn to look within yourself for the answers you seek. It would be a travesty to teach spiritual truth without the wisdom and intuition that comes from walking the path of knowledge," he said as he again held the pine needle out in front of him. "You must focus your mind upon the needle. It is to the pine tree as you are to that which you seek to remember." He studied Kim's face for a moment, and then smiled. "To struggle with it is to turn your feet to clay. We will remain here for as long as it takes to rebuild your strength and recover your memory," he said as he raised himself to his feet. "Finish eating the fruit in the bag while you rest. I am returning to your car to cover it with brush."

"Why are you doing that?" Kim asked as he looked into the bag.

"It is only a matter of time before you remember your true identity," the old man said as he walked toward the mouth of the cave. He stopped at the entrance and looked back at Kim. "When we leave the mountain your car will get us to the west coast where a freighter awaits. Our plan would be somewhat compromised if thieves made off with the vehicle."

"A freighter awaits? How can...I mean we don't...we don't know how long..." Kim stammered.

Hsuan Hsueh slapped his hand on the wall of the cave and cackled with laughter. "You are quite funny when faced with something inexplicable," he said after a moment. There is an electrical problem aboard the ship that is stopping it from leaving. It will leave for China when we are ready. Finish the fruit and focus your mind on the pine tree, not our transport," he said with a chuckle as he left the cave.

Kim spent six days on the mount with Hsuan Hsueh. The mornings were spent walking the mountain trails, observing nature and talking about the part man played in the natural world. In the afternoons they discussed the principles of meditation, mind expansion and the proper use of certain psychoactive plants. They spent the evenings sitting in front of the cave watching the stars and exchanging thoughts on subjects as diverse as world politics and time travel. Throughout it all Hsuan Hsueh dropped pearls of metaphysical wisdom cloaked in obscure language, laced with a spattering of humor.

On the last night Hsuan Hsueh sat in front of the cave with Kim and peered into the dark sky as the stars laid their claim to the night.

"Astronomers look into the sky and say they see billions and billions of stars, but they are only nibbling at the truth," the old man said as he gestured toward the heavens. "A countless number of tiny solar systems compose each star. Each galaxy contains billions of stars, and the universe contains billions of galaxies. This is a nameless spiral that man sees around him and believes he understands, but does not. To comprehend the truth one must be able to reach beyond the limits of ones perception."

A sudden gust of wind swayed the tree and sent hundreds of pine needles and a few small limbs showering down in front of them.

Hsuan Hsueh picked up one of the branches and handed it to Kim. "Each needle on the tree is like tiny soldiers in a constant battle with the elements. Soldiers died, and new ones are born to take their place on the front lines. The tree stands as a silent tribute to the ones that had fallen in the life and death struggle. The needles live and die, believing they are individuals, but they are not. They are part of something much greater, something that is beyond their comprehension."

Kim closed his eyes and listened to the old man's words echoing in his mind as a deep quiet filled his being. His intellect seemed to fade into a soothing stillness, which closed him off from the outside world as his breathing slowed and took on a natural rhythm. His mind was nothing, surrounded by darkness and within the dark void came a dim light and within that pale illumination came a silent procession of human figures moving in an endless line..."My God!" Kim shouted as he opened his eyes and jumped to his feet, letting the branch fall from his hand.

Hsuan Hsueh laughed gleefully as he stood up and looked at Kim. "You have found the fire from within!" he cried out happily.

"My God!" Kim repeated absently as he grabbed the flesh of his arm. "This body is but a receptacle for the reincarnating spirit that is me! I have seen my previous forms in an endless procession winding back through time! I have seen them! My God, I have seen them!" he cried out as tears started streaming down his face.

Sudden deceleration and the squeal of tires brought Kim out of his thoughts as the small jet touched down on the runway.

"Home away from home," Albert said as he applied the brakes. "It's not the Hilton, but there's hot water, warm food and comfortable beds."

"I'm just happy to be on firm ground, but I'd keep going if I could," Kim said as he stretched his arms out in front of him. "When do we get back in the air?"

"We're here for eight hours," Albert said as he pivoted the plane at the end of the runway and let it roll to a stop. "We'll be in the United States tomorrow an hour after sunset."

Steve put the cold can of Pepsi against his forehead as he watched Luther run the weed whacker and thought about the job awaiting them in the lab. He hated the kind of work that was going to be involved in the dismantling of the huge wooden crate. Removing the bolts holding the damn thing together was going to be a royal pain in the ass, but probably the easiest part. The beams were heavy and much too long to load onto Luther's lawn wagon. They'd have to be carried out one at a time, and that translated into a whole hell of a lot of work. He and Luther would both be nursing sore muscles for a couple days.

He wondered if the artifact was actually as frightening as Joyce thought. He suspected it wasn't. Her reaction to the thing was probably nothing more than the product of a stressful morning. Finding a dead body in a strange part of town had to be at the top of any list of things that could turn an ordinary day into something twisted and unnerving. Touching the thing and having it roll over right at your feet had to twist it just a little more. Maybe later they'd all have a good laugh about Joyce's low threshold of fright.

Luther finished with the trimming tool and walked over to the bench where Steve was sitting. "Damn, it's hot," Luther said as he plopped down on the bench.

"Hot isn't the word for it," Steve said as he handed Luther a can of pop.

"We sure could use some rain."

"Not just rain," Luther said as he opened the can of soda. "We need one of them thunderstorms that drops the temperature about twenty degrees."

"The lab's nice and cool. It'll be good working in there," Steve said.

"I don't know," Luther said tentatively. "I get the heebie jeebies when I think about that thing in the box. Joyce was real spooked about it, ya know."

"Luther, she found a dead body right before she discovered that artifact. Hell, a tiffany lamp would have spooked her. I'm betting we uncrate that thing and have a good laugh," Steve said with a chuckle.

"Boy, don't you know Joyce be a strong woman? There's somethin' in that box that we wasn't meant to see. I can feel it in my bones, an' my momma always said not to laugh at the dark things that you be feelin' in your bones 'cause they might come at night an' snatch you right out of your dreams."

"Hell, I don't want to get snatched right out of the middle of a good dream. We'll have to try not to laugh," Steve said with a snicker.

They both looked toward the drive when they heard a car horn. Martha Prince waved as she drove passed in her silver Lincoln Town Car. Steve and Luther both waved back.

"She must be meetin' Sam for lunch," Luther said as he put the cold can of pop against his neck.

Steve crumpled his empty can and tossed in into a bag of trash as he pulled a bandanna out of his back pocket.

"That means she's going to want to see the artifact when they get back," Steve said as he wiped the sweat from his face and neck. "We'll have to bust our asses to get it done."

"Then we better go get started," Luther said as he stood up and started walking toward the museum.

"I suppose so," Steve said as he stood up and returned the bandanna to his back pocket. "Don't forget. We can't be laughing at this thing," he said with a grin.

"If my momma was here she'd be slappin' the piss outa you for laughin' at her," Luther said over his shoulder as he started across the blacktop.

Steve followed Luther across the drive and waved at Martha again as he walked past the nose of the Lincoln. Martha smiled and returned the hand gesture just as Samuel pushed open the plate glass door.

"Hey! Are you flirting with my wife?"

"No sir, she was flirting with me," Steve quipped.

"Well, I guess that's okay," Samuel said with a chuckle. "We're going to go for a nice, unhurried lunch. We'd really like to see the artifact when we get back."

"Shouldn't be a problem. Have an extra beer or glass of wine just to make sure," Steve said as he disappeared around the back corner of the building.

"Hi, sweetheart," Samuel said as he opened the car door and slid in onto the leather upholstery.

"Hi, Babe," she said and kissed him.

"You been out here long?" he asked as he closed the car door.

"No, I just pulled in," she said as she dropped the shifter into drive. "I'm really hungry for a big salad. Is the Olive Garden okay?"

"Wherever you want to go is fine with me. Steve is supposed to have Joyce's artifact ready for our inspection when we get back."

"I can't wait to see it," she said as the car started back down the drive toward Market Street. "I finished the article this morning. I dropped it into the mail on the way to the museum."

"Great! Do you feel relieved?" he asked as Martha stopped at the end of the drive and waited for traffic.

"Yeah, but you know, I don't feel that sense of accomplishment I always got when I put a novel in the mail," she said as she looked left, then right, waiting for a break in the traffic. "I guess what I mean is that it was more like finishing up a good day at the office."

"So what's the next project?" he asked as she pulled out behind the last car in the string of traffic.

"I don't know," she said with a pensive smile. "Writing for the magazine this last year has been an interesting change of pace, but I have to admit I've missed the depth of involvement with a novel. Maybe it's time to take a couple months off, but then I'm not sure I could stand it. Writing is such a great outlet for me. What in the world would I do with my time? What do you think?" she asked tentatively.

"Oh, I definitely think you've seemed less content writing for the magazine. Maybe taking some time off isn't such a bad idea. It would give you a chance to relax your mind and see where your heart leads you. You've always got the option of uncovering the computer and going back to work if you feel the need. I'm sure the people at Viking would be happy to hear from you. It's a little different for me. Going back to work after a year would probably mean I'd be behind the counter at the hardware store."

"Does that make you afraid to retire?" Martha asked as she stopped for a red light.

"No," he said with a chuckle. "I'd never go back to work after retiring. There are so many things I've thought about trying, but have never taken the time. I wouldn't need a part time job to stay busy."

"That almost sounds like you've been giving it some thought," Martha said nonchalantly, trying to conceal her sentiment on the subject. She didn't want him to feel like she was pushing him, yet she didn't want to turn her back on a chance for a gentle nudge.

"Actually, I've been doing a lot of thinking about it the last few days. For a long time I thought I wanted to work forever, but I think I've finally came to my senses. Maybe it was Rudy's little stunt with the guards that put me over the edge. Joyce doesn't know it yet, but I've decided to turn everything over to her after I help her with the artifact."

"Will that end her teaching career?" Martha asked as the light turned green and she started through the intersection.

"I don't think the job is that much of a demand anymore. It's mostly public relations. She'll do both unless she gets tired of dealing with Rudy."

"So how long do you think you'll need to work on the artifact?" Martha asked as she turned into the Olive Garden parking lot.

"I suppose three weeks or so. I can't imagine it taking any longer than that," he said as Martha wheeled the car into a parking space at the front of the restaurant. "All I really want to do is help her establish that it's not some kind of hoax. She'll be crushed if it is. On the other hand, if it's real her career path will be defined until she retires."

"I suppose you know you've made my day," Martha said as she put the gearshift into park and turned off the ignition.

"I know," he said as he took her hand. "I guess I finally set my priorities. I'd rather spend my time with you than fighting with Rudy."

Joyce waited for the last of the students to leave the chemistry lab before she walked in. Jerry was on the other side of the room erasing a series of equations from the chalkboard. She watched him as she crossed the room and wondered if they were destined to have a sexual encounter. She was willing, and it was obvious he was interested, she just wasn't sure if he was ready to play by the rules. If there was any doubt in her mind they'd simply remain friends. She had no interest in letting him get hurt the way Mark did.

"I could never quite get comfortable with those damn chemistry equations," Joyce said as she came up behind Jerry.

Jerry set the eraser on the chalk trough and dusted off his hands as he turned around. "Maybe I should make you stay after school so I can tutor you," Jerry said with a lecherous grin.

"Would you teach me things, Mister Lansford?" Joyce squealed with feigned innocence.

"Oh, yes indeed, little girl," Jerry said and laughed with mock lewdness.

They both laughed at their impromptu bantering.

"Seriously," Joyce said after a moment. "I just stopped by to see if you had time for lunch and a trip to the museum."

At that moment Jerry was so taken by her beauty that he almost didn't catch the question. "I...I would like that," he stammered as he fought the urge to take her in his arms. His desire for her felt like a raging inferno deep within his soul. "Did the artifact finally show up?" he asked, trying to focus his mind on something else.

"They're dismantling the shipping crate as we speak. We should be able to grab lunch and go see it," she said with an edge of excitement in her voice.

"I've got a couple hours to kill," Jerry said as he glanced at his watch. "You ready to roll?"

"Ready," she said as she took his arm. "You want to drive the Porsche?"

"Are you trying to overload my pleasure centers?" he asked capriciously.

"Just testing them," she said with a smile.

Lieutenant Morgan had been at his desk for well over an hour reviewing the information taken from the files. He had read his notes over so many times that portions of them were committed to memory like poetry. He had combed through the facts carefully, and still nothing had clicked.

He leaned back in his chair and put his feet up on the desk as he closed his eyes. In his years on the police force he had seen his share of problems. He had investigated cases involving everything from drug abuse and robbery to rape and murder, but he had never been confronted with anything quite so bizarre.

The cases taken individually had no particular impact, but together they painted a disturbing picture. A private detective jumps out of a window; a wealthy woman with no history of drug abuse dies of a heroin overdose and a reformed alcoholic drinks himself to death with a mysterious bundle of money in his pocket, all within a week.

His town wasn't exactly quiet, but three bodies in one week was big news. And to top it off, the subsequent investigations found that two more people were missing. The dead woman's husband, who was a prominent member of the community, and his business partner were nowhere to be found.

Now, as if there weren't already enough knots in his stomach, an extra disappearance was thrown into the mix. With the new element came a bold connection that should have provided some direction to the investigations, but it didn't, and that boggled his mind.

He had a body, a disappearance, and a strange artifact at the same location, and no answers. To make matters worse he had a nagging hunch that refused to be silent, a hunch that all the bodies and disappearances were somehow connected. After twenty years of police work he came to value his nagging hunches. They were usually right on the money, and maybe that was what bothered him more than anything else. It was like having blank pieces of a jigsaw puzzle, pieces with no patterns to match up, only endless combinations of curved joints that made no sense.

He took his feet off the desk and put the files into a single stack as he wondered about the artifact. His officers gave him a vague description, but that simply wasn't good enough. He needed to see the thing for himself. He was certain it would add nothing, but he wanted to be thorough. Years of police work had taught him that nothing ever came easy. A good cop had to be willing to dig through the facts until there was nothing left. No rush to judgment and no lazy investigations, just the steadfast pursuit of the absolute, untarnished truth. The truth was out there somewhere, waiting to be found and he was going to expose it, no matter how long it took.

Terry sat in his chair and casually leafed through the pages of the new Playboy. He knew he was overdue to make his rounds with the time clock, but he didn't much care. As far as he was concerned Rudy could stuff the damn thing right up his fat ass. He could feel his visceral indignation building as he snapped the page of the magazine.

He had always been a dedicated employee, even in the face of the abuse Rudy continually handed out. He had always taken a great deal of pride in his job, even though it required little more than the ability to read and write. He had always been there to make sure the job was covered, and the thanks he had received was a two-week layoff notice.

His anger was becoming so intense and consuming that his eyes simply observed the pages flipping past without registering their contents. Even the pictures slipped beyond the grasp of his mind without notice. His body was locked into an automatic cycle of magazine browsing while his brain played out fantasies of revenge. The sounds of car doors and voices brought Terry back from the brink of murder.

He closed the magazine and tossed it up on the desk as he stood up and walked over to the display case. There was a part of him that wanted it to be Rudy and a guest. He didn't just want to have it out with him; he wanted to humiliate him in front of company.

He glanced around the corner and saw Sam and his wife coming through the door. He took a deep breath and tried to calm his anger, but he could feel it lurking in the dark corners of his mind.

"I'm back, Terry," Samuel said as they stepped into the lobby. "Is Steve still working downstairs?"

"I don't know," Terry responded sullenly. "Luther came running up the steps and out the door about twenty minutes ago, but I haven't seen anything of Steve."

Martha walked over to the display case and offered an awkward smile. "I'm so sorry about what happened to you and Ralph," she said. "If there's anything Sam or I can do to help you find another job, let us know."

Martha's warmth managed to get a little smile from Terry. "Thanks, Martha. Sam already offered his help, but it's nice to hear it again."

"Come on, dear," Samuel said as he took Martha by the arm. "Let's go see Joyce's artifact. This suspense is killing me."

"We'll see you later, Terry," Martha said as Samuel pulled her over to the top of the steps. They stopped when they saw Steve coming up from the basement.

"Steve, are you guys done? Can we see the artifact?" Samuel asked excitedly.

Steve stopped at the top of the steps and leaned against the wall. His face was pale and jaded with apprehension.

"Steve, you okay?" Samuel asked, suddenly concerned.

Steve nodded his head slowly. "Most of the lumber is still down there," he said in a shaky voice. "We...we'll get it moved out, but that thing has to be covered up first. Luther won't stay down there with it, and...and I can't much blame him. That thing's awful, Sam." He pushed himself away from the wall and walked across the lobby. He stopped at the plate glass doors and looked back. "Sam, don't take Martha down there," he said warily as he pushed open the door.

"He seems genuinely upset," Samuel said as he looked over at Martha. "You still want to see it?"

"Well, of course I do," Martha said firmly.

Samuel took Martha's hand as they started descending the staircase. He was experiencing a strange mix of anxiety and exhilaration that was growing more intense with each step. His mind was aflame with the same quandary that had plagued him from the onset. In a matter of moments he was going to either see a hoax that had fooled a talented professional or a paradox that was going to turn Anthropology and Archaeology upside down. He couldn't believe either, but one had to be true.

Martha could feel the tension as they moved across the lower chamber toward the office. She wondered if Samuel was as excited and preoccupied as he had been in Egypt so many years ago. She wanted the artifact to be the blaze of glory at the end of his career and not the catalyst that kept it going.

They walked into the office and stopped at the door to the lab. Samuel looked over at her as he squeezed her hand. "I've got butterflies the size of cows," he said nervously. "I'm glad you're here with me. You ready?"

"If you are," she replied.

Samuel opened the door and walked into the lab with Martha at his side.

The artifact was on the other side of the lab next to a pile of lumber that had been stacked haphazardly.

"Oh, my God," Samuel whispered as his eyes focused on Joyce's discovery. His mind went momentarily numb.

Martha stopped abruptly and took an unconscious step backward as she released Samuel's hand. She was struck by unexpected revulsion and a disquieting sense of dread as she reviewed the artifact from a comfortable distance.

Samuel felt like his heart was between his ears as he walked across the room on legs that suddenly felt rubbery. Each step seemed to be a desperate struggle between odd, almost morbid fascination pulling him closer and a strange primal fear holding him back. The last shuffling steps that put him in front of the artifact were driven only by professional will.

Samuel noticed his fuzzy bluish reflection on the face of the crystal, but it was the frame and its carvings that grasped his attention. The notion of a possible hoax faded from his mind as he reached out with a trembling hand and touched the petrified wood. He ran his fingers along the features of one of the carved faces as his brain struggled to explain the contradiction. As he stood in front of the artifact with his hands touching the cool surface of the frame he felt a surge of excitement he hadn't experienced in years. The realization that he was standing in front of what could be the most important discovery of his professional life left him almost breathless.

"This is no hoax," Samuel muttered with an unsteady voice. "I can't believe it. It's going to hit Archaeology like a ton of bricks."

Martha crossed the room timidly and stopped a few feet away from the artifact. "My God, it's the most...most horrendous thing I've ever seen. What is it?" she asked anxiously.

"My guess would be that it's some kind of totem...but...but the petrified wood doesn't fit," Samuel said tentatively. "It really distorts the time line. It may take years to unravel this puzzle."

"I've seen enough," Martha said nervously as she backed away from the artifact. She could almost feel the prospects of Samuel's retirement crumbling under her feet and there was nothing she could do.

"There's nothing that could have prepared me for this," he said as he backed away from the artifact. "This is going to get a lot of attention."

"I'm going home," Martha said as she slipped her arm around Samuel's waist. "Please don't stay here all night."

"I'll walk you out," Samuel said as they moved toward the office.

"That's not necessary. I know there are hundreds of things running through your mind right now. I don't want to break your concentration."

When they got to the door Martha put her arms around his neck and hugged him. "I don't like that thing," she whispered. "It scares me."

"I'd be less than honest if I told you it didn't give me the heebie jeebies, but I'm a professional. I have to remain focused on its potential importance." He raised her hand to his lips and kissed it. "Love you."

"Love you too, babe. See you at home," she said as she turned and went into the office.

She walked past Samuel's cluttered desk and wished Joyce had never discovered the artifact. In her heart she knew Samuel would delay retirement indefinitely. She felt like all her careful planning and exhorting was disintegrating before her eyes and she was helpless to stop it. Retirement would never work out as long as he was faced with a challenge. He simply wasn't the type of person to walk away from something he considered important.

She walked out of the office and moved past display cases of Indian relics. As she approached the other side of the room she saw Joyce coming down the steps, followed by a man she didn't recognize. "Joyce, I'm so glad I ran into you," she said as she walked toward them.

"Hi, Martha," Joyce said as they hugged. "I haven't seen much of you lately. Where's Sam been keeping you?"

"Chained to my computer," she said lightly.

"Martha, this is Jerry Lansford. We work together at the college. Jerry, this is my curator's wife, Martha."

"Hello, Jerry," Martha said with a smile.

"Pleased to meet you, Martha," Jerry said as they shook hands.

"Did you see the artifact?" Joyce asked excitedly.

"Oh, I saw it alright. It's the most grotesque thing I've ever seen," she said darkly.

"Oh God, I know. It's repulsive. I'm taking Jerry to see it now."

"Joyce, it's your discovery. Sam's too old to take on a new project, especially this one. I've finally convinced him it's time for retirement. If he gets too involved with that damn thing he'll keep working. I'd really like to see you take the lead on this and keep him in a support position."

"I promise I'll do what I can. He's a little stubborn sometimes," Joyce said.

"I know," Martha said with an accepting smile. "Thank you. Nice meeting you, Jerry."

"You too, Martha," Jerry answered as he walked toward the other side of the room.

Joyce watched Martha go up the steps and wondered how in the world she would ever be able to relegate Samuel to a support position. He was her mentor. She had too much respect for him to quibble over who would take the lead on the artifact, but Martha was right. He was too old to take on a long-term project.

She turned away from the steps and saw Jerry on the other side of the room gazing up at the buffalo hunt mural.

"It's an amazing piece of art," she said as she walked over to where he was standing. "I'm so use to seeing it that I forget how powerful it is."

"It's beautiful. You can almost hear the thunder of the buffalo herd."

"Follow me and I'll show you something that's not quite so charming," Joyce said.

Samuel was standing at his desk leafing through his address book as they walked into the office.

"Sam, what do you think about the artifact?" she asked confidently.

"I'm absolutely dumbfounded," Samuel said as he turned around. "Your description did it very little justice. It's so...so overpowering. I don't think Martha was too thrilled about it."

"Sam, this is Jerry Lansford. Jerry, this is my boss, Samuel Prince," Joyce said.

"Glad to meet you, Jerry," Samuel said as they shook hands.

"The pleasure's mine. Joyce has told me a lot about you," Jerry said with a warm smile.

"I hope some of it was good," Samuel said with a laugh.

"Jerry, go have a look at the artifact," Joyce said as she gestured toward the lab. "I need to talk with Sam for a moment."

"Okay," Jerry said as he moved out into the lab.

Joyce knew she had to talk to him while she had the chance, but had no idea how to begin. She appreciated Martha's position, but was afraid of hurting his feelings.

"Well?" Samuel asked as he looked at her quizzically.

"Sam, are you getting ready to retire?" she asked.

"Martha and I have had some fairly serious discussions about it. Why, you want my job?" he asked with a chuckle.

"No, not exactly..." she said and hesitated.

"Joyce, we've been together for a long time. Tell me what's on your mind."

"I...I want to take the lead on the artifact," she said quietly. "If you're planning to retire you don't need to be hip deep in this project."

"You've been talking to Martha," he said with a smile.

"Well, sure, but..."

"Joyce, it's okay," he said with a laugh. "I was going to suggest you take the lead anyway."

"Oh, God," she whispered with relief. "I was so afraid of hurting your feelings."

"Don't be silly. The artifact is your discovery, be tough. Lord knows you'll have to stand up to Rudy when I retire and you take my place," he said as he looked down at his address book. "When you came in I was looking for a contact with a solid background in Geology. I'm not at all familiar with that crystalline structure."

"Let's see what Jerry has to say about it. He said he took some Geology in college," she said as she stepped out into the lab.

Jerry was standing in front of the artifact running his hand across the crystal.

"What do you think?" Joyce asked as she and Sam walked toward him.

"This thing is really creepy. It looks like something right out of an Edgar Allen Poe nightmare. What the hell is it?" he asked as he looked over at Joyce.

"We were hoping you might tell us," Joyce said.

"Jerry, I understand you have a little background in Geology. Are you familiar with this crystalline structure?" Samuel asked.

"Not at all," Jerry said as he shook his head. "I think you need someone specializing in the study of crystals. I've never heard of crystal with rough surface texture like this, but then I'm not an expert either," he said as he ran his hand across the crystal again. "Crystals are smooth. If you look closely there are tiny pyramid structures rising from the surface. And there's one other thing," he said as he placed a finger on his chin thoughtfully. "Crystal usually forms within stone like granite or marble. I've never heard of it forming in slate before."

Samuel stepped up and examined the crystal closely. "I see what you mean. They really do appear to be tiny pyramids. I was so busy looking at the petrified wood that I didn't notice them until now."

"Now the frame is something a little different. I wrote a couple papers on the agatization process in college," he said as he ran his hand along the frame. "The age of petrified wood is usually thought to be somewhere around one hundred and fifty million years. In light of that I believe these carvings, and they are carvings, present quite a problem for Anthropology."

"Playing the Devil's advocate for a moment, how can you be certain they're actually wood carvings and not stone chiseling done sometime after the completion of the agatization process?" Joyce asked as she stepped toward the artifact.

"Oh, that's actually quite simple," he said as he looked over at Joyce and smiled. "Stone sculpture produces sharp transitions between individual cuts, like diamonds, for instance. These features are all somewhat rounded."

"I understand the reasoning about sharp features, like with diamonds, but how does less sharp translate into carved wood?" Joyce asked. "I want you to be right, and I'm sure you are, I just need to be able to answer that question if somebody asks."

"When the wood was originally carved the features were sharp. There's not much difference between the attributes of carved wood and chiseled stone at that point, but you have to remember how petrified wood is formed. Water seeps into the cells of the wood and, over millions of years, leaves mineral deposits. The wood eventually rots away to nothing, leaving only the deposits. Wood cells are like tubes running the full length of the wood, but they're incredibly small in diameter. There's a great deal of stress in sharp features and the deposits don't have enough strength as they're solidifying to hold that shape, so they tend to round off a bit. It's actually the exact same principal that keeps a knife edge from remaining sharp forever."

"Wow. I'm impressed," Joyce said with a smile.

"Yeah, well I'm calling you tonight if I have nightmares," Jerry said as he looked up into the gaping jaws of the beast at the top of the frame.

"Sam, I'm going to take Jerry back to school. How about calling some of those contacts of yours and finding an expert on crystalline structures."

"I'll find somebody," Samuel said as he turned and started walking back toward the office.

"You ready to go?" Joyce asked as she backed away from the artifact.

"Yeah, I'm ready," he said as he turned and found her watching him intently. "What?" he asked sheepishly.

"You ever play hooky?" she asked with a sensuous smile.

Jerry held her gaze as a sudden burst of lust surged through his body, leaving his insides trembling. At that moment he knew he would risk anything to have her.

"There were a few days when I was a kid. Back then it was fishing that held an irresistible attraction for me," he quipped.

"Why don't you call in sick this afternoon," she said as she took his hand and raised it to her lips. "There's a lake behind my place, but I doubt if you'll be interested in fishing," she said and ran her tongue along one of his fingers.

"Oh, God," he whispered as passion gripped his entire being. "Is there a phone I can use? I don't feel well."

"On my desk," she whispered as she put her arms around his neck and kissed him firmly.

Samuel glanced at his watch as he picked up the phone and punched in the numbers. He wondered if Martha was pacing the floor, waiting for him to get home. He knew she'd be relieved to find out Joyce had the lead on the artifact. A dozen roses and a bottle of wine might fit the occasion nicely, he thought as the phone started ringing.

"Colorado State University. How may I direct your call?"

"I'm trying to reach Professor Lippencott," Samuel replied.

"One moment, please."

Her voice was immediately replaced by soft elevator music.

He looked over at the scribbling on his work pad and was amazed by the number of fruitless calls he'd made. Apparently geologists specializing in crystalline structures were as rare as chicken teeth.

"Sir, Doctor Lippencott isn't in his office. Would you like for me to page him?"

"Yes, please," he responded as he shifted in his chair.

It had been a long day and he was tired. After spending the entire afternoon on the phone he was determined that Lippencott would be his last contact before going home. He leaned back in his chair and put his feet on the desk as he closed his eyes and wondered if there was any point to staying on the line. The girl was most likely going to come back and offer to take a message. He picked up his pencil and started doodling on his work pad as he waited patiently. After a couple minutes the music clicked off and was replaced by a man's voice.

"Hello, this is Professor Lippencott."

"Hello," Samuel said as he took his feet off the desk and sat up in the chair. "This is Samuel Prince. I'm the curator for a museum in Ohio. I've been trying to contact a geologist specializing in crystalline structures. I haven't had much luck, but your name has come up a couple of times."

"Well, Samuel, you're luck has evidently changed. What can I do for you?"

"We've come across an extremely unusual artifact which contains a very large crystalline structure," Samuel said as he got to his feet and started pacing back and forth next to his desk. "I've never seen anything quite like it."

"Surely there's someone in your area with a background in Geology," Lippencott stated curtly.

"Yes, of course. He suggested we seek out a specialist. It is very unusual. You need to see it."

"Samuel, what exactly makes you believe this thing is so unusual," Lippencott prodded.

"It's not the crystal itself that grabs your attention. Granted, it's quite large, and the structure seems different, but when you first see the artifact you hardly notice it. It's the framework that holds the crystal. Professor, I have a massive frame made of petrified wood that's covered with carvings."

"Chiseling designs into petrified wood really isn't any more difficult than working stone."

"Professor, these are carvings in wood that have later petrified."

Lippencott cleared his throat after a momentary pause. "What you're suggesting is...is crazy."

"Right, it is crazy," Samuel responded. "It's crazy and I haven't even mentioned the bluish crystal or the bed of slate in which it's embedded."

"Samuel, exactly where in Ohio are you?"

"Lima. It's about eighty miles south of Toledo. I really need your help," Samuel pleaded.

"I have to make some arrangements for my classes. Give me a number where I can reach you tomorrow."

Samuel gave him the number at the museum, thanked him for his time and hung up the phone. He dropped down into his chair and sighed with relief. Things were beginning to fall into place, he thought as he tore the top page from his work pad. He shook his head in amazement as he looked at the evidence of his afternoon on the phone. He wadded the paper into a ball and wondered why he didn't call Lippencott as soon as his name was mentioned. Reestablishing all his contacts was beneficial, he supposed as he tossed the ball of paper into the trash.

Samuel was startled by a rapping sound from behind him. He pivoted in his chair and saw a police officer wearing a gold shield standing in the doorway.

"Hello, I'm Lieutenant Morgan," he said as he stepped into the office and extended his hand toward Samuel.

"Samuel Prince," Samuel responded as he stood and shook the officer's hand.

"Is Joyce here?" Morgan asked.

"No, she's gone for the day. Is there something I can help you with?"

"Actually, I just dropped by to look at the artifact, if you don't mind."

"Help yourself," Samuel said as he gestured toward the lab. "I'm leaving, so if you have any questions you'll need to call tomorrow."

"You'll need an umbrella," Morgan said as he walked past Samuel's desk and stopped at the doorway into the lab.

"Are we finally getting some rain?"

"It's just starting. They're forecasting some severe thunderstorms for tonight," he said and stepped through the doorway.

Morgan walked across the lab and stopped in front of the artifact as an unfamiliar apprehension gripped his heart. He was no stranger to fear. He knew the icy touch of a near death experience, but he was a stranger to the dread that seized him as he looked at the abomination. His insides began to tremble as he gazed up into the carnivorous jaws of the beast and felt a deep primal aversion.

He backed away from the artifact slowly, as he considered its relevance in the cases on his desk. It was difficult to believe there was no connection, no matter how unlikely it seemed. He walked back to the office door and turned for a last look. It was like having a piece of a jigsaw puzzle that fit perfectly with the surrounding contours, but made no sense in the picture. He didn't like it when facts failed to fall together properly. It always left him with a nagging feeling that something had been overlooked.

Ralph broke the seal on the bottle of Jack Daniels and set it in front of him on the desk as he thought about his life. There was a time before the drug experiment when it seemed happiness was well within his grasp. There was even a year or two after his body was poisoned with the drug that he was optimistic about his chances for a fruitful life. That was when the nightmares only came once every couple months and he believed they would eventually go away.

All he ever really wanted out of life was a good woman who could be his best friend and the mother of his children. He never wanted a high-powered education or a position on some corporate ladder. He just wanted a family and if someone would have given him a choice between his military career and the family he always wanted, the Marines would have come up short. He would have taken his discharge and found a civilian job. If someone would have warned him about the dangers involved with the drug experiment he would have never volunteered.

He picked up the bottle and raised it into the air in a mock toast. "Here's to you, Rudy. You fat, overbearing son of a bitch. May your soul rot in hell," he said, almost cheerfully. He put the bottle to his lips and took a long drink. Murder and suicide were goals that required courage and to make sure he had plenty the whiskey would be gone by morning.

Ralph set the bottle back on the desk and opened his lunch box. He lifted the Colt out of the otherwise empty container and gazed at it with reverence. It was the tool that would first end Rudy's life and then his own suffering, he thought as he slipped the weapon inside the waistband of his pants.

His platoon was ordered to report to the infirmary and it was there, after a briefing, that volunteers were sought out for what was described as an experimental flu vaccine. Each Marine taking part in the program was to be given a two thousand dollar bonus, which was big money to everyone and impossible to resist. Later, after the entire platoon received the first dose of the drug, everyone was informed the program was actually a classified drug experiment and talking about it was prohibited.

In the weeks that followed there were daily sessions in which he was questioned intensely about the details of his dreams. He was unable to recall much, which seemed to be a major irritation to the medical team. It wasn't until months later, after the program was stopped, that he experienced his first nightmare.

He didn't even call them nightmares at first. They were simply recurring dreams about a crimson sky and strange animals that reminded him of the flying monkeys from the Wizard of Oz. He found the dreams troubling, but didn't begin to think of them as nightmares until the creatures got closer. That's when he stopped thinking of them as flying monkeys.

Over the next few years the nightmares progressed in frequency until they were coming about once a month. The nighttime visitations remained regular for quite some time. It wasn't until he started at the museum as a security guard that the cycle changed. After that they came about once a week, except when he worked midnights, and then it was more often.

During this last rotation on the graveyard shift things changed dramatically and the nightmares started coming every time he slept, but the increased frequency wasn't the worst of it. The horrid things were on him, slashing his body open with their talons and ripping away chunks of flesh with their jaws. It seemed like it could get no worse. That was before the hallucinations started. With the onset of the hallucinations came the sudden complication of not always knowing exactly where reality ended and the terrifying visions began.

Ralph pushed his chair back away from the desk, stood up and walked to the window. He looked out at the approaching storm front and listened to the distant rumble of thunder. Lightning made him nervous, especially at night when the flashes in the darkness were too much like strobe lights, too much like the nightmares. Light flashed through the window from somewhere in the distance as he turned away.

He walked back to the desk and picked up the bottle just as thunder rolled through the museum. His insides trembled with apprehension as he raised the bottle to his lips...

The hallucination struck without warning as his mouth fell open and whiskey ran down the front of his shirt. An instant later the bottle slipped from his hand and shattered on the floor in front of his feet.

He was stunned to find himself atop a white sand dune within a vast depression surrounded by steep cliffs. He looked around, wide-eyed, and saw hundreds of other dunes lining the walls of the crater. In the distance beyond the rim of the cavity were jagged mountain peaks rising into the cloudless crimson sky.

Unbridled terror gripped his heart as he heard the beat of leathery wings in the air above him. He whirled around, desperate for an escape route, and saw a fissure behind him in the rock face above the dune. The sight of Samuel's lab beyond the crevice paralyzed his mind as the terrifying sound from above closed in on him...

He suddenly found himself back in the security station, staggering from the impact of the hallucination and terrified that it wasn't over. He grabbed the edge of the desk to keep from falling as thunder rattled the museum.

Ralph struggled to control his panic as he stumbled out of the security station and across the lobby to the steps. He started down the steps as a dark cold fear settled into his heart. It was a fear of uncertainty, a fear that he might still be in the clutches of the hallucination. He covered his eyes and shielded them from the bright flashes as he made his way down the stairs and into the soothing blackness of the basement. He stopped at the bottom of the steps, clutching his pounding chest, waiting for some clue that the horrid vision had truly ended. If his mind was still in the grip of the hallucination he desperately needed it to end before he saw the creatures again. After a moment he moved away from the stairs and broke into a run for Samuel's office where he could wait for the storm or hallucination to end.

He hurried into the office, slammed the door behind him and was reaching for the door into the lab when a crackling lightning bolt vaporized a nearby transformer and plunged the museum into total darkness. He stumbled, lost his balance and fell through the doorway and out into the darkness of the lab. He got to his feet and was about to feel his way back into the office when he saw red crisscrossing lines that seemed to he hovering in the air on the other side of the lab. The lines swelled steadily and darkened until the strange display disappeared into the darkness of the lab. A moment later, as he looked on in horrified wonder, it seemed the air itself split open. Dull crimson light spilled into the lab as the split widened, exposing the familiar landscape of his nightmares and hallucinations.

He moved toward the alien scene on wobbly legs, driven by a frightening, irresistible curiosity. He moved forward, unable to stop himself, stepped up into the opening and out onto the top of the dune with his heart pounding in his ears. With each step the dune crunched beneath his feet, a sound which seemed to add a new dimension to his horror.

He was only vaguely aware of the drill and circular saw as he stepped forward, gazing at the red stain, shredded clothing and scattered bones ahead of him on the dune. At that moment he came to the staggering realization that he was standing not on a dune of sand, but brittle bone fragments.

Paralyzing fear gripped his soul as he heard the beat of leathery wings in the air above him. He tried to turn and run back toward the fissure in the rock face, but slipped and fell in the loose debris. He screamed out in terror as he crawled madly toward the opening, scattering bits of bone in all directions. He stopped suddenly and whirled around as he heard something drop onto the dune behind him. The creature continued to flap its leathery wings for a moment as it stabilized itself on the loose bones. It's large yellow, cat like eyes peered down at Ralph as it snarled, exposing deadly jagged teeth. It snapped its carnivorous jaws as it moved toward him with its sinewy arms outstretched, talons raised.

Ralph screamed and crawled backward away from the horrid thing, moving as fast as he could in the bony debris. In the next instant he remembered the gun in his waistband, which was a new addition to his nightmare. He ripped the gun from his waistband, pulled back the hammer and fired until the slide locked open on the empty magazine. The creature shrieked in agony, clutching at its bleeding chest and fell backward onto the dune.

He struggled to his feet and backed away from the lifeless beast, still pointing the empty weapon. He felt a tremendous release of fear and pent up anxiety as he looked down at the creature that had been the source of his personal horror for so many years. Now it simply looked like road kill.

His sigh of relief froze in his throat as he heard the brittle bones crunching behind him. He whirled around with the empty gun raised in firing position and saw the creature closing in quickly. He pulled the trigger and nothing happened. For a second he was amazed that it didn't fire. He just had time to wonder how a dream gun could run out of bullets and then the creature was on him. It drove its talons into Ralph's shoulders and lifted him into the air as blood ran down his arms and dripped onto the dune from his fingertips. Ralph screamed and kicked his legs as the thing snarled and opened its mouth. The almost casual bite removed most of his arm in a spray of blood as a lifeless hand dropped to the dune. His next scream was cut short as the beast snapped its jaws and removed the top of his head in a spray of blood, bits of bone and brain matter. The creature released its grip, dropping the nearly headless body onto the dune as more of the winged beasts dropped out of the sky to join in the feast.

CHAPTER NINE

The lights from the instrumentation cast a red glow across Albert's face as he checked his heading and air speed against the flight plan. He could only guess at how many times he had made the trip in the last five years. Often enough that he knew the corridor of airspace between China and the United States better than he knew his own house. It was always a relief to get back to the comforts of home and friends, but this time it was different. This time he was troubled by a vague sense of remorse he couldn't explain.

He grew up knowing the world was full of advantages for those willing to do what was necessary. You simply found the angle and exploited it regardless of the impact to others. There was no room for compassion. The game went to the one who didn't blink, no exceptions. You followed the simple rules, did whatever it took, and never, ever looked back.

Now, after years of chasing money and pleasure at the expense of others he was beginning to feel that something was terribly wrong with his life. He looked over at Kim as he slept in the passenger seat and wondered if there was a connection between him and the troubling thoughts. It didn't seem possible, but then there were other things that seemed beyond the realm of possibility. Things he'd witnessed with his own eyes. Things his mind still questioned.

"There is spiritual light within everyone. In some it is nothing but a dim flicker, but it is there just the same," Kim said suddenly as he sat up in the seat and looked at Albert.

"I thought you were asleep," Albert said as he put the aircraft into a moderate dive.

"If I was asleep I'd be awake now," Kim said anxiously as he gripped the armrests. "How long before we land?"

"About five minutes. I'm dropping the plane below the radar threshold now. What did you mean about spiritual light?"

"Within everyone burns a spiritual fire that drives us toward our destiny. Some have a raging inferno, and others have only a spark. Those feelings of remorse are driven by your spiritual fire. They will most likely diminish once we part company."

"You mean you're causing these feelings?" Albert asked as he shifted nervously in his seat.

"Indirectly. It's like putting a cold rock next to a campfire. The longer the rock sits by the flames the warmer it gets, but take it away and it cools off. Your spirit is simply reacting to my presence."

"I feel like there's a battle raging in here," Albert said as he thumped a finger on his chest. "Part of me wants everything to remain the same...but there's this new part of me that wants to throw it all away. That part wants to dump the drugs in the ocean and start a new life. If I did that they'd track me down and kill me like a rabid dog," he said apprehensively.

"True spiritual awakening and enlightenment usually occurs over the span of many lives, but on rare occasions it happens spontaneously. There is sanctuary for those who experience this conversion and find themselves at odds with the physical world," Kim said as he felt the plane level off. He looked out the side window and saw the moon reflecting off the rippling waves a few meters below the aircraft as his mind drifted back to his first days in Tibet.

The journey into the Himalayan Mountains was a brutal test of physical strength that left him totally exhausted. He had no memories of the last few hours and only dim recollections of their arrival in the place Hsuan Hsueh called the circle of Yu Wu. It was only after what felt like days of sleep that he emerged from the darkness of a stone lodge to find himself in a warm valley of lush vegetation and towering pine trees. The stark contrast with the memories of the climb through barren snow covered mountains left him feeling as though he was still in a dream world produced by a delirious mind. It was the soothing voice of Hsuan Hsueh that brought his mind into focus.

"It is a great joy to see the wonder in your face as you awaken for the first time within the circle of Yu Wu."

Kim looked up and saw his master sitting in the lotus position atop a large boulder a few feet away. "I don't understand this place," Kim said as he looked around, eyes wide with amazement.

"Join me," the old man said as he gestured toward a spot next to him on the rock. "We can talk while we eat. You will find grooves cut into the back of the rock."

Kim walked around the boulder, found a series of crude steps winding upward and started climbing. After a momentary struggle he pulled himself up on top of the rock and stood in silent awe as his eyes fell upon the beauty of the valley. A rolling meadow divided by a frothing stream and dotted with stands of giant pine trees spread out away from the boulder. An arched footbridge crossed the stream and connected sections of a winding cobblestone path that snaked through the valley and led to a stone monastery. Steep, forbidding cliffs surrounded the lowland, rising upward into the jagged peaks of the Himalayas where wind driven snow blanketed the sky. "It's beautiful," Kim said humbly. "But I don't understand. How can this be?"

"Sit and eat with me," Hsuan Hsueh said as he gestured toward a loaf of bread and several pieces of dried fruit.

Kim sat on the rock and picked up a piece of apple as his eyes scanned the valley. "I have so many questions," he said as he raised the apple to his mouth.

The old man laughed as he tore a piece of bread from the loaf. "You must remember to look within yourself for many of the answers you seek. To find the path of knowledge within your heart is to discover the treasure of wisdom," he said as he handed the piece of bread to Kim.

"Must I find all the answers within myself?" he asked as he took the bread and ate hungrily.

"Sometimes you ask truly stupid questions," Hsuan Hsueh said with a chuckle as he shook his head slowly. "The discovery of specific knowledge is not the treasure we seek, but the vehicle with which we pursue truth. Ask your questions. Some I will answer, and some I will have you ponder upon," he said as he picked up a piece of fruit.

"I don't understand this place," Kim said as he chewed the last bite of bread. "We are surrounded by barren rock, blowing snow and frigid temperatures, yet we are here in the midst of a vibrant garden. How does this place exist?"

"Later this morning we will walk through the valley, much as we did in the mountains of California. The Circle of Yu Wu lies within an ancient volcanic crater containing many sources of heat. To the north, between the farthest stand of trees and the cliffs, you will find a pool fed by hot springs. The water has great healing powers, should you ever suffer an injury. To the south of the valley are great pits of bubbling mud. These pits are not only a heat source, but also the birthplace of all the soil within the crater. These are the secrets of the valley that any fool could discover by simple observation.

There are other secrets upon which you must meditate."

Kim picked up another piece of fruit as his eyes scanned the surrounding valley. "My heart tells me that this is a holy place filled with many people, yet my eyes find it empty. Are we the only ones here?"

"No, of course not," the old man said with a laugh. "Later, when we walk you will meet others. Some are just beginning their journey upon the path of enlightenment, while others, like you, are on the threshold of nirvana. Now it is time to meet another of your teachers," he said as he pointed toward the other side of the rock.

The air around them took on a sudden chill as a sphere of swirling dust motes appeared a few feet above the boulder and quickly elongated into a miniature tornado. As the vortex touched down it began to take on human shape. After a moment the form darkened and organized into the body of a woman.

"This is Rishi," Hsuan Hsueh said as he presented the small woman with long black hair, high cheekbones and reddish complexion of an American Indian.

"Welcome home, Samadhi," she said with a tender smile. "It is good to see you here again within the Circle of Yu Wu."

"How...how did you do that?" Kim stammered.

Hsuan Hsueh looked at Rishi and laughed. "He has yet to remember everything. He teeters upon the brink of understanding Tat Twam Asi."

"Master, help me understand all this," Kim pleaded as he looked over at the old man. "How did she get here? Who is Samadhi? Why does she speak as though she knows me?"

"You are Samadhi," the old man said with a chuckle. "Western thought has so clouded your vision that you do not see that which is under your nose. Samadhi is your spiritual name just as Hsuan Hsueh is mine and Rishi is hers. Kim Lee will eventually grow old and die, but Samadhi will always be."

"I am Samadhi?" he whispered.

"Yes!" the old man shouted. "You are Samadhi, the ancient one."

"Master, I must know. How did Rishi get here?"

"Why do you ask me?"

He turned to Rishi, who was laughing wildly.

"I am in my other body," Rishi said, still laughing.

"I...I do not understand," Samadhi said uneasily.

"You will," she said as her body began to atomize. "You will remember."

"Better fasten your seat belt," Albert said, bringing Kim out of his thoughts.

Kim pulled the seat belt across his lap and fastened the buckle as he looked out at the stretch of desert highway coming into view below the plane. The road was lit with lines of flares along the berm and the headlights of a truck.

"Wait until everybody is involved in unloading the plane before you leave. I really don't want to answer any questions," Albert said as he lowered the landing gear.

"I won't let anyone see me." Kim said as he picked up the cane sword and laid it across Albert's lap. "I need you to do one last thing for me."

"Anything, just tell me," Albert said as he lowered the flaps and set the air brakes.

"First thing this morning I need you to ship the cane overnight express."

"To where?"

"I just planted a name and address in your subconscious. When you start filling out the shipping label it will come to you."

"Will I see you again?" Albert asked with an unsteady voice.

"If the spiritual flame within you remains strong I will free you from your oppression and deliver you to a place of sanctuary. If the flame fades I will leave you to your life. This is my promise to you," Kim said as the plane touched down.

The darkness of the desert swallowed Kim as he walked east along state route 50 and watched as the rising full moon silhouetted the Rocky Mountains. He could feel time slipping away with each step and knew there was little hope of getting to his friends before they stumbled upon the grisly secret of the crystal. The only way to protect them now was to enter their dreams and plant the seeds of action. He prayed their minds were still flexible enough to absorb the subliminal messages. In his heart he understood only too well that saving them could prove to be impossible. Their lives were a secondary consideration, as was his own. His responsibility was to seal the portal and save humanity from the unthinkable, and he had seen the price of his failure.

In that terrifying vision the crystal was exposed to the magnetic field of photographic lights, opening the doorway and transforming the museum into the focal point of unspeakable horror. Thousands of creatures poured through the aperture as darkness fell and the city became a place of death. Fleeing survivors told incredible stories of demonic creatures dropping from the sky and devouring victims.

The next day law enforcement from the surrounding areas investigating the reports found the aftermath of a mass slaughter, but failed to survive long enough to request assistance. The day faded into night amid confusion and fear as frantic calls went out from authorities in the surrounding counties to anyone willing to listen. By dawn the radios and telephones were silent and the circle of death had engulfed ten counties like a virulent plague. With each subsequent night the carnage expanded ten fold. By weekend civilization in North America collapsed into scattered pockets of terrified survivors as humanity regressed into a prey species.

As Kim walked along the edge of the highway he remembered Moksha and the day he began to comprehend his true destiny.

"You have learned much," Hsuan Hsueh said as he walked with Samadhi along the cobblestone path between the monastery and the footbridge. "When you first came to me in the mountains of California you were like a lost child wandering in the darkness. It has been a precious gift to witness your spiritual awakening and a great honor to have been your teacher."

"Master, you will always be my teacher," Samadhi said as he stopped and looked at the old man. "You are the one that set my feet upon the path of knowledge. It is you that has given me a precious gift."

"You bring tears of joy to the eyes of this old man," Hsuan Hsueh said as he moved toward the footbridge. "I will feel the loss of your company when you cross the bridge to be with your new master. We will not become strangers, but things will be different. Soon I will witness your return to a place within the Brotherhood of Ajnachakra. Go now, your new Master awaits on the other side of the stream," the old man said as they embraced. "Do not be fooled by Moksha's size. He is an extraordinary warrior worthy of great respect."

A look of sublime love and understanding passed between them for a moment, then Samadhi turned and started up the arch of the footbridge. When he got to the other side he found an empty path leading away from the stream toward the dense wall of pine.

"Master, are you here?" he asked as he looked up and down the stream. He stepped to one side of the bridge and looked back to where he had left Hsuan Hsueh standing. The old man was nowhere to be seen. Samadhi turned to go back to the path and was startled by the sight of a small figure in a dark hooded robe standing a few feet away.

"You are Samadhi," the small Oriental man said as he pulled back the hood of his robe, exposing long black hair with a streak of silver running from one side of a widow's peak. "I am Moksha," he said quietly.

"Master, you startled me."

"Yes, I know," Moksha said as they started walking away from the stream. "It is the beginning of your first lesson. You must always reach out with your mind as Hsuan Hsueh taught you. You must learn that the physical eyes are not always reliable. Had I been an enemy bent on doing you harm you would have found yourself at a terrible disadvantage."

"Master, where were you hiding and how did you move upon me so quietly?" Samadhi asked.

Moksha stopped and turned toward Samadhi. "I was not hiding and I did not move, I simply fooled your eyes by letting my body absorb the light. If you had spread the wings of your perception you would have found me. This is but one of many things I will teach you. Know this, Samadhi," Moksha said as they started walking along the path again. "The physical world is a very dangerous place. Your destiny is much too important to allow yourself to be in jeopardy. I will teach you how to flee danger as well as how to use the ancient Japanese martial arts. I will also teach you secrets that are unknown to the outside world."

Samadhi followed Moksha in silence as they walked the cobblestone path along the edge of the dense forest. After a few minutes they came to a narrow break in the trees.

"Enter this place with the knowledge that nothing of what I teach you can ever be passed on to another," Moksha said as he moved through the passage. After squeezing past several trees and ducking below a number of low limbs they came out into a large clearing in the center of the forest.

At one end of the clearing, where the forest grew against the stone face of the crater, was a small lodge built from rocks and logs. A few hundred feet from the lodge was a massive boulder surrounded by a ring of pine trees that towered above the rest of the forest. Several bulging burlap sacks hung from low branches in each tree and swayed gently in the breeze.

Samadhi followed Moksha across the clearing to a place between the lodge and circle of trees where fresh pine branches were piled. Moksha lowered himself down upon the branches and gestured for Samadhi to join him.

"This will be your home until you master all that I set before you," Moksha said as he wrapped his legs into the lotus position. "Within the lodge you will find a few necessary tools and a sleeping place. Everything else you need will come from the forest and from within."

"Master, Hsuan Hsueh has taught me that inflicting pain upon another is to also harm yourself, yet you are about to teach me to fight. Help me understand this paradox."

"Samadhi, I am not teaching you to fight, I am teaching you to survive in the physical world. Dhyana did not reveal the secrets of alchemy so you could be wealthy, and Rishi did not explain how to project your energy body so that you might do magic tricks. We teach you these things to insure that you will prevail in the physical world," Moksha said as he reached into his robe and took out a small cloth wrapped bundle. He set the bundle between them and opened it, exposing a pile of dried fruit.

"Eat," he said as he picked up a piece of apple and put it into his mouth. "Later I will show you how to find roots within the forest that will provide you with mental and spiritual energy, as well as nourishment."

"Master, if I am threatened with physical harm would it not be better to run than to fight and risk injury?" Samadhi asked as he picked up a piece of fruit.

"It is far better to run than it is to fight. I will teach you to run like the wind and disappear like a wisp of smoke, but there may be a time when this strategy is doomed to failure because of the circumstances. That is why there are four different actions that can be applied to each situation. The choice of action will require a decision based on more than your strengths as a warrior. It will require intuition driven by all the teachings of Ajnachakra."

"Moksha, I see but two choices. Run or fight," Samadhi said as he picked up another piece of fruit. "Can we speak of the others now?"

"If I told you to run to the monastery and return with more fruit would you run?"

"Yes, of course, Master."

"And if I told you to run to the monastery and protect Hsuan Hsueh from a band of outlaws?" Moksha asked as he picked up the last piece of apple. He broke the fruit in two and handed half to Samadhi. "It is the same with fighting. I will teach you to flee an attacker, but I will also teach you to injure that attacker, if justified by the circumstances. Running is best, but it is better to inflict pain than to allow yourself to be hurt, just as it is better to maim an attacker than to risk serious injury. The final option is to kill. Physically, it is a simple matter to take a life, but spiritually it is quite different. If you kill without a clear conscience it will have a profound affect on your karma and you will suffer in your next incarnation. "

"Master, you speak of a clear conscience. Is it possible to take a life and not feel a sense of guilt?"

"Samadhi, you must always have compassion in your heart, even in the midst of battle. The compassion of which I speak is for humanity. There will come a time when only you stand between man and a nightmarish fate. We are preparing you for that time. Any person or thing that stands between you and the fulfillment of your destiny must be handled in the most appropriate manner. A man who blocks your path and refuses to move is no more worthy of your concern than one of Rishi's mindless creatures."

"Mindless creatures?"

"Yes," Moksha said as he removed another bundle from his robe and set it between them. "One of Rishi's contributions to your training," he said as he opened the bundle and displayed a number of objects that looked like egg sized mud balls.

"Those are the creatures of which you speak?" Samadhi asked skeptically.

"They are like unfertilized eggs holding lifeless protoplasm until they become energized. Once they begin to grow they develop quickly into mindless creatures bent on killing."

"They have no spiritual force within them?"

"No," Moksha responded firmly. "They draw their will to live from the darkest of human emotions."

"Then these things which Rishi created are quite dangerous," Samadhi said apprehensively.

"Samadhi, they are not play things, they are ferocious creatures spawned by an ancient incantation. It is the ultimate warrior who masters their challenge. The boulder within the circle of trees is there for a reason. It is your only place of safety within the forest should things go awry."

"Master, how can I perfect non-lethal combat skills against such creatures?"

"The strength and tenacity of the creature is determined by controlling the amount of energy forced into the embryo. Hsuan Hsueh taught you to pull the energy from the surrounding ether inward to intensify your perception, and Dhyana taught you to channel the energy of the Earth through your body to transmute base metals into gold. I will teach you to pull the energy of the Earth inward and hold it within your body like a battery. Once you become sensitive to this plasma energy you will be able to store and release it as needed," Moksha said as he raised his hands in front of him and displayed a blue plasma charge that danced along his fingers. "Sometimes only a trickle is required," he said as a tiny lightning bolt jumped from one hand to the other, "and sometimes you need to release it with great force," he said as he pointed his fingers and released a swirling bolt of energy that split a tree on the other side of the clearing. "Always remember, when you are out of contact with the Earth, or with something that touches it, the energy will begin to discharge from your body. Anytime you fly in an airplane or balloon your body will lose its charge. It takes three full days to completely recharge your body after a significant length of time in flight," he said as he picked up one of the earthen vessels.

"It is this plasma energy that is forced into the embryo and determines its strength. This one will be somewhat passive," he said as he placed it in the palm of his hand and pointed with the first two fingers of the other hand. A crackling blue discharge jumped from his fingertips and twisted into the pod, transforming it into a pulsating fleshy blob. Moksha watched the churning mass for a moment, and then threw it toward the center of the clearing. It hit the ground with a flash of light. A moment later a cloud of dense crimson smoke engulfed the impact area as a pungent odor spread through the clearing.

"Do not move," Moksha said quietly as they watched a shadowy form take shape within the cloud. "The creature's vision is most acute when detecting movement."

Samadhi fought to control his inner terror as the cloud began to dissipate, exposing a hideous biped with a scaly muscular body and large reptilian head. Fiendish screams and howls shattered the tranquility of the forest as the creature thrashed the air wildly with its powerful arms. It ripped at the ground with its clawed feet and kicked up dust and shredded vegetation as it turned in a tight circle.

Samadhi's blood turned cold as the creature stopped suddenly and locked its cat like eyes on him. It growled viciously and snapped its savage jaws as it took a step toward him with arms outstretched and talons raised. It took another step, snapped its jaws again, and charged.

Terror gripped Samadhi's heart as the creature closed in with leaping strides. A vision of his life passed through his mind within the twinkling of an eye and he saw his own death as the beast lunged into the air for the strike. At the last instant Moksha raised his hand with fingers extended and released a crackling thunderbolt. The swirling blue discharge struck the creature in the middle of the chest and dropped it to the ground in front of Samadhi in a smoldering mass.

"Samadhi, we must refine your concept of not moving," Moksha said softly.

"I...I thought it was supposed to be somewhat passive," Samadhi said with a trembling voice.

"It was," Moksha said stolidly. He held Samadhi's gaze for a moment, and then smiled. "Do not be alarmed. You will learn much in the coming days and weeks," he said as he scooped up another of the strange mud balls and raised himself from the bed of pine branches. "You will master the skills you need to defeat those horrid things, even when they are their most powerful."

He gestured for Samadhi to stand, offered his hand and pulled him to his feet. "You will learn to fade into the background and not be seen and you will learn to move with more quickness than you thought possible," he said and flashed across the clearing to the boulder with its ring of towering pine trees. He pushed one of the hanging burlap sacks away from him and watched it swing back and forth. "I will teach you to strike with such force that no natural structure can withstand the blow." He moved with a blur of speed and struck with his fist as the bulging bag came back at him. The sound of hundreds of rocks clacking together echoed of the cliff wall after which a tiny trail of sand started sifting through the burlap material and falling toward the ground.

"You will learn all these things, but none as important as this. The eyes of a predator, like these creatures, are wired to detect motion, sustained motion. If you remain still and do not move you will be invisible to them. You can also move and remain invisible if your movements are brief and separated by pauses in which you again become motionless. To another human the movements would appear as some bizarre dance." He stepped forward and held the small earthen sphere out in front of him. "Please stand still so I might finish this demonstration."

He again released a tiny bolt of plasma into the ball and watched it begin to pulsate with life. After a moment he tossed the writhing mass into the clearing a few yards away.

Samadhi went rigid with fright as he watched the cloud of crimson smoke billow up from the ground. He listened to the horrible alien screams as the dark shadow within the smoke began twisting upward, taking form. As he watched, the smoke dissipated in the breeze, exposing another of the horrid things as it slashed wildly at the air.

To his horror Moksha began moving toward the creature. He took a small, slow step and moved his arms outward into a new position with slow, fluid motion. The movement was brief and ended as he stopped abruptly in mid stride, remaining motionless. After a second he moved again in the same manner and again stopped abruptly. He continued the odd, dance like movements as he circled the animal, at times moving closer only to back away a moment later. During the demonstration the creature moved about slowly as if stalking some unseen prey, its eyes sweeping from side to side.

The scene continued until Moksha stopped and waved his arms in the air wildly. The predator whirled instantly, charging with its talons raised for attack and leaped into the air. Moksha rolled to the side, came back to his feet and delivered a lethal kick into its side as it landed where he'd been standing only seconds before.

A quick toot from the horn of a passing semi jarred Kim from his memories. He watched as the truck slowed, pulled off onto the shoulder of the highway, and gave another quick toot.

Kim ran ahead, jumped up on the side of the cab and looked in at the driver. The driver looked back with a friendly smile illuminated by the dash lights.

"Where ya goin', Bud?"

"Ohio," Kim responded.

"I ain't goin' that far, but I can get ya to Denver."

"Sounds good to me," Kim said as he opened the cab door.

Randy Lippencott sat straight up in bed and stared wide eyed into the darkness of the room as his mind struggled to separate the tenuous residue of the fading nightmare from the unwavering face of reality. As the terror in his heart dissolved into oblivion it was replaced by the pain of an emotional wound that the passing years had failed to dull. A wound suddenly reopened by a cruel dream. He felt the sting of building tears, and before he could drive them back he began to sob uncontrollably. After a few moments he regained his composure, wiped away the tears and swung his legs over the side of the waterbed.

He never forgot her beautiful face, the warmth of her smile or the love and joy she brought into his life. He still remembered the sound of her laughter and the way his heart responded to her touch. They were memories he cherished more than anything else, but remembering was painful, and the pain he felt now was unbearable. It was like reliving the heartbreak of returning from Vietnam to the emptiness of a world without her.

After returning from Vietnam he spent months trying to locate her, but it was as if she'd vanished from the face of the earth. All he really knew was that she didn't stay around long after finishing her last quarter and she didn't return for graduation. The last contact the university had with her was when they mailed her degree to a post office box in Wounded Knee, South Dakota. Without a family or friends to supply leads the trail turned cold. The worst part of not finding her was the knowledge that she believed he was dead. The thought of how she must have suffered and the depth of her sorrow brought back the sting of building tears.

Randy Stevenson. The name haunted his memories like a restless spirit walking the halls of an ancient castle. He still remembered the numbness and shock that paralyzed his mind when he saw the name on his hospital identification bracelet. It was like looking into a mirror and seeing the wrong face. The real horror struck the next morning when he found out that he had been in a coma for three months. He always assumed it was Randy Stevenson's burned body that went home in his place. It was easier to believe in a simple mistake than to think misidentified remains were one of the ugly facts of war.

He eased himself off the side of the bed wondering why, after all these years, he had dreamed about Joyce. On the heels of that thought came the sudden realization that Kim had also been in the dream, along with something dark and terrifying. Something he was glad he couldn't quite remember.

When his hope of finding Joyce faded he turned the search toward Kim. His prayers were to find them together, but it wasn't to be. Kim contacted his family several times from Las Vegas and then vanished without a trace. He always wondered if he got careless with the wrong people.

He hobbled over to the closet and retrieved his robe from the corner of the door. Hanging clothes anywhere but a hanger was something he and Kim never got away with after Joyce moved in with them. There were other bad habits she purged from their lives, too. Dirty dishes didn't accumulate in the kitchen until the last glass was gone from the cupboard, bathrooms got cleaned on a regular basis and empty beer cans didn't collect on the coffee table.

He grabbed his cane from the corner, slid his feet into his slippers and headed for the kitchen, wishing for some kind of closure to the whole damn tragedy.

He filled the teakettle with water and put it on the stove as he picked up the plane ticket, checked the flight time and glanced up at the clock. There was still a couple hours before he had to start getting ready, but he knew there was little chance of going back to sleep now. He tossed the ticket onto the counter, pulled a chair out from the table and sat down as he waited for the water to boil.

Thinking back on the three years he shared with Joyce and Kim was disturbing because of the emotional agony the memories produced, but there was something else, too. Something so far removed from the scientific view of the world that it was almost like remembering a dream. The scientist in him demanded that the memories were flawed and should be discarded; yet there was another part of him that clung to them with resolute faith and certainty.

As Randy waited for the water to boil he let his mind drift back to the day he met Kim.

The commons in Cramer Hall was one of the more popular campus locations for students seeking a break from the academic grind. There were food machines for those interested in a quick snack and a kitchen manned by a small staff for anyone needing something more substantial, like a pizza or a burger and fries. Most of the students were transients, stopping in for a quick bite or just hanging out for an hour between classes, but there were others that were part of a more regular crowd. They were the ones that spent a disproportionate amount of their time playing cards or talking with friends instead of studying. The regulars usually only lasted a couple quarters before they flunked out and went on to a menial job until the draft board called. Randy was a regular.

Randy wasn't as bad as some, but his study habits were a disaster and any excuse to cut class was good enough. The only thing that separated him from the rest of the regulars in the Cramer Hall commons was a photographic memory and a willingness to cram thirteen weeks of reading into the week before finals. His technique was just enough to slide through with passing grades and left plenty of time to pursue his two main interests in life, sports and gambling.

Randy flipped the page of the Sports Illustrated and continued to read an article about the Chicago Bears as he scribbled a note in the margin of a point-spread sheet. When he finished writing he stuck the pencil behind his ear and picked up a slice of pizza.

"Mind if I join you?" someone asked.

Randy looked up from the article and saw a student who was unmistakably Oriental American with shoulder length black hair. He was standing at the other side of the table holding a Coke in one hand and a hamburger and fries in the other.

"Have a seat," Randy said as he pushed the chair away from the table with his foot.

"Thank you," he said as he set the food on the table and dropped into the chair. "I'm Kim Lee, what's your name?"

"Randy Lippencott, glad to meet you," he said absently as he returned his attention to the magazine.

"I've seen you in here before," Kim said as he picked up a couple fries. "You're always reading a sports magazine and making notes on those funny looking papers. What subject are you studying?"

"Football," Randy said without looking up from the article.

"This is for a class you're taking?"

"No," Randy replied in a slightly annoyed tone as he looked up from the Sports Illustrated. "I'm picking the teams I want to bet on this weekend."

"I'm sorry. I don't mean to bother you, it's just that I'm fascinated by what you're doing."

"It's okay," Randy said as he closed the magazine. "I need to rest my eyes for a few minutes."

"How does this betting thing work?" Kim asked as he picked up his sandwich.

Randy laid the game sheet in front of Kim as he pulled the pencil from behind his ear.

"The two teams on this line are playing this weekend," he said as he pointed with the pencil. "The number next to the Washington Red Skins is the point spread. That means the bookie thinks Dallas will win by three points. By spotting Washington three points the game is as even as possible. That means if you bet on Dallas they have to win by four points, since the bookie wins on ties."

"Okay," Kim said with a pensive look, "but assuming the bookie is out to make money, how does an even game work for him. Does he win that many ties?"

"He wins with more ties than you'd think, but he gets most of his money from playing the odds."

"I don't understand," Kim said.

"The odds of winning a single game are fifty-fifty. Right?"

"Right," Kim said as he picked up his drink.

"That means the odds of winning two games are four to one, three games eight to one, and so on. The bookie pays odds determined by the number of games you bet. All the teams you pick on a single card have to win for you to win the bet. You get ten to one odds if you pick four winning teams, but the actual odds of winning are sixteen to one."

"Oh, yeah," Kim said with a laugh. "I understand now. Pretty clever. What kind of odds do you get if you bet every game?"

Randy laughed.

"I don't know, but you'd have to be nuts to throw your money away like that. The actual odds of winning twenty six games are astronomical," he said as he started writing figures on the table. After a moment he put the pencil down. "Holy shit!" he said with a surprised look. "The odds are a hundred thirty million to one, give or take a couple million. God, I had no idea it would be that high. Like I said, you'd be giving your money away."

"Do you have an extra sheet?" Kim asked.

"Sure," Randy said as he took another sheet out of his pocket and handed it across the table. "You trying your luck?"

"I'm just playing around," Kim said as he picked up Randy's pencil and started circling teams. "What would happen if you bet all the games and won?"

"You wouldn't," Randy scoffed.

"Okay, but just for the sake of this discussion, what would happen?" Kim pressed as he continued to pick teams.

"I don't know," Randy said as he shrugged his shoulders. "You'd win a bunch of money, but I have no idea the kind of odds you'd get. But I'm sure of one thing."

"What's that?" Kim asked as he passed the sheet back to Randy.

"That bookie would never cover a bet of yours again. He'd be scared off. He'd probably think you had a clairvoyant touch or something," Randy said lightly.

"Don't loose it. I want to know how I did."

Randy closed his eyes and held the sheet to his forehead.

"I see you winning...thirteen games," he said with a laugh as he opened his eyes.

Kim pulled a dollar out of his pocket and slid it across the table to Randy.

"Just to make things interesting. If I win you buy lunch all next week."

Randy snatched up the dollar and stuffed it into his shirt pocket.

"If you win I'll buy your lunch every day for the rest of the quarter."

That weekend was much like any other football weekend for Randy. With the first kickoff he became something not unlike a stockbroker tracking investments. The game that held the most interest was on the television, but the radio was nearby to keep up on the scores of the untelevised gridiron contests, and at the end of each series of downs he ran through the channels and checked the progress of other battles.

It was the college scoreboard program between the first and second game that provided Randy with the first clue that he was about to witness something incredible. That was when he realized that Kim had, so far, picked eight winners and no losers. By halftime of the second game Randy had lost interest in any of his own bets and was watching Kim's sheet intensely, and by the final minutes of the game was pacing the floor like an expectant father.

Sunday morning when Randy awoke he rushed to the porch and tore into the paper looking for the score of a late starting west coast game. When he found it his mind went numb. Kim's string of wins was unbroken at sixteen.

Sunday afternoon was, for the most part, a repeat of Saturday, except Randy ignored his own bets and kept a careful eye on the remaining ten teams Kim picked as winners. By mid afternoon it was obvious that something unique was happening, and by evening Randy was so pumped with adrenaline that he feared sleep would escape him completely. The final score of the last game from the west coast came in the early hours of Monday and sent shivers up Randy's spine. When he finally fell into bed, exhausted from the stress, his greatest fear was that something would happen and he'd never see Kim again.

The next morning when Randy walked into the Cramer Hall commons he found Kim sitting alone at a table with a book spread open in front of him. He walked up to the table and pulled out a chair.

"How did you do that?" he asked as he dropped down into the seat.

Kim smiled as he looked up. "I thought I'd probably see you first thing this morning," he said as he closed the book.

"Are you just incredibly lucky or..."

"It's simply something I do," Kim responded.

"No," Randy said as he shook his head. "Walking across the street is something you do. Driving a car is something you do. This is completely nuts. What you did is fucking impossible!"

"Randy, if you allow yourself to think about it you'll go crazy. Linear thought has no place here. Simply accept that I can do this thing."

"I'm really having trouble with this."

"Only because you're thinking about it. Your thought process has been molded by western religion and science. Neither have any willingness to look beyond the world they define. All of your life you've been told that things like this are not real. Then I come along and provide you with substantial proof otherwise. The paradox will evaporate when you stop thinking about it."

"But..."

"But nothing!" Kim demanded. "I could continue to offer proof, week after week, but there's no point. I've already given you more proof than you can handle. Let the linear thinker in you go to sleep."

"It was no accident that you sat down at my table last week, was it."

"No. I've been watching you for awhile."

"Why?" Randy asked.

"I had to make sure you were the right person. I have a secret to protect and you have direct knowledge of this betting game. As long as we're careful and take only what we need we can provide ourselves with a fairly steady income while we're pursuing our education."

It was the whistling teapot that brought Randy back from his thoughts.

When Samuel turned into his parking spot next to Ralph's car he was an hour ahead of his normal morning routine. He couldn't remember the last time he had spent such a restless night. He simply couldn't get Joyce's artifact out of his head. It was the excitement of a mysterious discovery, the anxiety of seemingly unanswerable questions and the frustration of knowing it came much too late for his own career. He finally drifted off to sleep, but was awakened sometime later by the storm. It wasn't so much the storm that kept him awake the rest of the night, as it was his concern for Ralph.

The nightmares started up full tilt, just like they always did when Ralph worked midnights, but this time his stint on the graveyard shift didn't end when it was supposed to and neither did his personal cycle of torment. For weeks he watched helplessly as Ralph's state of mind deteriorated until his condition was well beyond clinical depression. And then, as if he needed one more thing to drive him over the edge, Rudy gave him two weeks notice.

Samuel felt uneasy as he got out of the car and walked toward the museum. The storm couldn't have come at a worse time for Ralph. His recurring nightmare was always set in the midst of a ferocious thunderstorm, making him extremely apprehensive about lightning. The circumstances had him set up for a night of living hell. He hoped he was able to cope with the stress without hitting the bottle, but it seemed unlikely. He supposed it really didn't matter in light of his approaching termination date.

When Samuel got to the museum door he was surprised to find it locked. He rapped his knuckles against the plate glass and wondered if Ralph was down in the office sleeping off a drunken stupor. After a couple minutes he gave up and walked around the back of the museum. When he got to the doorway into the lab he was shocked to find the remains of the sheet of plastic hanging in shreds.

He examined the plastic as he stepped through the opening. A series of long slices cut through the material from the upper corner, leaving tails of plastic flapping loosely at the edge of a gaping hole in the center of the sheet.

"Ralph," he shouted nervously as he walked into the lab. "Ralph, are you okay?" The lack of a response left him with the feeling that something was terribly wrong. "Ralph, can you hear me?" he yelled as he moved toward the office.

He stopped and looked down as he felt something crunched beneath his feet. Several pieces of what at first looked like popcorn were scattered across the lab floor. He stooped down and picked up one of the pieces and rolled it between his fingers. The particle was hard like ivory, but with a rough surface texture, as if from exposure to some hostile environment. One mystery at a time, he thought as he dropped the fragment into his shirt pocket and stood up.

As he walked toward the office the fear that Ralph was laying dead somewhere in the museum hit him like a punch to the stomach. He had to find him before everyone else arrived. If he was drunk he needed to get him on his feet and pour some coffee into him, and if it was worse he wanted to make sure his friend received the final dignity he deserved.

Apprehension filled his being as he stopped at the door to the office. He knew Ralph could have easily died of a heart attack while sleeping off a stupor. He took a deep breath and opened the door slowly. He was surprised and relieved to find the office empty, yet confounded that Ralph wasn't at least asleep at one of the desks. With no outside doors or windows it would have been a perfect spot to wait out the storm.

He went through the office without stopping and walked out into the display chamber. After a few feet the unmistakable smell of alcohol hit his nostrils and grew stronger as he approached the steps. He started up the staircase with the fear that Ralph was indeed dead, but at his own desk or close to it. As he approached the top of the steps the smell became an overpowering stench that seemed to state clearly that something had gone terribly awry. When he got to the top he was prepared for the worst. He walked toward the security station hoping that Ralph went quickly without suffering.

He stopped at the display stand and looked into the security station. He wasn't surprised by the shattered Jack Daniels bottle or the dark residue surrounding it, but was astonished that Ralph wasn't nearby. His lunch box was open on the desk next to a partial cup of coffee as if he had left and was coming right back.

After a moment he stepped away from the security station wondering if he was actually in the midst of some bizarre dream. He walked around the museum and looked in every possible corner for Ralph, but found nothing. After a few minutes he returned to the security station to use the phone, but decided he couldn't take the smell. He scribbled a note to Steve, taped it to the inside of the door and headed back to his office.

Samuel sat at his desk with one hand on the telephone wondering if a call to the police was warranted. He didn't want to get them involved just to find out Ralph had gotten too drunk to drive and had deserted his post in a taxi. He considered the scenario for a moment, then shook his head and picked up the phone. Regardless of the circumstances, he couldn't believe Ralph would simply walk away from his job without at least calling somebody. He punched a programmed dial sequence and put the phone to his ear as it started ringing.

"Hello," Joyce said sleepily.

"Did I wake you?"

"No," she said with a laugh. "You're just used to talking to me after I've had a cup of coffee. What's up?"

"I don't know how you had your morning planned, but I need you to stop here before you go to school. I'd like your friend Jerry to do a chemical analysis on something I found in the lab this morning," Samuel said as he took the fragment from his pocket and set it on the desk. "By the way, did Ralph happen to call you last night?"

"No. Why?" Joyce asked.

"His car is in the parking lot, but I can't find him anywhere."

"He's got to be there somewhere," Joyce demanded.

"I've looked everywhere for him. He's not in this museum. I've got a broken bottle of Jack Daniels in the security station, but no Ralph."

"I hope you can get Steve to clean up that mess before Rudy sees it," Joyce remarked.

"Yeah, I'll get it cleaned up, but what's Rudy going to do. Fire him, maybe?" Samuel grumbled.

"Not to change the subject, but did you hear back from our crystalline expert?"

"He's flying in this morning. He should be here when you get back from school."

"Great. I can't wait to hear what he has to say. Well, I better finish getting ready or I'm going to be late. See you in a little bit."

"Okay, see you then." Samuel said and broke the connection. He placed another call and leaned back in his chair as it started ringing.

"Lima Police Department, this is officer Donner."

"This is Samuel Prince at the museum. I seem to have a missing security guard. I think I'd like to make a report if you could send someone over to see me."

"We'll have somebody there as soon as we can, sir."

"Thanks," Samuel said and hung up the phone. A moment later he heard Steve call his name from the lab.

"In here, Steve," Samuel responded as he stood up and walked out into the lab. Steve was standing in the doorway looking at the shredded sheet of plastic.

"What the hell happened to this?" Steve asked as he stepped into the lab.

"I have no idea. I found it that way when I came in. Would you like to hazard a guess as to what this stuff is?" Samuel asked as he bent down and picked up another of the fragments scattered across the floor.

"Looks a little like popcorn," Steve said as he stooped down and picked up a piece. "Why does Ralph still have the door locked?" Steve asked absently as he examined the particle in his hand.

"I haven't been able to find Ralph," Samuel said as he turned and walked back toward the office.

"His car's still outside," Steve said as he followed him.

"Yeah, I know. There's also a broken Jack Daniels bottle upstairs in the security station," Samuel said as dropped the mystery fragment on his desk next to the other one. "I'd like for you to clean up the mess before Rudy gets here," he said as he took the piece from Steve and added it to the collection.

"I'll get on it right away. No sense in giving Rudy a chance to be a bigger fucking asshole than he already is," Steve said as he left the office.

Samuel sat back down at the desk and picked up one of the white chunks from the lab floor. There was something vaguely familiar about the stuff. He opened his desk drawer, retrieved a small magnifying glass and examined the piece closely. Under the glass it looked less like popcorn. Stress fractures and pockmarks within the irregular shape seemed to suggest that the piece had been dislodged from a larger structure while subjected to a tremendous crushing force.

Samuel went back to the lab and started picking up the rest of the fragments. To his surprise and bewilderment he found the most pieces in a concentrated area near the artifact. He went back to the office with his hands full, spread the pieces out across the top of the desk and started examining each one under the magnifying glass.

After inspecting most of the pieces his focus was broken by a knock at the office door. He turned in his chair and saw Lieutenant Morgan standing in the doorway.

"Morning Lieutenant," he said as he stood up. "I didn't expect them to send you to fill out the report."

"Someone else will be along for the report," Morgan said as he stepped into the office. "I'm here to talk."

"Have a seat," Samuel said as he gestured toward Joyce's desk.

Morgan walked around the desk, pulled out the chair and sat down with a troubled look on his face.

"What's on your mind?" Samuel asked as he returned to his chair.

"There's nothing magic about police work," he said as he removed his hat and set it on the desk. "You simply gather the facts and start looking for the obvious connections. It works that way most of the time. The last week or so has been one of those exceptions."

"I'm not much of a detective, but I'll be glad to help if I can." Samuel said as he opened his desk drawer and took out his pipe and tobacco.

"There isn't much that happens around here that falls into the category of unusual. Sure, we have drug dealers killing each other over turf, and we have robberies, burglaries, and bar brawls, but those are things a cop comes to expect. But let me tell you what's happened in the last ten days," Morgan said as he leaned forward.

"Ten days ago we found the body of a private detective that apparently jumped to his death from the tenth story of Cook Tower. No big deal. Maybe he just found out he had AIDS. Eight days ago we found the body of a woman, dead of a heroin overdose. No big deal, except the note pinned to her body indicated she was part of a love triangle that went bad. Even though we don't know where they are, we believe there are two more bodies, the husband and the business partner. Four days ago your assistant found the body of the old junk dealer. Two days ago a workman building the shipping crate for your artifact vanished into thin air. And now your security guard."

"Unless you just need somebody to talk to, I really don't see how I can help you, Lieutenant," Samuel said as he finished filling his pipe.

"Give me another minute and you'll see where I'm going with all this."

Samuel gestured for him to continue.

"Like I said earlier, police work is usually as simple as gathering facts and looking for the obvious. Well, the connection between most of the cases I just mentioned is sticking out like a sore thumb, but it makes absolutely no sense, and that's making me nuts. The connection is right out there," Morgan said as he gestured toward the lab.

"You mean the artifact?" Samuel asked in a surprised voice.

"I know...I know. It sounds crazy, but the artifact is a common thread that keeps turning up in these cases. Three people are either dead or missing, and they all had some connection to that thing out there in your lab."

"Lieutenant, I'm not sure what you're suggesting, but I can absolutely guarantee you that the artifact isn't capable of interfering in our lives. Regardless of how it looks, it's no more hostile than a bunch of dinosaur bones. What about the other bodies? Where's that connection?" Samuel asked and lit his pipe.

"Actually, there's a lot of evidence that strongly suggests that the artifact came from the bottom of a pond on the missing husband's property." He gave Samuel an awkward smile as he shook his head slowly. "I'm just trying to be a good cop. I'll be the first to admit the correlations I'm coming up with sound crazy as hell. But there's something else you don't know," he said as he raised himself out of the chair and picked up his hat. "The police station has been deluged this morning with calls about missing farm animals. It's getting real tough to come up with rational explanations for all this stuff," Morgan said as he put on his hat and walked toward the door. He stopped and looked back at Samuel for a moment. "Be sure and give me a call if anything unusual happens."

"Lieutenant. Maybe you should see something in the lab before you leave."

Joyce stopped in the open doorway and watched quietly as Jerry erased a series of strange equations and diagrams from the chalkboard at the front of the classroom. As she watched him move she felt desire for him deep in her body and wondered how long it would last. Her relationships with men always started with a month or two of torrid sex, and then they started looking for more in the affair than she had to offer. Steve was the first one to maintain some kind of emotional control. She supposed it was his youth. He was more interested in getting laid on a regular basis than looking for some kind of deep, meaningful intimacy.

"Good morning," she said as she stepped into the classroom.

"Morning, Joyce," Jerry answered as he continued to clean the board. "You're in here early."

"Maybe I stopped in for a quickie before class," she responded with a mischievous laugh.

He felt a jolt of sexual energy as an image of them making love on top of his desk bolted through his mind, driving a desire so intense that it seemed to set his soul ablaze.

"I'm all yours," he said as he turned away from the chalkboard and walked over to her. His being was suddenly alive with her essence as the smell of her perfume touched the memory of their afternoon sexual encounter.

"You're much too easy," she said with a soft laugh. "Actually, I do need you to do something for me," she said as she pulled an envelope from her purse and handed it to him. "I'd like you to analyze this stuff. Maybe I can think of some special way of thanking you later," she said with a suggestive smile.

Jerry opened the envelope, dumped the contents onto the table and picked up one of the pieces.

"It looks a little like bone or ivory that's been exposed to a tremendous crushing force. Where'd you find it?" he asked as he picked up another piece.

"Samuel found it at the museum this morning. We both think it's bone, but we want some verification. How long will that take?"

"If it really is bone it won't take too long," he said as he picked up another piece and rolled it between his fingers. "If it's not it could take a few days to design a battery of tests and pin point the composition."

"Does your lab have the capability of carbon dating?" she asked as she picked up one of the larger pieces and held it up to the light.

"Oh, sure. It may not be as precise as a better equipped lab, but I can get you within the ball park."

"Please, can you do it for me this morning?" she asked as she laid the piece in the palm of his hand and gently stroked her fingernails up his forearm.

"You drive me crazy when you do that," Jerry said as he pulled his arm back and rubbed away goose bumps.

"I know," she said softly.

"I can verify bone in a few minutes, but the best I can do on dating the samples is a couple hours. How about if I give you the results over lunch?"

"I'd love that, but it's going to have to be lunch only. There's a geologist coming to look at the artifact this afternoon and I need to be there."

"How about if we meet up town in that little bar behind the theater," he suggested.

"You mean Clancy's Place?" Joyce asked.

"Yeah. I've heard a lot about the place but never been there. Eleven-thirty okay?"

"That sounds good," Joyce said as she pulled him toward her and put an arm around his neck. "They make the best tenderloin sandwich in town."

"Somebody's going to see," Jerry whispered.

"So?" Joyce said as her lips found his. She held the embrace for a moment, and then pulled away. "I'll see you later," she said as she picked up her purse and briefcase.

"Clancy's Place," he said absently as he watched her turn and walk out of the room. He could feel his insides trembling and knew sleeping with her occasionally would never be enough. Falling in love with her was a bad idea, but it was too late to back away now. As he watched her turn the corner he wondered how long the pain of a broken heart lasted.

Lieutenant Morgan watched as the last of the detectives walked quietly out of the briefing room. There was none of the usual banter between cops that had known each other for years and there were no jokes, only scared faces. After thirty years of police work he could tell how bad things were simply by watching his men. He knew the faces of detectives tracking rapists, murderers, serial killers and cop killers, but the fear and confusion apparent in the men that just left the room was something completely alien to him.

He sat at the desk staring down at the pile of photographs in front of him and fought back the compulsion to scream out in despair. He picked up the top photo and looked at it again, hoping for some reasonable explanation to fall into place. The picture, which had been taken by an officer earlier in the morning, showed a large doghouse with the front and part of the roof ripped away. A heavy chain trailed away from the destroyed shelter and ended abruptly in a patch of blood stained gravel. It was all that remained of a two hundred pound Rottweiler Mastiff mix named Crusher who stood night watch at Miller's wrecking yard. He tossed the photo aside as he shuffled through the rest of the pile.

Most of the other pictures showed similar scenes of destruction and mayhem where dogs and farm animals had been brutally attacked. Little more than a patch of blood soaked ground or a few broken and splintered bones remained of any of the animals. The most disturbing photographs were on the bottom of the pile, and as horrible as they were, they were nothing compared to the actual crime scene. The brutality and horror of that place was something he could only hope to forget someday. As he stared down at the photos the memory of the bloody car unfolded in his mind again.

From a few hundred feet away the sight of the yellow Mustang convertible seemed normal enough. The car was pulled off the side of the road with the trunk open, jack under the back bumper and spare tire lying on the ground. The only indication of trouble was the flashing lights of the police car that was pulled off the road ahead of the Mustang. It wasn't until he pulled along side of the Mustang in his own patrol car that he noticed the splattered blood on the right window.

He stopped the cruiser, engaged the warning lights and pushed his door open. His gut instinct told him that something was terribly wrong, but it was the swarming flies that drove the point home. It was a point he didn't fully comprehend until he climbed out of the car and saw the bloodied remains of the convertible top. A series of long parallel slashes ended in a gaping hole in the center of the top where bloody pieces of twisted and broken cross members were visible. Blood was smeared across the front of the top, down the windshield and across the hood. The trail of blood continued on the road in front of the car with a line of red droplets. As he walked around the front of the mustang he saw the first officer on the scene, a rookie with three months on the force, in the weeds losing the contents of his stomach.

"You all right, officer?" he asked as he walked toward the driver's door.

The officer nodded his head and retched again.

He looked through the blood-smeared window and felt his own stomach turn. The interior of the vehicle was splattered with blood and strewn with bits of flesh and bone fragments, but it was the driver's seat that seemed to speak of unfathomable horror. Twisted springs and blood soaked padding protruded through deep slashes and rips in the back of the leather seat. Embedded in the destroyed upholstery were pieces of shredded clothing, chunks of flesh, part of an ear and a section of scalp with dark curly hair.

He started stacking the photos together and tried to think of something else, but his mind kept going back to the scene. It wasn't the blood and bits of flesh that haunted his memory, it was the slashes in the back of the seat and the convertible top, marks just like at the museum.

Randy watched the markings on the runway rush past the window as he felt the thrust of the jet engines push him back into the seat. The rapid thump of tires hitting expansion joints in the pavement ended abruptly as the aircraft lifted off the ground. As he watched the airport fall away in the distance he wondered what sort of mystery awaited him in Ohio.

He was no stranger to the task of identifying unusual bits of rock and mineral deposits, but the questions usually came from neighborhood kids returning from a trip to the mountains. He couldn't think of the last time an adult asked for identification, especially one a thousand miles away. The chance that there actually was a crystalline formation unknown to the world of science seemed so unlikely that he felt foolish boarding the plane. But there was something else that prodded him forward, something so unimaginable that he had to see it for himself.

The notion that logs had been carved into totems ahead of petrification sounded like something from the lunatic fringe. It was crazy, yet Samuel Prince checked out to be a highly respected Archaeologist who was exploring Egyptian tombs in the early Sixties. The thought crossed his mind that maybe the old geezer was losing it, but he sounded much too crisp and articulate on the phone. He supposed that was the thing that he found most unsettling. Samuel sounded like he had a firm grasp of the basics of Geology and he was certainly well versed in the chronology of the Human species. He knew petrified wood predated humanity by millions of years and still insisted the totems had been carved.

He refused to buy into the obvious paradox, and that only left two possibilities. Either petrification was achieved through an unknown process or Samuel Prince was as crazy as a loon. It was going to be a lot easier on the scientific community to learn that Samuel was demented.

Randy suddenly remembered a term Kim had introduced him to years ago. Linear thought. He described it as a thought process that locked the thinker into a well-established path by paradigms accepted by the scientific community. According to Kim the linear thinker was incapable of making the intuitive leaps required in the exploration of the unknown. Freedom from the bonds of linear thought started with questions that refuted knowledge accepted by society. He still remembered the two examples Kim used to demonstrate the principle.

What if there really was a complex conspiracy behind the assassination of John Kennedy? What if the government really was covering up the crash of an alien spacecraft in Roswell, New Mexico? The answers to the what if questions provided startling new descriptions of the world and fueled a series of long discussions that spanned several months.

Randy gazed out the window at a bank of dark clouds on the horizon and wondered how Kim's non-linear thinking would play out with the situation at hand. What if the crystal formation really was unknown to the scientific community, and what if the totems really were carved out of logs prior to agatization? The answers that came whispering from his own subconscious spoke of research grants, which could spit out cash faster than an ATM run amuck.

To his astonishment the exercise in non-linear thought left him with an overpowering sense of certainty that within his grasp was an enigma of unfathomable proportions. It was a sensation he remembered from another time in his life when the world seemed to be a mysterious and magical place.

He pulled the shade down on the window and closed his eyes as his mind drifted back to a drinking establishment called The Final Exam.

The Final Exam was one of the best-known taverns near campus and a long-standing meeting place for students at the end of the week and throughout the weekend. They made the best pizza around, the on tap beer selection was large enough to leave even the most worldly guzzlers dazed and a state of the art sound system played uninterrupted top 40 hits from the last ten years.

After the weekend the student crowd at the establishment was a little subdued, making Monday the slow day of the week. The beer was just as cold and the kitchen turned out the same tasty pizza, but the customers were more interested in quiet talk than reveling.

After picking up two thousand dollars from the bookie Randy was primed for a celebration, but quiet talk was what he wanted most. He desperately needed to know Kim better and understand as much as he could about the process that put a roll of hundred dollar bills in his pocket. In one weekend Kim won more money than he had over the last couple years. As preposterous as it was, he believed Kim had some kind of touch. From the moment he was given the list of teams a part of him knew something special was about to happen. It was as if he had stumbled onto a mystery of boundless depth and potential the day he met Kim in the commons.

When Randy walked into The Final Exam it seemed quiet, even for a Monday. Most of the waitresses were busy polishing brass railings or cleaning mirrors. The only one working the floor was carrying a pitcher of beer and a pair of frosted mugs to a corner table where Kim was sitting. He followed her to the table and pulled out a chair as she delivered the beer.

"You guys need menus?" the waitress asked.

"How about a large pepperoni pizza," Randy said as he lowered himself into the chair.

"Double cheese," Kim added as he picked up the pitcher and started pouring beer into a mug.

"Okay, that's a large pizza with pepperoni and double cheese. It should be out in about twenty minutes," she said as she walked away from the table.

"You hang around until she gets off and she'll take you home with her," Kim said as he set the mug in front of Randy.

"What makes you think so?" Randy asked as he turned and watched the girl walk toward the kitchen.

"Sometimes I get feelings, like waves of emotion. It's a little like the feelings I get when I know who's going to win a game."

"It's a sure thing I'm getting laid tonight if you're as good at reading emotions as you are picking winners," Randy said as he pulled a roll of bills out of his pocket and handed it to Kim. "You've got the touch or something. I still can't believe you hit. I mean, if I hadn't picked up the money myself...well let's just say you test the limits of my mental agility."

"Sometime we'll discuss linear thought and the limits it puts on your mind," Kim said as he unfolded the hundred dollar bills, fanned them out in his hand and examined them for a moment.

"Linear thought?"

"That's a discussion for another time. We have other things to talk about right now," Kim said as he refolded the bills and handed them back to Randy. "You keep this. We'll call it the first deposit into our operating fund."

"Operating fund?" Randy asked.

"I told you before it was no accident that we ran into each other, and it was no accident that brought you to this table with that wad of money in your pocket. It was all planned. I've shamelessly manipulated you from the very beginning because we each have skills that complement the other. Together we can accomplish much more than either of us can alone. To paraphrase Spock, together we are greater than the sum of our parts."

Randy smiled. "I'm a Star Trek fan, too. I'm flattered, but I'm not so sure I understand. Why would you want to work with someone else? You're the one with the touch. What do I have to offer?"

"Let's call it your street wisdom. I know nothing about bookies or the way they do business, and I don't want to learn. I want to be insulated from that end of it. And I have a secret to protect," Kim said as he raised his mug and took a drink. "I don't want anyone to learn about my gift, I don't want my picture on the cover of Time magazine and I don't want to be a lab rat for some scientific study."

"So you pick the winners and you want me to place the bets and collect the money? Sounds like a pretty easy job." Randy said with a chuckle.

"It's not as easy as it sounds. You've got to fool the bookies into believing it's nothing but dumb luck."

"How the hell do I do that?" Randy demanded.

"It's your job," Kim said with a shrug of his shoulders. "But a Bram Stoker novel does come to mind," Kim said with a calculating smile. "The only reason Dracula was discovered was because of the dead bodies he left behind."

"Sorry, I'm not making the connection," Randy said with a bewildered look.

"What if Dracula only took a little blood from each of many victims and didn't leave a trail of bodies?"

"I suppose nobody would have known.... Hey, wait a minute," Randy said with a sudden gleam in his eyes. "If we bet with enough bookies and do a healthy rotation of the ones we zap we leave no footprints!" he said and laughed. "We could even place losing bets as a smoke screen. No foot prints and no shadow."

"There are rules that have to be followed faithfully or we could both end up in a very dangerous situation," Kim said as he shifted in his chair.

"Yeah, stealing money from bookies, and that's how they'd see it, could be real unhealthy if we get caught," Randy said as he picked up his beer.

"If we take a reasonable amount of caution and follow the rules we have nothing to fear from a bunch of thugs."

"Okay, what are the rules?"

"It's not enough to know the rules, you have to understand them," Kim said as he reached down and pulled a book out of his backpack. "To understand you have to have a glimpse of a world I perceive and resolutely believe in," Kim said as he slid the book across the table.

Randy picked up the book and looked at it.

"I've never heard of Carlos Castaneda."

"He's an Anthropologist from Berkeley. His original intent was to do a field study of the Yaqui Indians of Mexico and their use of hallucinogenic plants. His study ended up being a vehicle that provided him with a completely different view of the world, a different reality. Read the book."

"Unusual cover," Randy said as he set the book aside.

"Unusual subject," Kim said with a smile.

"Can we talk about the rules or do we have to wait until I've read the book?"

"There are three very simple rules. First, we cannot use the money in such a way that another person is harmed. We can't invest in a drug smuggling ring and we can't give money to a wino when we know he's going to buy a bottle. Buy him lunch instead. Second, the money is to be used to help others whenever possible. If we neglect to help someone simply because we've earmarked the money for something else we're on a very risky path. Third, we take only what we need. To let ourselves be blinded by our own greed is to toy with devastating consequences. If we hold steadfastly to these rules we'll be protected by forces that are unknown to the world of science. If we falter those same forces will turn on us."

The pilot's voice on the intercom announcing their departure from Colorado airspace broke Randy away from his memories. He kept his eyes closed as he felt his body relax and drift toward sleep.

When Jerry walked into the dim light of Clancy's place it was as a stranger. He always heard stories about the elegant watering hole catering to judges and attorneys from the nearby courthouse but had never checked it out himself. The inside of the tavern seemed friendly and inviting with etched mirrors, brass railings and a long mahogany bar. Carved wooden signs hung from the ceiling in appropriate locations identifying features such as the side bar, the witness stand and the jury box. Another sign behind the bar above the expensive bottles of liquor listed three house rules. No lynching, no ex parte communications and no jury tampering.

"How about a beer?" Jerry asked as he walked up to the bar and pulled out a stool.

"What flavor?" the bartender asked as he finished drying a glass.

"You got Michelob Lite on tap?"

"Yep. Twelve or twenty four ounce?"

"I'll start with a twelve," Jerry said as he climbed up on the stool.

"Comin' right up," the bartender said as he walked toward the line of tap handles at the center of the bar.

"Don't think I've seen you in here before," the bartender remarked as he opened the tap and started filling the frosted mug.

"You haven't," Jerry responded. "This is a new place for me. I'm meeting a friend for lunch. She claims that your tenderloin sandwich is the best in town."

"Sounds like a regular," he said as he set the beer in front of Jerry.

"She might be. She works down the street at the museum."

"Tall with long, dark red hair and a great pair of legs," the bartender said with a big smile.

"Yeah, that's her."

"Beautiful woman," he said as he walked toward the other end of the bar where another patron was holding up an empty beer bottle.

"Yes she is," Jerry said to no one in particular. He raised the mug and took a drink as he thought of Joyce. She was more than just beautiful. She was in a category all by herself and he wanted to call the bartender back to his end of the bar and tell him so. He wanted the world to know how alluring she really was. He wanted to brag about how magnificent her body was and how good she was in bed. It was at that precise moment that he knew he had fallen hopelessly in love with her.

There was a part of him that needed to bare his soul and confess his feelings, but the fear of driving her away was simply too great. He wondered how long his heart could tolerate a purely physical relationship with her. His heart responded with a craving that felt as though a bottomless pit had opened in the center of his chest.

He knew he needed to focus his mind on something other than his emotions. The consequences of letting his heart set the pace of their relationship were simply unacceptable. He supposed the key was to throw himself into the physical relationship with total abandon and fuck his brains out. Maybe that much sex would deaden the pain of a tortured heart.

As he picked up his mug and raised it to his lips he suddenly remembered the reason for meeting her for lunch. The mysterious bone fragments. He was still baffled by the results of the carbon dating. The data seemed so unlikely that he ran the tests a second time just to verify.

Jerry looked up into the mirror as the door behind him opened and a shaft of sunlight spilled into the dimness of the tavern. For a fleeting moment he saw the silhouette of a woman pass through the doorway, then the door swung closed, eclipsing the light. Drifting on the breeze that whispered through from the outside was a scent that he recognized instantly.

"Could I interest you in some company," Jerry said as he pivoted around on the barstool.

"Oh, I'm not supposed to talk to strangers," Joyce said with feigned shyness as she walked toward him.

"Not even if the stranger has candy for a good little girl?" Jerry said, responding to the game.

"Well, I guess that's different," she quipped as she stepped up to the bar and rubbed up against him.

"Hello. What can I get you to drink?" the bartender asked as he walked up and set a napkin on the bar in front of Joyce.

"I'll take a small Miller draft and a couple menus at the table in the corner," Joyce said as she grabbed Jerry by the hand and pulled him off the stool. "I'm taking you to my table," she said as she led him along the line of bar stools. "I don't know if it's the luck of the draw or just a corner that most people don't like, but it's always empty when I come in. A bartender carved my name in the bottom of it one night when I was helping close up. So, like I said, it's my table."

"Is this place really a hangout for judges and lawyers or is that just a bunch of hype?" Jerry asked as he pulled a chair out and sat down.

Joyce took a quick look around the bar as she pulled out her chair.

"Out of the twelve or so people in here I count three lawyers that I recognize. That sounds like a fairly significant percentage. I don't think that's normal for just any bar."

The bartender walked up to the table, set a beer in front of Joyce and handed each of them a menu.

"Bobby, how many lawyers in here right now?" she asked.

The bartender looked around the tavern.

"I count five, but there are a couple people I don't know."

"Is that about normal?"

"Yeah, probably, except for election night. After the polls close this place looks like an ambulance chasers convention," he said with a chuckle as he headed back to the bar.

"There's your answer, pretty much straight from the horse's mouth."

"Since you know this bar so well and we're at your table, what do you recommend for lunch?" Jerry asked as he opened the menu.

"I've already mentioned the tenderloin. It's high on the list, but they make a Reuben that's out of this world."

"That sounds really good," he said as he closed the menu and laid it on the table.

"Bobby's starting to get busy. I'll put our order in since my schedule's running a bit tight," Joyce said as she stood up, grabbed the menus and walked toward the bar.

Jerry felt a burning desire for her as he watched her hips move under the slinky dress. She made him feel like he could make love to her all night and still want more. The memory of her dropping the silk robe at the side of her bed and slipping between the sheets with him exploded in his mind and fanned the fires of his lust.

"Okay, I put a rush on the sandwiches. They should be out in a few minutes," Joyce said as she returned to her seat. "What did you find out about the stuff I gave you this morning?"

"Real strange," Jerry said as he shook his head. "The pieces were definitely bone fragments, no doubt about that, but the carbon dating...I'm not sure what the data is trying to tell us."

"What do you mean?"

"You've had statistics in college. I'm sure you remember about the bell curve and normal distribution."

"Sure. The values from a sample are supposed to fall within the six standard deviations of the bell curve unless something real unusual is happening."

"Yeah, that's it," Jerry said as he nodded his head. "You gave me a sample of about sixty five bone fragments. About fifty five of those fragments tested to be between ten thousand and seventy thousand years old."

"Oh my God. Seventy thousand years? The oldest bones we have in the museum only date back about eight thousand years!"

"That's not at all my point," he said as he picked up his beer. He took a long drink and returned the mug to the table. "The age of those fifty-five fragments all fell within the six standard deviations. It was practically a text book case."

"And what about the other pieces?" Joyce asked.

"They were completely out of the ballpark. They were all less than a hundred years old, which pretty much represents the limits of my equipment. Those bones could have been dead for a week or a century. And there's something else that got my attention. There were microscopic bloodstains on almost every fragment. Those stains seemed very recent. There wasn't enough to test, but I'd bet my last buck they were no more than a day or two old."

"Ralph," Joyce whispered.

"What?"

Joyce shook her head.

"Ralph is a security guard at the museum. He was missing when Samuel arrived for work this morning. I was thinking maybe it was Ralph's blood, but that doesn't make any sense at all. I mean if it was Ralph's blood there'd be a lot more than a few traces on those bone fragments. And where in the hell did the fragments come from anyway?"

"I hope that was a rhetorical question because I don't have the foggiest notion. Maybe we should talk about something a lot less troubling, like seeing each other tonight."

"I'd like that," Joyce said with a smile. "I don't know exactly when I'll be getting home. Samuel might have plans to take our visiting geologist to dinner. I'll have to go if he does, but I can call you when I get home. Maybe you can pick up a bottle of wine."

"What kind of wine do you like?"

"Something with just a sweet touch. Some wines make me want to take off my clothes," she said with a sensuous smile.

Samuel raised the cardboard nameplate to his shoulder as the walkway door opened and arriving passengers began spilling out onto the concourse. He felt conspicuous as he tried to make eye contact with each passenger, but he supposed that was the whole point. He wanted to be noticed. This was the place to hook up with Dr. Lippencott, even if it meant standing in the middle of the isle yelling out his name.

The first class passengers were past him with no one giving him a second glance. He continued to watch the crowd, quickly passing over the women and children and focusing on the faces of the men. As more people moved past him he began to feel anxious and sorry they hadn't established a specific meeting place or discussed their respective appearance and attire.

After a few minutes the flow of people exiting the plane slowed to the point that he began to worry. Lippencott either walked past him without noticing the sign or missed the flight all together. When he saw the flight crew moving slowly behind a bearded man walking with a cane he knew something had gone wrong. He lowered the sign as he turned and looked around for anyone that seemed to be waiting.

"Samuel?"

He turned back and saw the bearded man with the cane walking toward him.

"Samuel Prince?" Randy asked.

"Yes. Dr. Lippencott?"

"Yes," he said with a smile as he extended his hand. "Please, call me

Randy."

"Randy, glad to meet you," Samuel said as they shook hands. "I was afraid I missed you."

"I should have told you I'd be the last one off the plane. Vietnam slowed me down a little," he said as he raised the cane in evidence. "I don't like to get in the way, so I just wait and follow the crowd."

"Not a problem," Samuel said with a laugh. "Can I take your bag?"

"No, it's okay," Randy, said as he repositioned the shoulder strap. "It's easy to handle."

"Do you have other luggage to pick up?" Samuel asked as they started walking toward the front of the airport.

"Nope. I travel light. If I don't have room for it in my duffel bag I don't take it."

"How was the flight?" Samuel asked as the worked their way past a crowd waiting to move through the metal detectors.

"Departure was right on time, I didn't lose my luggage and the plane landed in one piece. That doesn't leave a lot to complain about."

"No, not really," Samuel said with a chuckle. "Are you hungry?"

"Well, I missed a real breakfast. I thought I'd get something on the plane, but they served doughnuts, which I don't eat, and coffee that was strong enough to walk. The university must have booked me on a cheap flight. I'm hungry, but what I need most is a good cup of coffee."

"I'll take care of that," Samuel said as he turned in the direction of a coffee shop.

"I hope you don't mind the delay," Randy said as he followed Samuel's lead.

"Certainly not. We don't have any deadlines to meet. My assistant will be expecting us, but she can wait. Besides, I can't have you tired and hungry when you just flew a thousand miles to help us out."

"How far are we from the museum?" Randy asked as they made their way through a crowd waiting to retrieve luggage.

"It's about eighty miles, but it won't take long. It's interstate all the way. That's one of the penalties of living in a small city like Lima. If I need to fly on a commercial jet I have to drive to Toledo, Columbus or Dayton."

"Really, that's not so bad. The traffic around Denver is terribly stressful, especially if you're trying to get to the airport for a flight," Randy said as they walked into the coffee shop.

"I've never wanted to live in a high population center just because there's so many damn cars. Work weeks are long enough without sitting in traffic every day," Samuel said as he stopped at a table and pulled out a chair.

"You know, after talking with you on the phone there were some things about your artifact that I found very troubling," Randy said as he moved to the other side of the table. "I was concerned you might be a little crazy."

"Oh, I'm not crazy," Samuel, said as he shook his head.

"I'm afraid I have to agree," Randy said as he pulled out a chair and sat down. "Based on what I've seen so far you seem to know where all your marbles are. That's good for you, but it leaves us with a perplexing problem. There's something about the artifact that doesn't quite add up."

"Let me guess. You're having trouble swallowing this thing about carved totems and petrified wood. Right?"

"Then you've already questioned this obvious paradox?"

"Of course. It kept me awake the best part of last night," Samuel said as a waitress walked up to the table.

"Hello, gentlemen. What can I get you?" the woman asked.

"I'd like a cup of black coffee. Do you have pie?" Randy asked.

"We have apple pie with cinnamon ice cream and pumpkin pie with whipped cream."

"I'll have the apple."

"And you sir?" she asked as she looked over at Samuel.

"I'll have the same, except I'd like cream and sugar for my coffee."

"Thank you, gentlemen. I'll be right back with your orders," she said and walked away from the table.

"I know this contradiction puts Archaeology at odds with Geology," Samuel continued, "but I have to be honest in my assessment. I've examined the totems closely with this problem in mind and I remain steadfast in my opinion. The features are carvings done prior to the onset of petrification."

"I have to go into this with an open mind, no matter what science tells me. If I examine the artifact and conclude the same thing it will require expanding or possibly even rethinking some very basic theorems. I'm after the truth and I hold no professional prejudices. If it takes an archaeologist to point out that something has been overlooked in the science of Geology, so be it."

"There's something else you may find quite troubling about the artifact," Samuel remarked. "We spoke at length about the frame because it was easy. We have a common base of knowledge about petrified wood, but the crystal is different. I've made observations that I find impossible to express. I don't know the language, I just know it's very unusual."

"Yes, of course, the mysterious crystal that nobody has ever seen before. I feel obligated to point out that a newly discovered mineral simply opens a new category. It doesn't play havoc with what we thought were the rules of nature."

"You simply don't understand yet, and that's my fault. Let me try to fumble my way through an explanation," he said as the waitress came back to the table carrying a tray with their order.

"The coffee just finished brewing, so it's hot. Enjoy the pie. I'll be back to check on you in a few minutes," she said with a smile.

"Thank you," Samuel said as she walked away from the table.

Randy grabbed his fork and took a quick bite of the pie.

"Oh, God, Samuel. This pie is delicious! It's certainly not typical of airport food."

"Maybe you're just exceptionally hungry," Samuel said with a laugh.

"Maybe so," Randy said as he raised his cup. "You were about to fumble your way through some kind of explanation about the crystal."

"Yes, I certainly was," he said as he tore open a packet of sugar and dumped it into his coffee. "Every crystal I have ever seen has had quite similar characteristics. There is always some kind of geometric shape, and the faces are always smooth, like glass. I've never seen a crystal with surface texture like this, until now."

Randy fixed a troubled gaze on him as he lowered his cup slowly.

"You just gave a very simplistic text book definition of a crystal. Atomic composition will manifest distinct differences in the color and shape of the crystals, but they always have smooth surfaces. There should be no exceptions."

"I'm afraid you have another problem, if there are truly no exceptions to that rule," Samuel said as he added cream to his coffee. "This artifact is going to prove to be a real problem for you."

"Samuel, you're making me crazy," he said as he leaned forward. "Gather your thoughts, take a drink of your coffee and tell me what's captured inside this frame."

Samuel had a pensive look on his face as he picked up a spoon and started stirring his coffee slowly. After a moment he set the spoon aside, raised his cup and sipped at the hot brew.

"You don't have a real good reference to size since you've never seen this damn thing, so I'm going to back up a bit," he said as he returned his cup to the table. "The frame is approximately twelve feet high and seven feet wide.

It's very imposing, both in size and appearance. It literally looks like something right out of an Edgar Allen Poe nightmare. Within the enclosure of the frame is a slab of black slate that is probably about eight inches thick. The crystal is embedded in the slate. The crystal itself is about seven feet high and three feet wide. It has the traditional geometric shape, but the surfaces...the surfaces aren't smooth, they have a roughness. Under close examination I found tiny pyramid shapes protruding from the surface."

Randy stopped the pie-laden fork half way to his mouth and gave Samuel a blank stare. After a moment he lowered the fork back to his plate without taking the bite.

"Samuel, that...that's impossible," he stammered. "Crystals have smooth faces because of the way the atoms build on each other. They have smooth faces, no exclusions."

Samuel shook his head slowly. "Either I have an exception to that rule in my lab, or...or it's something other than a crystal."

"Samuel, finish your pie," Randy said anxiously. "I need to examine that artifact."

The early morning sun reflected off the chrome of the big rig as it careened around the curve with tires squealing and thick black exhaust spewing from the twin stacks. Inside the cab a pulsating ribbon of plasma passed from the palm of Kim's hand to the center of the driver's chest. The driver's face was frozen in a maniacal grin as a lightning storm of firing neurons raged through his normally befuddled brain. Acute visual and tactile impulses, arcane equations and transcendental visions flashed through the shared cerebral matter as it processed information and channeled electrical responses through nerve fibers at the speed of light.

Kim looked into the driver's murky awareness and knew he was experiencing nothing more than the thrill of a roller coaster ride. There was simply no connection between the flickering consciousness languishing in the primitive recesses of the medulla oblongata and the semi streaking along the mountain highway at speeds well beyond its design limits.

He felt the driver's heart beating wildly and knew the body was on the threshold of total collapse. The heart was pushed well beyond its ability to recover, the adrenal glands were withered and dry and the nervous system was approaching complete overload.

The eighteen-wheeler began to slow as the driver applied the air brakes and worked through a series of downshifts. After several long skids the truck came to a shuddering stop on the outskirts of Estes Park as smoke billowed up from smoldering tires.

The driver slumped against the steering wheel and gasped for air as Kim withdrew the plasma nexus. He raised his head slowly as he struggled for breath and looked at Kim, offering a weary smile. "Did we make it?" he whispered as he tried to sit up. After a momentary fight for balance he collapsed back onto the steering wheel. The damaged heart muscle continued beating for a moment and then fell silent.

Kim raised the driver's lifeless torso off the steering wheel and pushed him back against the seat. He was a simple man who was transformed by a fleeting glimpse of the inner light, a man who begged for a chance to redeem himself by offering up his life for humanity. The sacrifice could not go unrewarded, he thought as he closed the man's eyelids and straightened his hair.

Kim opened the door, climbed out onto the running board and looked back as the driver's soul separated from the corrupted body and passed through the ceiling of the cab. In that instant he understood that the man's karma had been purged of negative energy.

Kim closed the door, dropped down to the ground and started walking along the edge of the highway toward the mountain community. He was acutely aware that time was critical and every moment he spent on his feet pushed his friends closer to a hideous fate. As he walked along the pavement he reached out with his mind, probing for anything useful.

Two old men in the back room of a nearby Sunoco station bantered over politics while trying to outwit each other from opposite sides of a chessboard. The young man working the gas pumps was cleaning the windshield of a red pickup while gazing at the legs of a beautiful blonde behind the wheel. His body trembled at the thought of touching his lips to hers while fondling her breasts. The woman took great pleasure in teasing the youth as she casually moved the hem of her skirt and exposed more of her inner thigh.

The manager of the Howard Johnson's motel across the street from the Sunoco station was in his office splitting up seven kilos of cocaine with the owner of a Boulder ski resort. He snorted two long lines of the powder and passed the drug-laden mirror to his partner. They both spoke of retiring to Hawaii with the profits, but neither knew the toll the drug had already taken on their circulatory systems.

The proprietor of the Red Rocks Grill and Tavern next to the motel watched nervously as six members of an obscure motorcycle gang took turns picking at the waitress who was trying to clear their table. His hope that they leave quietly after eating their steak and eggs faded as they ordered two pitchers of beer.

Kim watched as a faded blue 1973 Corvette convertible with loaded luggage rack slowed as it went passed and signaled a left hand turn. After waiting for traffic for a moment the deteriorated sports car turned into the Red Rocks parking lot. As he probed the mind of the woman behind the wheel he found a graduate Doctor of Veterinary medicine on her way to Indianapolis and a new practice. Kim checked for traffic and trotted across the highway as he projected a tiny bolt of plasma toward the woman with the short brown hair.

Jamie Lawson had been on the road for four hours when she saw the sign in front of the Red Rocks Grill and Tavern advertising steak and eggs for seven dollars. She had a good nights sleep at the Motel 8 in Steamboat Springs, but leaving at five o'clock in the morning before any of the local restaurants opened was a mistake. Now, after nearly two hundred miles of desolate winding highway, she wasn't going any further without breakfast.

She turned into the parking lot and pulled the car into a space at the front of the log building next to a line of motorcycles. After doing a quick hair check in the rearview mirror she shut off the engine, pulled the keys from the ignition and was struck by a sudden and profound sense of deja vu. The intense sensation was overpowering. She unconsciously let the keys slip from her hand and fall to the floor as she struggled to clear her mind and focus her thoughts. A moment later the tenuous remains of a fleeting memory faded, leaving her distracted and confused.

She tried to reconstruct her thoughts directly prior to the episode, hoping to grasp onto some thread of the mental images, but it did no good. The more she pressed for some recollection the more vague and remote the experience became. After a few seconds she gave up and let the incident slide away into oblivion.

She grabbed her purse from the passenger seat and was about to open the door when she saw a man standing near the front of the car. A gust of wind tossed the man's long black hair as he looked at her with dark, intense eyes. At that moment a wave of powerful feelings and memories flashed through her mind with such force that she was momentarily stunned. The sudden flood of recollection was relentless as a dynamic bond engulfed her mind. She knew this place and she knew the man who was looking at her.

She opened the door and climbed out of the car as quickly as she could, ready to reacquaint herself with the man from somewhere in her past. The feeling of familiarity began to fade as she pushed the locked door closed. A moment later the phantom memories were gone and she was left standing in front of a total stranger with a bewildered look on her face.

"Are you all right," Kim asked as he stepped toward her.

"I...I'm not sure," she stammered. "I just had the strangest feeling...like I'd been here before and...and I knew you."

"I don't believe we've ever met," Kim said as he extended his hand toward her. "Kim Lee."

"Jamie Lawson," she said with a smile as they shook hands. "I can't shake the feeling that I know you from somewhere, but I can't put my finger on the memory either. I wouldn't mind the company if you'd like to have breakfast with me. Maybe I can remember where I've seen you before."

"I don't know. I've got to keep moving."

"Aw, damn it!" Jamie cried as she opened her purse and started digging around.

"What's wrong?" Kim asked.

"I think I locked my keys in the car," she responded as she continued to search her purse.

Kim walked over to the car and shaded his eyes as he peered through the window.

"You sure did. They're laying on the floor in front of your seat."

"Damn it, I don't have time to sit around waiting on a locksmith," she said as she stopped her search and walked over to the car. "I don't even know if a locksmith can help me."

"Go get a table, I'll get your keys for you and we'll have breakfast."

"How do you plan to get my keys? I'd rather wait on a locksmith than have a broken window," Jamie said cautiously.

"I can get into your car and I promise I won't break your window."

"How?" Jamie demanded.

"Trade secret. I use to repossess cars for a living. Get a table and I'll be along in a minute."

"How do I know..."

"Trust me," Kim said as a transparent thread of plasma passed between them.

The cautious expression on Jamie's face melted away and was replaced by an indulgent smile.

"Okay," she said as she turned and walked toward the tavern.

Kim watched Jamie as she moved up the steps, crossed the veranda and disappeared through the doorway into the Red Rocks. After a moment he turned back toward the car and placed a hand with two extended fingers near the lock cylinder. A tiny bolt of plasma crackled as it jumped from his fingers and flashed into the key slot. A small wisp of smoke curled up passed the window on the inside of the car as Kim opened the door. He waved the smoke away as he stooped down, retrieved the keys and relocked the door.

When Kim stepped into the Red Rocks a moment later he found a typical tavern complete with dim lighting and a jukebox belting out the twang of Country Western music. It was only the smell of charbroiled steak hanging in the air that seemed to lay claim to the grill part of the name.

"Over here," Jamie said from a table in the corner near the bar.

Kim walked over to the table and dropped the keys beside Jamie as he pulled out a chair.

"Charming place," he said sarcastically as he looked over to the far corner where the owners of the six motorcycles were gathered around a large table drinking beer and bragging loudly about their exploits.

"Yeah, they're assholes. They all whistled when I walked in. I only stayed because I knew you were on your way. Thanks for getting my keys."

"Happy to help," he replied as the waitress walked up to the table.

"I have to apologize for the crowd over in the corner. They're certainly not regulars. I just wish they'd leave," she said with a troubled expression. "What can I get you folks?"

"I'd like coffee and the steak and eggs breakfast. Over easy on the eggs and medium on the steak. One check," she added.

"And you sir?"

"Scrambled eggs and wheat toast, please."

"Coffee for you, too?" she asked.

"I'll just have water," Kim responded absently as he watched the group in the far corner. A man with a shaved head and chains hanging from a sleeveless denim jacket gestured toward their table. The others turned for a look and started laughing. A man with a leather vest and tattooed arms smiled and nodded his head before turning around. A man wearing a World War One pilot's headgear and goggles pulled up on his forehead offered a wide smile, exposing golden front teeth.

"I can't shake the feeling I know you from somewhere," Jamie said as she studied Kim's face. "Have you ever been to San Francisco?"

"I have to be honest with you. We've absolutely never met, but I am responsible for those feelings that hit you outside."

"What in the world are you talking about?"

"I projected my thoughts into your mind and created a flash of memories."

Jamie started laughing as the waitress walked over to the table and set a steaming cup of coffee in front of her and a glass of water in front of Kim.

"I'm sorry," she said as the waitress walked away. "You'll have to excuse me for laughing, but that's funny, and if you really believe it, you need help. I suppose you're going to tell me you can read my thoughts, too," she said with a snicker.

"How else could I possibly know that you're moving to Indianapolis to open a veterinarian hospital?"

The smile disappeared from Jamie's face as her jaw dropped.

"How...how did...you know..." she stammered.

"I know I'm scaring you," Kim said as he reached out and touched her hand. "But don't be afraid, I mean you no harm," he said in a reassuring tone.

"I don't understand. Who are you?" Jamie demanded.

"I will explain as much as I can, but not right now. We are in an unstable situation that requires the utmost caution. I didn't reach into their minds until I sat down," he said as he gestured toward the motorcycle gang. "Those people are dangerous and we should leave."

"We can't just get up and leave. We've got breakfast coming and I'm starved. Besides, I'm having more than just a little trouble buying what you're telling me. Maybe we do know each other from somewhere. Maybe that's how you know where I'm going."

"See the guy with the tattooed arms that just walked over to the jukebox?" Kim asked.

"Yeah, I see him," she said as she tore open a packet of sugar and dumped it into her coffee.

"He's coming over here with intentions of getting you out on the dance floor. He's showing off for his buddies and won't hesitate to use force if required."

"You're going to look real stupid when he walks back to his table and sits down," Jamie said as she stirred her coffee. She watched in disbelief as the man turned away from the jukebox and looked at her with an impure grin. Patsy Cline was singing about her man with the cheatin' heart as he took his first step in the direction of their table.

"Oh, my God," she whispered. " What should I do?"

Kim pushed her purse and keys over to her forcefully.

"Run for the car," he said as he stood up and pulled her to her feet. "Wait for me."

"But..."

"Go!" he said as he shoved her toward the door.

"Hey, bitch, where you goin'," the tattooed man yelled as he tromped in her direction. "I played that song for you!"

"She's not interested," Kim said as he whirled around and faced the man.

"Fuck you, I'm talkin' to her," he said as he continued his pursuit.

Kim stepped to the side and pushed him back.

"Hey, you slant eyed motherfucker," he screamed as he regained his balance. He stepped to the side and let loose with a thunderous right hook.

Kim sidestepped the punch, grabbed the extended arm and twisted it back behind the man as he screamed out.

"This can be as easy or as hard as you want," Kim said as he forced the man back toward the center of the tavern. "We're leaving the place to you." He released the man's arm, pushed him toward his table and backed away.

"You're one dead son of a bitch," the man growled as he stopped short of running into the table. He turned around and stepped toward Kim as the others stood up around the table.

"Kick his ass," someone yelled.

"I'm gonna do more than kick his ass," he screamed as he picked up a chair and threw it aside. "I'm gonna have that pretty hair of his. I'm gonna do the scalp thing," he said as he pulled a long knife out of his boot. He threw another chair aside as he moved in toward Kim with the knife swaying back and forth in front of him.

Kim sidestepped a lunge and backed away.

"Call the police!" the proprietor yelled from the kitchen doorway.

"Touch the phone and you're dead," the man with the golden teeth growled.

The tattooed man lunged again with the knife.

Kim sidestepped the blade, grabbed the man's wrist and snapped his arm at the elbow with one smooth, quick motion.

The man's face was filled with confusion and shock as he stared at his ruined arm. The knife slipped from his hand and fell to the floor as he began screaming.

"Billy, I want you to cut this fucker's liver out," the man with the shaved head said as he pounded on the table.

The man with the headgear and goggles pulled a knife from each boot as he stood up.

"Hey, China boy," he mocked. "Man says I gotta cut ya," he said with his golden grin as he stepped forward.

"Gut 'em, Billy," the tattooed man cried as he leaned against the wall clutching his broken arm.

Billy closed in on Kim with menacing speed as he raised the knives to the top of their deadly slashing arc.

Kim plunged his hand toward Billy's chest with fingers extended, released a small bolt of plasma and held it for an instant before backing away toward the door.

Billy went ridged for a moment before falling to his knees. Both knives fell to the floor as he teetered momentarily, then fell forward on his face.

When Kim ran out the door he found the Corvette waiting with the passenger door open. He glanced back at the line of motorcycles as he jumped into the car.

"Go!" he yelled.

The old sports car had seen better days but it still had enough to smoke the tires as it screamed out of the parking lot.

One of the other men from the gang ran to the door and got a glimpse of the speeding Corvette as it fishtailed through the intersection.

"Got 'em!" he yelled back into the tavern.

Inside the Red Rocks the man with the shaved head stared at Billy's body in disbelief.

"Can you ride?" he asked as he looked over at the tattooed man who was cradling his broken arm.

"I don't know," he cried.

"Al, help him get back to the garage, then come back for the other bike," he said as he shoved the table out of the way and ran toward the door. "You two are with me. Get the sawed off loaded up, we're going to even this score right now," he bellowed as they rushed out into the parking lot.

"They went that way in an old blue Corvette," one of the men yelled as he jumped up on his motorcycle and hit the start button. The engine cranked, soon followed by another cranking engine and a third. All three motorcycles continued to crank, but no cylinders fired.

"What the fuck!" the man with the shaved head screamed as he jumped back off the motorcycle. He crouched down next to the machine and looked at the engine. "What the fuck," he repeated as the others were dismounting their Harleys. The spark plug wires crumbled in his hand as he reached in to examine them.

"Son of a bitch," he screamed as he stood up and kicked the machine.

Steve felt heat rising off the blacktop in waves as he walked up the drive toward the museum carrying a bag from Wendy's and two cans of Pepsi.

"It's way too hot for that walk," he said as he stepped off the drive and crossed the grass to the bench where Luther was sitting.

"It be damn hot," Luther said as he looked up at the clear sky. "Hot enough to be wishin' for more rain," he added.

"This lucky streak of yours isn't right," Steve said as he handed Luther a can of pop and plopped down on the bench. He retrieved his sandwich and handed the bag to Luther.

"I'll tell you what not be right," Luther said as he raised the Pepsi to his lips. He took a long drink before lowering the can. "Ralph's car jus' sittin' there like...like a dead body. That ain't right. Why don't somebody move it or somethin'. It be spooky."

"I heard Rudy talking with that Pinkerton guy. I guess nobody knows where the keys are," Steve said as he raised his can of pop and took a drink.

"An' that's somethin' else that not be right," Luther said as he took his sandwich out of the bag. "Those men in their fancy uniforms that come in here this mornin'. They jus' come stormin' in like...like the FBI or somethin'. Rudy don't care nothin' 'bout what happened to Ralph, he jus' wants to get things normal again. Ain't nothin' normal 'bout that man sittin' in Ralph's chair."

"You don't have to go in and out as much as I do, so you really haven't had to deal with that prick. I have to sign in every time I go in for something and sign back out when I leave. And he really has this attitude, you know, like he's in charge of the whole damn place or something. I swear, if they could train a monkey to punch a time clock they could put one to work as a guard," Steve grumbled.

"Poor ol' Ralph. What you suppose happened to him? You think he got kidnapped by aliens or somethin'?" he asked as he unwrapped his sandwich.

"I don't know, Luther. Alien abduction sounds a little far fetched, you know what I mean? For people to claim they were kidnapped is one thing, but we've got a missing person here."

"Them people was missin' while they was gone!" Luther protested. "Ralph can't tell us about his kidnappin' 'cause he ain't back yet. It's what happened,

I can feel it in my bones."

"How can you know something like that?" Steve demanded as he pulled a rag out of his back pocket and mopped the sweat from his forehead.

"Boy, it be in my bones, I tell ya. An' when these ol' bones of mine start talkin' I be listenin'. They told me all 'bout that artifact thing of Joyce's down in the lab. That thing be trouble, nothin' but bad trouble," he said and took a bite of his sandwich.

"I don't know about your bones, Luther. I think they give you bad signals sometimes. Joyce's artifact is creepy looking, no doubt, but that's all. There's nothing dangerous about it, unless it fell over on you," he said with a laugh as he unwrapped his sandwich.

"There be somethin' lots worse about that thing," Luther demanded. "It gives me the willies deep on the insides."

"Hey, there's Sam," Steve said as he noticed his car waiting to turn into the drive.

"Where's he been?" Luther asked with a mouthful of Wendy's cheeseburger.

"He went to Toledo to pick up somebody. I guess the guy's going to look at the artifact or something," he remarked as the Thunderbird turned into the drive. "I better go tell Sam about the change in the security team," he said as he set his sandwich aside.

"This is my home away from home," Samuel said as he turned the car into the drive.

"Impressive. I expected the museum to be surrounded by tall buildings, not real estate. I bet a lot of work goes into keeping the grounds in good shape," Randy said.

"There's the two guys that keep the place from falling down around our ears," Samuel said as he honked the horn and waved at Steve and Luther. "Doesn't look like Joyce is back yet," he said as he wheeled the car into a parking place.

"Joyce?"

"My assistant curator. You'll like Joyce. She's probably about your age," he said as he shut off the engine. "She's the one who actually discovered the artifact. Poor girl found a dead body at the same time. It wasn't a real good morning for her."

Randy felt his heart stir at the mention of the name. For a brief moment he considered asking more about the woman, but dismissed the notion that she might be Joyce Robbins as insane.

Steve and Luther walked up to the car as Samuel opened the door.

"Any word about Ralph?" Samuel asked as he eased out of the car.

"Not a thing," Steve said as he closed the door for Samuel.

"Guys, this is Randy...uh..."

"Lippencott," Randy said with a smile.

"He flew in from Denver to take a look at the artifact. Randy, this is Steve and Luther. Steve looks after the building and all its needs and Luther takes care of the grounds."

"Hi, guys," Randy said with a wave of his hand from the other side of the car. "Nice to meet both of you."

"You, too," Steve said with a nod.

"You come all the way from Denver jus' for that awful thing?" Luther asked.

"Yeah, I did," Randy said with a smile. "Doesn't sound like you care much for it."

"No sir," he said as he shook his head slowly. "That thing be nothin' but bad business. You be understandin' when you see it."

"Come on, Randy. I'll show you the artifact so you can form your own opinion. See you guys later," Samuel said as he started toward the museum.

"See you guys around," Randy said as he moved to join Samuel behind the car.

"Sam, things are a little different in there," Steve said as Luther walked back to the bench.

"Different how?" Samuel asked as he stopped and turned around.

"Pinkerton security is on duty," Steve replied. "Three guards and their supervisor showed up right after you left. Everybody's gone now except for Wyatt Earp."

"I guess I'm not surprised. Why are you calling him Wyatt Earp?" Samuel asked.

"Just the way he acts. You'll really like him," he said sarcastically.

"Thanks for the heads up," Samuel said as he turned back toward the museum.

"Something unusual going on?" Randy asked as they continued across the blacktop.

"Last week our managing director gave our security guards two weeks notice of termination based on his intent to bring in Pinkerton to replace them. This morning when I got here we had a guard missing, so he brought them in ahead of schedule."

"Is that who you were asking Steve about?"

"Yeah. When I got here this morning the doors were locked, just like he never left. His car is still sitting over there," Samuel said as he opened the plate glass door and held it for Randy. He continued to hold onto the hope that Ralph was sleeping off a drunk somewhere, but he knew the clock was working against that particular theory. He knew it was past time for him to be wandering back to the museum for his car.

Samuel followed Randy into the museum and felt the relief of the cool air.

"Feels real good in here," Randy said as he stepped into the small lobby.

"Yeah, it does," Samuel said as he gestured toward the stairwell. "We're going downstairs. Sometimes it gets a bit chilly down there," he said as they moved toward the steps.

"Excuse me, you both have to sign in," came a gruff voice from the security station.

Randy stopped and looked at Samuel.

"You've got to be kidding," Samuel muttered as he looked back at the security station. A tall man in a Pinkerton uniform with closely cropped hair and a thin mustache was looking back.

"You both have to sign in," the guard repeated.

"This is bull shit," Samuel said as he turned and walked toward the security station with Randy following.

The guard grinned smugly as he turned a log sheet toward Samuel.

"Logging in and out is a requirement now," he said as he took a pen out of his pocket and laid it next to the log.

"Do you know who I am?" Samuel asked in a tense voice.

"No sir, and I don't really care. Security may have been somewhat lax in the past. As a member of Pinkerton Security the door is my responsibility and signing in is a requirement."

"Oh, and whose requirement would that be?" Samuel demanded.

"That would be my requirement based on Mr. Van Burg's direction that traffic in and out of the building is one of my basic responsibilities," he responded firmly.

"I'm Samuel Prince, head curator for this museum and I won't sign in and out. Furthermore, I'll tell everyone else to refuse to sign. This isn't a military complex, it's a museum and your job is to key a set of time clocks every hour, not to keep track of the location of everyone who works here!"

"If you don't sign in I'll be forced to log you in myself and report your attitude to Mr. VanBurg," the guard announced.

"Yeah, you do that. Have Rudy come and see me if he doesn't like my attitude," Samuel said as he turned and walked toward the steps. "Come on Randy, let's go have a look at the artifact."

"And what's your name?" the guard demanded as he glared at Randy.

"Randy, don't pay any attention to that moron," Samuel said as he started down the steps.

"Sorry," Randy said with a shrug of his shoulders. "I guess I'm not supposed to sign in." He offered a curt smile as he turned and followed Samuel down the steps.

As Joyce approached the museum she continued to probe her thoughts for an answer that might explain the bone fragments. Finding bone debris scattered in the lab seemed unusual, but not to the point of being mysterious. There were certainly plenty of bone sources within the museum, and while it was difficult to imagine a way they might have gotten scattered through the lab during the night, she could hardly deny the possibility. It was also possible that if there were stray fragments they might have been quite old, although it seemed unlikely. Unlikely, but possible just the same. So there was a very slim chance of explaining the presence of fifty thousand year old bone fragments in the lab, and if that was possible most all of the others could be accounted for also. And that was the rub. A successful theory had to explain all of the fragments, not just most of them, and there was simply no way to rationalize the one hundred year old sample with the blood stain in the context of the other debris. And that threw the whole question right back into the enigmatic fog she was trying so hard to work through.

She pushed the bone fragments to the back of her mind as she turned into the museum and wondered if there was any word about Ralph. When the car got to the crest of the drive she noticed Steve and Luther sitting on their bench. She let the Porsche roll to a stop and set the brake as she powered down the window.

"Hi, guys," she yelled. "Any news about Ralph?"

Steve jumped up from the bench and trotted across the grass to the blacktop.

"Not a word," he said as he stooped down next to the car. "Rudy brought Pinkerton in already. It's like he doesn't give a shit about Ralph or what happened to him. It's just business as usual."

"You didn't really expect his actions to have any kind of human quality, did you?"

"Yeah, I guess that's a good point," he said absently as he gazed upon the beauty of her face and thought about the long legs that were just beyond the car door. "I haven't seen much of you the last couple of days. I miss your face...and some other parts," he said with a mischievous grin.

"I know. School was keeping me busy enough, and then things really got hectic when I found the artifact. It seems like things have been non-stop since then. We need to get together, there are a couple things I want you to do for me," she said as a sensuous smile spread across her lips.

"You make me crazy when you smile at me like that," he said as he felt her sexual presence taunting his manhood. "I'd like to return the favor," he said and licked his lips slowly.

"Stop that," she cried softly.

"You better go see your boss. There's a visitor from Denver looking at your artifact," he said as he stood up and adjusted the fit of the front of his pants.

"Looks like you've got a problem," she said with a laugh as she released the brake and pulled away. She turned the sports car into a parking space next to Samuel's Thunderbird as she wondered how she was going to manage two relationships and two jobs without going crazy. She shut off the engine and climbed out of the car laughing to herself at the thought of quitting both jobs.

She started across the blacktop toward the museum as her mind went back to the bone fragments. Her thoughts immediately fell back into the same paradigm that always led to the same bewildering dead end. When she pulled opened the door and stepped into the museum she realized the only theory that might explain all the fragments was an act of vandalism. The thought of a bunch of kids tearing through the plastic covering at the outside doorway into the lab and scattering bone fragments about just for kicks suddenly sounded like the ravings of a lunatic. It was at that moment that she realized she had arrived at the absolute end of the road. There was no answer, she thought as she started down the steps.

"Excuse me. You have to sign in."

Joyce turned and looked back at the security guard with a confused expression.

"I'm sorry, what did you say? My mind was a million miles away."

"You have to sign in," the guard repeated.

"Sign in?" she questioned as she walked back to the security station.

"What in the world are you talking about?"

The guard turned the log toward her as he pulled the pen from his shirt pocket.

"Signing in and out is a requirement now," he stated bluntly.

Joyce looked down at the log sheet for a moment.

"That's not Sam's writing," she said as she looked up.

"I was forced to sign him in myself. His uncooperative attitude is going to be reported to Mr. VanBurg."

"Doesn't look like his visitor signed in either. I guess you're not having much luck today," she said as she turned away.

"Hey, you didn't sign in," the guard protested.

"Guess you better tell Rudy," she said and laughed as she moved across the lobby. She ignored the repeated demands for her name as she started down the steps trying to understand why there was no apparent answer to the bone fragment riddle. Having no answer was impossible, yet it was the only thing that made sense.

She left the steps and moved out into the room as she wandered around the display cases waiting for an intuitive flash that might give her a new approach to the problem. After gazing at the bones in each of the display cases she shook her head and walked toward the office hoping Sam might come up with an answer.

When Joyce walked into the office Samuel was standing at his desk leafing through a thick book.

"Sam, you're not going to believe the test results I got on that stuff you found in the lab this morning," she said as she walked to her desk and set down her purse. "They were all bone fragments."

"How's your Latin? Ever hear of something called Antitheus Vitrum?" Samuel asked absently as he looked up from the book.

"Sam, you're not listening to me! What you found in the lab this morning were bone fragments, and the data from the carbon dating is unexplainable!"

"Yes, dear. I heard you," Samuel said as he turned away from the book. "Unexplainable bone fragments. We'll have to discuss that when we have time. Right now there's a geologist in the lab examining the artifact. According to him we have the only example ever discovered of something called Antitheus Vitrum. He said it's a crystalline structure that was predicted to exist by an archaic Numerology based science a couple thousand years ago. Go introduce yourself while I go back to this mathematics book from the library. He says I might find a brief entry about it in the section on imaginary numbers."

"What's his name?" Joyce asked as she moved toward the doorway into the lab.

"Randy...Randy something or other. You know how I am about names."

"Yeah, I know. Sometimes I'm surprised you remember mine."

When Joyce walked out into the lab she saw the back of a tall man with a cane standing in front of the artifact.

"Have you ever seen anything quite so gruesome?" she asked as she walked toward the man.

After all the years that had passed Randy recognized her voice immediately. It was a moment that was filled with disbelief, denial and finally shock. The sudden realization that Joyce was standing behind him hit like a runaway train.

"Joyce Robbins?" he managed to choke out as tears welled up in his eyes. "I tried so hard to find you when I got back," he said as the tears found their way down his face.

"Do we know each other?" Joyce asked as she watched the man turn toward her. Her eyes embraced his, and for a moment time stopped, frozen between the present and a past that seemed like a different lifetime. The face was older; the hair shorter, there was a graying beard and a scar above one eye, but it was Randy. The world suddenly turned ashen gray and began to spin out of control.

Randy lunged forward and caught Joyce as her legs buckled and she fell toward the floor.

"Samuel!" Randy screamed as he eased Joyce to a prone position.

"My God, what happened?" Samuel demanded as he came running out of the office.

"She fainted. We need smelling salts," he responded as he cradled her head and wiped the tears out of his eyes.

Samuel ran back to the office while Randy felt for the pulse in her neck. Her heart rate was fast, but beginning to slow and her respiration was steady. "Wake up, sweetheart," he said softly as he stroked her cheek with the back of his fingers and watched her eyelids for any sign of returning consciousness.

"I don't understand why she fainted," Samuel said as he came rushing back into the lab. "She was fine a minute ago!"

"Joyce and I know each other," Randy said as he looked up.

"But why in God's name did she faint?" Samuel asked as he knelt down next to them holding an ammonia capsule in his hand.

253

"She thought I was dead."

Samuel's face turned pale as he looked over at Randy.

"Oh, my God...you're the Randy that was killed in Vietnam?"

"Almost killed. Certainly a mistakenly identified casualty."

"Oh, my God," Samuel whispered as be broke open the cap and waved it under Joyce's nose.

A second later Joyce pulled away from the inhalant as her eyes fluttered open. She looked at Samuel with a blank, disoriented stare for a moment before bolting upright into a sitting position and turning toward Randy.

"Oh, my God!" she cried out as trembling hands covered her mouth. "You're dead!" she screamed and began to cry. Samuel helped her to her feet as she took several steps back away from Randy and began to sob hysterically. "You're dead," she shrieked as her entire body began to shake.

"Come on," Samuel said as he pulled her back toward the office. "I need to get you off your feet," he said as she continued to wail. "You better stay here in the lab for awhile," he said as he looked back at Randy.

Randy watched helplessly as they disappeared into the office amid Joyce's mournful sobbing. He wiped tears away from his eyes as he listened to Joyce cry uncontrollably. Seeing her again after so many years filled him with such joy that he felt lifted beyond human experience, yet mixed with the joy came the pain of witnessing her devastating emotional breakdown and the fear of what might follow.

Samuel walked her into the office, guided her around the desk and lowered her down into her chair as she continued to sob. He took a handkerchief out of his pocket and handed it to her.

"Oh, my God, this can't be. He's dead. I must be going crazy," she cried with a trembling voice.

"I don't know what happened, but he's really out there in the lab."

"He can't be," she screamed angrily. "He's alive after all this time? Why the hell didn't he look for me?" she demanded.

"Maybe he tried," Samuel responded in a soothing voice. "I remember you telling me about how you ran from the pain. How long did you wander around the country before you came here?"

Joyce shook her head as she tried to remember the time she spent wandering the country aimlessly. It seemed so long ago. It suddenly hit her that there were a number of years before she met Samuel and settled in Lima that she was nothing more than a transient. She found herself wondering if anyone could have found her during that time.

"I'm feeling so many different things right now," she said as the tears began to slow. "I'm angry, I feel betrayed, but mostly I'm just confused. I feel like the world isn't spinning quite right. It's like the first few seconds after waking from a dream and not knowing what's real."

"You've had quite a shock. You'll be all right, but it's going to take some time."

"Sam, I think I need to get out of here for the rest of the day. I think I'll go home by way of Clancy's and get drunk," she said as she stood up.

"What about Randy?" Samuel asked.

"I don't know. I can't really think about it right now. Maybe tomorrow after I recover from my hangover I can deal with it," she said as she handed the handkerchief back to Samuel. "Sorry, it has my makeup all over it. I bet my face is a mess."

"It's dark in Clancy's," he said and kissed her on the forehead. "You take care of yourself, I'll deal with Randy."

"Thanks, Sam. I'll see you in the morning," she said as she picked up her purse. She offered an awkward smile as she moved past him and walked toward the door.

Samuel watched her walk away, hoping she might stop and come back, but she continued out of the office. He walked over to his own desk and dropped down into the chair as he wondered how to explain things to Randy.

"Randy, come on in here," Samuel shouted as he closed the mathematics book and pushed it aside.

A moment later Randy stepped into the office cautiously as he looked around for Joyce.

"She left, Randy. Come on in and sit down," he said as he gestured toward Joyce's desk.

"She's gone?" Randy asked with a shaken voice as he moved toward the desk.

"Yeah. I'm afraid it was all a little too much for her. She's pretty much a basket case right now. I think she just needs some time to herself. I hope she'll be a lot more stable tomorrow."

"I feel so bad about what happened," Randy said as he went around the desk. The lingering smell of Joyce's fragrance tormented his heart as he lowered himself into her chair. "I really did try to find her when I got back, but with no family to contact it was hopeless. I had no idea what her social security number was and the school absolutely refused to give it out. The only thing they offered me was the address in Wounded Knee where they mailed her degree. I went there and actually found a few people who knew her, but they had no idea where she went."

"I'm not sure she knows where she went. I believe losing you was far more devastating to her than losing her parents in the car wreck."

"We were so much in love," Randy said as he wiped a tear away. "I can't even begin to tell you what I felt when I found out I had been reported as killed in action. I was numb. I couldn't even think."

For the next half hour Samuel listened intently as Randy talked about college and a life three friends shared, the last summer they spent together, the personal tragedy of Vietnam and the long fruitless search for Joyce when he got home. Finally his tale of lost love came back to the present.

"I always dreamed of finding her someday, but I never thought about how traumatic it would be for her to see me after believing I was dead. I'd give anything if this could've happened differently."

"I'm an old man. I've seen a lot of terrible things happen during my years, but this is awful. My heart is broken," Samuel said as he struggled with his own emotions. "The only way to fix my heart is to get you two back together where you belong," he said as he stood up and looked at his watch. "I think I know where she went."

When Samuel walked into Clancy's it took a moment for his eyes to adjust to the dim light, but he knew exactly where to look. As soon as he saw the silhouette of a woman sitting at the table in the corner he knew it was Joyce. As he approached the table he saw her staring absently into a mug of beer. Between her and the mug were a neat line of six shot glasses, four empty and two containing an amber liquid.

"Mind if I join you for a minute?" he asked as he walked up to the table and pulled out a chair.

"Sam, what are you doing here?" she asked as she looked up from the mug.

"Checking on you," he replied as he dropped down into the chair. "Looks like you've got a good start on tomorrow's hangover."

"Yeah, good old Wild Turkey," she said as she picked up a shot glass and raised it in front of her. "Here's to the people, whoever they are, who got us involved in Vietnam. May they rot in hell," she said loudly, downed the shot and slammed the empty glass back on the table. "I'm very sorry for leaving you to take care of things. Is Randy okay?"

"He's a basket case, just like you, maybe not quite as bad. After you left the museum he started talking about his college days and his relationship with you and Kim. I just let him talk. I figured it might help for him to bare his soul. He told me a lot about that time in your life, stuff that I never heard from you. Now I understand why you found it so difficult to talk about. The three of you had a very special relationship, the kind that most people only dream about. I'm just now beginning to understand the true depth of your pain. He told me about what happened in Vietnam, and he told me something else, something you need to hear. He really did try to find you when he got back. He looked for you and Kim both, but after a few years he gave up the search. He always hoped he'd run into you someday, but at some point I think he stopped believing it would ever happen."

"Where is he?" she asked as she pushed the last shot of Wild Turkey over in front of him.

"Thanks, I'm sure I need it worse than you do. He's outside in the car," he said and downed the shot. "He really wants to see you."

"I want to see him, too. I feel bad about running away like I did."

"I wouldn't give it a second thought. I think you had a very normal reaction to a severe emotional shock," he said as he stood up and pushed in the chair. "I'll send Randy in, then I'm heading back to the museum. It might be a good idea to call a taxi when you're ready to leave."

Joyce stood up cautiously, put her arms around Samuel's neck and hugged him tightly.

"You're the sweetest man I know," she whispered. "Thank you for caring about me enough to try to set things straight."

"I just want you to be happy," he said as he hugged her back. "I'll go get Randy."

She stood next to the table watching Samuel cross the bar and suddenly her heart was awash in a sea of emotions. She felt a love for Samuel that had once belonged to her parents, a love she hadn't allowed herself to feel for so long. She also felt a stinging bitterness for the years that had been ripped from her life by the war in Vietnam, a bitterness that was tempered only by the unexpected regret she felt for refusing to face the emotional pain in her life. As the emotions flooded her heart she finally understood the terrible price she paid for not allowing grief to run its natural course. It was a price counted by broken relationships and the misery of a life without love.

Light spilled onto the floor and surged momentarily into the darkest corners of Clancy's as the door swung open and the shadowy outline of a tall man hobbled into the bar. The door closed behind the figure, eclipsing the light and returning the tavern to the pseudo twilight.

Joyce stood there looking across the bar at Randy and felt her body trembling as her heart began to race. After a moment she took a cautious step toward him as she struggled to counter the affects of the alcohol. She grabbed the back of a nearby chair and steadied herself as she watched Randy move toward her slowly.

Randy moved toward Joyce slowly as he felt his pulse pounding in his throat. It was as if his heart was suddenly alive with songs of love. With the songs came a flood of memories that brought tears to his eyes and trembling to his body. His soul was on fire as he moved closer to her and prayed that it wasn't all simply another cruel dream from which he was about to awake.

They both came together in a firm, weeping embrace that rendered up their years of separation and brought a measure of peace to both their hearts. They cried together, their tears mixing on their cheeks as they held each other, both afraid to let go, and then they kissed. The touch of their lips brought harmony to their souls and melted away the icy cold fingers of death that had separated them.

"I need to understand what happened," she said in a shaky voice as their lips parted. She wiped tears away from her face as she took Randy by the hand and led him back to the table. She returned to her chair and pushed the empty shot glasses aside. "I think you've got some catching up to do."

"I'm surprised you can still walk," he said as he glanced at the shot glasses.

"Yeah, me too. I think I'll stick with beer for the rest of the afternoon."

"Welcome to Clancy's," the bartender said as he walked up to the table. "What can I get you?"

"A pitcher of Bud and a bottle of Cuervo. I think we only need one shot glass," he said as he looked over at Joyce.

"Yeah, just one. I don't think Tequila and Wild Turkey will mix too well. You can take these," she said as she pushed the empty shot glasses toward him.

"Ok, pitcher, Cuervo and one shot glass coming up," Jimmy said and grabbed the glasses. "Looks like we have some kind of reunion going on here. The pitcher's on the house," he said as he backed away from the table.

"Thanks, Jimmy," Joyce said as she watched him walk back toward the bar. After a moment she turned back toward Randy as her hand went across the table to his.

"I know we have a lot to talk about, but there's something I have to know first. Are you in a relationship?"

"No. I've tried a few times, but there was always something missing, something I just couldn't deal with. Maybe I was never able to move on because I knew you were out there somewhere. I was surprised when Samuel told me you were still single after all these years."

"When I lost you something in me died, or at least I thought so. I never even wanted to try to be as close with anyone else as I was with you. Oh, I wasn't ready for the convent, I've had plenty of physical affairs, but I never let anyone get too close. I thought the part of me that felt love was dead."

"Two crippled hearts wandering aimlessly through life. It's a terrible thought," he remarked as the bartender came back to the table.

"I started a tab for you," Jimmy said as he set the pitcher of beer, bottle of Cuervo and glasses in the center of the table. "I'm not going to come back here and disturb you two, so let me know if you need anything."

"If Joyce owes anything for her drinks put it on my tab."

"You got it," Jimmy said as he walked away from the table.

"I don't want you doing that," Joyce protested.

"Don't be ridiculous. I'm the reason you came down here to get drunk," Randy said as he picked up the pitcher and filled both mugs. "At least let me pay for it."

"It's not necessary, but thank you," Joyce said as she picked up her mug and raised it in a toast. "Here's to mending crippled hearts."

Randy raised his mug, touched it to Joyce's mug gently and consummated the toast with a long drink.

"That's the best beer has tasted to me in a very long time. There must be a connection between taste buds and happiness."

"Tell me what happened in Vietnam," Joyce said as she returned her mug to the table.

"After all these years, even after all this, it isn't easy to talk about," he said as he picked up the bottle of Tequila and twisted the cap, breaking the seal. He pulled the shot glass over in front of him, filled it and set the bottle aside. "The Vietnamese called the mountain Dong Ap Bia and the press called it Hamburger Hill. We just called it hell. There were about eighteen hundred men from five battalions that went in after the bombing runs and artillery batteries stopped the pounding. The price we paid for that piece of real estate was horrific." He picked up the shot of Cuervo, tossed it back in his mouth and refilled the glass. "My platoon was one of the first to go in. They dropped us into an area that was nothing short of hell on earth. There were bodies of Vietcong and North Vietnamese soldiers still smoldering in their foxholes.

The stench and smoke of burning flesh hung in the air like the smog in Los Angeles. As we moved up the mountain I remember shell bursts exploding in the air above us, the sound of automatic weapons all around and the screams of wounded men calling for medics. It's all pretty much a blur. I really don't remember many specifics and I have no memory of being wounded. I remember waking up in a hospital bed with a nurse changing the bandage on my leg. She yelled for a doctor and pretty soon this guy was in the room shining a flashlight in my eyes and asking me a bunch of stupid questions. Later that day one of the nurses told me I'd been in a coma for about three weeks and I was the only survivor in my platoon."

"Oh, my God," Joyce whispered as she watched him down the shot and chase it with a drink of beer. "Is that the wound that almost killed you?" she asked as she gestured to the scar above his eye.

He nodded his head as he refilled the shot glass, emptied it and refilled it again. "I've got a steel plate in my head right there," he said as he touched the scar. "And there's another one in my leg."

"Does either of them bother you?" Joyce asked.

"Sometimes my leg aches when it's cold or if I walk too much."

"Why did the Army report you as dead?"

"I was laying in my hospital bed a week or so after I came out of the coma wondering why there were no letters from home. It really had me depressed. For some reason I looked at the plastic wrist band the hospital put on me and I was stunned. It wasn't my name. I'll never forget the feeling of hopelessness that hit me. I knew then why your letters stopped and I was devastated. I was a total basket case and when I tried to explain the mix-up to the nurses they thought I was having a relapse from the head wound. So, of course they immediately sedated me. It was another few days before I was lucid enough to make them understand that I wasn't Randy Stevenson. It was another month before they let me out of the hospital and flew me home. When I got off the plane I prayed you and Kim were there with my family, but I knew you weren't."

"I'm so sorry," Joyce whispered as tears started again. "If I would have stayed with Kim and faced my emotional pain instead of running from it things would have worked out."

"I started searching for you as soon as I was able. The only help I got from school was the post office box in Wounded Knee where they mailed your degree. I drove to South Dakota and after a couple days I actually found some people you'd stayed with for awhile."

"The Lamberts," Joyce said as she wiped tears away from her face.

"Yes. Nice people. When I told them who I was they were shocked and then devastated because they didn't know where you went and couldn't help me find you. I stayed with them for a couple days and then turned my efforts to finding Kim. In my desperation I thought I might find you two together."

"Did you find him?"

"No. After talking with his family I traced him to the Las Vegas area. I found his house. There was a week's worth of mail stuffed in his mailbox and newspapers piled up on the porch. The door was unlocked, so I went in. There was a Mercedes in the garage, food in the refrigerator, cash lying around and a couple real healthy bank deposit books on his desk, but Kim was nowhere to be found. It was like he left for a walk and never came back. I think he was working the casinos, got careless with the wrong people and they killed him."

"He begged me to stay with him," Joyce said as more tears came. "If I had..."

"Don't beat yourself up over the past. Life's too short," he said as he wiped a tear away from her cheek. "It's hard to believe I found you after all these years. Time's been good to you. You're still the most beautiful woman in the world."

"You're so full of shit," she said with a slight smile.

"Not to change the subject, but I'd like to talk about the artifact."

"Good sound scientific work and the light of day usually expose the truth within a mystery. This one seems to become more complex to the point of being a paradox," she said as she blotted her eyes with a handkerchief.

"This discovery of yours is going to hit the scientific community like a ton of bricks," he said as he picked up his beer and took a drink. "There's an archaic science based in Numerology that barely gets even passing mention in the history books anymore because of its outlandish predictions about nature. One of those predictions was the existence of an aberrant crystalline structure that was called Antitheus Vitrum. My Latin is a little rusty, but I believe that translates into English as Devil Glass. Your artifact contains a large crystalline structure that I've never seen before and fits the profile that was established for Devil Glass."

"So even the paradox gets more complex," Joyce remarked.

"Actually not. Remember how Kim used to talk about something he called non-linear thinking?"

"Yeah, I do remember that."

"Okay, let's suppose for a moment those early scientists weren't as stupid as everybody ended up thinking. What if their mathematical scheme of the world was accurate? One of the basic theories about Devil Glass was that it warped time."

"Warped time?"

"Yes. It was actually one of the primary reasons why the entire discipline faded into obscurity. Nobody thought it possible."

"I have to admit I have a little trouble swallowing it myself," she said with a laugh.

"Our concept of time is a little different than it was a couple thousand years ago. We're much more inclined to think of it as a dimensional coordinate and because of that the term time warp conjures up images of time travel. Back then time warp meant the acceleration of natural processes. Suppose for a moment that the theory about Devil Glass warping time, in that context was true. How would that affect what we believe about the artifact?"

Joyce thought for a moment before a surprised look crossed her face. "Oh, my God! The crystal could have accelerated the agatization process. The petrified wood might not be as old as we thought."

"Bingo. Your paradox just crumbled."

"I can't believe it. If we accept the theory that Devil Glass warps time the mystery begins to unravel. You made it sound like there were other characteristics."

"Yes, there were several, but that's the only one that was ever talked about. The others were simply mentioned as being too absurd for discussion."

"How would we go about proving it's actually Antitheus Vitrum?" Joyce asked as she picked up her beer.

"We'd probably start by proving it's nothing remotely familiar. Once we've established that, the scientific community is going to be looking at us very closely, especially if we suggest a thorough reexamination of the Antitheus Vitrum theorem. I really think we can turn this artifact into a career for both of us. There will be papers to write, lecture tours, my God, I can even see a new branch of science based on the Robbins and Lippencott Antitheus Vitrum Artifact! We need to start documenting everything. I think one of the first things we should do is find a good photographer. There's a lot of detail in the frame we need to capture."

"Sounds like you're looking for a partnership," Joyce responded.

"Yeah, I guess I am," Randy said with a smile. "What do you think? Partners?"

"Partners," she said as she offered a handshake.

Randy took her hand, held it in both of his for a moment as their eyes locked. "I never stopped loving you for a moment. I know it's been different with you."

"You're the only one I ever loved. When I lost you my heart simply withered away. Now I'm filled with emotions that I haven't felt in years. I'm so afraid I'm going to wake up to find it's all been a dream."

"I know," he said as he kissed her hand. "If this is a dream I never want to wake up."

"I think I'm ready to get out of here," she said.

"Yeah, I need to get checked into a hotel."

"Don't be stupid. You're staying at my place."

"You sure you're ready for that?"

"There's no way I'm letting you out of my sight."

CHAPTER TEN

Joyce pushed her plate aside and set the remains of her cup of coffee in its place as she watched Randy work on the last of the stack of pancakes. She was astonished by the subtle changes that were occurring around her. Changes that individually might have gone unnoticed in the rush of day-to-day living. She couldn't think of the last time she slept so soundly or awoke so refreshed. The colors of the morning seemed more intense as the sunlight glinted off the lake and played across the kitchen ceiling like shimmering reflections of a bejeweled treasure. The birds sang in a remarkably sweet chorus that seemed more glorious than she could ever remember. She supposed the only real changes were within her. The sunlight was the same as were the bird songs, she was simply taking time to smell the roses. Love was such a wondrous and intoxicating thing.

She remembered the way her body responded to Randy's gentle touch during the night, remembered how they'd made love between lapses of sleep in which they held each other and remembered laying awake in the early morning watching his face as he slept. It suddenly occurred to her that there was an utterly vast difference between having sex and making love and on the heels of that thought came the memory of her intense orgasms during their love making. She smiled as she wondered if Randy had marks in his back from her fingernails.

"Good breakfast," Randy said as he picked up his last piece of bacon and pushed the plate aside. "You certainly haven't lost your touch in the kitchen. Reminds me of one of the reasons Kim and I wanted you to move in with us."

"It didn't take much culinary skill to overcome the lure of cold pizza and beer for breakfast," she said with a laugh. "It took a little more effort to get you guys to give up those damn bologna sandwiches."

Randy laughed with her, but pangs of sorrow passed through him as he reflected upon the memory of their friend and the love the three of them shared. The pain he felt in his heart for Kim was tempered only by the joy of finding the woman he thought had slipped from his life forever.

"I miss Kim," Randy said as he took a bite of the bacon. "It's too bad he's not with us, like we'd planned."

"I know. I miss him too, now that you've come back to me. Last week he was just part of some old, faded memory. Today he's the missing corner of a triangle. I suppose, in a way, you've revitalized those memories and made them stronger for me. Let's promise not to stop talking about the old days just because it's a little painful. I want to keep the memory of him alive, now that I have someone to share it with. Promise?"

"Yes, of course I promise," Randy said as he took another bite of the bacon.

The cat, which had been sitting next to the table waiting patiently for a dropped scrap of food rose up on its back feet and nudged Randy's thigh with both front paws.

Randy looked down at the cat in surprise.

"Your cat just punched me in the leg," he said with a laugh.

"Yeah, he loves bacon, but I'm amazed he's bothering you. He's a little spooky around strangers. I guess he's accepted you as part of the family."

Randy reached down and stroked the cat's head, then offered the remains of the bacon. He smiled as the cat took the meat from his hand and ate it quickly.

"I've never known a cat to eat bacon."

"He loves pepperoni, too," Joyce said as she watched the cat rub against Randy's leg. "Looks like you've made a friend."

"Can he call me Dad?" Randy asked as he scratched the top of the cat's head.

"Yeah, I think that would be appropriate," Joyce responded as she stood up and moved to the side of Randy's chair. "I love you," she said as she bent down, cupped his face in her hands and kissed him on the lips.

"I love you, too," Randy said as their lips parted.

"I've got to make a few phone calls. Just leave the dishes on the table. I'll take care of them when I'm through. There should be a morning newspaper on the front porch. Samurai will want to go out, which is fine. Put a disc in if you want some music."

"Remember to contact a photographer."

"It's on my list, that and burning a couple bridges," she said and kissed him again.

"Burning bridges?"

"My life has taken a completely new path in the last twenty-four hours," she said as she ran her fingers through Randy's hair. "There's a couple relationships, if that's what you want to call them, that are going to end this morning. I'm going to end them and not look back. That's what I call burning bridges."

Randy watched her walk into the bedroom and close the door as he thought about the first time he saw her sprawled on the ground from their collision in front of the university bookstore. He still remembered being gripped by the fear that he might have injured the beautiful young girl with the dark red hair. He never believed in love at first sight, but something certainly came over him that day as he pulled her up off the ground and onto her feet, something he never experienced before. Whatever took hold of him grew into an intense love that never dissipated over the years, a love that now had complete control of his heart.

As he took his cane from the back of the chair and stood up he realized the years had been much more kind to her than himself. Time had brought maturity to her beauty that was undeniable.

He hobbled through the kitchen and out into the living room as Samurai ran ahead to the front door. Randy laughed as the cat stopped and looked back as if to ask what was taking so long. When he finally opened the door the cat ran out onto the porch and quickly disappeared into the bushes. He bent down and picked up the paper as he noticed a Federal Express truck moving slowly up the street. The deliveryman was probably looking for a particular address, he thought absently.

Randy retreated back inside, closed the door and tossed the paper over next to the chair as he moved to the stereo. The compact discs were arranged in alphabetical order by artist in a tower next to one of the tall speakers. As he scanned down the collection he found groups like Allen Parsons Project, The Beatles, Crosby Stills and Nash, The Doobie Brothers and The Eagles and realized he could have been looking at his own collection of music. He stopped the search with the Eagles as he pulled out "Hotel California". After fumbling with the box for a moment he slipped the disc into the machine and pushed the play button. As the group started playing the title song he was reminded of Cincinnati and the concert in Riverfront Stadium in the summer of 1978.

He moved to the chair and was about to settle in with the paper and listen to the music when he heard the doorbell. He laid the paper down, went back to the door and pulled it open. A man in a Federal Express uniform was standing on the porch holding a clipboard and a long box.

"Package for..."

"I hope I can sign for it," Randy said as he interrupted the deliveryman. "I'm the only one available at the moment."

"I really don't care who signs," the man said as he leaned the package against his leg, dropped a pen onto the clipboard and handed it to Randy. Randy quickly scribbled his name on the line and returned it back to the deliveryman. The man took the clipboard and handed the box to Randy.

"Thank you, sir. You have a good day," he said as he turned away and started walking back toward his truck.

"You have a good day, too," Randy said as he closed the door, leaned the box against the wall next to the door jam and went back to the chair. He picked up the paper and started with the front page, reading thoroughly, more from the need to kill time than curiosity as the familiar music filled the room.

After consuming the front section of the paper he moved to the comics, taking time to read even the ones that held little interest. He was half way through the section, leaving his favorites for last when he heard Joyce open the bedroom door.

"That's one of my all time favorite discs," she said as she walked into the living room and over to Randy's chair. "I wore the album out, then replaced it with the disc when I bought the new system," she said as she went to the back of the chair, draped her arms over Randy's shoulders and kissed him on the ear. "I knew who they were but never had any of their music until after I saw them in concert. God, they were great. The stage was set up to look like the front of the album cover. Cincinnati really rocked that night."

"Oh, my God!" Randy cried as he turned around in the chair. "Riverfront Stadium in 1978! I was there! I was at that concert!"

"Oh, you liar," she said with a laugh as she slapped him on the shoulder.

Randy got to his feet as quickly as he could and raised his right hand. "I swear to God, I was there! How else could I have known the year?"

"You were really there!" Joyce squealed. "I've got goose bumps all over my body."

Randy put his arms around her and pulled her into a hug as he kissed her on the cheek. "God, I wonder how close we were to each other?"

"It doesn't matter," Joyce said as she hugged him back. "We have each other now, that's all that counts."

"Oh, yeah. You had a package delivered while you were on the phone," Randy said and kissed her on the forehead.

"I wasn't expecting anything."

"It's over there next to the door," Randy said as he returned to the chair and picked up the paper.

"We're supposed to meet the photographer at the museum about noon," Joyce said as she walked around the chair, picked up the box and moved toward the couch. "Maybe we can get the guy started and take the rest of the day..." She stopped suddenly and looked back at Randy, who had returned to the comics. "Randy...this...this package is...this package is addressed to you," she stammered as a bewildered look crossed her face.

"How can that be?" he demanded as he dropped the paper.

"I...I don't know, but see for yourself," she said as she handed the package to him. "It was shipped from Redding California two days ago."

"How is that possible?" Randy asked as he laid the box across his lap and looked at the shipping label. "I didn't know I was coming to Lima until yesterday! Sure as hell nobody else knew! This doesn't even make sense," he said as he pulled at the shipping tape with little success.

"I'll get a pair of scissors," Joyce said as she ran to the kitchen. A moment later she came back, handed the shears to Randy and stood next to the chair watching.

Randy used one of the blades to slice the tape, handed the scissors back to Joyce and pulled the box open. The inside of the carton was stuffed with large wads of newspaper. While he started pulling out the wads of paper and tossing them into a pile on the floor Joyce ran back to the kitchen and returned with a plastic garbage bag.

"The Redding Sentinel from five days ago," Joyce remarked as she examined one of the wads for a moment before dropping it into the bag.

The box was half empty when he finally exposed a long bundle of the daily publication wrapped about itself like a giant cigar. As he lifted the bundle from the box he could feel something solid beneath the paper. He started peeling away the layers of the newsprint and handing them to Joyce as he worked to free the thing concealed within. As the roll got smaller the shape of the object began to show itself as a long cylinder with a tapering diameter and a larger spherical end. He gasped as he removed the last sheet of newspaper, finding a beautiful rosewood cane with a large brass lion head handle.

Randy cradled the cane in his hands and stared at it for a moment as he started trembling.

"What's wrong?" Joyce asked when she noticed his hands shaking.

Randy opened his mouth and tried to speak, but the words refused to form. The colors of the room suddenly turned pale as a wave of dizziness passed over him and the music seemed to fade away into some distant background.

"Randy, what's wrong?" Joyce demanded in a frightened voice as she dropped to her knees next to the chair and grabbed his arm. The cane slipped from his grasp and dropped to the floor as she shook him. "Randy," she pleaded.

"I'm okay," he whispered as he slumped back into the chair, put his hands over his eyes and wiped them down across his face. "I'm okay," he repeated.

"My God, you don't look okay. All the color is gone from your face. You look like you just saw a ghost," Joyce cried.

"I had a sudden flash of memory...memory of a dream I had a couple nights ago. It was just like the dream, except very vivid, almost like a hallucination," Randy said as he pulled himself up in the chair, leaned forward and looked at the cane lying on the floor in front of him.

"I don't understand what happened. You were fine until you saw this thing," Joyce said as she reached over and picked up the walking stick.

"Be careful, don't touch the handle," Randy said as he held out his hands.

"Why?" she asked as she handed him the cane carefully.

"It's dangerous," he said as he pointed it toward the door, engaged the trigger on the handle and released the long spring-loaded blade from the end of the walking stick with a powerful metallic sound.

The sound and sudden flash of steel startled Joyce, causing her to jumped involuntarily.

"My God, how did you know it did that?" she demanded.

"Kim was in the dream. He gave me the cane and showed me how it worked," he responded as he engaged the trigger again, withdrawing the blade back to its hidden position within the walking stick.

"I don't understand any of this," Joyce said with an uncertain voice.

"Nor do I," Randy said as he examined the intricate design on the lion head handle. "But I'm not going to put a lot of energy into figuring it out either. We need to stay focused on the artifact. There's a lot of work ahead of us."

"What are you going to do with it?" she asked.

"I don't know," he said tentatively. "But it feels good in my hands, almost like it was made for me. I guess I'll use it for a while. It's not like I have no use for a cane."

"The whole thing gives me a case of the willies."

"I'm sure if you think back it's not the weirdest thing to ever happen in your life. Right? Remember how we met? Kim and I went to the bookstore because he dreamed we were going to meet somebody. Just accept these inexplicable events without question. What else can we do? Kim would probably tell you to let the linear thinker in you go to sleep."

"I'll try," she said as she cast a troubled gaze upon the walking stick.

Jerry Lansford sat at his desk and stared out the window, watching absently as the towering pine trees swayed in the wind. He felt emptiness in his heart as he tried to remember her exact words and wondered what he might have done to bring about the unexpected end of their budding relationship. He understood the rules, kept his distance and didn't allow himself to move beyond physical intimacy, even though his heart demanded more. It was impossible to deny he was in love with her, but it was his burden and his alone. And keeping it to himself wasn't easy, but he understood the consequences of any confession. With Joyce he experienced the best, most torrid sex of his life and he wasn't willing to give it up simply to unburden his heart. That's what he told himself, but now, after her phone call he wondered if it would have made any difference.

He found himself wondering if he had simply been a poor judge of her character. Maybe she was nothing more than a seductress, taking what she wanted from the men attracted to her and moving on, leaving behind emotionally scarred victims. His mind wondered, but his heart soundly rejected the notion. She was a beautiful woman who simply loved sex and wanted to have no complications. He didn't understand it, but he accepted it just the same.

He knew something was wrong when she failed to call like she'd promised over lunch. It wasn't like her to bargain with a sexual tryst and not deliver, especially after the sought favor had been carried out, not that the promise had been his motivation. It was simply beyond his capacity to say no to her.

It all seemed so uncharacteristic of her, especially breaking her teaching contract, and maybe that bothered him as much as the break up itself. Seeing her at school and knowing their sexual liaisons were over may have been traumatic, but never seeing her beautiful face again except in some chance encounter somewhere was inconceivable. The thought of never again being able to touch her hand or stroke her stunning red hair as they walked to her classroom left him feeling heartsick and disconnected.

He knew if there was any way to mend the relationship he had to find out what went wrong. The thought of going to the museum and trying to talk to her felt awkward and foolish, yet it seemed the only hope he had. They had to talk, and it had to be soon.

He'd call her, he thought as he sat up in his chair and grabbed the phone book. After a momentary search for the number he stopped and threw the book back on his desk. Trying to speak with her on the phone was the wrong thing to do; it had to be face to face.

He glanced at his watch and realized his next class was still three hours away. The time was set aside for reading through the pile of term papers on his desk, but his mind and heart were elsewhere. The thought of getting in front of students and trying to focus on their educational needs while distracted by emotional stress left him feeling compromised as a teacher. He knew he had to resolve the situation, either by mending their relationship or accepting its termination. He looked at the stack of term papers on the corner of his desk as he picked his car keys and wondered where his heart would be when he returned.

He walked out of his office, again prodding his memories for something that might explain her actions, but nothing came to mind. He tried to put a positive spin on the whole thing as he stopped next to the elevator and pushed the button. Maybe it was just a misunderstanding. Maybe she began to want more out of their relationship than she was prepared to accept. Maybe it scared her and she just needed to talk. Yes, that was it. She just needed to talk, he thought as he boarded the elevator.

As he left Galvin Hall and walked toward his car he tried to focus his mind on something that would divert his attention from the fear that was gripping his throat and creeping down into the emptiness in his heart. It was the fear that the sexual bond between them was truly fractured beyond reconstruction and the deeper, more meaningful relationship he had dreamed of in the future was gone forever. He desperately wanted to maintain the positive spin he'd fixed to Joyce's phone call, yet the fear continued its unabated intrusion into his thoughts.

As he climbed into his car, seared by the hot summer sun, he hardly noticed the stifling heat. He started the car and pulled out of the parking space with his soul possessed and mind locked into an endless search for the magic words that would return Joyce to him and bring peace to his aching heart.

With his mind besieged by turmoil the drive to the museum was nothing more than a blur of street sights and sounds of which he was only dimly aware. He was oblivious to the pedestrians who scurried across the street in front of his vehicle and other drivers who used horns and hand gestures in display of their annoyance with his inattentive driving.

When he arrived at the museum and turned into the drive he saw a photography studio van and wondered if they were taking pictures of the artifact. When his car crested the top of the drive and he saw Joyce's Porsche on the other side of the van the fear gripped him with full intensity. As he pulled into a parking spot he suddenly felt as if he was trespassing into another persons life and wondered if Joyce would even be willing to talk to him. An angry response was the worst thing that could happen, he supposed as he climbed out of his car and closed the door...

When it was new and still bright red the Radio Flier wagon was a prized toy. Years later, after a lifetime of faithful service in the hands of some child it had scrapes, dents and rust holes in the bed, but the wheels still turned, the tongue and axle still pivoted and it still had a job as Luther's lawn tool transport. It usually carried a shovel, rake, weed whacker and other miscellaneous lawn tools, but this day it was part of an urgent plan to avoid the clutches of the sweltering heat. Steve pulled the old wagon past the self serve gas pumps at the Sunoco station next to the museum and stopped in front of the ice storage freezer as the relentless sun blazed down from the cloudless sky and cooked the fresh blacktop.

"This one was only four bucks," Luther declared as he came out of the building carrying a Styrofoam ice chest and two six packs of pop, one cola and one root beer.

"Do we get a free bag of ice for each six pack?" Steve asked as he opened the freezer door and stuck his head in for a few seconds of cool relief from the heat.

"I don't be thinkin' so." He set the cooler in the wagon next to a Wendy's bag and removed the lid. "I asked but he said nope, jus' one per customer," he said as he separated the cans from the plastic retainer and set them in the bottom of the Styrofoam box.

"So, it's a free bag of ice with a six pack, but not each six pack," Steve remarked as he pulled a bag from the machine, tore it open and dumped it on top of the pop. "But if we each got a six pack we'd get two bags. That doesn't make a lot of sense to me. What about you, Luther?" he asked as he looked into the cooler and found space for more ice.

"It don't be makin' no sense to me either."

"You must have heard him wrong," Steve said as he quickly grabbed another bag, dumped it into the cooler and replaced the lid. "Let's go. If the pump jockey saw me take the second bag we'll claim we were confused." They moved with the wagon but nobody came running after them. A moment later they were moving along the sidewalk in front of the museum with the wagon in tow.

"Does it seem to you like it's gettin' hotter than it use to be?" Luther asked as he walked along side Steve and put his hand on the coolness of the retaining wall. "I been hearin' a lot about somethin' called the greenhouse affect an' it's got me thinkin'. I don't remember summer bein' this hot when I was a youngster."

"Yeah, things are supposed to be getting warmer because of certain gases that are being released into the atmosphere, but it's only supposed to be noticeable by comparing the temperatures over hundreds of years. My guess is that you notice it more because you're an old fart and you can't take the heat any longer," Steve said with a laugh.

"You laugh now, but you be as old as me some day, if some old person like me don't shoot you first, that is."

"Luther, you wouldn't shoot me. You know damn well you'd be lost without me to talk to."

"Maybe so," Luther said as he pulled a cigar out of his shirt pocket and started removing the cellophane wrapper. "But I could always have somebody else do it for me," he said with a chuckle. "I could bury you down in my old fruit cellar an' then I could talk to you any time I wanted," he said and added a feigned maniacal laugh.

"Luther, you've got to be more than just a little twisted to even think of something like that," Steve said as a van from the Learman Photography Studio rolled past them slowly and turned into the museum.

"Who's that?" Luther asked as he watched the van move up the drive and pull into a parking place.

"That must be the photographer Samuel said was coming to take pictures of Joyce's artifact."

"What they want with pictures of that awful thing?" Luther demanded as he bit off the end of the cigar and spit it out into the street.

"I don't know, Luther. I guess there's something special about it," Steve said as he turned the wagon into the drive and started pulling it up the hill.

"That Randy guy came all the way from Denver to see it."

"Yeah, well that guy must've made her mad or somethin'," Luther said as he stuck the cigar in his mouth and started pushing the back of the wagon. "Remember how she went tearin' out of here yesterday without sayin' a word to nobody? She was mad as a wet hen."

"She wasn't mad, Luther. There was something else going on."

"Now how do you know that?" Luther challenged.

"Because I talked to Joyce this morning," Steve responded as he turned around and started walking backwards as he pulled the wagon up the drive.

"Boy, I been with you all mornin' an' I ain't seen nothin' of her. When did you talk to her?"

"Remember when Sam came out and got me this morning?"

"Yeah."

"She was on the phone."

"What was so important that she was callin' you before she got here?"

"It was nothing," Steve said as he guided the wagon off the blacktop and across the grass toward their bench.

"Boy, I'll be dipped if that don't sound like you got some kinda secret. Now what'd she call you for?"

"Luther, it was really nothing, so just drop it," Steve said as he pulled the wagon up into the shade, dropped the handle and sat down on the bench.

"I'm not gonna be droppin' it until you fess up. If it was me with the secret you'd be buggin' the dog shit outa me an' you know it. Now what's goin' on?" Luther persisted as he grabbed the Wendy's bag from the wagon and sat on the other end of the bench. He took Steve's sandwich out of the bag and handed it to him. "I be waitin'", he said as he took the lid off the cooler, dug down into the ice and pulled out a can of pop. "It be your turn to talk," he said and handed Steve the can.

"You're really not going to shut up about this, are you?"

"Nope," Luther responded as he reached into the cooler for another can of pop.

"This goes no further," Steve said as he popped the tab on the can. "And I really mean it. If Joyce finds out I told you I'll be pissed off at you for the rest of my life."

"I won't be sayin' nothin' to nobody," Luther said as he set his pop on the bench and put the lid back on the cooler.

"Joyce called me this morning to put an end to something that's been going on between us for about eight months or so."

"Boy, what you meanin' when you say somethin' goin' on between you two?" Luther asked with a troubled expression as he took the unlit cigar out of his mouth and set it on the bench.

"God, Luther, do I have to draw you a picture? Joyce and I have been going to bed together. We've been having sex!"

Luther stared at Steve for a moment as his mind absorbed the confession. "You...you an' Joyce been...been screwin' around?" Luther stammered as he popped the tab on his can.

"Don't make it sound like something dirty, because it wasn't. We were friends, and still are. Our friendship simply had another dimension to it."

Luther picked up his Pepsi, took a long drink and put it back on the bench. "Was you in love with her?"

"I could have been, but it wasn't what she wanted and I respected that. Yeah, I do love her, but as a friend not a lover. Does that make sense?"

"I guess it make jus' as much sense as anythin' else you been sayin'. How come she called an' ended it?"

"I don't know many details, but Randy, the guy from Denver, was an old boyfriend from college. She was real upset when she left because she thought he was dead. She wants to put things back together with him."

"Thought he was dead? No wonder she left the way she did," Luther said as he shook his head slowly. "Boy, all this got you hurtin'?"

"No, she's still my friend, I still love her the same way I did and I'm happy for her. She really sounded different when I talked to her like...like she was truly happy for the first time in her life."

"So how come you been keepin' this secret from me? How come you didn't tell me? I wouldnta told nobody."

"Joyce made a real big deal out of not telling anybody. She didn't want you to know and she especially didn't want Sam to know."

"Oh, you know that be right. Sam's jus' like a Daddy to her."

"Sh," Steve said as he cocked his head to the side and listened. "I hear her car. She's about four blocks away, just getting ready to cross Main, I think."

"Boy, I don't hear nothin'."

"That's why I've always told you to wear those ear muffs when you cut the grass. She'll be pulling in the drive in a minute and you better not be acting funny like you know what's been going on between us. And don't be acting like you know about Randy either."

"I ain't repeatin' nothin' an' I ain't actin' like I know nothin'."

Ancient Elm trees grew along both sides of Market Street and branched outward high above the pavement forming a nearly complete tunnel in the two blocks between the Penn Central tracks and Main Street. The darkness of the passage was punctuated by a series of turn of the century street light reproductions set in the center of a string of islands separating the four lanes. The sunlight glinted off the hood of the Porsche as it emerged from the gray shadows and sped through the Main and Market intersection.

"I can't get over how beautiful certain sections of this city are," Randy said as he looked back at the wooded passageway fading behind them.

"I saw a great deal of the country in those years after I lost you and wandered aimlessly from place to place," Joyce said as she shifted gears and dropped her hand to Randy's thigh. "But this is the place that I was drawn to. The funny thing is I'm not really sure why. It's a nice city, but certainly not the most elegant or beautiful. Actually, Lima probably has more than its share of ugly spots, but I suppose it has enough character to make up for it. Maybe I was drawn to its rich history," she said as she downshifted and stopped for a traffic light.

Randy took her hand, raised it to his lips and kissed it softly. "Or maybe you were drawn to this place by God because he knew this was where we'd meet again."

"You always were a romantic," she said with a smile as she watched the light turn green. The Porsche moved forward through the intersection and accelerated quickly as she shifted to second. "Remember the first time we met?" she asked with a giggle.

"How could I forget? I ran into you and knocked you down in front of the campus bookstore. I was so embarrassed. I was so afraid I hurt you."

"It was all my fault," she said with a laugh. "I was so busy checking you out I'm surprised I didn't trip over my own feet."

"And I was only there because Kim said he dreamed we were going to meet somebody."

They both laughed in delight as she slowed the car and turned into the museum. "There's our guy," Joyce said as she drove the car up the blacktop lane and watched a man talking on a cellular phone climb down out of the van from Learman Photography. She gave the man a quick wave acknowledging his presence as she rolled the sports car past the van and turned into the next parking space. "His name is Dennis Learman," Joyce said as she shut off the engine. "He's supposed to be real good at close ups of animals in the wild."

"That's good. I'm going to need some real close shots to expose the details on the surface of the crystal," Randy said as he pushed his door open.

Joyce noticed Steve watching as they climbed out of the car and felt a bond with him that she hoped could remain unspoiled by the sudden and profound changes that were occurring in her life. He was always more that just a lover, he was a friend and she wanted to do whatever she could to insure the friendship remained healthy.

She stopped at the back of the car and waited for Randy to come around from his side.

"It's really hot," Randy said as he hobbled around to the back of the car with his new cane.

"Yeah, I know. I don't understand how Steve and Luther deal with it. The relief from that storm night before last didn't stay long," Joyce said as they walked around the back of the van together.

The man from the photography studio was just ending his call when they walked around the back of the van to where he was standing. He was noticeably thin with baby fine blonde hair tossed into disarray by a slight breeze.

"You must be Dennis," Joyce said as she walked up to him and extended her hand. "I'm Joyce Robbins, this is Randy Lippencott. Randy, Dennis Learman."

"Glad to meet both of you," Dennis said as he shook their hands. "I'm ready to start unloading my equipment if you show me where we're going to set up."

"Randy, why don't you take Dennis to the lab. Show him the artifact. I want to talk to Steve and Luther for a minute."

"Come on, Dennis. I'll let you take a look at your subject," Randy said as they moved toward the museum.

"I'll be there in a couple minutes," Joyce said as she stepped off into the grass and walked toward the bench where Steve and Luther were sitting. "Hi, guys. What's in the cooler?"

"Pepsi and Hires Root beer," Luther said as he scooted over and made room for Joyce to sit.

"You're more than welcome to a can of pop if you want one, we've got plenty," Steve said as he looked around Luther and made eye contact with her. He was instantly aware of her radiant beauty and wondered if she seemed more alluring because their sexual affair was over. It occurred to him that there might be some connection between the way her voice sounded on the phone and her striking appearance and then he suddenly understood. She seemed to be at peace with herself as if a great burden had been lifted from her heart. She was happy and he knew it was because of Randy.

"No thanks," she said as she sat on the end of the bench next to Luther. "I just wanted to say hi and suggest you guys come to the lab and get your picture taken with the rest of us around the artifact."

"Why you be wantin' pictures of that awful lookin' thing? The world'd be a better place if you jus' dug a big ol' hole an' buried it."

"You're right, it's awful looking, but it's also very unusual and we're in the process of documenting its existence. That's the reason for the pictures. If you found a UFO landing in your back yard you'd be reaching for a camera so you could document the occurrence. It's the same kind of thing with the artifact."

"I ain't gonna be around that thing," Luther said as he shook his head. "It be givin' me a bad case of the willies ever since it got here."

"Well, I'm not quite as superstitious as Luther. I'd love to be in the picture," Steve said.

"Boy, I ain't superstitious, I jus' be knowin' when somethin' bad. You go have your picture taken, but don't be yellin' for me if somethin' bad happens, 'cause I won't be comin'."

"I hope you change your mind. I'd like to have all my friends for one quick picture, but I promise I'll understand if you just can't," Joyce said as she got up from the bench. "Steve, if you've got a second I'd like to show you something on my car and get your opinion on how to clean it off."

"Sure. Be back in a second, Luther," Steve said as he got up from the bench and followed Joyce.

Joyce stopped behind her car and looked back at Steve as he walked across the blacktop to join her.

"I don't see anything," he said as he stopped next to her and looked at the back of the car.

"Don't be stupid," she said with a smile. "I just wanted to talk to you for a second. Are we okay? I want us to remain friends. I hope that's possible."

"Of course we're still friends. I refuse to pretend I won't miss the best sex I've ever had, but friends are forever," he said with a sincere smile as he casually took her hand. "I'm happy for you."

"Thank you," she said and kissed him on the cheek. "Finish your lunch while I go find Randy and the photographer." She backed away from Steve as he held onto her hand until the last moment.

"He better be good to you."

"He will," she said as she turned away and walked toward the museum....

Randy felt the cool air against his skin as he moved into the museum, wondering if the guard was going to give them a hard time about signing in.

"It feels good in here," he said casually as he held the door and waited for Dennis to pass.

"It certainly does," Dennis said as he stepped into the lobby. "Going back out to the van for the equipment will be tough."

"We're going down to the basement," Randy said as he gestured toward the stairwell. "I'm a little slow going down steps, so I'll let you lead the way."

Randy glanced toward the security station as Dennis started down the steps and was surprised when the guard looked their way and said nothing. He followed Dennis, certain the guard would come running after them at any moment, yelling for them to sign in but everything remained quiet except for the sound of his own hobbling footsteps. When he got to the bottom of the stairway Dennis was standing off to the side looking at the mural above the doorway to the office Samuel and Joyce shared.

"I've never been here before," Dennis remarked quietly as he studied the painting. "It's beautiful. Do you know who did the work?"

"I don't have the foggiest notion. Yesterday was the first time I saw it myself," he said as they started walking toward the office. "You'll have to ask Joyce. I'm sure she can tell you."

"I guess I got the impression you and Joyce had worked together for some time," Dennis said as he stopped and looked into one of the display cases.

"I came into town specifically to examine the artifact. Joyce and I have known each other since college, but this is the first time we've worked together."

"Are you both Archaeologists?" Dennis asked as he looked over the collection of arrowheads, spear points and stone knives displayed in the case.

"No, I'm a Geologist, well actually I'm a teacher now. I'm the head of the Geology department at the University of Colorado in Denver."

"Archaeology and Geology seems to be a strange paring," Dennis said.

"I think you'll understand when you see the artifact."

"This stuff is thought provoking," Dennis said as he studied the weapons.

"These pieces of stone are like tiny snapshots in time. When I look at them I can almost see the Indian craftsman sitting at his workplace chipping away at the piece of flint until it suits his mental design. The outcome is nothing short of a record of his talent. I don't think it's that much different from what I do when I'm working."

"Sounds like you should have been an Archaeologist," Randy said with a laugh as they moved past more display cases containing bones, pottery and artwork. "I think you'll find the artifact intriguing."

"I'm already fascinated. I've heard you and Joyce speaking of this object, yet I don't really know what it looks like beyond her vague reference to a totem pole. It's like speaking to someone on the phone and trying to imagine what they look like."

"I could go into more detail, but I think I would be doing you a disservice. I think you'll be much better prepared to capture its essence on film if I let you see it with no preconceived notions of what to expect," he said as he opened the office door. "I really doubt if you'll ever forget your first look at it."

When they stepped into the office Samuel was walking through the other door from the lab.

"Afternoon, Randy. Sounds like everything worked out okay for you and Joyce yesterday," Samuel said as he stopped next to his desk.

"Yes, definitely. I owe you."

"Nonsense. My payback was hearing the happiness in her voice on the phone this morning."

"Samuel, this is Dennis Learman. He's doing the photo shoot for us. Dennis, this is Samuel Prince, head curator and Joyce's boss."

"Glad to meet you, Dennis," Samuel said as they shook hands.

"The pleasure's mine," Dennis replied.

"I was just taking Dennis to see the artifact."

"I've been doing a close examination of the carvings and decided I better start taking some notes. Where's Joyce?" he asked as he grabbed a pad of paper and pencil from his desk and moved back to the doorway into the lab.

"She'll be here in a minute. She stopped to talk to Steve and Luther.

"By the way, did you guys have any trouble with the security guard when you came in?"

"No. He didn't say a word to us. I was surprised, especially since we weren't with Joyce."

"You haven't had the pleasure of meeting Rudy VanBurg yet, have you?"

"No, but I've heard enough about him from Joyce that I know what sort of person he is."

"Well, I had it out with him over his Pinkerton flunkies when I came back from Clancy's yesterday. I'm glad I got through to him," he said as he turned and walked out into the lab with Randy and Dennis following.

"There's your subject," Randy said as he pointed toward the artifact.

"Oh, my God!" Dennis cried as he came to an abrupt halt. "I had no idea it was so big and...and...my God, it looks like something right out of a nightmare."

"We get that a lot," Samuel said with a chuckle as they crossed the lab to the artifact.

"I've never seen anything so...so hideous in my life," Dennis said as stepped over to the object. He reached out and touched the petrified wood as he studied the carved faces. "The detail is magnificent. It will be an honor to capture it on film. Thank you for giving me the opportunity to work with it," he said as he looked up into the gaping jaws at the top of the frame.

"Thank you for appreciating it the way we do," Joyce said as she walked up from behind them.

"I'm amazed, awe struck and...and just a little frightened all at the same time," Dennis said as he turned toward Joyce.

"That's the kind of reaction we get from everybody," Joyce said with a laugh. "Our grounds keeper swears he won't come near the thing, even for a group picture."

"Luther's a bit superstitious," Samuel said as he set the pad of paper and pencil on the workbench next to the artifact. "He wouldn't even think about walking past a graveyard at night and I'm afraid the appearance of this thing plays right into those fears. I like the idea of a group picture, but I just don't see it happening with Luther."

"Dennis, let me show you some less obvious detail we need to capture on film," Randy said as he moved up beside him and reached out to the crystal. "The face isn't smooth, it has tiny pyramid shaped protrusions rising off the surface."

"Yeah, I feel them," Dennis said as he ran his fingers across the crystal. "I noticed a slightly frosted look, but I thought it was color. Isn't that unusual?"

"Very unusual. It's part of the reason we're doing the photo shoot. We need to get some close ups of the surface and expose the texture."

"That shouldn't be a problem," Dennis said as he went back to examining the carvings.

"Let's take the sheet of plastic down from the hole in our wall and let Dennis bring his equipment in that way," Samuel said as he stepped away from the artifact and walked toward the back of the lab with Joyce. "They're supposed to be here tomorrow to put in the new set of doors."

"God, so much has happened it seems like weeks ago that they took the old doors out. I'm glad they're getting it done. It gives me the creeps to think about the critters that could be coming in under the plastic," she said as they stopped at the covered opening. She reached up and removed the top corner of the plastic from the nail holding it in place while Samuel released the edges of the sheet. "I noticed Ralph's car is gone from the parking lot," she said as she went to the other side, released the top corner and lowered the plastic to the floor.

"Rudy didn't waste much time getting it out of here. A wrecker picked it up first thing this morning. You know, it's really hard to get closure with him disappearing like that. I keep hoping he'll turn up, but it's been too long. I'm afraid we're all going to have to except that he's probably dead, I just wish I knew how it happened."

"I know," Joyce said as they folded the sheet of plastic and laid it on the floor next to the opening in the wall. "I keep thinking there must be some connection between his disappearance and the bone fragments you found here in the lab, but it doesn't make any sense."

"In all the excitement about Antitheus Vitrum I nearly forgot about the bone fragments," Samuel said as they turned and started walking back toward the front of the lab where Randy and Dennis continued to examine the artifact. "Next week we'll set some time aside to review the carbon dating data and try to establish what it's trying to tell us. There's probably some perfectly logical explanation we're failing to connect with, but to be honest I don't see how the fragments could be connected to Ralph."

"Yeah, I know what you mean, but it's difficult to think of it as just a coincidence."

"Let's talk about something that's not quite so hard on the head for a moment," Samuel said as he stopped walking. "It's not going to be long before I sign the papers and retire. Martha needs me at home more that you need me here, besides I'm getting tired of dealing with Rudy's bullshit. It's your turn."

"Oh, thanks a lot," Joyce said as she smacked him on the arm.

"My whole point is I want to take something of this place home with me. I want a picture, a picture of everybody around the artifact. Rudy excluded, of course. So how do we get Luther to come down here long enough to pose for the picture?"

"Maybe just like that," Joyce responded. "The picture will be your retirement present from all of us. How can he say no. I'll talk to him when Dennis starts bringing his equipment down."

"You're a real sweetheart. I'm really going to miss you. You have to promise to stop by occasionally and see Martha and me."

"Of course I promise," she said and put her arm around his shoulder and started moving to rejoin the others. "You just have to make sure Martha keeps a supply of her homemade chocolate chip cookies on hand for me."

Rudy VanBurg walked into his office, closed the door and tossed a stack of unopened mail in the center of his hand carved mahogany desk as he moved to the window. He separated the blinds slightly, peered out and watched as a thin man with blonde hair walked across the parking lot with Joyce. The man stopped at the back of a van and opened the doors as Joyce continued on and disappeared behind the lawn equipment shed. He didn't have to see her to know she was joining Steve and Luther at their bench under the old oak tree. It was quite the chummy little club they all had, he thought resentfully as he watched the man with the blonde hair unloading equipment. Whenever Samuel Prince challenged his authority they were all hiding behind him laughing and making fun. He knew the games they played. He detested Samuel and his fucking working class hero bullshit, but he knew all he had to do was bide his time. Samuel wasn't going to put off his retirement for much longer and once Joyce took his place as curator things would get much easier to control. He knew she'd try to continue in Samuel's footsteps but he'd put the redheaded bitch in her place before Samuel cashed his first social security check.

He turned his back on the window, dropped himself into the prematurely worn black leather chair and pulled the stack of mail over in front of him as he continued to brood over Samuel's latest interference in his affairs. The bastard simply couldn't stand it when his security guard buddy was given his termination notice. The Pinkerton guards weren't part of his private little club so he made a big deal out of the security log. There was nothing wrong with the idea of everyone signing in and out. He had the right to know about the movements of everyone on the museum payroll. It was outrageous that Samuel used the log to flaunt his defiance in the face of the new security team. There was a definite need to restore his credibility and demonstrate to the Pinkerton people who was actually in charge.

His contempt for Samuel and need to even the score continued to fester in his gut as he started sorting through the mail. The bills went into a pile next to the checkbook and the junk mail, from bleeding hearts wanting money for whatever cause went to the trash, unopened.

Rudy stopped for a moment, surprised by an unusual yellow envelope with red markings. The distinguished looking envelope had a textured feel and a small red pyramid in the upper left hand corner. Below its base in bold black letters was the name Pyramid Movers and a local return address. He was totally unfamiliar with the group and wondered why he'd never heard of them before. He started to toss the envelope into the trash along with mail from The Boy Scouts, Green Peace and The United Way, but stopped. There was something about the name Pyramid Movers that intrigued him. It didn't matter what charity they represented and he had no intentions of giving them money but his curiosity was aroused. He threw the envelope on the corner of the desk and went back to sorting the mail. When he was finished with the bills he'd go back to the fancy envelope and have a look. It was always more fun to trash junk mail when you knew who was wasting money on postage.

Steve stopped near the outside entrance into the lab and looked back at Luther as he crossed the driveway and stepped off into the grass.

"Luther, it's only a damn picture. You look like a man on his way to be executed," he said with a laugh. "We'll be in and out of the lab in five minutes."

"Boy, I'm only doin' this 'cause Sam be wantin' a retirement picture. Don't know why it had to be around that artifact thing," Luther grumbled as he stopped next to Steve. "I must really love that man."

"I know this is real tough for you, but Sam has done a lot for you and everybody else. Just think of it as payback for the motor he got so I could repair the lawnmower you fucked up. You know damn well Rudy would've fired you over that fiasco if he'd found out."

"Yeah, I be knowin' you an' him saved my job. It's jus' that...that thing be nothin' but bad business."

"Okay, let's get this over with," Steve said as he moved toward the opening into the lab.

"Lord, keep me safe," Luther muttered as he followed Steve.

When they stepped into the lab Joyce and Randy were at the front of the room leaning against a granite laboratory table talking while Samuel helped Dennis position the light towers next to the artifact.

"I've got him here for the picture, but he's more than just a little squeamish," Steve said as they walked toward the front of the lab.

"Hi, Luther," Joyce said cheerfully. "I'm glad you decided to join us."

"I wouldn't be doin' it for nobody but Sam," Luther said as he glanced warily at the artifact.

"Thanks for coming, Luther," Samuel said as he backed away from the portable lighting fixture.

"I promised him we'd be in and out in five minutes," Steve said.

"Sounds like we better get started," Dennis said as he locked the wheels on the light tower and walked over to the tripod holding the camera. "I want everyone to move in around the artifact."

"Are we going to get a sunburn?" Randy asked as he and Joyce moved past the light tower.

"I don't think so," Dennis said with a laugh. "I'm only going to use the camera flash for the group picture. Joyce, I want you and Randy at the center of the artifact. Sam, I want you in front of them, and I want Steve and Luther kneeling down in front of you."

Everyone moved to their positions as Dennis stepped to the back of the camera, peered through the viewfinder and focused the picture.

"Luther, move toward Steve a couple inches and try to relax a little bit," Dennis said as he looked around the camera. "You look like you're scared to death."

"Can't help it. My insides be tremblin'."

"Somebody needs to make him laugh," Dennis said with a chuckle.

Steve grinned and looked over at Luther.

"Luther, remember the limburger cheese we put on the muffler of Rudy's car?"

Luther nodded his head and they both broke into laughter.

"Oh, my God...that was you guys?" Joyce said with a snicker. "He took a beating when he traded that car because they couldn't get rid of the smell."

Samuel shook his head and smiled.

"Okay guys, that's good. Let's tone it down to a simple smile now," Dennis said as he stepped away from the camera holding the remote shutter button. "Say cheese," he coaxed. The flash from the camera flooded the room with an instant of bright light.

"Everybody stay in place for another..." Dennis paused as his attention was drawn to a red pattern of crisscrossing lines spreading across the face of the crystal behind Joyce and Randy. The lines darkened for a moment, then faded and disappeared. "That was strange," he muttered absently. "I want to get a couple more shots."

Dennis took two more pictures and watched as the red lines followed the exact same pattern as before. "I'm getting a real unusual refraction of light on the crystal. I've never seen anything quite like it."

Everybody except Luther craned his or her neck to look back at the artifact.

"I don't see anything," Joyce remarked.

"It only lasts for a few seconds. Let me get one more shot and I'll show you. Okay, Luther, last one. Everybody say cheese." Dennis triggered the camera and again the crisscrossing lines spread, darkened and faded.

"I can't see anything but blue spots from the flash," Joyce said as she looked back at the crystal.

"Me neither," Randy said as Luther jumped to his feet and bolted toward the doorway.

"Thanks for being in the picture," Joyce yelled.

Luther raised his hand, waved and disappeared through the opening in the wall without turning around.

"I don't think I've ever seen Luther move so fast," Joyce said as Steve stood up and brushed off the knee of his pants.

"You guys have no idea how upsetting he finds that artifact. I think it's a little irrational, but that's Luther. I was surprised when he agreed to be in the picture. I guess it's a tribute to how much he cares for Sam."

"Thank him again," Samuel said as he clapped Steve on the back.

"I will when I catch up with him. I've never seen him move that fast either," Steve said with a laugh as he trotted toward the doorway. "See you guys later."

"Don't work too hard in that heat," Joyce said as Samuel and Randy joined Dennis at the camera.

"Okay, show us this light phenomenon," Randy said as they turned and looked back at the artifact. Joyce was standing next to the light tower looking down at the coiled electrical cord connected to the pair of light fixtures.

"Joyce, you want to see this?" Dennis asked.

Joyce ignored the question and continued to gaze down at the electrical cord.

Dennis shrugged his shoulders and triggered the flash. They watched closely as the red lines spread across the face of the crystal, darkened and faded away.

"That's remarkable," Randy said in a surprised voice. "But I'd expect to see more than just red if it was actually light refraction. I've never seen anything like that before, but until yesterday I'd never seen a sample of Antitheus Vitrum either. We're pretty much in uncharted territory. It could be a natural reaction to the bright light."

"Something like a photoelectric cell?" Samuel asked.

"Yeah, it could be. There are so many possibilities to be explored it's a little mind boggling. It's going to be a research gold mine," Randy said as he looked over at Joyce as she bent down and picked up the end of the cord.

"Joyce, what are you doing?" he asked as she cradled the end of the cord in both hands.

"Deja vu..." Joyce responded absently as she examined the plug.

"What?"

"The most intense deja vu I have ever experienced," she announced. "It was like...like a hallucination. I glanced at the electrical cord and...and flashed into this...this vision or something."

"Vision of what?" Randy asked.

"There was something very specific about this cord but it's gone now. It's gone but...but I remember something...an impression. It was like something physically passed through my mind."

"That's weird," Dennis said.

"Are you okay now?" Samuel asked.

"I think so, but there's something about this...I just can't quite put my finger...oh God, there it is," she whispered as she put her hand across her eyes. She stood there with her eyes covered, holding the electrical cord for a moment before dropping her hand and looking back at the others. "This is really strange," she said as she walked away from the light tower trailing the cord behind her. "I've got a sudden, overpowering compulsion to plug this in, right after I tie it to the laboratory table."

The others watched in silence as she looped a section of the cord through a drawer handle, secured it firmly and pulled the free end toward the receptacle in the far wall. When the plug failed to reach the wall she dropped it and walked back to the table. After adjusting the loop for more slack she returned to the wall and pushed the plug into the socket leaving the cord stretched knee high between the table and wall.

"Are you going to leave it like that?" Samuel asked as a puzzled expression crossed his face.

"Yes, I am," Joyce said as the moved back toward the others. "I have no idea why I was compelled to do that, but it has to stay that way. I don't want anyone messing with it."

"Seems pretty strange, but that's the way the last couple days have been going," Randy said with a smile as he tapped his new cane on the floor.

...Jerry moved across the drive toward the museum filled with apprehension that gripped his heart like a vise. He felt the most profound need to talk with Joyce, yet every step seemed to plunge him deeper into the fear he was desperate to avoid, the fear that their relationship was truly nothing more than a fading memory.

He wanted to again feel the happiness of passionate love and bask in the thrill of sharing the joys of life. He wanted to believe his heart would soon be unburdened. He wanted these things and was ready to strike any bargain God demanded to bring peace to his aching heart, yet he felt only despair.

He stepped up to the door to the museum and reached out for the handle when he heard running footsteps. As he turned toward the sound he saw the grounds keeper racing across the parking lot as if chased by the hounds of hell. After watching for a moment he pulled the door open and felt the cool air hit his face. He took a couple steps into the lobby and noticed the security guard rising up out of his chair.

"Afternoon, sir," the guard said as he stepped over to the display case. "Guests are asked to sign in our visitation log," he said as he took a pen out of his pocket and laid it on the logbook.

"I'm here to see Joyce Robbins," Jerry said as he stopped between the security station and the stairwell.

"You must be here for the artifact, too," the guard said as he picked up his pen and returned it to his pocket.

"Yes...yes, I'm a consultant."

"Just about everybody else in the museum is down there. You may as well join them," the guard said with a sigh and wave of his hand.

"Thank you," Jerry said as he turned and started down the steps, wondering if he had chosen the right time and place to approach Joyce. In his office the thought of going to the museum and talking to Joyce seemed so simple and rational. Now it was beginning to sound complicated and ill timed, yet he pressed on, prodded by the hope of rescuing their relationship.

When he got to the bottom of the steps and again witnessed the radiant grandeur of the buffalo hunt mural on the far wall above the office door he remembered the only other time he'd been in the museum. The memory of their leisurely walk through the chamber as they held hands and looked into the display cases sent a wave of emotions flooding into his heart. As he moved past the same displays he remembered her fragrance and the softness of her beautiful hair as it brushed against his arm. He stepped into the office, stopped at the front of her desk and looked over at the telephone he'd used to cancel his classes that afternoon when she suggested they return to her place. His mind was tumbling helplessly into the memories of that first sexual encounter when he heard the sound of heavy footsteps. A moment later a portly man in a blue pinstriped suit burst into the office from behind him.

"Get the hell out of my way," Rudy growled as he pushed Jerry toward Samuel's desk and bolted into the lab. "Prince, what the hell is this?" he screamed.

Jerry regained his balance and eased into the lab behind the fat man as he fought to hold back his anger. He wanted to confront him, yet he feared losing his chance to speak with Joyce. From his position near the door he caught a glimpse of Joyce before she moved in front of the man and out of his line of sight. He had an unobstructed view of Samuel and a stranger walking with a cane as they moved toward the big man. Another stranger with blonde hair was on the other side of the lab walking toward the artifact.

Samuel looked at Rudy with a blank expression. "I really don't have the foggiest notion of what you're yelling about," he responded.

"This!" Rudy screamed as he shook the fist holding a piece of crumpled mail. "Four thousand dollars to have that piece of shit moved here! It's nothing more than trash from the set of some cheap horror movie. It sure as hell doesn't belong in my museum!"

Dennis shook his head in disgust as he stepped over to the light tower. He wasn't sure who the fat man was and he didn't care. He was spouting nothing but dribble, he thought as he depressed the foot switch and felt the instantaneous heat from the lights. He was a photographer, not an archaeologist, but he was educated enough to know the artifact was something other than discarded movie junk.

"You're not an archaeologist, don't try to act like one!" Samuel responded sharply. "Don't try to do my job!"

"Or mine, you overbearing pig!" Joyce added indignantly.

Dennis stepped over in front of the artifact and watched as red crisscrossing lines spread across the face of the crystal. The lines darkened, but instead of reaching a zenith and fading away as before they continued to darken and expand until the entire crystal was an unfamiliar color that seemed to suggest black tinged with red. Purple on steroids, he thought.

"Your ignorance is outrageous," Randy asserted as he stepped toward Rudy. "This artifact is one of the greatest scientific discoveries of the last hundred years...and you think it's movie junk?"

"I don't even know who you are or what you're doing in my museum, so you better stay out of this and shut your yap," Rudy bellowed as he jabbed a finger at Randy.

"I've got something pretty strange going on here," Dennis said as he turned toward the group, but nobody was listening. Only a stranger standing near the door to the office seemed interested in the changes taking place with the crystal.

"He happens to be the head of the geology department at the University of Colorado and my guest," Samuel said, raising his voice. "I will not stand by and let you insult him! I'll have the entire board of directors down here and then we'll find out who's really in charge!"

Dennis turned back toward the artifact and watched in astonishment as the color of the crystal started to break apart, grain at a time and dissipate, slowly exposing a distinct image in the background. Prehistoric photography, he thought as he saw jagged mountain peaks and a crimson sky come into view. The cycle concluded with the exposure of what appeared to be the top of a sand dune in the foreground at the bottom of the picture.

"Don't threaten me, you old bastard. You had no right to do this without my approval!" Rudy yelled as he threw the crumpled piece of mail on the floor.

"You...you guys sh...should stop screaming at each other long enough to...to see this," Dennis stammered as he turned toward the group again.

"We don't need your approval to do our jobs!" Joyce asserted. "If we need a box of paper clips or a new door we'll check with you."

As Dennis stood there wondering if he should repeat himself to get their attention he heard a heavy flapping sound from behind him that was reminiscent of the huge Fox Bats of Africa. He turned back toward the artifact, as the sound grew louder.

"You best stay the hell out of this," Rudy snapped. "This is between Samuel and me."

"Bullshit!" Joyce screamed. "I'm the one that had the artifact shipped to the museum. Your fight is with me."

Dennis's heart froze in terror as he witnessed a single winged creature drop out of the crimson sky and land on top of the sand dune. It was a horrid beast with heavily muscled limbs, leathery reddish-brown hide and cat like eyes. The features of its head and face were feline, the menacing jaws more shark like. The thing beat its wings against the air with powerful thrusts as it moved across the dune with short hops.

"Oh, I see. You think you'll stand up and take the blame to protect Samuel. Well I've got news for you. I just might fire both of you for misappropriation of museum funds."

Dennis tried to scream as he backed away from the artifact but the sound died deep in his throat. The creature hopped through the opening and landed on the floor as it curled its lips back into a hideous grin, exposing deadly teeth. Behind it more of the beasts were dropping onto the dune from the alien sky.

"I think it's safe to say you're not scaring either of us," Samuel asserted. "Let's get the board of directors involved and see what they think."

Dennis made one more futile attempt to scream before the thing reached out for him, sank its talons into his shoulder and pulled him back. Blood sprayed across the floor as the beast snapped its carnivorous jaws and severed his right shoulder and upper arm. His hand and forearm fell to the floor with a thump as the thing consumed the bite. His last optic impressions were of more creatures coming through the opening, and then everything went black as the creature took a bite from his head in a burst of blood and bits of bone.

When Jerry saw the dark color in the crystal dissipate and expose the alien landscape his mind went into a frantic scramble for some bit of stored knowledge that might explain what he thought was a picture. A picture somehow generated by the strange crystal within the artifact. When he saw the creature drop onto the sand dune his pulse quickened as his mind fought to explain movement within the still picture. When he saw it hop through what wasn't supposed to be an opening his brain staggered into shock. He fell back against the wall and raised a trembling hand as he pointed toward the artifact. He tried to scream, but all that came out was the whimper of a tortured mind as it tried to deal with the sudden rift in reality.

"You bastard. My aunt's money put this museum here and it's my job..." Rudy's attention abruptly shifted toward the other side of the lab. He squinted his eyes as he tried to focus on a disturbance near the artifact. When his sight finally embraced the scene it captured a brutal, mind-numbing event that left his intellect struggling for balance. His eyes were suddenly wild with horror as the color drained from his face and he took several shuffling steps back away from the group.

Joyce's tumultuous anger melted into confusion as she watched the terror cross Rudy's face. When he backed away from the group she caught her first glimpse of Jerry cowering against the wall, face contorted in horror. Time seemed to collapse in on itself as her mind registered the aghast expressions. Terror struck her own heart as she came to the stark realization that something behind her had the two men in the clutches of incapacitating fear. She glanced over at Samuel and caught an apprehensive cast to his face as he stared back. She saw Randy turn slightly and look toward the artifact. When he turned back to her his eyes were filled with panic.

She pivoted around and a faint gasp escaped her throat as her eyes fell upon an incomprehensible sight. Grotesque beasts beyond the limits of sanity were somehow coming out of the artifact and fighting over something tattered and bloody. They made low-pitched guttural sounds, snapped their jaws and clawed at each other as they struggled for a share of what she suddenly understood to be Dennis Learman's mangled remains. One of the creatures turned away from the melee and started moving in their direction with blood dripping from its muzzle and talons. A few others followed with shreds of bloody clothing hanging from their mouths. They moved with unmistakable purpose as they opened and closed their raised talons, bared their carnivorous teeth and snapped their jaws.

Her muscles went rigid with fright as she backed away from the approaching horror, feeling her lucidity slipping away. She felt herself lapsing into a trance like state as mysterious memories began crowding into her mind. She was only remotely aware of her body as it began to make slow fluidic movements toward the wall, broken by momentary inanimate pauses.

"Don't run," she heard herself yell out.

Randy was sliding into a similar daze as he felt unfamiliar memories intruding into his mind. An instant later his body started making the same strange dance like movements toward the other wall.

When Samuel whirled around his eyes captured a horrific scene that struck his heart with mortal terror and sent his mind plunging toward insanity. He heard Joyce's warning not to run but it came too late. A primitive part of his intellect responded to the advancing threat with an overpowering command for flight. His spinning maneuver toward the office sparked a similar response in the other two men. The three of them collided in a panic-stricken sprint for the exit that sent Rudy falling into Jerry and crushing him into the door as it slammed closed. The impact with the door twisted Jerry's head around and snapped his neck like a brittle twig. His death was swift and merciful.

The sudden movement sent the approaching carnivores into a savage frenzy. Some ran while others leaped into the air and spread their wings. They fell upon Rudy with ferocious blood lust. They shredded his suit with slashes of their talons and ripped bloody chunks of flesh from his body with their jaws as he cried out in agony. He struggled to protect himself, but his fight was short and came to an abrupt end as one of the beasts took a bite that removed his face in a gush of blood. His body slumped back as his tongue flopped to the side of the gaping hole in his head like a dead fish.

The feast began amid alien growls and savage fighting for a feeding spot as Joyce continued with the peculiar movements and slowly made her way to the wall. As she maneuvered along the wall the limited portion of her intellect that remained coherent yet isolated and encumbered saw one of the creatures closing in on Samuel. That part of her was desperate to help him but powerless to do so and at last accepted his doomed fate. In the same instant she also saw Randy approaching the other wall using movements identical to her own. With unexplainable clarity she understood he was not in danger.

Samuel's eyes were crazed and wild with insanity as the carnivore came for him. He pummeled the creature with demented boldness, striking again and again until his fists were broken and bloody. The beast stopped its approach for a moment and regarded him with its cat like eyes. It growled and bared its teeth as it hopped to the side. It lunged with blinding speed as it slashed its talons across Samuel's chest, leaving a gaping wound. Samuel clutched his bleeding chest and tried to scream as blood spilled from his mouth. He staggered backward as the thing lunged again, snapped its jaws and removed the top of his head in a spew of blood and tissue. His body slumped into a heap as other creatures came for a share of the catch.

The remnant of Randy's perception that remained coherent teetered on the brink of madness as he stood motionless with his body pressed against the wall and watched more creatures coming through the artifact. Most of the beasts seemed to search for a way beyond the confinement of the walls while some pushed their way into the feast in the midst of ferocious competition for feeding spots. A few grabbed chunks of bloody flesh or limbs still wrapped in shredded clothing and backed away to devour the treat unhindered by the ongoing territorial disputes.

Randy caught a momentary glimpse of Joyce through the horde of roaming carnivores and was immediately engulfed by an urgent compulsion to be at her side. He understood with perfect clarity the sanctuary of his location yet he grappled with the extrinsic thoughts and memories controlling his mind and body. After a momentary struggle he began moving away from the wall with the bizarre stop and go movements. His insides cringed as he entered the snarling mob of roving brutes and slowly danced his way through their midst.

Joyce moved along the wall toward the taut electrical cord, blind to all but the singular purpose ahead of her. Her grief for Samuel was muted, as was the consternation she felt for Randy and herself. In the murky depths of her secluded awareness she understood her fate was intertwined with the fate of mankind and her failure would usher in the final days of humanity. When she was a few feet from the taut cord she halted her unfamiliar stride and bolted. She went through the cord like a runner crossing the finish line, pulling the plug from the wall and killing the electricity to the light towers. As the lights faded the volatilized crystal began reforming along the edges of the opening in the center of the artifact.

In that instant the feast stopped. The carnivores raised their blood smeared faces as they sensed the permuting crystal. The ones roaming the lab reacted in the same manner. The room was suddenly wild with movement as every creature bolted for the opening in the artifact. Some ran while others jumped into the air, spread their wings and flew toward the portal.

The intense comfort Joyce felt as she watched the creatures withdrawing was short lived and collapsed in on itself when she caught a glimpse of Randy in the middle of their mad rush.

Without warning Randy was caught in the midst of a throng of creatures withdrawing toward the artifact. He was in the path of a stampede and nowhere to hide. There was no time to ponder the motivation for their flight and there was no time to run. His only defense was swift reaction within the raging torrent of alien predators.

Screeching carnivores brushed past him as he made quick evasive sidesteps to avoid collisions. Others passed inches above his head as they beat their wings and flew toward their destination. In the next instant he came to the heart stopping realization that his conventional movements were drawing attention as a creature came toward him with eyes focused, bloodied teeth bared and talons raised. At the last possible moment he raised his cane and pushed it into the chest of the creature, keeping it from coming any closer. The thing screamed out in rage as it slashed with its talons and snapped its jaws only inches from Randy's face. The strength of the predator pushed him closer to the artifact as the others continued to rush past and disappear through the closing portal.

At last only one creature remained in the lab and it continued to reach out for Randy as it pushed him perilously near the narrowing passage in the crystal.

As Randy struggled to keep the predator at bay an intense sense of deja vu flooded his mind. The thing snapped its jaws in front of his face as he suddenly remembered something special about the cane. After a momentary fumbling search his fingers found the trigger in the handle of the walking stick. The creature screamed out in anguish as the blade released and penetrated into its chest. Randy reversed the trigger, recoiling the blade back into the shaft of the cane and released it again. The blade plunged again and again until the creature staggered, lost its balance and fell forward into Randy. The momentum carried them both through the portal just before it closed completely, sealing the rift between the two worlds.

Joyce was alone in the lab when her horrified scream finally escaped her throat and reverberated through the museum.

His spiritual essence returned through the timeless void, carrying with it the resonance of her scream and a momentary glimpse of an alien world as his senses began reintegrating with his physical body. The sound of the scream faded into oblivion as the noise of passing traffic and the deep rumble of the idling Corvette stimulated his auditory system. The pungent smell of exhaust fumes drifted to his nostrils as his body began to detect the solid support of the bucket seat. He was suddenly aware of someone watching him. He opened his eyes slowly and saw Jamie crouched down between the open door and the car holding his hand. Tears were making there way down the soft features of her face as the breeze ruffled her short brown hair.

"Oh, my God! Are you okay?" she cried as she wiped away the tears. "We were talking and you just stopped in mid sentence and didn't say anything else. You wouldn't even answer me when I spoke to you. It was like you were in a trance or something. You were like that for a few minutes and then you yelled out 'don't run' and your whole body started trembling. I thought you were dying and I didn't know what to do. I was so scared. I pulled out of traffic and stopped the car as quickly as I could."

"I'll be okay, I just need to rest for a minute," he whispered in a barely audible voice.

"I don't understand what happened."

"The explanation is simply beyond your comprehension. You've seen me do things that can't work in the world defined by your system of beliefs, yet you've accepted them based on what you've witnessed. I can't expect you to grasp something when you have no point of reference, so don't try. Set aside your college education for a moment and accept without reservation what I say. Can you do that?"

"You've already opened my eyes to things that I would have dismissed as insane a few days ago. Tell me."

"The threat to humanity of which I spoke yesterday manifested itself and I had to intervene to keep things manageable. My physical body was here in the car with you, but my mind and spiritual essence were projected ahead to our destination."

"I don't understand how you could do that, but it doesn't make any difference. I believe you and...and.... Oh, sweet Jesus. Those...those things you told me about were loose?" she asked as a frightened expression crossed her face.

"Yes, they were loose. I stopped them for the moment, but everything didn't go as I planned. Where are we?" he asked as he pulled himself up in the seat.

"About two hundred miles from the Indiana-Ohio line."

"Get in the car, we need to talk," Kim said in an urgent tone.

Jamie stood up, closed the door and rushed around the back of the car.

"Do you trust me?" Kim asked as she slid into her seat and closed the door.

"After spending this time with you I know one thing. My life will never be quite the same. I may not understand how or why I've changed, but I feel it in here," she said as she put her hand on her chest. "You probably kept me from getting raped or worse back in Colorado. I'd do anything for you and I'd trust you with my life."

"The world is safe for the moment, but the action isn't complete and one of my friends is trapped. I underestimated the love that drove his power of will. He struggled free of my control and now he's trapped in a hostile world."

"I'm ready to do anything. Just tell me what you need."

"We can get there in a little over two hours, but I have to do more than act as a radar detector. I have to be in your mind."

"I don't understand."

"I've been able to tell you where the cops are because I can reach out and probe the minds of the other people on the road. I can probe their minds and control their thoughts for a moment. I can keep them from pulling out in front of us when we're doing a hundred, but I have to be able to control your actions too, because it all has to happen at the speed of light. The fusion of our minds can be dangerous if it lasts too long. It's like running four hundred volts through a nine-volt electrical system. I can protect you, but you have to be beyond worrying for your personal safety. You have to put your life in my hands. You have to trust me."

"You do whatever you have to do. I love you, I trust you and I put my life in your hands."

"When our minds become one you'll see some of the things I've seen. Some of it will be very frightening, but you'll be okay, the memories can't hurt you. The memory of what you'll see will fade and peace will return to your mind, I promise. Are you ready?"

"Yes. Will it hurt?"

"Only a slight tingling," Kim said as a ribbon of plasma extended from the palm of his hand and danced in the air between them.

Jamie's body jerked back against the seat as the projected energy entered her chest and merged with the network of nerves in her solar plexus. She took a deep breath and then relaxed. "Oh, my God..."

"Don't be frightened," Kim whispered reassuringly. "These are only memories and can't hurt you. Quiet your mind and put your trust in me."

Jamie dropped the transmission into gear and pressed the gas pedal to the floor. The corvette lurched forward with tires smoking and soon disappeared in the distance.

Steve sat on the bench and watched absently as the throng of onlookers parted, allowing the second ambulance access to the museum driveway. His hand trembled as he took a cigarette from the pack being offered by Lieutenant Morgan. Luther paced back and forth on the lawn a few feet from the bench where they sat.

"I quit smoking almost five years ago," he remarked as he put the filtered end of the cigarette between his trembling lips.

"I wish I had a good stiff drink to offer you," Morgan said as he cupped his hands around the flame from the lighter and put it to the end of the smoke.

Steve took a long drag on the cigarette and blew the smoke to the side away from Morgan.

"I know this is a difficult time for you, but I need to ask you some questions," the Lieutenant said as he returned the lighter to his pocket and watched the paramedics wheeling Joyce to the ambulance. He could see her wide eyes staring up at the sky as they loaded her into the vehicle. "I need to know who was in the lab and what the hell happened to them. Just tell me everything you know."

"I told them that artifact thing was nothin' but bad business," Luther cried out suddenly as his pacing brought him near the bench.

"Did he see anything?"

Steve shook his head as he drew in more smoke from the cigarette and expelled it over his head.

"He didn't go back in the lab after...after we heard her scream. I love him like a brother, but he has wild theories about everything. But in light of all this, who knows..."

"I see," Morgan said as he took a small notebook out of his pocket. "Why don't we start with this group picture you mentioned? Who was in the lab then?"

"There was the photographer, I don't remember his name."

"The truck is registered to a Dennis Learman."

"Yeah, that sounds right. Dennis was behind the camera and the rest of us were around the artifact. There was Luther and I. We were only in the lab long enough to take the picture. Samuel was there along with Joyce and her friend from Denver, Randy something."

"Randy Lippencott," Luther said as he moved passed the bench again.

"What about a guy named Jerry Lansford?" Morgan asked as he jotted Randy's name in his notebook. "We've got a car in the parking lot registered to him."

Steve shook his head.

"The name sounds vaguely familiar. Maybe he's the guy from the college Joyce was working with. She had a part time position there. I don't remember seeing him."

"Okay, you left the lab after the picture was taken. How long before you heard Joyce scream?"

"Five minutes, I guess. Maybe ten."

"Joyce screamed and you ran to the lab. What did Luther do?"

"I really don't know. We looked at each other and I took off running. I know he didn't follow me. He's really spooked about the artifact. It was like pulling chicken teeth to get him down there for the picture."

"When you got to the lab what did you see?" Morgan asked as he watched the ambulance transporting Joyce pull away.

Steve lowered his head and stared at the ground.

"Blood," he whispered. "There was blood everywhere and Joyce was slumped against the wall just staring out into space. Samuel and Joyce are my friends," Steve said as he looked over at Morgan with tears welling up in his eyes. "I can't understand what happened to them. I think...I think Samuel was in that pile of shredded body parts in the corner," he said and started sobbing.

"It's okay, kid," the Lieutenant said as he put a hand on his shoulder. "You've answered enough questions for right now. Maybe you ought to go have that stiff drink I couldn't offer you." He stood up and walked to the edge of the drive as the other ambulance crew came out of the lab rolling the stretcher toward their vehicle. A bloody sheet covered an oddly shaped pile of what he knew to be body parts. He saw one of the paramedics stop at the edge of the drive and lose the contents of his stomach. He crossed the drive toward the museum and tried not to look at the morbid cargo being loaded into the back of the ambulance, but his eyes seemed to have a will of their own. He felt his own stomach churning when he noticed a broken and bloody hand dangling from under the sheet and swaying with the movements of the stretcher. As he stepped off the edge of the drive and into the grass he felt the anxiety of not understanding what the body of evidence was saying to him. It wasn't like there was a lack of evidence. There was plenty, but none of it made any sense. In his gut he knew the artifact was somehow connected to this incident and more in the worst ten days of his law enforcement career. He knew it sounded crazy. Inanimate objects simply didn't make very good suspects.

When he got to the doorway to the lab he met one of his detectives coming out of the building carrying a camera.

"Get that film developed right away. Maybe the pictures will shed some light on all this," Morgan said.

The detective nodded his head. "I've never seen anything like this," he said with a grim expression. "I just can't put a handle on it. What happened to those people?"

"If I could answer that I'd probably sleep a lot better tonight. Did anybody locate Mr. VanBurg?"

"No, but judging from his description we got from the security guard I'd say what's left of him is leaving with that ambulance."

"That would make it five dead and one who I hope will be able tell us what the hell happened. I'm going to have a look around the lab and talk to Charlie for a minute, and then I'm going to the hospital and try to talk to the woman. When I get done there I'm coming back here to spend the night. I want you to go back to the station and pick up a thermos of coffee, a shot gun, a box of double aught shells and a mobile phone. I'll get someone to bring me something to eat later."

"You want company?"

"No," Morgan said as he moved toward the doorway. "I just want to be a fly on the wall."

"You got it, boss."

When he stepped into the lab he found the forensics expert in his white lab coat studying the smeared red trail leading from the blood-splattered corner to the artifact.

"Got any ideas for me, Charlie?" Morgan asked as he walked over to where he stood.

The doctor looked up at the Lieutenant and shook his head. "I've made some startling observations, but I'm completely out of ideas."

"Tell me about your observations."

"You'll have to draw your own conclusions because I'm not going where the information is trying to take me. It's...it's too crazy," he said as he pointed toward the trail of blood. "This trail is really smeared, but you can make out an occasional foot print. There," he said as he pointed to a strange looking track. "That looks like a print from some kind of animal. It appears to show three toes in the front, one in the back and a claw on each one. It looks like the print of a five hundred pound canary, for Christ sake. This blood trail ends abruptly at the artifact. That doesn't make a whole lot of sense to me. It's like whatever made the tracks jumped out of a window or something, but there's no damn window. What I find even more troubling is the condition of the remains of the victims. It appears that these people were ripped apart and consumed by one or more large predators. I've seen wounds this morning that are fairly consistent with large animal attacks. You know, like bears or big cats."

"Charlie, you're not helping me a whole lot. I haven't seen any big animals running around town. Have you?" he asked, as he thought about the Mustang convertible with its top ripped open and its interior shredded and bloody.

"No, but I've been hearing some real crazy talk," he said as he followed the trail of blood. "Look," he said as he pointed to a dark green splatter in front of the artifact. "What's that?"

"I don't know..."

"It was a rhetorical question. I didn't expect you to be able to answer. I don't know either, but I'm going to test it. Except for the color it reminds me of blood. And look over there," he said as he pointed toward a blood splatter a few feet from the artifact. "One of the victims died there except all we found were his...his shoes. They still had feet in them."

Morgan looked at the splatter of blood and remembered the picture of the four hooves lying in the center of a circle of blood stained grass that was apparently all that remained of a horse.

"And we've got this stuff that looks a little like popcorn scattered throughout the lab," Charlie said as he bent down and picked up a piece. "It appears to be bits of bone," he said as he rolled it between his fingers. "But it looks way too old to be connected to whatever happened here," he said and handed it to Morgan.

"Samuel Prince, who I believe is one of the victims, showed me some of this stuff Tuesday," he said as he examined it in the palm of his hand. "He found it here in the lab and had no idea where it came from."

"Why were you here Tuesday?"

"A security guard disappeared during the night and has never turned up. A few minutes ago you told me you weren't going where the evidence was trying to lead you. Just between you, me and the lamp post, I want to know what you think this crime scene is trying to tell us."

"It's way too crazy to even consider," Charlie said as he shook his head.

"I want to know what you think, off the record."

"Lieutenant," he said as he pointed to the artifact. "This crime scene is telling me...it's telling me that fucking thing walks around and eats people."

Morgan shook his head as he tossed the bit of suspected bone back on the floor.

"I told you it was nuts," Charlie said and shrugged his shoulders.

"Of course it's nuts, but that's not what bothers me. I've got access to a lot more information than you do and I'll be damned if it's not trying to take me to about the same conclusion. How the hell do we rationalize all this? That artifact doesn't get up and walk around. I know it and you know it, but..."

"Yeah, this is definitely a strange one. Strange to the point of being a little spooky. I've got a crew on the way to get samples of all this stuff. I'm going to stick with what I know and maybe something useful will come to light."

"God, I hope you find something that doesn't lead to another bunch of fucking questions. I'm tired of not having answers. Let me know right away if you come up with anything new. I'm going to the hospital and try to talk to my only witness," Morgan said as he turned and walked toward the doorway.

"Good luck."

"Thanks, Charlie," he said as he stepped through the doorway and into the bright light. The hot sun felt good on his face. It felt normal and he needed as much of that as he could get, he thought as he walked over to his car and opened the door. As he slid in behind the wheel and closed the door his mind started running through the facts again. He knew he had no real hope of coming up with anything new, but his mind continued to drive at the problem over and over.

He turned the car around in the parking lot and moved it slowly down the drive toward the people remaining along the edge of the street and thought about the apparent suicide in front of Cook Tower, wondering if the private detective really had anything to do with the rest of this case. Maybe he was a red herring and had nothing to do with anything but his own death. Maybe it was just one hell of a coincidence that he decided to off himself at the start of a very bad ten-day stretch.

He turned onto the street as his mind went to the next link in the chain of events, the discovery of Marion Aster's body. Lima had its share of violence, but two bodies in as many days was more than a little unusual, especially since the note pinned to the body suggested a love triangle gone bad and made reference to two more bodies that would never be found. Again he wondered if there was any real connection with the case other than the evidence suggesting that the artifact came from the bottom of a pond on the Aster property.

His mind went on to the death of the old junk dealer, again wondering it there was any real relevance to the case. There was a definite connection to the artifact, but the old guy died of alcohol poisoning. He didn't vanish into thin air and he didn't succumb to a violent end, he simply drank himself to death.

And that was what he considered to be the first part of the equation. One bizarre looking artifact and evidence of five deaths in as many days in a town that might have three of four murders over the course of a year. It was enough to raise the eyebrow of a good cop, but not much more, he thought as he stopped for a traffic light.

The second part of the equation was much more potent, especially in light of the latest event, he thought as he watched the traffic light. The first link in the series of events was the disappearance of a workman employed by a company named Pyramid Movers. He vanished while building a box around the artifact for shipment to the museum. People die in their sleep, they get run over by trucks or they get murdered, but they don't normally disappear without a trace. Maybe he got cold feet and decided to duck out on his approaching marriage. Maybe he was really laying on the beach in Aruba soaking up the sun. Maybe his disappearance was just another coincidence, he thought as the light turned green and he drove through the intersection.

The next link in the bizarre chain of events was a collection of incident reports tied together by one particular night. A dark night in which a line of violent thunderstorms rolled through the area. He thought again about the Mustang convertible with the jack lifting the left rear corner. He imagined the driver being very apprehensive about changing the tire in the middle of a barrage of lightning bolts. Then something happened. Something horrible. He remembered how the top was ripped open and the interior was torn to pieces, but the most vivid part of the memory was the blood, the bits of flesh and the pieces of bone covering the inside of the vehicle. It was a bad night with multiple disappearances of dogs and farm animals. It was also the night the security guard at the museum vanished. People only disappear in magic shows, he thought as he turned the corner and saw the hospital up ahead.

The incident today brought the total to twelve people either dead or missing, one witness that looked to be in bad shape mentally and an unknown number of missing animals. The only suspect he had was that grotesque looking artifact, he thought as he pulled into the hospital parking lot and noticed he was again at the same mysterious dead end.

When he got out of the car and started walking toward the emergency entrance he realized his mind was starting all over with the death in front of Cook Tower. He knew if he continued chasing himself around in what seemed to be a closed loop of evidence he was going to drive himself nuts. He moved through the automatic doors leading to the emergency room and forced his thoughts toward his approaching two-week vacation that he badly needed. It would be good to feel the Florida sun cooking his hide as he fished from the back of a boat. A good tussle with a big Marlin and he might forget about this case for a while, he thought as he walked up to the administration desk.

"Can I help you, sir?" the nurse asked as she looked up from the paperwork in front of her.

"Lieutenant Morgan with the LPD," he said as he pulled out his badge and held it up for her to see. "I believe a woman by the name of Joyce Robbins was brought in about half an hour ago. I'd like to speak with her. Is she still here?"

"Yes, Lieutenant, she's still here. We're waiting for the psychiatric ward to transport her. She's down the left corridor in room 6B," the nurse said as she gestured in the direction of the room. "I wouldn't expect to get much out of her."

"Thank you, nurse." Morgan said as he moved away from the desk and started down the hall. He was always amazed by the smell of hospitals. Medicine, sickness, death, he wasn't sure, but it was always the same, he thought as he walked along checking the room numbers. When he got to 6B he walked into the room and was surprised to see a woman with white hair lying in the bed. He stepped back into the hall and checked the room number as a doctor was walking passed.

"Excuse me, Doctor. I was looking for Joyce Robbins, but the nurse sent me to the wrong room."

"Are you a family member?" the doctor asked.

"Lieutenant Morgan of the LPD," he said as he showed his badge.

"Sean Reed," the doctor responded as they shook hands.

"I need to ask Joyce some questions if you can help me locate her."

"You found her," Reed said as he stepped into 6B ahead of Morgan.

"This isn't her," Morgan insisted as he followed the doctor into the room. "She has red hair."

"Look again," he said as he stopped at the end of the bed.

"Oh, my God. That's her," he said as he focused on the face and the blank, staring eyes.

"It's an amazing case. Her hair was definitely a dark red when she came in. It virtually turned white during our assessment. I always thought hair turning white after a severe shock or scare was an old wives tale, but it's apparently true," he said as he walked along the side of the bed. "Joyce," he called as he picked up her hand.

Joyce continued to stare at the ceiling without responding.

"I didn't think I was going to get a response, but I thought I'd try," he said as he lifted her arm to a forty-five degree angle where it remained after he released her hand. "She's in what we call a persistent catatonic state," Reed said as he lowered her arm back to the bed.

"It doesn't look like she's going to be able to answer my questions any time soon," Morgan said quietly as he gazed at her emotionless face. "Do you have any idea what caused this?"

The doctor shrugged his shoulders. "She experienced something that her mind simply couldn't deal with. Sometimes this type of patient will come back, but most of the time they don't."

"Thanks, doctor," he said as he handed him a card. "I'd appreciate a call if her condition changes."

"I'll pass this along to the psychiatric ward when they pick her up."

Morgan walked away feeling disappointed by the lack of new information and distressed over the condition in which he found Joyce. He only remembered speaking to her once but it was enough to know her as a beautiful woman full of life and vitality. Now it seemed she was nothing more than a body deprived of its mind, a body simply existing in limbo and he felt a degree of responsibility for not understanding the facts.

The automatic doors parted as he stepped out into the heat wondering if maybe a vacation wasn't what he really needed. Maybe it was time to get out of the police business all together. Maybe it was time to trade in his badge and gun for a set of golf clubs and a Florida driver's license.

Jamie felt the sting of building tears as she turned the corner and caught sight of the museum looming ahead atop its terraced hill. Her heart ached for the loss of companionship that was about to occur, the companionship with a man she'd known for barely two days, the man who touched her more deeply than anyone she'd ever known. From the time Kim ended the bizarre and mysterious linking of their minds at the edge of town she'd denied her tears, pushing them back and refusing to let them fall. Now, with the end of her strange journey at hand, and the terrifying visions still fresh in her mind she could no longer contain all of them and some escaped, making their way down her face as she pulled the Corvette over to the curb. Across the street yellow crime scene tape danced with the breeze.

"I guess this is it," she said as she pushed the gearshift lever into park and turned toward Kim with tears flooding her eyes.

"Don't cry," Kim said as he wiped the tears from her face.

"I can't stand the thought of never seeing you again. You've opened my heart and soul to so many things and...and I'm worried about you. Those visions I pulled from your mind...what I've seen...you're in so much danger. I love you and I'm afraid for you," she said and struggled to control the sobs that seemed to be pounding on the door to her heart. "I'm afraid for all of us."

"Everything will be okay, I promise and the memories of those visions will pass. Tomorrow peace will return to your mind."

"I don't want to say goodbye," she said and choked back the sobs that were trying to escape her control.

"It's not goodbye and never will be. There's an everlasting bond that ties us together now. Our minds have been one and because of that I'll always be with you. Your thoughts will find me and bring me to you if you ever need me. No one will ever harm you," he said as he cupped her face in his hands and kissed her lightly on the lips. "I love you, too," he whispered and pulled back. "Get your oil changed and stay the night somewhere in Ohio. There's a daily state lottery. Play it in the morning. Play the numbers that come into your mind. Your winnings won't be large enough to poison your dreams, yet if you invest the cash wisely your golden years will be more than comfortable."

"I didn't help you expecting a reward," she said as she wiped at the tears that continued to fall.

"It's not a reward, it's a gift from my heart. There's one other thing I'll ask before I leave."

"Ask it. I'll do anything for you."

"My friend has a beloved pet, a cat that will not be able to make the trip to Tibet. On our return journey I want to stop at your veterinary hospital in Indianapolis and give you the cat as your own, to love and nurture. Will you do this one last thing for me?"

"You ask so little of me. Of course I'll take the cat. I'll care for it and love it as I love you."

He cupped her face in his hands again and kissed her tenderly.

"I'll see you in a couple days," he said as their lips parted. He opened the door and climbed out of the Corvette without any other words. He stood by the curb and watched her drive away as he felt the anguish of her heart in his own. He watched until the tattered sports car was out of sight, and then he turned his attention to the building across the street.

He could feel the final terrified moments of the latest victims still emanating from the building. It was like a fine blanket of cold, suffocating fog that clawed at all his senses and numbed his mind. They perished while in the grip of wild, soul splitting horror and only now did he truly understand that vague, unruly portions of their life force would likely walk the corridors, stairways and rooms of the museum forever.

As he stepped off the curb and started across the street he felt something else. It was a mind filled with confusion and unanswered questions, a mind determined to stay in the building until the truth was discovered. He probed the man's thoughts as he continued across the street and saw his fear and understood all that he had seen. Through his memory he saw the place where the crystal and the encasing frame warning of the danger was pulled from the ground, he saw the pictures of places where dogs and farm animals had been slaughtered and he saw the Mustang convertible with its top ripped open and interior shredded and bloody.

When he got to the other side of the street he stepped up over the curb, crossed the sidewalk and slipped under the crime scene tape as he continued to probe the man's mind. The man was a law enforcement officer with an unshakable commitment to finding the truth and Kim knew he had to prevent the kind of interference he was likely to generate. He would protect the man to a point, but the consequences of failure dictated that he was just as expendable as anyone else. As he moved up the drive toward the vehicles left abandoned by the deaths of the latest victims, he probed deeper into the mind, searching for a pathway into the depths of his intellect where the magic that could save his life would be worked.

Morgan sat on the floor in the lab with his back against the wall and a shotgun across his lap. He had watched as the forensic samples were taken and afterward he had witnessed a small army of housekeeping people from the hospital work their way through the room with mops, rags and buckets. Now, with the body parts and blood splatters gone there was nothing left to suggest that some kind of horrible tragedy had occurred.

Everything seemed normal except for the artifact that towered above him on the other side of the room and there was nothing in the world that could have made it seem less threatening to him. He felt a strange, nameless fear gnawing at his insides as he peered at the grotesque features carved into the frame and remembered what Charlie had said earlier about the thing walking around and eating people. It was a laughable notion that belonged on the bottom of any long list of theories, yet so far it was the only explanation that fit the evidence. Most of the evidence, anyway, he thought as he considered the Mustang with its convertible top ripped open and the slaughtered farm animals with nothing left but their hooves. He supposed it wasn't quite enough for the damn thing to walk around. It also had to fly, since some of the carnage occurred fifteen miles from the museum.

Sometimes he felt like it all had to be a bad dream and maybe he'd wake up soon, wake up and curse the late night pepperoni pizza that caused the nightmare. It was the most reasonable explanation for everything, except the Remington shotgun lying across his lap was real. The stench that came rolling out of the Mustang when he opened the door had been too sickening to be something conjured up by the mind during sleep. The sound of crazed flies buzzing around the chunks of flesh and blood soaked upholstery had been too clear for a dream. And in this very room the sight of the pile of shredded body parts and the bloodied walls had been too nauseating for something imagined.

And suddenly, while thinking of these horrors he had the sensation that someone was looking over his shoulder, watching him, listening to him breathe. A quick sweep of his eyes told him he was alone in the room. Nothing but a case of the heebie jeebies, he supposed and what the hell did he expect, sitting here with that artifact on the other side of the room and thinking about things that were best forgotten.

He felt the sensation again, this time more intense and accompanied by something else. It was as if he drifted toward sleep, but his mind was alert. He felt his muscles relax as the feeling engulfed him like the warming rays of the sun. He closed his eyes as the warmth soothed his body and he felt himself drifting deeper into relaxation, but his mind was alert. It was alert and floating upward.

He could hear the waves pounding on the beach just as they had done for millions of years. He could feel the breeze from the ocean caressing his skin as the warmth of the sand radiated up through the blanket and into his body. And his mind floated upward, bathing in a peaceful glow with only the sound of the surf and the cries of the seagulls keeping him from drifting away into the clutches of sleep.

Now the waves rocked the surfboard gently as the sun's rays continued to bake his flesh and the sea birds cried out against the air currents that carried them aloft. There was another here on a surfboard, being carried along by the same tide and pitched back and forth by the same waves. And now he spoke with a kind voice filled with deep compassion and understanding. These were dangerous waters infested with a most dangerous species of carnivorous marine life. Even at the very edge of the water the danger awaited to take the unwary. The surfboard was a small island of safety. As long as he stayed on it and didn't dangle his limbs in the water he could avoid being grabbed by terrible jaws and reduced to a quick meal. He had to leave but promised to come back and help him out of the treacherous water.

The notion of being eaten alive by a thing that lurked below in the dark shadows of the water, something unseen and vicious, struck terror deep in his heart. He would wait on the surfboard, wait with all his limbs tucked under his body, wait for his new friend to return.

Kim listened to Morgan's entranced thoughts as he quietly moved close and crouched down next to him. He was relieved that the officer had gone under so easily. He probed into the depths of his mesmerized mind and found him enraptured in soothing repose. The expression on his face was one of complete surrender and isolation. Kim knew immediately he was well beyond rational thought and would not initiate any interfering actions as long as he was held in the trance.

Kim stood up, turned toward the artifact and studied the features carved into the frame as he felt the icy fingers of fear slipping around his heart. His focus moved from the carvings to the crystal captured within the frame as he struggled to fight back the consternation that threatened his power of will. This was the portal through which passed the death bringers, the butchers of humanity, the creatures that were the embodiment of horror. He stepped toward the artifact and as he did felt the immense and portentous burden. Now he was in the clutches of the cold, dark fear that had pursued him relentlessly throughout his journey, the fear that he would falter and allow humanity to suffer a horrible fate, a fate that could make instantaneous nuclear obliteration seem like a pleasant alternative.

He reached out and ran his hand along the rough surface of the crystal as his heart pounded in his chest and he felt the fear creeping through his body, filling his limbs with the compulsion to escape. He pressed his forehead against the crystal as he fought to control the terror building in his heart. After a brief struggle with his anxiety he closed his eyes and began a shallow, rhythmic breathing as he released his consciousness into his etheric body and projected it into the crystal. His awareness transmuted into a bright shaft of light growing progressively smaller as it flashed through a black void until it became a dimensionless point and erupted out into a dull crimson glow. As his energy body slowly took form in the alien world his senses began to distinguish his surroundings.

He stood motionless atop a high dune of what he instantly knew to be bones that had been crushed into coarse bits of shapeless rubble over thousands of years. The backside of the dune was piled against a shear rock face in which the crystal was embedded. Lying on the dune a few feet out from the stone escarpment where it had fallen was the body of the creature that had gone after Randy during the crazed exodus from the lab. Next to the body was the broken cane weapon that Randy had used to protect himself. Further out on the top of the dune were the sites of two recent kills where dismembered skeletons and pieces of shredded clothing were scattered about in the center of large bloodstains. A drill and power saw still attached to a severed electrical chord were lying near one of the bloody sites, a discharged Colt .45 automatic was laying near the other. He found Randy a few feet away laying face down in the skeletal debris. His hair and beard were as white as freshly fallen snow. He looked dead, but Kim detected a weak life force emanating from his body. He probed his mind and found a rudimentary intellect and a conscious mind crippled by the insanity of what he'd witnessed. The higher functions of his brain were shut down, which Kim knew had saved his life. Any movement would have drawn the creature's attention and they would have descended upon him like a plague of locusts.

Knowing Randy was in no immediate danger he withdrew from the wrecked mind and scanned the alien world. The pile of crushed bones upon which he stood arose from the floor of a vast depression surrounded by shear stone faces extending upward into jagged mountain peaks, peaks which ascended into a dull crimson sky. There were hundreds of other crystals inlaid in the cliffs throughout the cavity at different levels. Most of them had similar dunes of varying sizes rising from the rocky floor but there were a few below which nothing was piled. High above the jagged mountain peaks in the crimson sky was a dark cloud slowly swirling in a circular motion. Tenuous strands of darkness seemed to be reaching out from the cloud and touching the jagged peaks.

Kim understood his responsibility and knew delay risked failure, yet he was driven to penetrate the mysteries of this place and behold its secrets. His energy body atomized and reformed into a shapeless mist as he ascended into the dull crimson atmosphere above the depression and floated toward the dark churning cloud. As he entered the swirling darkness he suddenly understood its composition. The dark mass was made up of thousands of creatures soaring in a circular pattern high above the depression. The mass continued to expand as more of the horrid beasts left their jutting perches among the rocky peaks and merged into the periphery of the living maelstrom.

He probed into the mind of one of the creatures soaring near him and discovered the horrible simplicity of this place. He found a dark, instinctive intellect that joined all of them together. There was no emotional element to them and there was no drive to create an evolving society from which a great culture could rise. There was only the instinct to sleep, awaken from sleep to fly above the depression in an endless circle and to feed voraciously whenever the opportunity presented itself. There was no energy devoted to reproduction.

They had no sex and did not copulate. Within each creature was a nucleus of cells, which, upon the death of the host, would begin growing a reproduction of the individual. The maturing clone simply used the decaying body as a nutritional source until it was strong enough to claw its way through the leathery hide and take its place within the group.

Suddenly a piercing sound like fingernails on a chalkboard was transmitted through the network mind and he understood at once that one of the crystals below in the depression was changing state and opening a portal into another world. He withdrew from the mind to focus upon the horror that he knew was about to take place.

After a moment the center of the pack began to extend downward like the funnel of a huge tornado. Downward they swooped in the spiraling column, landing atop the dune of bony debris and moving through the doorway as the piercing sound stopped. Minutes later some of the beasts began returning with hairy, primitive looking humanoid victims, some of which continued to struggle and scream out in agony as they were devoured. He continued to observe the ghastly spectacle and watched as fed creatures returned to the periphery of the circling cloud and took the place of the ones that moved toward the center where they awaited their turn to feed. The horrific scene continued with its orderly procession of slaughter until the piercing sound returned and the crystal began to close. All the individuals returned to the soaring mass, going back to their circling flight as they awaited the next feeding. Below he watched as the crystal reconstituted itself, beginning at the edges and working inward. The flurry of molecular rephase along the edges, mending the crystal and closing the opening, cast a ghostly luminescent glow over the top of the dune. He knew any flesh, whether human or not, coming in contact with the transmuting matter would be instantly vaporized.

He knew there was but one more secret this God forsaken place had to give up. As he arose from the swirling mass and moved upward through the crimson atmosphere and into the blackness of the outer regions surrounding the world, he reached out with his senses, probing far out into the dark space and found nothing. There were no other stars and no other planets, only the blackness of a boundless void. He drew back toward the crimson world and saw the single dim star about which it orbited. As his energy body streaked back into the atmosphere he came to the stunned realization that there were hundreds of depressions scattered across the surface of the dark world, each with a swirling mass of creatures above, awaiting the opportunity to feed.

His energy body flashed downward through the layers of dense atmospheric gas, past the dark mass of soaring creatures, and back to where Randy lay clinging to life. He hovered above the dune as he again probed into the network mind and waited for the piercing sound of a doorway opening somewhere in the depression. He waited patiently, knowing a feeding cycle with its distraction was the best time to move Randy. The sound finally came, spreading through the group mind like a raging fire. A moment later the center of the dark mass started spiraling downward toward another transmuting crystal.

His energy body vaporized and returned through the crystal from whence it came.

Kim staggered back away from the artifact as his energy body slammed through the crystal and reintegrated with his physical body. He regained his balance, turned and ran toward the other side of the lab where the electrical cord for the light towers had been plugged into the wall receptacle. As he grabbed the plug and pushed it into the socket he knew the success of Randy's rescue and his own safety was going to be a matter of impeccable timing. He turned and watched the artifact as the light towers came alive, illuminating the immediate area as well as the darkest corners of the lab. As he watched red crisscrossing lines spread across the face of the crystal he felt numbing fear strike his heart. The doorway was opening and it was exposing his world, if only for a moment, to a horrible and terrifying end.

He waited until the portal was fully opened, then jerked the plug from the wall and dropped it to the floor as he ran for the artifact, knowing the doorway was beginning to close. He ran through the opening and out onto the edge of the dune where he stopped and began slow rhythmic movements broken by brief inanimate pauses as he approached Randy's prone, motionless body. When he got to him he stooped down slowly, guarding against any quick or sustained movements, placed a hand on his shoulder and slowly rolled him over on his back. He placed his hand in the middle of Randy's chest, but before he could join their minds to insure he remained motionless he became partially conscious and started to thrash about wildly.

"Oh, my God, no," Kim screamed as he threw himself on top of Randy and tried to hold him still, but it was too late. He knew without looking that the movement had attracted the creatures and they were spiraling down toward them. He jumped to his feet, grabbed Randy under the shoulders and started dragging him across the top of the dune toward the closing portal as fast as he could, feet kicking bits of bone into the air and crunching down into the debris with each step. Randy continued lashing out with his arms and kicking wildly with his legs as they went.

The sound of heavy, leathery wings was above them, coming closer as Kim continued to drag Randy past the discharged gun, past the bloody stains on the dune, but the force of his wild movements jerking from side to side was slowing them down. He had plenty of time to leave him and escape, but he couldn't. Better to be trapped in this world by the closing portal than to leave his friend behind. He knew if it came to that he could still destroy the crystal from this side and save his world before suffering the horror of those carnivorous jaws. And he'd known all along that his own life was something expendable in the greater scheme of things.

The sound of the flapping wings was growing louder as he stopped momentarily and released a tiny bolt of plasma that jumped from his hand and into Randy's head, knocking him back into unconsciousness. He was moving again, dragging Randy, plowing through the bony debris. There was still plenty of time before the crystal closed the portal, but now the flapping was becoming a heavy thumping as he felt the wind generated by the leathery wings ruffle his hair and heard the gentle whistle of air rushing past his ears. He charged toward the opening, dragging Randy and ignoring the horrid sound and the unbridled terror ripping at his heart. He ignored everything except the direction and distance of the fissure leading back to their world until he heard the crunch of bones as something dropped onto the dune next to him.

Kim stopped, heart frozen with terror and looked in the direction of the sound. One of the creatures was standing on the dune a few feet away. It snarled, exposing deadly teeth as it focused its cat like eyes on Kim and advanced with its talons raised. Kim released Randy's shoulders as he moved to the side, drawing the thing away from his friend. The beast snapped its carnivorous jaws as it closed the distance between them with a series of short hops. It snarled again and slashed at Kim with talons that cut the air inches from his face as he jumped back away from the blow. As his feet landed back on the dune he moved toward the predator in a blur of speed and delivered a bone splintering punch to its chest. The thing screamed out in surprise and then agony as it clutched at its shattered breastbone and fell back onto the dune in a writhing heap. The creature twitched and cried out as Kim watched, poised to strike again. It fell silent as the sound of more of its kind dropping down from above found his ears.

He turned as two more of the horrid creatures landed on the dune and started advancing with their teeth bared and talons raised. The thumping sound of more winged beasts descending toward them was becoming a heavy drone as the predators moved across the dune and closed in toward him with jaws snapping and yellow eyes fixed in deadly stares. The first one leaped into the air and landed on the dune inches from Kim with its teeth bared and jaws open. Before it could strike Kim raised a hand and released a twisting bolt of plasma into its chest, knocking it back and dropping it into a smoldering heap on the other side of the dune. Five more winged predators dropped onto the dune behind the other beast as it lunged into the air. Kim released another bolt of plasma that caught the thing in mid-air and sent its fiery mass plummeting toward the dune.

The creatures spread out as they approached amid snarling growls and snapping jaws. More landed behind him as he backed up toward where Randy lay, oblivious to the ring of horror that was forming around them. One of them leaped into the air with talons extended, jaws open and was coming down on Kim. The talons on its grasping feet shredded his shirt and raked across his chest and abdomen as it came down, leaving bleeding wounds in his flesh. He grabbed both of the creature's arms before it could strike with its talons and delivered a devastating front kick, which broke open, its chest cavity and knocked it back off its feet. It fell onto the dune thrashing and screeching as more predators dropped out of the air and landed between him and the crystal.

Now they were completely surrounded, cut off from their escape route by the approaching abominations and more of them were dropping out of the air. They were caught in the midst of a snarling ring of death as the creatures approached, closing the circle, pushing and struggling with each other for a place at the feast that was about to begin.

The creature positioned between them and the portal suddenly shrieked in agony as its chest exploded outward in a spray of greenish blood and bits of flesh and the roar of a gun shot echoed through the depression. As it fell forward into a heap Kim saw Morgan standing on the dune just beyond the opening holding the Remington, smoke still rolling out of the barrel. His crazed eyes were like tiny windows into a mind ravaged by insanity. The shotgun bellowed again, sending lead pellets ripping through another of the creatures.

"Go behind me!" he screamed as he shot again, clearing a path to the closing portal.

Kim grabbed Randy under the shoulders and started dragging him toward the opening that was now barely wide enough to move through. The luminescent glow from the mending crystal cast a ghostly silhouette around Morgan as the Remington thundered again, sending small projectiles shredding through alien flesh. The creatures growled, snarled and snapped their jaws as their ring reformed and started closing again. Kim dragged Randy past the destroyed bodies of two creatures as the shotgun bellowed three more times in rapid succession and fell silent. They went past Morgan and started through the narrow opening as he began swinging the empty shotgun like a baseball bat, splitting open the head of one of the creatures as dozens of others dropped out of the air and landed on the dune.

"Come on," Kim screamed as he moved through the fissure. The sleeve of his tattered shirt brushed against the glowing edge of the opening, vaporizing the material in a puff of smoke. "Morgan," he screamed again as he dragged Randy out onto the floor of the lab.

Kim looked back through the opening, which was now too narrow for passage and saw Morgan surrounded by the predators. He was swinging the Remington with one hand and pulling the Glock from his waistband holster with the other. A series of shots rang out and then the gun fell silent as the horrid circle fell in on him. He screamed out in agony. Blood and bits of flesh sprayed upward from the center of the pack as the creatures struggled with each other for a share of the prize. The crystal closed amid the sound of horrifying growls, ripping flesh and breaking bones.

Kim's body began trembling as he stood beside Randy's prone figure and looked down at the bleeding wounds in his chest and abdomen. He stripped off his ruined shirt and used it to wipe at the blood that was running down the front of his body as his mind grappled with the memory of the other world and the horror he had witnessed. He wanted his mind purged of the sights and sounds of the horrid place, but for now they had to be his burden. There were other, more important things to do.

He winced against the pain as he directed tiny threads of plasma into his injuries. The pain was incredible and the smoke from the sizzling flesh was rolling up into his face and burning his eyes as he cauterized the wounds one by one. The smell was almost sickening, but it helped put everything into the proper perspective. The horror was over and the relief was beginning to wash through his entire body. When he finished with the treatment of his wounds there were four long, blackened furrows running downward from his chest.

He bent down, grabbed Randy by the shoulders and dragged him across the floor to a safe distance from the artifact where he pulled him up into a sitting position and leaned him against the wall.

As he moved back across the lab he raised his hands in front of him and held them a few inches apart, palms facing each other as if he was carrying an invisible package. A tiny strand of winding plasma jumped the gap between his hands and formed a pulsating blue arc. With each step the twisting bolt grew denser, oscillating faster, expanding in circumference and forcing his hand apart as it lengthened. When he stopped a few feet from the artifact the swirling blue energy was shaping itself into a luminescent sphere the size of a medicine ball. He forced more energy into the ball through his hands. Tenuous fibers of plasma leaped from everywhere on his body and jumped into the ball, each tiny bolt pulsating and growing more concentrated. More strands jumped until his body faded from view at the center of a luminous orb of pulsating blue light. He continued to force more energy into the sphere surrounding him as the oscillation accelerated and the luminance intensified. When he was no longer able to contain the raw power he released it. Instantly a tremendous bolt of swirling plasma slammed into the crystal with a deafening clap of thunder.

The crystal absorbed the power, taking on its brilliant color and pulsating at an ever increasing rate until the room was flickering with irradiant blue light at a dizzying rate. A moment later the crystal exploded into a fine, silvery dust that filled the air and drifted downward toward the floor like powdery snow.

It was over, he thought with a sigh of relief as he looked at the slab of black slate with a depression where the crystal had been.

He went back across the lab to where Randy was sitting and stooped down next to him as he probed his mind. He was slowly returning to a limited state of consciousness in which he could be directed in simple tasks, yet completely dependent upon whatever input was provided.

"Randy, can you hear me?" he asked as he withdrew from his mind.

Randy looked around the room with empty eyes, finally focusing on Kim.

"Kim," he whispered.

"You stay here. I'll be back."

"Stay here..." Randy muttered softly as he closed his eyes.

Kim knew one of the cars outside in the parking lot had to belong to Joyce and he knew her mind as well as he knew his own. She wasn't the type to get caught unprepared and he knew she had an extra set of keys stashed somewhere in her desk. He went into the office and immediately felt her energy emanating from the desk to his right. He moved around the desk and dropped down into her chair as he started looking through the drawers.

The search didn't take long and after a few minutes he returned to the lab with the keys and a white lab coat that had been hanging on a hook next to her desk.

When he put on the coat he found it a couple sizes too big, but it was all right, he just needed something to cover the injuries in his chest and abdomen. He buttoned up the front of the jacket and rolled up his sleeves as he went back to Randy.

"Randy, can you stand up for me?"

Randy opened his eyes again and looked at Kim with a confused expression. "Kim," he said with a lifeless voice.

"Can you stand up?"

"Stand up..." he whispered as he slowly got to his feet.

Kim moved with him a step at a time as he took him out through the doorway, into the bright sunlight and across the driveway. When they got to the Porsche Kim helped Randy work his way into the back seat, which was little more than an upholstered luggage compartment. Once he got in past the back of the front seat he was able to shift into a comfortable position sitting sideways across both seats, completely avoiding the small, almost non-existent leg room.

Randy said nothing on the way to the hospital and was still in his reclined position with his eyes closed as Kim pulled the car into the hospital parking lot.

"I'm going in here to get Joyce. You stay here," Kim said as he climbed out of the sports car.

"Stay here," Randy muttered.

Kim made his way into the psychiatric ward, distracting the staff nurses when necessary and slipped into Joyce's room. He probed into her mind and found an intellect suffering from crippling mental trauma. Her brain was completely shutdown except for the areas controlling her involuntary biological functions.

Kim joined their minds and began working her body like a puppeteer, getting her out of bed and dressed. He felt her returning to a limited state of consciousness as she stood in front of the mirror working a brush through her long white hair.

"Joyce, can you hear me?" he asked as he withdrew from her mind.

After a moment she turned toward him, looking into his face with dull, emotionless eyes. "Kim," she whispered.

"Can you walk with me?" he asked.

"Yes...walk with you."

They left the room, walking slowly down the corridor holding hands. Behind them nurses were scurrying out of the nursing station and running down the hall as doors to rooms automatically closed in response to the sounding fire alarm. They continued moving along the passageway leading to the exit with hospital staff paying little or no attention to them as they hurried past.

The fire alarm system was sounding the all clear as they moved through the door and out into the bright sunlight.

Kim led her to the Porsche, opened the door and lowered her down into the passenger seat where she sat silently as he moved to the other side of the car and slid in behind the wheel.

Kim drove the sports car across town as Joyce sat quietly, staring ahead with empty, expressionless eyes. Behind her Randy remained motionless in his cramped space. After a few minutes Kim pulled the car into the driveway at Joyce's condo and shut off the engine.

"I'm going in here to pick up a few things," Kim said as he opened the door. "You guys stay here."

Joyce turned and looked at him with a vacant stare.

"Stay here," she whispered.

When Kim returned to the car a few minutes later he had a small leather duffle bag stuffed full of clothes slung over one shoulder, a cat laying across his other shoulder and a bag of cat food under one arm. He opened the passenger door, laid the cat in Joyce's lap and tossed the leather bag and cat food in the back with Randy. When he got back in the car Joyce was stroking her hand slowly across the cat's head and back.

"What a beautiful cat," she said as the cat nuzzled her arm.

"Joyce?" Randy cried out in surprise as he sat up in the back seat and looked at her with a bewildered expression.

"Randy! I...I don't understand?" she said as she looked over her shoulder. "What are you doing here? I thought you got on the bus...hey, you've got a beard and...and all your hair is white, even your eyebrows."

"My God, yours is too," he said as he looked into the rearview mirror.

"It is?" she asked as she grabbed a handful of hair and examined it.

"I'm so confused," Randy said. "Where are we? I thought you guys just said goodbye to me at the bus station. Where's the Cadillac?"

"Yeah," Joyce said as looked over at Kim. "Where's the Cadillac? And where'd you get this car?" she asked as she continued stroking the cat.

"God, you guys ask a lot of questions," Kim said as he started the engine and began backing the Porsche out of the driveway. "We've got plenty of time to talk. For now just enjoy the ride."

"Where are we going?" Randy asked as he went back to his reclining position.

"Road trip across the country!" Kim said with glee. "You guys might want to take turns in that back seat."

"God, it seems like we just did that, except in a bigger car," Joyce said.

"Yeah, that was thirty years ago," Kim said as he backed out onto the street.

"How can that be?" Joyce demanded.

"Don't try to figure it out, just let the linear thinker go to sleep," Kim said as he slipped the gearshift into first and pulled away from the condo. "We're on our way home and maybe someday you'll both understand everything that happened."

EPILOGUE

Kim made one more stop on the way out of town. He stopped to see me. It had only been about three hours since I was notified of Samuel's death and I was in no condition to see anyone. I was devastated. My husband of forty-five years was gone and apparently nobody was willing to give me straight answers about what happened. In retrospect I now understand their hesitation and vagueness in answering my questions. Not only was he gone, but there was very little left of his body. So when Kim showed up at the house I was in no way ready or willing to speak to a stranger.

He immediately eased my burden by putting me into some kind of trance and I was quite suddenly with Samuel. These were not memories of Samuel. I was with him somewhere. I never gave much thought to the spirit world, but now its different; and Kim did something for me that was much more than a last visit, he gave me the ability to see Samuel anytime I want. It's certainly not like having him in the physical world, but it's better than not having him at all. Our visits are much like dreams without the surrealistic quality. I actually have vivid memories of our time together.

Kim did something else during his brief stay. Through some strange linking of our minds he gave me the entire story you just finished reading. He said I had to give the story to the world. It has taken me two years working with a hypnotist and another writer to get it out, and now you have it. There were a couple other things he wanted me to tell you, but first let me bring you up to speed on other more mundane matters.

When Lieutenant Morgan failed to answer calls on his radio officers went to the museum to check on him. They found his car still in the parking lot. When they went into the lab they found everything in it covered by a layer of fine, powdery dust. They found a nearly full box of shotgun shells and a thermos full of coffee, but Morgan was gone.

After a couple weeks it was apparent that the Lieutenant was the last person to disappear into the depths of the dark mystery that had been plaguing the city. Although his friends continue to look for him, holding onto the hope that he'll turn up, the police department had a memorial service and said goodbye to him.

When the hospital realized that Joyce had apparently walked out of their facility they were frantic. They immediately searched the hospital grounds. Shortly thereafter they elicited help from the police department. After a brief investigation they concluded that there was no foul play involved and that she simply went back to the museum, got in her car and left town. The investigation was closed and the hospital went back to its normal routine.

The Board of Directors wanted to reopen the museum as soon as possible, starting with a memorial service. It didn't take them long to realize there were only a couple people that knew anything about the museum. They hired Steve as the managing director and Steve in turn hired Luther to replace him as the maintenance man. He also hired a college student named Sandy to take care of the grounds after he explained that he was actually the one who found the artifact while working on a construction crew.

After a few weeks the media caught wind of the story upon which Lieutenant Morgan had placed a tight lid. The ensuing investigation uncovered sketchy details of a story that was simply deemed much too wild for serious journalism. A brief story, which reported on the outcome of the investigation, and raised more questions than it answered, appeared in The National Inquirer a few months later.

When Kim was ready to leave I walked to the car with him. I was shocked when I realized the white haired woman in the passenger seat was Joyce. Nothing had been said about her and I assumed she died in the bizarre attack with Samuel and the others. What shocked me even more was that she had no idea who I was.

As Kim opened the car door and slid in behind the wheel he turned to me and said that it was of the utmost importance that the world understood something very clearly. When he left Tibet on his journey everyone thought there was only one crystal when, in fact, there are thousands. There may or may not be more of them here in our world. We must all be ever diligent in watching for the discovery of any other crystals with the tiny pyramid projections rising from surfaces that should be smooth. The exposure of any of these aberrant crystalline structures to a constant electromagnetic field will doom humanity to an unthinkable fate.

He told me one more thing before he left. He said nobody should think of him as a hero, because in the end he did falter. He let his love for Randy cloud his vision. In the greater scheme of things he should have destroyed the crystal without attempting to rescue him. The true hero was Lieutenant Morgan. He's the one who laid down his life and saved humanity.

Martha Prince
August 26, 1999

Printed in the United States
1419500002B/49-132

9 781592 862023